FROM THE BEST-S
THE NEW MADRID
ROUSING, ROLLIC...

The Road To Key West has all of the energy and adventure of the wild and wacky '70s, and only an author who lived those raucous times at full throttle could deliver it so honestly. It's a hell of a ride, propulsively cinematic in its story-telling—sort of Ken Kesey crossed with Clive Cussler, *Electric Kool-Aid Acid Test* meets *National Treasure*, in a story that will make you laugh and gasp, and yearn for an adventure of your own.
— *Ronnie Clemmer, Longbow Motion Picture Productions, Los Angeles*

A treasure trove of outrageous personalities and impossible situations that tumble along in perpetual motion. All the Caribbean feel and flare of a Buffett or a Hiaasen read, with descriptions so poignant and enticing they'll leave you booking a ticket for the islands.
— Melanie Bowles, best-selling author of *The Horses of Proud Spirit* and *Hoof Prints.*

Every blue-blooded Boomer who "adventured" their way through the 70's will love this descriptive recollection of the time. This book is intoxicatingly reminiscent of those wondrous days before responsibility overtook our lives!
— *The Log Cabin Democrat*

Readers looking for evocative writing, ribald humor, and a peep into '70s will find it all here. When you turn the last page, you'll be disappointed that your romp with all of Reisig's extraordinary characters has come to an end.
— *Linda Hicks, The Searcy Sun*

OTHER BOOKS BY MICHAEL REISIG

THE ROAD TO KEY WEST

BACK ON THE ROAD TO KEY WEST

ALONG THE ROAD TO KEY WEST

THE HAWKS OF KAMALON

THE NEW MADRID RUN

If you have enjoyed Reisig's best-selling "Road To Key West" novels, you will love his new "Caribbean Gold" series:

CARIBBEAN GOLD — *THE TREASURE OF TORTUGA*

CARIBBEAN GOLD — THE TREASURE OF TIME

CARIBBEAN GOLD —THE TREASURE OF MARGARITA

THE ROAD TO KEY WEST

Michael Reisig

CLEAR CREEK PRESS

(reisig@ipa.net)
1st Edition, May 2010
Cover design by Powell Graphics

Manuscript consulting by Cris Wanzer

Published by Clear Creek Press
P.O. Box 1081 Mena, AR 71953
1-479-394-4992

ISBN (print book): 978-0-9713694-9-8

To my old partner, Bill, who helped me make so many
of the stories in my life.
And to my lady, Bonnie Lee, who patiently listened to them,
time and again....

Genuine adventure isn't available mail order. It isn't delivered to your door like pizza. You have to apply imagination and actively seek the extraordinary if you want great barroom stories.

The truth is, most real adventure is the raw unearthing of experience when you're least prepared for it, and those who have spent any time at the endeavor will tell you, harrowing exploits are usually appreciated more in retrospect, and in the company of fermented beverages.

Almost everyone has a golden recollection in their past, from which they draw to refuel life in the present. Very often, those memories are the product of instinctive initiative and some stretch of their imagination—a few moments in their life where they chose to believe in the impossible.

— *Kansas Stamps*

"I can't believe in impossible things," said Alice.

"I daresay you haven't had much practice," said the Queen. "When I was your age, I always did it for half-an-hour a day. Why, sometimes I believed in as many as six impossible things before breakfast."

— Lewis Carroll

Contents

FOREWORD

Mac practically skidded the floatplane to a stop about twenty yards from my partner, who still drifted motionless, face down in the ocean. As I swung my door open and jumped onto the pontoon, Angie grabbed the pilot by the hair and thrust the broken bottle neck against his throat, drawing blood. "Don't even think about touching that throttle," she whispered with deadly vehemence.

I hadn't even hit the water when the officers in the Cuban gunboats realized what was happening and a cannon round struck the remainder of the boat Will had been piloting. The explosion threw a maelstrom of fiberglass and metal into the surrounding sea. A moment later the first of their 50-caliber machine guns came into range and bullets slapped the surface next to the aircraft.

Angie tightened her grip on Mac. "Relax, sweetheart, we're not going anywhere."

In seconds I was at Will's side, flipping him over and looking for wounds. A bad gash on his forehead was leaching blood into the water, and his eyes were closed. He didn't appear to be breathing, but there was nothing I could do at the moment. I put him in a cross-chest carry and dragged him toward the floatplane.

The gunboats were closing on us—puffs of smoke from their 20 mm deck cannon heralded the whine of fresh rounds, the explosions ripping holes in the ocean around us, showering the Cessna with water and shrapnel.

I dragged Will aboard—pale, still unconscious. Angie pulled him into the back seat and began CPR as Mac hit the throttles. While the plane shuttered and bounced on take-off, a burst of machine-gun fire stitched the starboard wing with the snapping sound of popcorn in a microwave. As frightening as it was, Angie never even missed a beat with Will. A cannon round exploded to our right and the aircraft shook from the shock wave, cantering up onto one float for a moment. Mac cursed under his breath as he fought with the rudder and ailerons for control. Finally, as the rhythmic slap of the water on the floats ceased and we became airborne (and I exhaled the breath I had been holding), three or four 50-caliber rounds slammed into the fuselage and shattered the rear window about a foot from my head. That time I cried out. There was another sixty seconds of dramatic tenseness as we rose into the darkening sky, but at that point, it appeared we'd made it out.

I turned and looked back at Angie. She was still furiously working on Will, but I could see the fear in her eyes when she glanced at me. My stomach lurched at that look of desperation. I don't remember feeling more helpless in my entire life—I was watching my closest friend die. That sudden emptiness—the pain and the terrible reality—were overwhelming. Angie paused, tears streaming down her face. She began sobbing, hammering Will's chest frantically and crying out, "Don't do this Will! Oh God! Don't die, please...don't die..."

I reached back, I don't know why, and took my friend's hand. There were so many things I wanted to say, but my mouth was dry as sawdust...

I awoke with a start in the darkness of my room, a sheen of sweat bathing my face, heart thumping, breaths coming in small, quick gasps. I had to still myself. It was a long time ago, a long, long time ago.

I lay there in the stillness for a moment or two, remembering, and being reminded of what a remarkable life we had lived. More luck than talent, that was for sure. Outside, the moon broke through a battery of powdery gray clouds and painted the room in soft chartreuse. I exhaled quietly and a smile began to edge out the tenseness around my mouth. Not only had we experienced extraordinary adventures, but we had been fortunate enough to share powerful friendships, dance in the rum-soaked moonlight in more exotic places than Elvis, and live through one of the most unique, absolutely spectacular eras of our times.

The late '60s, early '70s were a social anomaly—much like a two-week vacation in the history of America. We converted a symbol of war into a symbol of peace that would be remembered for generations; provided the first true blending of cultures in this country; and designated free love as a sign of the times—garnished with flowers and embraced by the newly braless. We nurtured rock music as it made its evolution into substance and power, and ardently participated in a garish, uninhibited, tambourine-accompanied symphony of communal living, drugs, and sex, all while undergoing a rebirth of faith that turned Jesus Christ into a superstar. It was a wondrous, remarkably contradictive experience that provided a spiritual and cultural bonding like this country had never before seen.

There's no question that history is measured in eras, but within those same frames in time are geographic microcosms, creating their own unique flavor. During the '70s there was San Francisco, Denver, New Orleans, and dozens of other locales, each offering its own definition to an extraordinary epoch. I don't know whether it was coincidence, karma, or just amazing good luck, but I ended up in the Florida Keys in August of 1971.

The Keys—haven of scoundrels, smugglers, and pirates for over 300 years—a bastion for independent thinkers, benign crazies, adventurers, and visionaries. But the '70s brought a new sense of freedom and imagination, and the Florida Keys became magical, like Oz—rife with characters and experiences beyond ordinary vision. Kurt Vonnegut, Joseph Heller, or even Jimmy Buffett would have struggled to match the residents of that distant time.

CHAPTER ONE

Crab Races

My name is Kansas T. Stamps and I can say without reservation I have lived, loved, won, and lost with equal fervor in this lifetime, and there's nothing you could offer me that I would trade for the experience. I've been fortunate to have encountered a number of remarkable people with whom I have shared this journey. In my early years there were several notable relationships—first loves, first friends, and a handful of people who taught me the rules of life—but when I look back on the days of my youth, the person I count myself lucky for knowing was a guy named William Baltus Bell. He was my business partner and friend in what became a carnival of extraordinary experiences that lasted for almost a decade in the land of Oz.

Will and I met during our last semester at St. Petersburg Junior College, in English Literature—one of those electives you get when you're not paying attention to what the guidance counselor is saying. You're looking through the office window at the backside of the blond in the hallway, bent over her floor-level locker like a living, breathing, erectile dysfunction test. There are words coming out of the counselor's mouth and you're nodding, trying to keep the blond in focus over his shoulder but the damned guy keeps moving his head. The next thing you know you're in English Literature.

The year was 1970, but I don't recall exactly how Will and I became friends—probably because guys are always a little awkward when it comes to establishing bonds. I think I remember us attending a couple of parties with mutual acquaintances and getting fairly snockered—that has a tendency to loosen up a soul and let personality show through. I had taught guitar for the last couple of years. Will was living in a room at his parents' motel and working for his father. Both of us were looking for the beef in life.

We had a mutual penchant for the outdoors, particularly the ocean, and I recall we went fishing off the Sunshine Skyway Bridge one afternoon. As soon as the portable radio was turned on, the baits cast out, and the rods propped securely against the rail of the catwalk, Will lit a crooked cigarette with a sweet, green scent and drew deeply. Jimi Hendrix growled out "All Along The Watchtower" in the background. Will handed it to me. "Here, try this."

"There must be some kind of way out of here," said the joker to the thief.

I knew what it was, but somehow I'd never gotten around to trying it.

"There's so much confusion, I can't get no relief."

"Cool," I said, staring at it with sort of a first-sex anticipation.

"No reason to get excited," the thief he kindly spoke.

(Hey, man, there aren't many bad reviews on this, just step up to the plate.)

"There are many of us here who feel that life is but a joke."

On one hand, it was a lot less complicated than first sex. But this, was sort of—illegal.

"But you and I, we've been through that, and this is not our fate. So let us not talk falsely now, the hour is getting late."

Then I remembered that sex turned out to be way better than the best of reviews. "Gimme that sucker," I said.

"Outside in the distance a wildcat did growl. Two riders were approaching and the wind began to howl…"

We didn't catch much that evening, but it didn't matter. Everything took on a warm, decidedly amusing glow and I had more fun just trying to grab the baitfish in the bucket than I did at my senior prom. The sun bled into the ocean in a riotous chorus of Degas pastels that left me stunned and agape, and suddenly I could feel the pilings of the bridge come alive, vibrating through the soles of my feet as they fought the churning rush of the new tide. Twilight turned the green waters into frothing obsidian, and as James Taylor crooned about having a friend, we ate two entire buckets of Mr. Chickie's Charcoal-Baked Chicken under the glow of the yellow bridge lights.

Will looked at me with slightly glazed eyes and that infamous, crooked smile of his. "Don't get much better than this, dude." I agreed at the time, but it wasn't long until we'd both discovered that it did.

We were complete opposites in appearance. Will was tall and gangly with a curt, unruly shock of sandy hair and deep blue eyes. He had an easy nature and a clever, Steve Martin wit, which often led him to the nexus of any gathering (especially if alcohol or a little herb were added to the equation). I was short and stocky with long, almost shoulder-length dark hair, hazel eyes, and more of a type-A demeanor, but no less entertaining when plied with the proper personality-enhancing chemistry. We had this weird, cosmic connection almost from the beginning—playing off each other as if it were rehearsed, knowing what was coming before the other said it. We shared a passion for the mischievous, constantly looking for something to challenge our wit and whet our slightly twisted humor. We were benign rogues, Peter Pan pirates, searching for a sail on the horizon, a ship to board, and as our two-year intellectual odyssey neared an end, we came to realize we simply viewed the world differently than those around us. They envisioned dental colleges, accounting offices, and brokerage businesses. We saw sails in the distance—and they carried us south/southwest.

A few weeks after graduation, Will and I, along with a friend of ours named Glen Fryer, decided to take a camping excursion to the Florida Keys. The trip was a hallmark for each of us, and it was somewhat of an adventure unto itself.

Will and I had taken a scuba diving course and received our certification in Saint Pete several months before the trip. We both loved the ocean, but in the process, we discovered that diving, for us, ran a close second to Mr. Chickie's Charcoal-Baked Chicken. We had purchased gear and were looking forward to exploring the clear, aquamarine waters of the Keys. Our buddy wasn't certified, but had done some diving and managed to borrow some equipment for the junket. For Glen, a quiet, husky fellow of medium height with blond, curly hair, this was to be the last hurrah before starting veterinary school in the fall. He intended to make the most of it.

We left late one evening and drove all night, taking turns at the wheel. It was a long, eleven-hour trip down the twists and turns of old Highway 27, but a glorious, yellow sun rimmed the horizon and welcomed us as we entered Key Largo.

In each life there are a couple of absolutely indelible moments that unequivocally ordain a portion of your future. Most guys will tell you those moments generally involve nice teeth and shapely figures. But as that weathered stretch of U.S. 1 arched across a limpid, blue-green bay bordered by mangroves, I watched a flock of egrets rise gracefully into the air—delicate, black and white wings showcased against the distant, gray and crimson morning clouds—and something inside me changed. As I savored the poignant, salty tang of the ocean and the mangroves, a fishing skiff turned out of a small cut and skipped lithely across the clean, clear water. Something clicked and whirred inside my psyche, and suddenly locked into place. It wasn't at all like experiencing wonderful and new—it was like coming home.

Our first day was spent in an *Alice in Wonderland* montage of first-time sights, smells, and sounds. After breakfast at a little clapboard restaurant encased in red bougainvillea and yellow hibiscus, we continued south, pausing here and there to cast a lure, or snorkel in the pristine waters, exclaiming to each other with muffled gurgles and urgent gestures as a kaleidoscope of sea life surrounded us. Rainbows of colorful tropical fish cascaded in and out of our reach, while grotesquely shaped, vividly embellished crabs scurried away from overturned rocks. Small, wary octopuses stared out from dark cubbyholes in the coral, an array of unlucky crustacean husks adorning the mouths of their lairs, and occasionally a bantam barracuda drifted in amongst the small snapper that gathered around to see if we might uncover a meal for them. It was nothing short of exotic—a wonderland for real.

By afternoon we had reached the Middle Keys. We shared a hasty lunch of sandwiches from our cooler, then decided to push into Key West—garrison of ganja, bastion of stunning beaches and bare breasts, and last but not least, Duval Street; the dimly lit cakewalk of music, liquor, and liaison—heady stuff for young hormones.

We found a campground on Stock Island just as the sun began to burn a fiery hole in the layered gray and rose horizon. By seven o'clock the evening breeze appeared like magic, washing away the heat from the island, and as the shadows lengthened, we emerged from the campground feeling frisky and hopeful. Glen had dressed a little for the occasion, wearing tan bellbottom jeans and a long-sleeve maroon shirt he'd somehow managed to keep fairly wrinkle-free—blond hair combed straight back and blue eyes alight with anticipation. I went with a Rolling Stones T-shirt and blue jeans. After a quick comb, I let my hair succumb to gravity, the longest of it just reaching my shoulders. I looked over at Will, who had begun to slow-dance himself over to the car while fondling his own ass and singing "I Think I Love You." I had to smile. The guy was a "Paint Your Wagon" Lee Marvin in a tropical shirt and khaki shorts—younger of course, and a little less aggressive, but he had that same sandy blond hair and lanky, casual rhythm about him—the same irresponsible sense of self-composure, reckless grin, and dry wit. If I could keep him in form, the night would undoubtedly be interesting.

We hopped into my old Ford Falcon and headed downtown, parking near the foot of Duval Street by the docks. I can still remember stepping from the car and pausing, captured by the essence that was Key West. The last of the crimson sky rose above distant squall clouds and silhouetted the outriggers of shrimp boats and the masts of sailboats at harbor. The pungent odor of drying nets and lobster traps mingled with the aroma of conch fritters, Cuban *Picadillo*, and the tart, sweet smell of key lime blossoms. It was that intoxicating contradiction of flavors that I would come to know as the Keys. Like the ocean, which could be so serene one day and so totally unforgiving the next, I would learn that the Keys were always the same and never the same.

As we strolled onto Duval, bathed by pale street lamps and humid evening air, the cross-section of humanity around us represented a vibrant blend of Bahamas sea-people, enterprising and excitable Cubans, and a cacophony of adventurers, misfits, and ogling tourists from across the country and around the world, all searching for their own slice of key lime paradise.

We spotted Sloppy Joe's (which was really sloppy, then), and as we got closer, we could hear a guitar being beaten upon rhythmically and someone crooning about a great filling station hold up costing him two good years. As we went inside and found seats at the bar, the crooner had begun something about a piano player from Miami and a Cuban crime of passion—messy and old-fashioned. I remember thinking the guy with the long, sun-bleached hair and guitar certainly had some interesting themes.

We spent about an hour in Sloppy Joes, listening to the music, drinking, and trying to separate strays from the herd. We were having a great time, but none of us were finding the girl of our temporary dreams, and it was seventy-five cents for a Miller, so we decided to move on. We drifted across the street, to Lou's Bar (later to become the Bull and Whistle, and probably the epitome of a Key West bar in those days.) Casablanca ceiling fans churned the thick, smoke-filled air above batteries of small, weathered tables loosely surrounding a huge center bar. Tall windows faced the street and provided a free stage show for those inside and outside. Bartenders and waitresses, as high as they could afford to be and still function, scurried about in a frenzy of splashing liquid, sliding bottles, and clanging registers. From a small stage in the back, a three-piece group with a guitar, bass, and a conga pounded out sensuous, driving rhythms and the place virtually writhed to the tempos. But Lou's was fast and loud that night and the crowd was so thick it was a challenge just to get a beer, let alone a date, so we hit the street once more. Two bars down on the right there was a sign that read:

Hermit Crab Races Tonight
(Bring your best crawler)

Now that caught our attention—particularly Will's, because he had somehow slipped ahead in the unannounced race for inebriety. "How in the hell are you gonna race a hermit crab?" he mumbled. "You'd have to have really itsy-bitsy little jockeys, man." Showing an inch of height with forefinger and thumb, he squinted through the window. "Itsy-bitsy jockeys."

The place wasn't quite as packed as the Bull and Whistle, but there was a good crowd gathering in the back around a long, narrow table. It had a fluorescent light above it, with a notice that read:

Touch a crab during a race, get "The Hook" for 10 minutes
(And you buy all runners a drink)

I noticed that in one corner of the bar there was a huge gaff hook attached about six feet up the wall, and there, sure enough, was a guy dangling by his collar. I took another look around and realized the clientele was distinctly different from the last bar. There were a lot of burly-looking bikers, and biker chicks with that hard sensuousness that says *I can suck the chrome off a handlebar, but when I'm finished with you, I'll sacrifice you to the god of Harleys.* I felt like I should instantly go get a tattoo and come back later. Actually, I was on my way out when Will grabbed me. "Crab races, man! Let's watch the crab races!" He was already stumbling in that direction.

A race was just about to begin and all the "runners" (guys and girls with crabs—wait, let me clarify that—all the guys and girls who had entered crabs in the race, regardless of their present hygienic afflictions) were gathered around the track. Will was almost to the table when he stepped on a piece of discarded lime and stumbled into a long-haired girl in a saffron halter top and white bellbottoms. Her crab went flying, hit the ground, and Will stepped squarely on it. There was a crackling, squishy sound, followed by a collective gasp and the room went totally quiet. The only sound was the jukebox in the back, playing a Creedence Clearwater Revival tune.

I see the bad moon rising.
I see trouble on the way...

Someone in the background whispered, "That was Little Mike's crab."

I thought, *No, that was the cute little girl's crab, and besides, if it's Little Mike's he'll just have to accept an apology.* Suddenly, the men's room door swung open and all eyes riveted on it. Silhouetted in the doorway was this little guy in Dockers and a T-shirt, curly hair, somewhat frightened eyes. *Ahhh, Little Mike. I'll take care of this.*

I see earthquakes and lightnin'
I see bad times today...

All of a sudden, a huge hand from behind the door swatted the little fellow in the back of the head, knocking him halfway across the bar. Then this "thing" stepped out—much like a shaved gorilla on steroids—hair pulled tight and braided in a long pigtail down his back, one really fierce-looking eye (the other gazing upward, glazed, and indifferent—very spooky), ice pick acne, dressed in blue jeans, chains, and tattoos, roughly six and a half feet tall.

The crowd opened up, the little girl put her hands together. "I didn't do it, Mike!" She swung around fiercely and pointed at Will, who held the broken remnants of his future. "He did it! He knocked Little Charlie out of my hand and stepped on him!"

Don't go around tonight
Well, it's bound to take your life...

I thought, *Oh my God, the damned thing had a name! Sweet Lord, we're in trouble—or Will's in trouble,* which made me feel guilty, but better. Will, being a sensible, intelligent person, did the only thing he could; he began pleading for his life, babbling about buying Little Mike a new crab, several new, larger crabs, or a new Harley, then lapsing into "Please don't hurt me! I loved Little Charlie!"—then back to a new crab with a tattoo of his choice, or a dog—a dog would be good. Suddenly I found my feet moving toward them. I don't know why. I was telling them to stop, but they just weren't listening. Little Mike picked up a pool cue with no intention of playing billiards, and I was suddenly facing him, standing in front of Will.

I fear rivers overflowing
I hear the voice of rage and ruin...

"Mike, sir," I said.

Mike tested the cue on the table next to me. It apparently wasn't heavy enough because it shattered. I'll admit a little shriek burbled out of me. He picked up another one. "Whadda you want, you little weasel? You want a beatin' too?"

"No! No sir," I said in a squeaky voice that didn't remotely resemble mine. "I want to replace your crab with the best, fastest crab around." (*I didn't know where the words were coming from—someone had possessed me. Where was I gonna get a friggin' hermit crab in the middle of the night, let alone a fast one—or one that wasn't scared shitless of Little Mike*?)

Don't go out tonight

There's a bad moon on the rise...

Mike stopped and gave me his Cyclops gaze. "I don't think so. I wanna beat him."

"But Mike, sir. Wouldn't you like to win more often?" I pointed at the wall. "The chart says Little Charlie was rated tenth in the top twenty. A guy like you can do better than that—you got a reputation. I'll make a deal with you. If I bring you a crab and he wins the race you enter him in, you let my buddy go. If the crab loses you can beat him to a pulp."

I heard a high-pitched whine from Will behind me, and felt his fingers biting into my side.

"Are you frigging mad?" my partner hissed. "Whose side are you on?"

Hope you got your things together

Hope you're quite prepared to die...

Mike thought about it for a moment. We got the Cyclops gaze again. "If he loses, I beat you both to a pulp." He smiled, knowing the odds were way on his side and he was probably going to get a two-for-one ass-whooping. Then he grabbed me by the front of the shirt, (surprisingly fast for a big guy.) "Okay, you got a half hour to bring me the crab. You're not back by then, you can pick up the pieces of your friend in the back alley, and we'll be lookin' for you!"

Looks like we're in for nasty weather

One eye is taken for an eye...

A moment later Glen and I were out the door and into the street.

"Where in God's little green acres are you gonna get a hermit crab—a fast hermit crab?" Glen practically shouted. "This is a serious bummer! They're gonna beat you guys bald-headed, and I'm personally so very glad that I don't know you. Where? Where are you gonna get a frigging crab?"

I shrugged helplessly. "I don't know, dude. Let's walk, I need to think."

We'd cruised along the street for about ten minutes, looking in bushes and checking out trees in people's yards—hell, I didn't know where hermit crabs hid. I didn't even know there were hermit crabs until a half hour before.

About that time, someone shot Glen with a BB gun while he was rummaging in a flower garden. He was getting pissed and scared. He glared at me. "Man, you better come up with something quick, 'cause the minutes are ticking away. This is a stone-cold bummer, dude. Where you gonna get a crab? And how are we gonna win—"

I started to reply, when I looked over his shoulder and saw the sign in front of a distant bar:

Crab Races Every Saturday Night.

"C'mon," I said. "I know where the crabs are."

The racing setup in the Laughing Turtle was just about the same. The crab races were at one end and there was a big bar at the other. A handful of tables were dispersed in between. The place was pretty well packed. Two guitarists on a small stage in the corner were doing a fair version of The Doobie Brothers' "Listen To The Music," and about a dozen runners were getting ready for a race. The musicians finished their song and announced a short break.

I turned to Glen. "Okay, we need a diversion. Order two double shots of 151 Rum and meet me at that table," I said, pointing at the one closest to the races.

"So you're going to get wasted? That's your answer?"

"Just get me the shots, okay?" I looked around and saw a girl standing alone by the bar—not that pretty, but dressed hot—tube top, miniskirt, platforms, long dark hair. I walked over. "Hi."

She nodded and smiled.

I cleared my throat. "Listen, how'd you like to make twenty bucks?

Her expression turned to disdain. "Get real, little cowboy."

"No, no. You just have to do one thing—"

"Twenty bucks? Don't insult me again."

"No, no. I just want you to scream when I tell you to."

"How about I moan while we're doing it? I'll say something like, 'Oooh baby, oooh baby, you're the one.' But it's still gonna cost more."

"No, no. I don't want to do it. It's just—"

She straightened up, hands on her hips. "What? I'm not good enough for you? What are you—one of these weirdos who just wants to ogle and play with your—"

"No! For God's sake! All I want you to do is to stand right here and scream when I nod to you. Can you do that—for twenty bucks?"

She shrugged indifferently. "It's your money."

"Loud," I said handing her the twenty. "Loud."

"Whatever turns you on."

Glen showed up with the drinks and I told him what I wanted. He agreed on the condition that later, when we were arrested, I would admit that it was my idea. Then he drifted into the crowd.

I waited until the crab race started, then I took the first shot of 151 and belted it down. When I stopped gagging I grabbed the second shot, splashed it across the table, struck a match and tossed it. The tabletop went up like a faulty gas barbecue. I looked at the girl by the bar and nodded. She did much better than I expected. Right behind her commendable screeches, I yelled, "Fire! Fire!"

Glen, from the other side of the room, did a remarkably good high-pitched scream and cried, "Save the women and children!"

For a few moments, no one was paying attention to the crab race. People surged at the door as a waitress ran from the bar and sprayed the table with a fire extinguisher. I just strolled by the racing platform, snatched the crab closest to the finish line, and kept going.

I thought I'd made a clean getaway, but by the time I reached the entrance, the panic had ebbed. Suddenly one of the bouncers stepped in front of me—six feet, muscle shirt, no humor.

"I saw what you did, dude, and now I'm gonna—"

"Meteorite!" I cried, pointing upward. He glanced reflexively at the ceiling. I kicked him in the nuggets and bolted through the door.

A few minutes later I found Glen hiding behind a dumpster and we headed back toward Little Mike and Will. We had six minutes. Setting out at a trot, Glen and I made three blocks before settling into a fast walk. The bar was only two blocks away. We were going to make it. Then, of course, we had to win a race, but I figured one thing at a time. We were walking by an alleyway when a voice hissed at us from the shadows.

"Hegh, man, help me! Help me!"

Glen and I stopped and turned, moving a little closer. We shouldn't have. A guy with a gun leaned out of the dimness—a Latin in his mid-twenties, dressed in a pair of worn khaki shorts and a tie-dyed T-shirt. He had hair that fell in dark curly ringlets around his forehead and ears, a swarthy, pockmarked face that reflected some African heritage, an Errol Flynn mustache, and anxious dark eyes. "Chu get chur ass in here, now, man!"

Hector Zarapata, the consequence of a liaison between a Haitian hooker and a Salvadorian fisherman who shipwrecked in Cuba, was a pickpocket, burglar, and former resident of Cuba's *Quivican* Prison. He was having a bad day, even for Hector. Actually, he'd had another bad week—it was all kind of blending together in a collage of rotten luck. The "pluckin' *touristas*" he tried to rob had lost or already spent their money. One lady spit on him, another kicked him in the *cojones*. He got bit by a "pluckin' dog" while breaking into a house, and for a week he thought he had rabies. *Son-a-bitch! When was it gonna end?*

Three months ago he thought his luck had changed. He managed to escape while on a work detail outside *Quivican* prison. A friend had told him about the raft—only room for five, a week in the right current and they hit Florida. It was all planned for Saturday night, when most of the guards who watch the docks were drunk anyway. Saint Nicolas, the patron saint of mariners, took them in his arms and eight days later, they're burned to a crisp and each ten pounds lighter, but they're drinking *cervezas* in Key West. He and Ramos got jobs cleaning traps on the docks. Ramos was fairly content, but Hector Zarapata "was no meant for clanin' stinkin' traps." That was partly because Hector had a terrible lisp that was exacerbated when he spoke his thoroughly mauled version of English with Cuban and Haitian inflections. The boss had a tough time understanding the twisted dialect, and teased him some. Hector decided it would be easier to make a living robbing people. There was less conversation. At least that was the theory.

"Chu get chur pluckin' ass in here or I'ne dwena choot chu."

I looked at Glen. "Chu chu? Is he talking about a train?"

Hissing from the shadows. "Dimme sus walletas or I'ne dwena choot chu twice, man."

"The Conch Train is on Simonton Street," said Glen, trying to be helpful.

"No! No! Idiota! Sus dinero! Dinero!"

"The son of a bitch is trying to rob us!" I muttered to no one in particular.

"No," said Glen. "My Spanish is pretty good. I think he just wants us to buy him dinner."

"Chit! Chit! Chit!" whispered a frustrated voice from the shadows.

Glen took two dollars out of his pocket and handed it to the outstretched hand. "Have a good *dinero* and a *bueno dias*, *amigo*," he said with the same condescendingly earnest tone you use when the dog pees in the right spot.

As we slowly backed away and moved off, the voice in the shadows was still moaning, *"Coño! Coño! Coño!* Thas it! I'ne dwena buy bullettes. I'ne dwena buy real pluckin' bullettes!"

We ran the final distance and entered the bar two minutes late. Still, our timing was good. Little Mike and two of his buddies were just marching across the barroom toward Will, who was dangling helplessly from the gaff hook on the wall. Mike had a new cue stick.

We worked our way through the crowd and confronted them just as they reached Will.

"We've got your crab," I said, a little out of breath.

Mike paused and lowered the cue. "Yeah? Let's see it."

I pulled the little fellow from my pocket and held him up. He came wiggling out for a moment, then quickly ducked back into his black and yellow-striped shell (which is basically the first impulse anything would have when it saw Mike). He reached for the crab and I pulled back. "You get it when the race starts. I gotta protect my interests, man."

Mike snorted. "You gonna get it when the race ends—if he doesn't win. Your friend stays where he is till it's over." He reached over and picked up some guy's tequila off the table next to him, shot it, dropped the glass and lumbered off to the bar.

I breathed again for the first time in thirty or forty seconds, then Glen and I walked over to Will. "What's happenin', man?"

Will looked down. "Nothin', just hangin' around."

I noticed his Hawaiian shirt was partially ripped open in the front, and his pants were askew on his hips, zipper halfway down. I looked up.

"They made me dance on the tables for the biker bitches." He sighed. "You can only be fondled so much before your dignity is lost."

I looked at him.

"Okay, I liked it. But I still suffered the loss of my dignity."

"You didn't have any dignity to begin with," Glen said.

Will grinned. "So you got a crab, huh?"

"Yeah, he's so fast I had to break one of his legs so the race wouldn't look fixed."

Will brightened. "Really?"

"No, you dumb shit. I wouldn't know a fast crab from a tampon."

"Well, how in the hell is he gonna win the race?"

I paused and glanced over to a darkened corner of the bar where two shady-looking characters sat. "I got a plan."

My partner exhaled, exasperated. "Well, it better be bitchin' and quick because the race starts in seven minutes."

"Try to keep your pants up for a little longer, dude. Glen will keep you company. I'll be back."

I had watched the two guys earlier, hard faces, expensive clothes, gold chains, leaning close, talking earnestly, drinking shots of tequila and following them with limes. But they were following the limes with little white lines they were laying out on the table and snorting discreetly through a straw when they thought no one was watching. I may have been somewhat of a virgin when it came to drugs, but I wasn't stupid. I walked over casually, when they were between snorts. "It's none of my business, *amigos*. But I just heard the bartender say something about the DEA headed over this way. Just thought you might like to know. You dig?"

I blinked and the seats were empty. I reached down and with the edge of my little finger, gathered some of the cocaine residue on the table into a tiny pile. I put our crab down next to it, with the open part of his shell facing the pile, and blew.

I'm not exactly sure what I expected, but nothing happened, nothing at all. I peeked into the shell. The little guy was still tucked way into the back. I sighed. Maybe if I got Mike to hit me in the head right away, I wouldn't remember the rest of the beating. The bell rang for the next race and I heard Mike bellow, "Where's my friggin' crab?"

I was so certain that Will and I had about five minutes before being pounded into jelly, I just numbly handed Mike the crab. He smiled (or something similar to a smile.)

"This is a win-win situation for me," he growled. "Makes me feel so good, I'm gonna call him 'Lucky.'" Then he grabbed me by the shirt again. "Don't wander away."

I stepped back.

Mike turned and held Lucky at the starting line, as did the handful of other runners. The starting gun sounded, everyone released their crabs and stepped away.

Some contestants came out running, some set out a tentative leg or two, checking the turf before getting underway, some just wiggled a little and rolled over on their backs, then drew themselves upright and entered the contest like the seasoned racers they were. One just lay there.

Shit! I killed him! I killed him!

As the fastest crabs neared the halfway mark of the track, the momentum of the crowd rose. People were yelling and screaming, money was changing hands as percentages altered, jostled drinks bathed onlookers and shelled participants, fights broke out. Two crabs reached the three-quarter mark with four more close behind. The crowd roared. I looked around and Glen was gone. I was about to make a dash for Will—*if I can get him off the hook we might make the door*—when suddenly I saw Lucky's shell tremble. I figured someone jarred the table. I stared. *C'mon Lucky!* There it was again. The damned thing was vibrating. The next thing I knew, Lucky was clawing his way out of his shell like he had a grease fire in the kitchen. The little dude popped out, completely forgot his house and ran two feet as fast as a rat before realizing he was ass-crack naked. The crowd howled with excitement, but that spooked him and he swung around, starting to drag his ugly, curled little body back toward his shell.

Suddenly Mike lumbered forward, slammed his hand on the table, put his face down in front of Lucky and screamed, "Run, you little son of a bitch! Or I'll eat you! I'll friggin' eat you!"

With the blast of cocaine and one really good look at Little Mike, Lucky decided to book a flight to the other end of his known universe, which happened to be the finish line about twelve feet away. I'm pretty sure I heard him scream. He rose up on his back legs, balancing on his butt sack, and shot off as if someone had spit him out of a blowpipe. He knocked out two contestants on the way, zigzagged into one side of the raceway, then crossed the track and careened off the other side, took out a third crab with a final body slam, and crossed the finish line three inches ahead of the closest contender. The crowd went wild. Mike picked up Lucky at the winner's circle and I brought him his shell, which he scooted into gladly.

There was some argument that Lucky won without his shell—no one had ever seen that happen before. Someone in the back said there was nothing in the rulebook about it. *(What friggin' rulebook?)* Most importantly, there was Little Mike to contend with, so it was declared an official win. Mike was happy. Will and I were thrilled. Glen suddenly appeared saying he must have had to go to the bathroom when all the excitement started.

Mike hoisted Will off the hook and bought us a round of drinks, then told us, "Don't come round here again till you got tattoos." We thanked him for the drinks and the advice, shot our rums, and quickly left.

It was one o'clock in the morning when we stepped back out on the street and began working our way toward the car. That old pirate moon, round and gold as a doubloon rose up over Duval, reminding us of the fortunes that had been won and lost for over 300 years right where we stood. And I realized then, even at this late date, there were still fortunes to be won or lost. The game was just a little different. But I could learn to play it. Yeah, we could learn to play it.

CHAPTER TWO

A Cool Place To Live, If You Could Make A Living

The following morning dawned clean and cool—the sweet, rich aroma of mangroves and sea blended with wood fires and sizzling bacon drawing us from our sleeping bags. For just a moment I lay there savoring it all—fluffy, cream-colored clouds drifted indifferently across the soft blue sky, seagulls laced through the azure stillness calling to each other, and there was just enough breeze to caress the palm fronds above my head. It was like a Michener book (with the other fifty pages of the description torn out). Softly, somewhere in the background, I could hear a radio playing James Taylor's "Fire and Rain." I remember thinking if it got any better than this, I hadn't experienced it.

While sharing a pot of coffee, we decided that having survived Key West with a memorable tale, it was on to some serious diving and fishing. After a little breakfast, we loaded our gear and headed north, exploring a little, and snorkeling here and there. A boat rental was beyond our pocketbooks, but everyone said the diving off the bridges was magnificent, so toward afternoon we agreed to take a shot at Kemp Channel in the Lower Keys. Arriving as the tide was coming in and the water was as clear as an aquarium, we sat on the seawall that abutted the bridge, watching huge green and red parrotfish picking a snack here and there from the underwater foliage while blue angels floated effortlessly next to them against the current. All this was no more than a dozen feet below us.

A grizzled old conch was fishing next to us—no shirt, grimy, knee-length shorts, a faded Dodgers ball cap, leathered skin, and enough lines around his eyes to resemble a topographical map of Brazil. He heard us talking about diving. He checked the line tension on his rods, then turned to us with an appraising glance. "You boys ain't seasoned at this, are ya?"

"Well, we have our diving certification cards," I said a little defensively.

He spit into the slowing waters below us. "Well, that's good. Take that with you so you have something to wipe your ass with when ya get in a dither down there and crap your pants."

Will sighed, combing back his shock of blond hair with the fingers of one hand in a nervous concession. "Okay, we don't know diddly-squat about diving a bridge."

Without preamble, the old man began. "Bridges are great places to dive and tricky places to dive. The tide moves at a good clip most of the time, but when it's slack at high or low, you got about a half hour of still water before it begins to move again. When them waters pick up and near their peak—and it happens quick—they'll wash you out to Hawk Channel quicker than the flick of a grunt's tail. But the trick is to be gone before then and checkin' your catch on shore." He pointed. "Best place to get in is under the bridge, there, where all that cement and rocks meets the water." Then he smiled, just a flicker. "Don't mind Rufus. Now get going. Tide's gonna ebb in fifteen minutes."

We went back to the car and grabbed our gear, then worked our way down the abutment to the seawall that ran underneath the bridge. Shaded from the sun in the dim stillness of the grotto-like structure, we all stopped, staring. In the back of the man-made cavern was a structure of some sort—an old Maytag washing machine box embroidered with palm fronds and a variety of drift line flotsam. There were sheets of Styrofoam, ragged beach towels, driftwood, and No Trespassing signs, all woven into some kind of dwelling. Something rustled in the rear of the box. We all took a step back. The silence was punctuated with the reverberation of a car running over the bridge above. There was another rustle and a cough. A thin veil of smoke drifted from the nest and the distinct smell of marijuana pervaded the air. Suddenly, from out of the lair crawled a spindly-looking, light-skinned black guy clothed in a ragged, yellow Captain Tony's T-shirt and a baggy pair of khaki shorts. He had shoulder-length dreadlocks and weird gray eyes that looked as if he'd probably consumed sufficient pharmaceuticals to be listed in the "Who's Who of Experimental Laboratory Vermin."

"Hello, mons! Hello, mons!" he called with a warm, gap-toothed smile. "Welcome to you that you should meet me—gondolier of good tidings and grand messenger for the wisdom of ganja." He smiled disarmingly once more and bowed. "I am Rufus. May your life egg break cleanly and the great tortoise grant you a moonlit path to the sea."

Will, who was very quick and enjoyed psychobabble anyway, put his index finger and his thumb together, making the sign of the moon and drew his hand in a full arch across his chest. "When the eyes of beauty fall lightly on dawn's faint scent, the wind will smile."

Rufus' eyes lit up as if he'd just discovered a separated-at-birth sibling. Extending his arm, he made a peace sign, then reversed it and placed the two fingers against his forehead. "Only the clever blowfish treasures the darkness of the moon."

Will opened his mouth to counter when Glen interrupted. "Okay, okay, enough with the clever blowfish. Are we going diving?"

We sat on the rocks and donned our diving gear, while Rufus explained that he bully-netted lobster in the backcountry for a living, but he had lost his boat, which was sort of an interim home as well, during a recent storm. He'd been living in his Maytag abode for about three weeks—a temporary setback in the life of a free spirit. Rufus wished us "great joy and infinite revelations" on our dive, assuring us that he would guard our clothes after Will struck a deal with him for two packages of Hostess Twinkies.

I'll always remember entering the sea and feeling that sense of weightlessness and wonderment. There was still just a little current. I gave my body a moment to adjust to the temperature, found Will and Glen to my right, then lifted an easy kick out into deeper, green-blue water and drifted gently down into a world that would possess me for the rest of my life. There was, of course, the anxiousness of entering a domain in which you are no longer entirely in control, where life can be measured by the air you carry and the creatures you meet. But in moments I was immersed in the magic of it all—captivated by the silent rhythm of the tide, the sway and cadence of all about us, and the movements of an insanely colorful, complex dance that I could only view with wonder, for I was a stranger in the strangest of lands.

We moved out a little farther and found one of the grottos cut by the changing tides—a ragged hole perhaps twenty feet long, a dozen wide, and six feet deep, with three-foot ledges worn back into the sand at the bottom. Fire coral flamed up in brittle fingers along the lip, and staghorn jutted out along the sides. All around there was a symphony of movement. Snappers sailed in sleek schools with instant intuitive synchronization. Camouflaged grouper cruised confidently along the bottom, or shared the deeper ledges with clusters of crayfish that scuttled for position in their hideaways. Indignant moray eels poked their heads out of dark, foreboding holes and bared their teeth like cats, and an array of florescent tropicals moved about or slipped away from us with practiced ease. Each turn around piling or pocket presented an extraordinary new experience, another vision from the underwater book of Alice. For the next thirty minutes I was mesmerized, immersed in a baptism by the sea from which I would emerge forever changed.

When we felt the tide subtly switch and move toward the sea, we knew our time had passed. As I reached the shallow water of the shoreline, I removed my tank and crawled over the rocks, avoiding the sea urchins embedded in and around them, helping Will and Glen behind me to the dry, coral shore. Strangely enough, Rufus was nowhere to be found. We all sat there for a few moments, savoring the experience, watching the rising momentum of the tide as it coursed between the pilings, and eagerly trading the visions of our quest. The setting sun buried itself behind the bridge, only to reappear moments later as it descended beneath one of the arches, flickering gold and silver across the weathered concrete and the darkening waters. It was nothing short of magic. I looked over at Will and I saw that he was lost to the moment, raptured in paradise. I suspected that he was having one of his own indelibly ordaining junctures, without a shapely figure or nice teeth anywhere. It was pretty cool. He smiled strangely. "You know, I like this place—I really like this place."

I nodded, trying not to be too enthusiastic. "It'd be a far-out place to live—if you could make a living."

About that time Rufus showed up again, heralded by the rich, green smell of ganja. "Hey, mons! You got Hostess Twinkies? It's a very tired and hungry job guarding clothes!"

As Rufus bent down to help me with my dive tank, an amulet on a leather band slipped from the neck of his T-shirt. It was shaped like a pyramid, onyx colored, maybe an inch long. The last of the sun caught it and for just a moment. I was certain I saw it glow—light up as if it had just been plugged in. "Where'd you get that?" I said pointing.

Rufus wrapped his hand around it. "Family heirloom," he said matter-of-factly, eyes subtly changing for a fraction of a second. He looked out at the graying horizon. "Even the one-eye toad has visions of truth when he squints at the moon."

We packed up our gear and worked our way back along the coral pathway to the car. Evening was setting and the coconut palms leaned over the walk like old men, reflecting the last of the orange and red horizon. By the time we had gotten Rufus his Twinkies and loaded up, the trees were rustling silhouettes in the evening breeze. We said farewell to our Jamaican friend. With a half-eaten Twinkie in hand, he extended a final peace sign. "Cool driftings, mon. May you always nest peacefully amongst the soft down of life."

Will and Glen looked at me, smiled, and we all returned the salute.

"Don't take any wooden blowfish," I said.

That evening we stayed at The Kemp Channel Campground—running water, showers, daughters of campers....

The following day, after refilling our tanks at a local dive shop and getting a little insight into the area, we moved northward and explored Big Pine Key for a while. We discovered it was one of the largest islands—almost five miles long—with a beautiful, high interior of pine trees and palms. There were a few businesses and a couple of small subdivisions, but much of the island was still undeveloped.

We snorkeled the shoreline of Big Pine in a couple of places, then made a scuba dive off the southern end of Spanish Harbor Bridge. Once again we were astounded by the array of sea life, in particular all the incredibly colorful tropicals. Unable to refrain, we gestured frantically and gurgled incomprehensible words to each other at each new sighting. When the tide began to turn and the dive was over, we exited the water by the overpass of the bridge, as before. Once again, we discovered company. As I peeled off my wet T-shirt, I noticed another diver in a full wetsuit had just come out of the water about thirty yards from us and was bent over, working with a clear hand net of some sort over an Igloo cooler. I looked at Will and Glen, then walked over to him, the others in tow. The fellow, perhaps in his early forties, face still pinched with a red circle from his mask, hair damp and matted, glanced up and nodded, then returned to his project. He had a clear Visquene hand net with a square, eight-inch throat. The handle and the throat of the net were made of what looked like quarter-inch aluminum tubing. He was in the process of shaking out a variety of beautiful, small tropical fish into his ice chest, which was half-filled with water. The creatures darted back and forth, and huddled in the corners, displaying stunning combinations of shapes and designs.

"Dude! Those are wicked incredible," said Glen. "What are you gonna do with them?"

The fellow spoke without looking up, getting the last of his fish in the cooler. "I sell them—for aquariums. A wholesaler out of Miami buys 'em from me and ships them all over the country."

"Are there other people like you doing this?" I said as casually as I could.

"A few."

There was a heavy stillness in the air, a brief moment of incandescence.

"A cool place to live," I whispered to Will, who stood next to me.

He cocked his head and smiled. "If you could find a way to make a living."

CHAPTER THREE

New Homes and Rabbis

As we settled in that night at the Big Pine Key Fishing Lodge, Will and I began to discuss the possibility of coming back down to the Keys to live and earning our livelihood diving for tropical fish. Hell, if that guy could do it, surely we could! What a life! Diving for tropical fish in the Florida Keys! Sadly for Glen, the plan did not include him. He was committed to veterinary college in the fall. His course had been mapped long before, by him and his parents, both of whom were doctors.

We took the next few days to leisurely wind our way back up the Keys, but before heading north, we spent a little more time on Big Pine. Aside from being centrally located between Marathon and Key West, there was just something about that island that seemed like the right place. We took an hour or two trying to find a house to rent, but they were few and far between, and somewhat high for our budget.

On the plus side, we were able to locate another tropical fish collector on the Key—a fellow named Robert Bunter. With directions from a little lady running the dive shop on the island, we ended up at a small bungalow on the edge of a canal that led out to the gulf side of the Key.

As we pulled up, there was a guy leaning over a large fiberglass-coated plywood tank near the canal behind his house. Attached to the tank, leading into the canal, was a line of PVC tubing, and we could hear the hum of a water-circulating pump. The fellow was probably in his late twenties—tall, blond hair, blue eyes—tanned like a surfer, wearing a faded pair of Hang Ten shorts and flip-flops. He scooped up some seaweed floating in the tank and tossed it into the canal, then turned toward us as we got out of the car and walked over.

I smiled. "Hey."

"Hey." There was a pause. "Can I help you?"

I looked into the tank. There were dozens of tropicals darting in and out of broken conch shells and foot-long pieces of three-inch-wide PVC tubing on the bottom.

"Man, that's too cool!" I said with more awe than intended. "Did you catch those?"

He gave me a look that said we weren't the first members of "Family Feud" to grace his door. "No. I put a molar in the tank last night and the Tropical Fish Fairy left them."

"Okay, stupid question. How about I try again?"

"Okay, I'm game."

"We're divers. We heard you collected tropical fish. Truth is, we just wanted to see what it was all about, you know, catching fish." I paused. "Man, I've been in the water with these guys and it seems like it would be the equivalent of putting salt on a bird's tail."

Robert wiped a little sweat from his forehead with the back of his hand. "Not much easier, at first. You just get better with practice, or you starve." There was a pause. "I guess you guys have been diving for a while?"

I glanced at Will. "Oh yeah, seems like forever."

"But there are times when it seems like just a few days," said Glen with a grin. "So much to see, and all..."

"Yeah," said Bunter with a chuckle, totally picking up on us. "Lots of stuff out there. No two dives the same, never know what you're going to see." He straightened and stretched a little. "Got chased out of the water yesterday by a small hammerhead—ten, twelve feet. But then I'm sure you guys have dealt with that before."

"Oh yeah, no big deal as long as you pay attention," I said, while my mind screeched, "*A twelve-foot friggin' hammerhead shark! Are you absolutely mind-numbed crazy? If you hurry back, you can still get a job at your uncle's shoe store!*"

I looked over at Will, whose eyes were very clearly making some significant points.

"*You never told me about no twelve-foot friggin' sharks chasing you out of the water. One good attack and you're pushing your chomped-up ass around by your knuckles on some skateboard, they're feeding you from the table like the family dog, and your new name is Shortbones, or for the really game beach dudes, Little Big Bite.*"

Trying to keep my voice casual, I said, "Just out of curiosity, about how often does that happen around here—you know, shark chases?"

Our new acquaintance tossed a couple more pieces of seaweed into the canal. "Aahhh, who's counting? You know, maybe a couple times a month, but hardly anyone gets eaten—well there was this one guy..."

A svelte, attractive lady with brown eyes, short dark hair, and a very small, yellow bikini stepped from the open sliding glass doors on the patio, walked over, and chidingly whooped Robert on the head with a newspaper. "Robert Bunter, don't be scaring these dudes off with your lies." She looked at us. "You hardly ever see big sharks here, and no one really gets bothered by them. They're all too well fed thanks to all the schools of fish in Hawk Channel and the Gulf Stream. The things you've got to watch out for are more like sea urchins, fire coral, and Man-O-War jellyfish, or an occasionally pissed-off moray." She paused. "So, let me guess. You guys thinking of becoming collectors?

"Well, it's crossed our minds," I said.

A soft chuckle escaped her lips. "Aaahhh, yes—the life of perpetual sun, sea, and all that money just swimming around out there just waiting for someone to scoop it up." She tapped Robert again with the newspaper. "Well, this lazy old dude could probably use some competition. By the way, I'm Dede."

Robert sighed. "It ain't as glamorous as it looks. It's not all cloudless skies and clear water. There's lots of hard, windy days in murky water, and wait until winter—talk about a bummer. I don't give a shit if you've got two wetsuits—" He caught himself and grinned, watching the setting sun turn the canal into flickering, wind-swept gold. "Like I'm going to run you off on a day like this." He paused again, as if making a decision. "It just so happens there's a new wholesaler out of Miami looking for collectors—Global Marine Life. You wouldn't be cutting into my sales if you hooked up with them. Truth is, I'm only planning on being here another year anyway, so what the hell. Then I'm headed back to California and law school."

We stayed and talked about the Keys and the business for about a half hour, then excused ourselves, thanking Robert and Dede for their time. As we started to walk away, on impulse I turned back, "Tell me, you wouldn't know of any place to rent on the island, on a canal?"

Robert thought about it for a moment. "Nah, not off the top of my head. You just have to watch the paper."

Dede held up her hand. "Wait a minute. I heard someone say something about a trailer for rent on Hibiscus Street, about three canals over from us. You might just check that on your way out."

We did, and sure enough, there was a small trailer with a "For Rent" sign in the window. We drove over to the local convenience store and called the number. The owner met us at the trailer ten minutes later. The mobile home turned out to be early '60s vintage but was well maintained. It was forty-five feet of extruded, pop-riveted aluminum painted a baby-puke green—eight feet wide, two cubicles called bedrooms, one claustrophobic bathroom with a stall shower just large enough for bathing bulimic meerkats, and a small living room/kitchen up front. Neither Will nor I were actually certain whether the refrigerator was in the living room or the couch was in the kitchen, but we figured it would work either way. The trailer was situated on a small rectangle of barren, sun-blasted coral rock garnished with a single coconut palm, bordering a small canal.

After we'd been given a tour of the place, Will looked at me with that crooked smile of his.

"You sure?" I said.

"Yeah."

"Okay," I replied with a grin of my own. "Welcome to paradise."

We gave the owner a deposit, promising to return in two weeks with the first and last month's rent. We had a home in the islands and we were going to be tropical fish collectors! When we left I was also absolutely certain that Robert Bunter was the "rabbi" we needed to work our way into this business.

It was a remarkable leap of faith when I look back on it. We were considering striking out into an area we had explored for a paltry five days, based on the assumption we could actually make a living because we'd seen a handful of tropical fish in a fiberglass tank. The fact that we had never once captured a single tropical fish in our entire lives didn't seem to cross our minds at the time.

I did, at least, have the forethought to contact Global Marine Life as we drove through Miami on our way home. The owner said they would welcome two more collectors—especially experienced divers like ourselves. Okay, I lied a little.

Two weeks later, Will and I had sold all of our possessions that weren't absolutely essential to survival in our new world. I sold my car and bought a slightly used VW bus, which we felt could be used as our mobile diving station. After a long, but highly anticipatory drive down from St. Petersburg, we arrived on Big Pine Key just as the sun was setting, casting the last of its magical, golden tendrils across a pale blue sky. It was August 17, 1971.

CHAPTER FOUR

Of Buccaneers Who Shook Their Booties

Our first few months in the Keys were spent enthusiastically encapsulated in a learning-experience thing. As we had hoped, Robert Bunter and Dede became great sources of information for us. They explained how to read the tides, showed us how to build our own Visquene hand nets, holding tanks, and pumping system, and how to pack our fish for delivery to Miami once a week.

We couldn't afford a boat right away, but we figured bridge and shore diving could support us in the beginning. With a little of Will's technical expertise and my ingenuity, we rigged up dive tank and gear racks, and Igloo holding coolers in the VW bus. We spent weeks just driving up and down the Keys, ferreting out those valuable dive spots within our reach that others hadn't bothered with, or hadn't discovered. We lived in Speedos and flip-flops, and when we wore out our rubber sandals we went barefoot until our feet grew so calloused that the punishing coral rock could no longer draw our attention. The sun bleached our hair and burned us brown, and our eyes grew accustomed to its glare. We talked to all the old-timers, bought them beers, and listened raptly to the secrets they were willing to share, and slowly but surely, we became tropical fish collectors.

Those days were a continuous collage of new experiences—each morning represented another opportunity to discover life at the threshold. We fished for pup shark off the beach at Long Key, pole-netted shrimp by the full moon off canal bridges on Big Pine, or caught the early morning tide and tossed fiddler crabs at tailing bonefish on the backside of No Name before heading out for a day's diving. At the end of the day, we often speared a grouper and grabbed a few lobsters for dinner, grilling great slabs of fish and split tails on the barbeque, and washing them down with a couple of beers while watching the setting sun turn the horizon into a Caribbean light show. I have never felt so connected to the elements—so alive and content at the same time.

The Keys nights had a magic all their own. Old amber street lamps cast hazy summer shadows as the humid evenings enveloped us in subtle fragrances of jasmine and mango. Trade winds caressed the palms, and they murmured back with their distinctive, somnolent rustling. Lizards scuttled in the dry leaves of sea grapes. Insects clustered around porch lights in erratic weaves, whispering to each other, humming melodies lost in an ancestry of gossamer wings. Full moons were mystical as their brilliance turned the sea chartreuse and they pulled at the waters in their ancient, perennial fashion. We fell victim to the quiet splendor of it all, and it freed us.

We survived the first winter—a mild one, fortunately—and by the spring of 1972 we had acquired a good degree of knowledge and a small boat. That same year, John Lennon and Yoko Ono actively demonstrated against America's Vietnam policy and were given a deportation order, *Grease* became the top Broadway attraction, Alabama Governor George Wallace was shot and paralyzed during a presidential appearance in Maryland, and Will and I discovered a Spanish treasure on the backside of the reef at G-Marker.

Our somewhat aged, sixteen-foot tri-hull was slightly underpowered with a fifty horsepower outboard, but it opened up wonderful new vistas for us. We finally had access to the mysterious and bountiful Hawk Channel that wound along the edges of the Florida Keys, and the aquamarine waters of the famed Keys' reefs became our playground. The quintessential scent and sensation of the ocean engulfed us—one part salt, two parts life on the edge—ceaseless casualty and rebirth at the very nexus of existence.

I can still recall that first trip out to the reef in our slightly used, heavily mortgaged *Pegasus*. Rolling gently in one and two-foot swells, the waters glimmered like shards of glass christened by a brilliant morning sun. Seabirds cried out, weaving precariously, plummeting into the shimmering waters as they assaulted schools of pilchards and glass minnows buried in the rise of the waves. Translucent-winged flying fish burst from the water and joined the fray, soaring effortlessly beside us. Hawk Channel's soft, current-scrolled sands and colorful patch reefs rose up at us from the clear waters, and an occasional, narrow weed line garnished the sparkling surface, stretching in a lazy coil toward the Gulf Stream. It wasn't just alluring, it was resurrecting.

I stood there, hands on the windshield brace, legs flexing to each light crest the bow pushed through, and looked over at Will. He held the wheel confidently, a soft smile curling the edges of his mouth—the sun in his eyes and the breeze ruffling his long blond hair. I knew he had fallen victim to the moment as well—another indelible juncture. We had joined the ranks of an elite brotherhood, a fraternity of adventurers who, for scores of generations, had sought their fortunes from Mother Nature's most mystical and capricious personality.

We dove through the summer, learning the ways of the reef and discovering an array of fascinating new creatures. Whether it happened in one day or a million years, I came to realize that the ocean is the creator's finest work—the detail, hues, and sheer artistry. It is the effort of an infinite imagination and the continual process of a power beyond the manipulation of man.

It was late September, when the waters lie down and become exceptionally clear for days at a time—perfect for reef diving. We had worked on the outboard engine for a few hours one morning, then decided to do a one-tank dive before the day got away from us. We packed our gear and were clearing Spanish Harbor shortly after the sun had reached its zenith. Will had the wheel and I relaxed in the passenger seat as we sailed out across the mirror of blue ice, headed for G-Marker, one of our favorite diving areas.

Will looked over, raising his voice above the sound of the engine. "What say we dive a little deeper today, hit the back side of G, where it starts to drop off."

"Yeah. Sounds good. I heard Bunter say there's lots of Rock Beauties and Cuban Hogfish out that way now."

We rolled past the aging and rusted tower that marked the reef, anchoring about a quarter-mile farther into blue water. The anchor line indicated a depth of roughly fifty feet. We donned our gear, grabbed our hand nets, then with a nod to each other, dropped into the ocean, gliding down in slow-motion freefall into a mysterious world that is never the same on any two occasions—where the situations and the possibilities are endless.

We spent the first twenty minutes working a fifty-foot radius around the anchor, bagging a dozen Rock Beauties and a couple of Cuban Hogfish. I motioned Will toward deeper water. He nodded and I lifted the anchor, carrying it out another thirty feet. The bottom was dropping off rapidly and our anchor line was more vertical than horizontal, providing less of an angle for the hook to lock in and secure, but we felt it was okay as long as we stayed in sight of the boat. I noticed a narrow coral ledge to the right of us, perhaps fifteen yards long and three feet high, decorated with brain coral and sea fans. I motioned to Will and we swam over, exploring around and under it. Spotting a Queen Angel scoot quickly into a hole at the back, I wedged myself under the ledge, trying to fan the sand back a little to get my net near the small crevice. As I did, I caught a glimpse of something out of place. There was a strange glitter for just a moment. I paused, and gently fanned the sand again. When the fog of sand dust settled there was a dull, gold-colored nub extending from the area I had just excavated. It had a curiously familiar shape. My heartbeat clicked up a notch. *Gold?... Gold?* We always carried in the back of our minds the possibility of stumbling upon some sort of sunken treasure. Hell, we were diving in one of the most heavily seeded areas in the world for lost ships. There was a part of me that never really thought it would happen, but there was another part of me that expected it.

I reached over and slowly slid my hand into the sand, around the object, grasped and pulled. It was heavy, but it gave with surprising ease. I moved out from the ledge and examined my find in the light, rubbing it clean with my gloved hands. My heartbeat suddenly hit the six-minute mile. It was a small golden statue, perhaps six inches tall and two inches wide. It had that heavy, square-featured Central American relief. Adorned with a headdress of some sort, the body had thick arms and legs, a wide face, and a prominent nose. But the most striking feature was the lustrous green, gemstone eyes.

Will was already swimming over to me when I looked up. He came to a stop, fanning his arms for balance. He stared at the statue for a moment, then looked up at me, his eyes wide. I handed it to him slowly—because of the weight. The realization came to him fully when he held it. Suddenly he did this little demented slow-motion jig, then came to his senses and motioned to me—*where?* I pointed to the end of the ledge, and in seconds we were burrowing under it like two lunatic sand eels. It was obvious that the coral had grown around something. It had deteriorated before being encrusted, but there was some shape left, and when I hammered the gnarled growth with the handle of my net I uncovered the rusted remnants of what might have been metal bindings and hinges—*a small chest.* We quickly explored the sand in that immediate area, trying to avoid stirring up too much of a cloud, and in mere seconds we were rewarded. I dug my hands into the spot where I had discovered the statue and my fingers closed on a mass of hard, flat objects. I pulled out a handful of gold coins. I hadn't even had time to react when Will suddenly emitted a garbled shriek and drew an ornately carved, five-inch gold cross from the same location. My heart was hammering against the rubber vest of my wetsuit. My mask was fogging, and I was gasping air through my regulator like I'd just had beach sex with Bo Derek. It was, undeniably, one of the most incredible experiences in my life. It was as glorious as all the treasure stories I had ever read, as spectacular as anything I had ever imagined. (Well, okay, not anything—I had imagined the Bo Derek beach sex once or twice, and that was pretty amazing, but when you're dreaming in these leagues, one out of two is still great.) I was praying for another find with each thrust of my fingers, while at the same time, silently begging I wouldn't awaken and find myself staring at the ceiling of our trailer, breathless, trembling, and bummed to tears.

In no more than ten minutes we recovered over sixty gold coins and another small idol, all from a spot no larger than a kitchen sink. We tried digging away from that location but the powdery sand yielded nothing. Regardless of our elation, we knew we had to quit. Our tanks were nearly empty and we were sucking the last vestiges of air. I motioned to Will (finger across throat) and pointed up at the surface. He nodded reluctantly and we headed topside—our dive nets filled with gold.

Once in the boat we ripped off our masks, quickly shifted out of our backpacks, then paused, staring at the booty on the deck in front of us.

"Holy mother of God," Will whispered. "Is it real?"

I bent down and picked up one of the idols. The sunlight glistened off its yellow surface and the emerald eyes sparkled in reflection. I took my dive knife and dug the point into the base of the statue. The soft metal yielded just a little. I looked up. "I'm not an expert, but I'll bet you dollars to donuts, this is gold, dude."

It registered then, and suddenly we were whooping, hollering, and dancing around our tiny deck like madmen. However, when I paused to catch my breath, I noticed we were a good distance away from the reef line. The anchor had pulled loose and we had been drifting into water too deep for the 150 feet of rope we carried. I wasn't really concerned. We had only to pull the hook, start the engine and head home. We were very rich people.

"Get the anchor line, Will. I'll get the engine," I said with a smile. "I can hear a bottle of expensive rum calling us."

"Oh, yeah! Right on!" my partner cried enthusiastically, stowing the gold in the console pockets and moving to the bow, while I secured the gear and hit the engine switch.

The engine cranked but didn't start. I tried again but it still didn't catch. I sighed, frustrated. "I thought we had this fixed."

"If I didn't think we had it fixed, we wouldn't be out here trying to start it in the middle of the frigging ocean," Will said, with equal concern. He pumped the ball on the fuel line. "Try it again now."

I gave it some throttle and cranked. Still no fire. "We may have flooded it."

"Pop off the cowling and I'll pull the spark plugs," he said, reaching for our small toolkit. A moment later, Will had a wrench on the plug. "We'll get this one out and have a loo—" There was an audible snap and the wrench spun freely. Will glanced down at the engine. "Lord! We broke the spark plug!"

"Not 'we,' Lone Ranger."

"Yeah, well, that may be true," he said looking at the darkening banks of cumulus in the distance. "But 'we' are stuck on this frigging ocean with an offshore wind. By morning 'we' could be in the Bahamas."

"Somebody'll be by, coming back from fishing. We'll get picked up."

I was right on one out of two. A big sports fisherman cruised by an hour later, about a quarter-mile out. We waved enthusiastically. They waved back enthusiastically and continued on their way. We found ourselves sitting out the rest of the afternoon and watching the sea for deliverance. Will pulled out the gold and we began to examine what we'd found.

"This is Spanish for sure," I said, studying a coin.

"And the cross has a Spanish inscription," Will replied. He paused, wiped the sweat from his forehead and looked at me. "Do you think there's more down there?"

I tossed the coin back into the pile. "Who knows? But my gut feeling is, there wasn't a ship there. I just didn't see any relief to indicate something big had been covered with coral, and there were no ballast stones anywhere. Most importantly, we're not the first people to work that section of bottom. If there was a galleon lost in that location, somebody would have known about it before now. My guess is, a long time ago someone dumped some personal treasures into a chest. Maybe it was on deck when a storm hit and they lost it, or maybe they managed to get their chest into a lifeboat before the sea swallowed them. I think it hit just right and rolled against that ledge. The box deteriorated and spilled the contents before the coral conveniently grew around it."

"That's a lot of maybes. Like those archeologists who draw a whole dinosaur with nothing more than a tooth in their hand."

"You know, the only important thing is, that you have the tooth, man." I smiled and held up an idol. "And we got the tooth."

As we sat there, contemplating the possibility of our bright future and the certainty of our present plight, the sun was sucked into the gray turbulence on the horizon. The clouds were momentarily rimmed in gold (our favorite color), then it was gone. We drank a little water from our boat jug and split the last of a tuna sandwich Will had brought, watching lightning pierce the somber heart of that distant storm. Night crept in, shadowing the waters with trepidations even golden idols couldn't dispel. We put our booty in one of our Igloo coolers and covered it with wetsuits and fins. I recalled an old pirate saying: "You put a bar of gold a'tween two men in a room, and no one sleeps that night."

I can tell you no one sleeps really well.

Cries of seabirds awakened us the following morning. The sun was just climbing off the horizon and the gilded, slate-gray seas began their metamorphosis to pale blue. It was apparent that with the brisk offshore breeze, we had been drifting south-southeast, pretty much fulfilling Will's prophecy. There was no land in sight. The day's conversation began with each of us assuring the other that a multitude of ships traveled that region, but by midday, talk had deteriorated to cheeseburgers, and how especially good they were when the cheese had melted down onto the toasted bun. And dill pickles. And man, a milkshake—you know, when it's really cold and you can hardly suck it up through the straw.

We were just into defining the myriad qualities of a good French fry when we saw the boat. It was nearly upon us when we noticed, because it had come up from behind and we were locked into a discussion regarding the importance of crispness and the absolute necessity of fresh condiments. We waved, and the boat slowed. It was an old shrimper design, lapstreak hull, forecastle amidships, but there were no net booms. The name on the bow was *The Black Lilly*. I noticed there were two hookah rigs on board, one on each side of the wheelhouse. Hookahs were the most advanced way to dive professionally—a gas engine that ran a compressor, feeding air into a volume tank. A couple of reinforced rubber hoses, about 150 feet in length, ran off the tank. They attached to the second stages of dive regulators, built into a backpack harness. You could dive for hours on end within a 150-foot radius of the boat—economical and safe. With the hookahs it was a sure bet that they were diving for crayfish—Caribbean lobster.

There were three young guys on the bow, all of them in cut-off shorts, no shoes, tanned and hard. Two of them had close-cropped hair and beards, and appeared to be twins—one of those wore an eye patch, both had numerous tattoos. The third guy was a little younger, no beard, shoulder-length, sun-bleached hair, no apparent tattoos. They returned our waves with more curiosity than excitement. As the boat came abeam of us, the engine stopped and the wheelhouse door opened. Out stepped a vision that might have been hatched by Robert Louis Stevenson on acid—a little character barely five feet tall, early forties, with a dark tan and a tattooed, barrel chest. He had a gleaming, shaved head, a sun-lightened beard, and a large gold earring that dangled from his left ear—no shirt, baggy pants, tennis shoes.

We had drifted up to where the boats were almost touching when suddenly I heard a high-pitched voice from inside of the wheelhouse. "Grubby buggers! Cut their 'willies' off and feed 'em to the 'cudas!"

The small guy swung around angrily. "Shut up, Pecker! Let me take care o' this, ya seedy little weasel." He turned back to us, looked down and smiled. It was a strange smile. His upper teeth looked like they didn't get along with each other. They were too large and there was too much space between them, as if they belonged in someone else's mouth—maybe a troll. His eyes looked like they never got the message his lips were delivering. Those eyes were a bizarre green—like the emeralds on the idol we had tucked away—but with jet-black pupils, indifferent and zealous at the same time. "Ahoy mates." he cried out, putting a thumb in the waist of his pants and stepping over to the rail, raising an eyebrow and jutting his chin as he peered down at us. "Aren't ya just a wee bit deep fer pleasure divin'?" His voice carried that growling, crusty, timber of an old salt. (Looking back on it now, it was like Danny DeVito gone pirate.) There was a part of me that wanted to say, "Just getting a little sun. We'll be just fine. Thanks for stopping."

"We developed engine trouble off Big Pine in the Keys," Will shouted. "The wind carried us out…"

"Aaahhh," he said with a sage nod, eyebrow still not coming down. "Then ya best cleat 'er off at the stern and come aboard."

One of the twins ran back and cast us a line. We pulled the boat around, tied off, and climbed up.

"They call me Calico Curk," said the small fellow, shaking our hands. "These be me boys, Lenny, Kenny, and Bennie." Lenny and Kenny were the bearded twins—Kenny had the patch, Lenny had a curved scar under his chin that also distinguished him. They were considerably taller than their father, maybe five-foot-seven, with marginally better teeth and equally strange, green eyes.

"Kansas," I said. "Kansas Stamps. This is Will Bell."

I noticed Bennie, the shorter and slighter of the three, seemed to be in constant motion—shoulders shifting, head nodding just a little as if he was listening to music the rest of us weren't hearing. His eyes were pale blue and carried a strange distance about them.

Calico Curk saw me glancing over and spoke. "Never mind Bennie. Ya might say 'e dances to a wee bit different tune—but 'e dives well enough, and cooks a mean grouper."

"Thanks for picking us up," I said, changing the subject. "There's a lot less traffic out this way than I expected."

"Aaaahh, that be true," said Calico. "So how long ya been driftin'?"

"Working our way toward twenty-four hours," Will said.

"No water or grub?" he said, eyebrow going up again.

"Some water. No food," I replied.

"Well, I suppose we can fix ya up there." He nodded to the twins and they headed for the galley. "What about yer boat?"

Bennie's left leg had started subtly bouncing—keeping a steady beat unto itself. Everyone tried to ignore it.

"Broke a spark plug. Do you have any?"

Bennie's shoulder had just begun twitching to the inaudible beat. Calico looked back at our skiff. "Probably so. But it's getting ya back to where ya want ta go, that's the trick."

Little brother's eyes had started blinking, that left leg still doing sort of a subtle little early Elvis. I was certain he was going to need a piece of leather to bite on any minute. Calico suddenly reached up, snatched him by his long blond hair and pulled him down.

"No more 'Born to be Wild,' son—a little 'Green Eyed Lady,' or 'A Horse With No Name,' okay?" He released Bennie and turned back to us. "His mother was hit by a jukebox when she was carryin' him. He gets tunes stuck in his head and sometimes we 'ave to help him change the selection."

"A jukebox, huh?" said Will.

Calico grimaced. "Not a story ya want to tell lest ya got some rum in ya."

Bennie had calmed down a little. There was a small amount of spittle on the side of his mouth, but he was smiling and quietly humming "A Horse With No Name."

"Where are we?" I asked. "And where are you headed?"

"We're on the edge o' Cay Sal Bank, about seventy miles southeast o' Big Pine. We're outta Key West. Been doin' a little lobster divin' on the bank. We'd planned ta stay a couple o' weeks, but there's a bit o' weather brewin' just east of Puerto Rico. They 'aven't named it yet but it looks like a good blow, so we'll work a few more days and hightail it back to the Keys. We'll secure yer boat and I guess you can hitch a ride. If yer up to it, ya can do some divin' with us. Make yerself a little coin."

I looked at Will. He nodded. "Sure, works for us."

We had just reached the forecastle when someone on the inside yelled, "Yer all a buncha greasy, fish-oiled pelican turds! Quit pettin' your willies and get ta work, ya lazy buggers!"

Calico sighed angrily. "Shut up, Pecker!" he yelled as he stepped through the portal. "We got guests."

Perched on the wheel in the console was a huge, green, yellow-naped Amazon parrot that fluffed up and screeched at the sight of us. "Bugger a Sunday nun! Guests we have! Guests we have!"

Will and I looked at the bird and smiled as we entered.

"Try ta pet him and you'll lose a finger," Calico warned. "Pecker ain't exactly got a pleasant disposition, but he commands more words than me ex-wife. He's got the run of the roost, gets into everything, and nothin' is sacred, but I keep him around 'cause he reminds me of the boys' dearly departed mother. He paused. "He was her pet—aaahhh, that he was."

"What happened to her?" Will asked.

"Lost to a particularly bad storm she was."

The boys looked up from the galley. Calico gave them a quick glance.

"Most likely she had a little rum in her and missed her step when the ship canted. No one knows fer sure."

The boy's eyes quickly went back to the sandwiches they were making.

Calico reached over to the ship's radio. "I best put a call into the Coast Guard and let 'em know we got ya safe and sound, lest the whole friggin' Navy be lookin' fer us—again."

We bolted a couple of sandwiches each and washed them down with some Pepsi. Lenny took us down into the hold and showed us to our bunks. There was a third bunk on the opposite side of the berth. "That's Bennie's bed," said Lenny. He glanced at the bunks then back to us. "It ain't Howard Johnson's, but it'll keep ya dry, and after a day of lobster diving, you'll sleep well enough, regardless."

We noticed he didn't have as much of the vernacular as his

father. I couldn't resist. "I hope you don't mind me asking, but where'd your dad get that salty accent?"

Lenny looked at us. "What accent?"

Will and I glanced at each other. "Never mind," I said, quickly shifting subjects and getting to a point I was certain weighed heavily with Will as well. "I guess we'll go get our gear off the boat and stow it, so we don't lose anything if a storm rolls up."

"Yeah. Best do that. Waves out here can kick a little craft like that around. We're headed into the bank again. Probably anchor up and do a dive in an hour or two." Lenny paused. "You ever dive lobster?"

"We've caught enough to have the trick down," said Will.

Lenny nodded. "See ya topside."

As soon as he was out of sight, I leaned over to Will and whispered, "We need to get that cooler down here, before anybody decides to see if we have anything they want."

Will nodded. "No joke, man! I feel like we're somewhere between Neverland and Treasure Island. God! I'm waiting to see the frigging alligator with a clock in its stomach."

Our timing was good. Lenny and Kenny were rigging up their spare hookah on the stern, for Will and me. Bennie was watching a pod of bottlenose porpoise playing off the bow. Calico was at the wheel, in a heated argument with the parrot. We managed to get our gear onboard, but when we were taking the cooler into the wheelhouse Calico asked. "What ya got there, mates?"

"Dive gear," I said.

"Best to stow that topside, so it don't get wet down there."

"Just going to lubricate some zippers, check our regulators—getting ready for our dive this afternoon," said Will. "When we're done we'll bring it up."

Calico cocked his head and stared at us for a moment, then shrugged. "Do what ya gotta do. We'll be anchored and divin' inside the hour."

We took the gear down to our berth, and while Will watched the stairs, I cut a gash in the bottom of the old mattress on my bed, pulled out some of the stuffing and crammed the gold inside. I was standing there with wads of cotton in both hands when Will motioned urgently—someone was coming down. I glanced around in a panic. Will was pantomiming something to the effect of, "Move it, you dumb shit!" I could just see the legs on the stairs when I bent down and crammed the stuffing into an inch-high curved arch under the small chest of drawers. The dresser was bolted to the floor with only that small aperture in front.

Bennie ambled down and stopped in front of us. He was humming "Alone Again," by Gilbert O'Sullivan. He pointed to the dive gear on the floor, then pointed up to the deck, turned around and trudged back up.

"Quite the conversationalist," I said.

Will nodded. "Very possibly a member of the Key West debate team."

We felt the boat slow. A moment later the engine shut down and we heard the anchor feed out.

There are a multitude of techniques used when diving lobster, from the laborious to the illegal. Calico and the boys chose the illegal. When we got on deck, Will and I were each handed an eighteen-inch piece of wire coat hanger that had been straightened. At one end a large bait hook had been welded, with the barb filed off. With this device you simply eased up on the crayfish and gently tickled them with the hook until they moved forward, out of the hole or crevice they were in. Then, when you had the point under the tail, you hooked them, grabbed the crayfish and tossed him in your catch bag. It worked like magic and was so easy it had been declared illegal almost everywhere.

We dove on a pristine reef in waters clearer than Smirnoff for the next two hours. Crayfish were everywhere—so plentiful we only had to move the boat once, for new territory. There were thousands of exotic tropicals weaving in and out of brilliant, multi-colored coral formations, and huge grouper and hog snapper were everywhere. It was exciting diving, and we thoroughly enjoyed ourselves, while bagging over fifty crayfish each.

Will and I were washing down the dive gear when Lenny came up last with a 15-pound grouper for dinner. "Nice, man!" I remarked. "I've never seen an area with so many big fish."

"That be the truth, matey," Calico growled. Then he smiled, the same bent-toothed trollish grin that never reached his eyes. "Tomorrow we'll do a little fishing—get a few o' those ta sweeten the pot."

The boys chuckled.

Will and I stowed our gear, then went down to our berth to change, and make sure our treasure was still there. Gold makes you very nervous. We took the following hour topside to remove and replace the damaged spark plug on our skiff with one from Calico's hookah parts supply. Bennie filled two five-gallon containers with fuel for us, which we lashed to our gunnel. Calico had explained that in a day or so, when we got back into Keys waters, they would be heading for Key West. They would cut us loose about twenty miles out and we'd set a course for Big Pine. Our engine started on the second turnover, purring as if it was fresh out of the box. Will looked at me, incredulously. I just shrugged my shoulders.

An hour later, Kenny had filleted the grouper and Bennie had marinated thick squares, grilling them on the barbecue by the stern. We all sat there in lawn chairs, drank a few beers, and watched the sun melt into a fiery, turquoise horizon. Then we ate baked beans and fish until I thought we'd burst. I've had a lot worse times. But that wasn't the end of the evening, by any means.

After the sun set, Calico broke out the rum. We sat in the twilight, knocked down shots of Myers and lime, and traded outrageous stories while trying to dodge Calico's horrendous bean farts. When the downsized sea dog wasn't scorching the furniture, he dipped pieces of banana in rum and fed it to Pecker, who sat on his shoulder. Occasionally someone had to slap Bennie on the head and recommend a new song, to keep his legs from walking off without him, but he took it in stride.

The full moon gleamed like a freshly hammered piece of eight, glistening constellations littered the sky, and magical bursts of green phosphorescence danced across the waves as they caressed the hull. From my rapidly developing haze, it seemed like a combination of Brothers Grimm and Disney World—weird, but not unpleasant. About that time, Calico turned on the stereo and slapped in an eight-track tape of Santana. The haunting, melodious rhythm of "Black Magic Woman" floated out across the waters, and as everyone began to move with the cadence of methodical bass and sensuous guitar, Calico pulled the tarp off a set of congas next to him. He set up Pecker with a shot of rum and a couple pieces of banana, put him on the table, then began an excellent accompaniment to Santana. Lenny and Kenny began to sway, raising their hands above their heads and snapping their fingers to the beat. As we rolled into "*Oye Como Va*" it occurred to Will and me almost simultaneously that Kenny was no longer wearing his patch—it was now firmly fixed over Lenny's right eye. Will glanced at me with a giddy, questioning look and raised his eyebrows.

"There are no rules in Neverland," I whispered a little drunkenly.

He grinned. "Yeah, I bet Tinkerbell is here somewhere."

Truer words were never spoken.

The bottle of rum was being passed around once more, and a raucous "Hope You're Feeling Better" began to pound the stereo speakers. Suddenly Bennie came bounding around the corner and flung himself into the light of the gas lantern on deck. I may have been drunk, but I wasn't drunk enough for that vision.

And I hope you're feeling better.
Yes I hope you're feelin' good...

Bennie, complete with Max Factor eye shadow and red lipstick, pirouetted into the moonlight in a green miniskirt and a sheer white, long-sleeve blouse that tied just above his bellybutton. I can safely say it took my breath away.

Is that you? Look across the ocean.
Is that you? Searching for a good time.

It was like one of the Pod People hookers had invaded his body. This was easy, slightly epileptic Bennie capering across the deck in crotch-tossing gyrations, up against the sea rail like a Chihuahua on grandpa's leg. Calico and big brothers hooted and whooped, coaxing him on. Pecker screeched, "Aaawwkk! Pet your willie, pretty boy! Aaawwkk! Pet your willie!"

And I hope you're feeling better.
Yes I hope you're feelin' good.

I'd seen a lot of strange things, and found myself in a bizarre situation once or twice, but that set a brand new benchmark for weird. Will took one look at Bennie, snatched the rum bottle out of my hand and upended it.

As soon as Bennie finished Act I, Santana swung into "You've Got To Change Your Evil Ways." Lenny and Kenny sandwiched him in a conga line, hooting, hollering, and trading a bottle of rum back and forth. I grabbed Will's bottle and bolted a shot—then one more. My last clear recollection was of Calico standing on his congas, shaved head gleaming in the moonlight, swaying, with his hands in the air, revival style, as the last vestiges of a satiny "*Samba Pa Ti*" wafted over the night breeze.

The next morning I awoke to the sound of retching—my own. The fact that there was no toilet in our berth was only just becoming significant. There was no sign of Bennie. Will, a seasoned veteran of unabashed self-abuse, had recovered sufficiently to crawl up to the galley and get some coffee. If I'd had the strength, I would have simply thrown myself overboard, just to end the pain. A half hour later I was able to stand without assistance, and swallow some coffee. I could hear Calico yelling up above, and the anchor being pulled as we moved the boat in preparation for the first dive.

I don't remember much about that morning, other than I caught about half as many lobsters as I should have, and I threw up in my regulator several times. No one mentioned a word about the night before or acted the least bit different for it—except that Lenny still wore Kenny's eye patch, and Kenny showed no ostensible need for it. Will and I decided to adopt the "If we don't ask the questions, we won't have to hear the answers" philosophy.

By midday, after a good lunch, I was feeling pretty much my old self again, except for the image of *Cabaret Bennie* still dancing in my head. But I got to thinking about it as I dove that afternoon. Hell, out of the whole bunch I liked Bennie best. What did I care if he looked better in a miniskirt than my ex-wife, or if he provided the floorshow for the cruise. It was his business. It sure as hell didn't seem to bother anyone else on board.

We dove until about three o'clock, when Calico brought us all up, saying it was "time to do a little fishin'." We were still in our wetsuits, standing on the deck outside the wheelhouse when Calico opened a small drawer from under the console and reached inside.

"Seein' as how that blow's getting worse east o' us, we're gonna pull out tomorrow—maybe one dive in the marnin' then we're gone," he said with his back to us. He quickly stepped out onto the deck and turned around, displaying two apparently live grenades—one in each hand. "So let's go fishing, mates!"

The older brothers laughed and clapped.

"Heavy metal Thundaaar!" shouted Kenny.

Bennie was starting to bob and weave in anticipation.

Lenny slapped little brother on the head before Elvis took over and cried excitedly, "Yeah, darlin', gonna make it happen!"

For a moment Will and I just stood there, one part aghast and two parts freaked out. I understood the principle. An explosion like that would stun hundreds of fish, probably rupturing their bladders and causing them to rise to the surface. But I could see Will's face, and none of this set well with him either. Calico caught our looks and arched his eyebrow again.

"It ain't your call, so ya might as well ride with it, cause there ain't no percentage otherwise." He laughed, pulled the pin on a grenade and tossed it twenty yards off the port bow.

Will glared at him. "You miserable son-of-a—"

There was a muffled explosion and a huge 20-foot effervescent bubble erupted into a fountain of water that showered us all. Calico just laughed again and threw the other to starboard. In just a few moments, large grouper and snapper began to rise to the surface, belly-up.

Calico looked up at us. “Okay mates, I’ve done me part. Now you boys drop in and bag up anything what’s not twitching. We’ll make this a good haul after all.”

“You’ve killed hundreds of reef creatures you can’t even use,” barked Will.

Calico just sighed condescendingly. “Aaahhh, matey, ya got yer glass half empty. There’s hundreds creatures out there ya can use. And ya best get to baggin’ ’em up afore they go ta waste. Ya wouldn’t want that, would ya?” He was smiling, but his eyes were hard as agates. “Always remember mateys, life’s a game o’ snooker—ya gotta know when ta play easy, and when ta play hard. But most of all, ya got ta have the balls to play!”

Unfortunately, Calico was right. The damage was done. If we didn’t help, half the fish killed would drift away before the others could collect them. I looked at Will. He sighed angrily and nodded.

Two hours later, we were all back on board and the fish had been put on ice with the lobster in the forward hatches. A squall rose out of the southeast and light rain pelted the ship as we drank a beer or two and ate a supper of baked hog snapper and canned vegetables in the galley. When the storm passed, Calico and the boys headed for the stern with a bottle of rum. Will and I declined, opting for our berth—one night of watching Crosby, Stills, and Bennie do “Love The One You’re With” was enough for us. Besides, after the grenade affair, we were both beginning to feel somewhat uneasy, and I felt the distinct need to stay a little closer to our gold.

When we got to our bunks, I made a quick, casual check of our riches. Will looked at me. I nodded. He breathed a small sigh.

“Damn, man! Is this crazy or what?” he whispered tersely. “We find a ‘not so small’ fortune and suddenly get marooned with a miniature Blackbeard and the friggin’ Steppenwolf brothers—not to mention an epileptic cross-dresser with a damaged jukebox for a brain. All we need now is the Tin Man and the Lion. By the way, I heard something ticking by the hull last night.”

I chuckled. “Don’t be losin’ it on me now, man. I’m gonna need you. We still got to get this stuff off the ship and away from here before Blackbeard finds it and decides maybe we had just a wee bit too much rum in us and missed our step in a particularly bad storm.’”

“No man,” Will said after a swig of beer. “We gotta pull this off.

I want to live to spend this booty. There's a really nice, little red Mustang calling to me from Key West Ford."

Calico and entourage once again refused to go quietly into the evening. It was well after midnight before Santana, Iron Butterfly, and Edgar Winter quit hammering the hull. But by eight o'clock the next morning everyone was up and having breakfast. One last dive, then back to the Keys.

"We'll spend about two hours bottom time here, and that's it," Calico said, looking up from the plate of eggs he surrounded with his elbows. "So grab as many o' them spiny little buggers as ya can and be back on deck by ten. I want ta take advantage of this flat calm and be back ta Key West by sunset."

The relief was once again spectacular and the lobsters were everywhere. We'd been diving for about an hour and a half when I surfaced to get my bearings from the boat. I noticed the brothers were already on board and out of their wetsuits. Bennie was on the forward deck and Calico was talking to the other two in the wheelhouse. I thought it was strange that no one had pulled on our hoses to call us in, but if they were finished, so were we. I went down, got Will, and we headed back. Ten minutes later we were out of the water and had our crayfish in the hold, but there was something amiss.

The stereo was cranked up, Buffalo Springfield's "For What it's Worth" resonated throughout the ship, and everyone was having a beer.

There's something' happening here.
What it is ain't exactly clear.

Kenny and Lenny had suddenly become smug, as if there was a joke they weren't sharing; and Calico was almost condescending. "Did me favorite castaways have a nice final dive ta remember their Bahama vacation by?" he said with a hollow smile. "Get yourself out of those shabby ol' wetsuits and relax. 'Ave an iced tea—'cause we be on our way ta better times."

Paranoia strikes deep.
Into your heart it will creep.

Will looked at me. We stripped down and dried off, then after a few moments of irrelevant conversation, casually excused ourselves and drifted down to our berth. The first thing I did was check on the gold. Lifting the mattress I reached under and stuck my hand in the hole. Nothing. My stomach did a little backflip. I jammed my arm into the mattress—still nothing. Will saw the look on my face and melted. "Oh, sweet Lord! No!"

You better stop.

Hey, what's that sound.

"They took it!" I hissed. "The sons of bitches took it!"

Generally, Will had an easy disposition and an excellent sense of self-preservation. He rarely did stupid things that could cost him important points in the game of life. But this was an exception. Without a word he turned and headed up the stairs with a determined look.

"Damned right!" I said, and followed.

We reached the cabin and stopped. Calico sat on a stool at the galley bar with a Cheshire smile, flipping and catching one of our gold coins. Bennie and Lenny stood at the port entrance to the wheelhouse and Kenny stood at the starboard door, casually leaning on the butt of a loaded spear gun—point of the shaft on the floor.

Stop, Hey, what's that sound.

Everybody look what's goin' down.

Calico reached over and turned down the stereo a little, then turned to us. "Here you boys are, rich as Solomon, and not a word to us—the kind souls what rescued ya and took ya in," he drawled. "I think that's purely selfish."

"Give us back our gold, you little maggot," Will spat.

Calico straightened. "Or what? It ain't your gold no more. Here's the truth, treasure don't belong to no one. We just borrow it fer a space in time, then it moves on its way. Yer time was short. Actually, ya owe it all to Pecker, who kept bringin' me wads o' cotton—and got me curious."

I noticed Lenny had a fillet knife in the belt of his pants as well. The situation was not looking good. I decided to negotiate, stepping forward a little. "Look, let's make a deal—split the treasure. We each get half. Everybody wins."

Calico appeared thoughtful for a moment, then looked up. "Or we could give you two a couple lungs-full o' brine, and keep it all." He paused to let that sink in. "But what we might do is this—we'll tie ya up and let ya sit this trip out here in the galley. When we get ta Key West, I'll take the gold ashore and Kenny will watch ya for an hour or two, then let ya go—cause in an hour that treasure's gonna be gone from yer life and there'll be no way ya can prove that it ever existed."

"You greedy little bastard," I hissed through gritted teeth.

The diminutive pirate just smiled, arching that eyebrow again.

"It can be the easy way or the 'missing at sea way'—your choice."

"I'm not giving up my Mustang," Will whispered tensely behind me. "I need a diversion—now."

I don't know what happened to me exactly, probably gold fever, but I reacted without thinking. Stepping over a few feet, I snatched Pecker off his perch, grabbing him around the neck like a chicken and holding him out in front of me. "Nobody moves or the bird gets it!" *(I couldn't believe I said that.)*

The parrot shrieked, "Aaawkk! He's got the Pecker! Aaawkk!

Calico was definitely taken aback, but he recovered quickly. "It's just a bird, mate. You think I'm gonna trade him for the gold?"

I saw his eyes glance to Kenny and the spear gun, and I realized I was running out of leverage. As Kenny's hand slid down the aluminum stock of the weapon, I did the only thing I could think of—I threw the parrot at him. Pecker hit him squarely in the face—and that was a very angry bird. I suspect Kenny still has the scars today. While he was struggling to pull the parrot from his head, I rushed in and body-slammed him. Kenny, with Pecker still attached, went stumbling out onto the deck and over the railing. I had little time to take satisfaction in my good fortune. Lenny and Bennie grappled me as I rose to my feet and we all went down in a pile. Through the melee of arms and legs, I caught a glimpse of Will stiff-arming Calico, sending him flying off his stool, as he headed for the console. A moment later, as I bit Lenny's fingers, which were crawling up my face toward my eyes, I heard Calico yelling, "He's got a grenade! He's got a friggin' grenade!" That pretty much halted all the action. Everyone stopped in mid-gouge.

Will stood next to the console drawer, grenade in hand, his countenance a mixture of anger and triumph. Holding the handle down, he ripped out the pin and hurled it across the room, brandishing the small bomb in the air over his head. "Now we're going to do it my way, you sons of bitches, or I swear I'll blow this frigging boat into kindling."

I shook myself loose from Lenny and Bennie.

Calico got up slowly from the floor. "Take it easy, mate. We can talk about this. We can make a deal."

"Here's the frigging deal," Will shouted, lost to the fury and indignation of the moment. "You're gonna get our damned gold right now, or the last thing you're ever gonna remember is this rolling between your legs. Now, all of you, into the center of the room."

Damn. I was so impressed I started to move into the galley with the rest of them.

"Not you!" Will barked, exasperated.

"Right," I mumbled. "Wasn't thinking."

Will began to move around them, back to the wall. "Now, you're gonna take that duct tape on the counter and start binding the family's hands. You make one wrong move, you even breathe too fast and I'll—" He raised the grenade up for emphasis and accidentally banged his wrist against one of the columns that supported the galley table. The grenade bounced out of my partner's hand and rolled into the doorway of the hold, tumbling down the steps below—thunk, thunk, thunk. There was an absolutely pregnant moment of silence as Will looked at us with an expression that wended its way from deep shock to sincere apology, but ended up somewhere closer to "oh shit!" In the next second, everyone was bounding for the exits with *Titanic* enthusiasm. Calico and his two boys went over the starboard rail, Will and I, the port.

There was a muffled roar in the hold and the planking on the sides bulged as the center keel of the ship blew away in a maelstrom of wood and metal. *The Black Lilly* lifted up in the ocean for a moment, then settled and began to take on water at an alarming rate. Fortunately, Will's keen sense of self-preservation was back in place. I had barely begun to tread water when I saw him hauling himself aboard our little skiff and cutting the line to the ship. Calico acted with equal haste, shouting at his sons to untie and cast off the rubber life raft attached to the top of the forecastle, then drawing himself over the gunnel of his boat, which was by then only a couple of feet above sea level, and dashing to the radio, where he got off a Mayday and a position to the Coast Guard. The water was around his ankles before he finished. I saw him look desperately at the hold, but the treasure was gone—blown into a thousand-foot trench in the Gulf Stream. Will had already fired up the engine on the skiff and pulled away from the boat—so the others couldn't reach him. He quickly came alongside and hauled me in. Calico made the raft with his sons and they pushed off just as the *Lilly's* wheelhouse filled with water and she began to go under. Two minutes later the ship was gone, littering the sea with buoyant flotsam and jetsam, and an oil slick. We quickly snatched up two bobbing five-gallon cans of gasoline as we made our way over to the life raft.

Pecker landed with a flurry of feathers on the end of the raft as Calico watched us approach. The old pirate ignored him as he glared at us. "You blew up me boat, mate. You sunk me friggin' ship!"

"No. You sunk your ship, you slimy little weasel—you and your greed," Will said.

Calico sighed, knowing he had no place to go with that conversation. "Ya can't just leave us out here, mate. Ya gotta take us with you."

"Not enough room for all of you. We'd flounder. You got off a distress call and a position. They'll come for you."

Calico was getting desperate. "Then just take me. I can pay me way." The others swung around at him as he pulled a small leather pouch from his pocket and opened it, spilling a handful of our gold coins into his palm. He looked at the others. "So I tucked a few away—for a rainy day."

"Toss us the coins and we'll think about it," Will said.

"Oh no, matey! Ya got ta agree before I give ya the coins."

"Whatda think you're doin'?" cried Kenny. "You ain't gonna leave us here!"

"No deal, buddy," Will said decisively as he swung the wheel around and revved the engine. "Goodbye."

"Okay, Okay! I'll give ya the coins," Calico pleaded as he quickly stuffed them back into the pouch.

"No you won't!" cried Lenny and Kenny in strident harmony.

Calico took a look at his mutinous crew and jumped into the water, quickly swimming over to us. "Here!" he said, grabbing our gunnel and handing the pouch to me. "Just take me with ya."

Will suddenly turned and hammered Calico's fingers with a PVC fishing rod holder. As the fellow yelped and let go, Will gunned the boat away from him.

"Ya said you'd take me if I gave ya the coins," the little man wailed.

Will put the shift back into neutral. "No. I said I'd think about it." He paused for a moment, in contemplation. "Okay, I've thought about it. The answer's no."

Calico's shaved head turned crimson when he realized he'd been had. He treaded water and began to hurl curses. "Ya piss-assed skinny sea turd! Ya sackless little weasel, I'm gonna—"

"Shark!" yelled Will, pointing urgently behind Calico. The old sailor stopped dead in the middle of his curses and did an instant pirouette, head craning.

"Big Mako!" I cried out, pointing as well.

That was it. For a little guy he was an amazing swimmer—actually it was more like skimming because I don't think he really touched the water much on his way back to the raft.

Will turned to me with a smile. "Have you ever seen that National Geographic show where those little lizards can actually run across the surface of the water?"

I nodded. "Yeah. There's a good chance he may have some lizard in him."

When the wannabe pirate was once more confined to his rubbery transportation, glowering bitterly, we pulled over. I cleared my throat. "Well, this is goodbye boys, so I'm going to leave you with a few words—especially you, Calico. Life is like a game of snooker—played with integrity it's a pretty straightforward contest, but if you deliberately tilt the table, you can just as easily snooker yourself." I smiled. "Have a nice day, 'mateys.' I hope you brought plenty of suntan lotion." Without a word of goodbye or a whisper of concern, Will whipped the boat around and headed northeast.

My last glimpse of the *Black Lilly* gang was that of Calico inadvertently slapping Bennie on the back of the head. "That's before ya even get started," he yelled. "This is a small friggin' raft. No Hendrix! No Vanilla Fudge! No funky shit at all!"

For the next eight hours we plodded along, barely keeping the skiff planed and using as little fuel as possible. If it hadn't been an extraordinarily calm day, battling the Gulf Stream waves would have long since consumed our fuel. We began with fifteen gallons in the built-in tank and twenty more in jerry jugs, but by the time we sighted smears of land in the haze of a distant horizon, our engine was sucking the last dregs. We were scorched, parched, and spent. Only three boats had come within sight, and they were too far away to hail. As the sun began to ease into the banks of outlying evening clouds, the elephant onboard whispered of a stilled engine and another offshore wind…

Will turned to me. "Have I mentioned to you how much I like cheeseburgers?"

"Hourly since about eleven o'clock."

"And cherry Cokes—with lots of ice."

The outboard engine sputtered. I shuffled the throttle forward a little and it settled down.

"Eskimo Pies," I said. "The first thing I'm gonna do is buy every Eskimo Pie on Big Pine, lock myself in the walk-in freezer at Jen's Stop n' Shop and eat 'em all."

The engine sputtered again.

Will looked back. "Maybe if we hold our breath."

"All the way to Big Pine?"

The engine coughed and died. My partner exhaled. "Didn't work."

I hit the starter, but it wouldn't cooperate. The elephant sighed with resignation. I paused and wiped the sweat from my forehead, then turned it over again—still nothing.

Will pulled out the leather pouch. "Have I mentioned to you we have ten Spanish gold coins?"

"Hourly since about eleven o'clock."

A few minutes later the sun was lost to the horizon and the water was starting to take on that heavy gray of dusk seas. The evening offshore breeze lifted itself from the ocean and whispered a murmur of intimidation.

My partner took a coin from the bag. "I've read about lost sailors sacrificing a piece of their treasure to the sea—for rescue. What would you think if I threw this coin back into the sea and asked to be saved?"

"I'd think that I'd be better off with a one-eyed monkey holding my coins, you flippin' idiot."

"It's the lack of sugar. I really need a milkshake." Suddenly Will straightened up. "But I might do it anyway. What have we got to lose?"

I was about to say, "A friggin' gold coin!" when he drew back his arm and turned toward the islands in the distance. He was preparing to throw. I was preparing to leap at him when he stopped, dead still, and pointed with the coin.

"It worked," he said quietly. "It worked." In the distance, coming up from behind us was an old 24-foot, flat-top commercial fishing boat. It was weird looking, I'll admit. The small forecastle was covered with palm fronds that were stretched down and around the two forward windows, making it look like a thatched hut—but it was headed our way. We began to wave madly and shout. As the craft got closer, I saw there were a couple of electric fishing reels mounted on the gunnels, and a trap-puller, but the windows appeared to be fogged and we couldn't make out the pilot. The boat was still fifty yards off when the breeze carried the sweet scent of ganja to us. I wondered what kind of seedy individual might own a tramper of that sort, and visions of our last encounter scrolled through my head. Still, we needed a tow.

The boat dropped off plane and slowed to a drift. The proprietor of the odd vessel stepped from the wheelhouse and hollered, "Hello mons! Hello mons! Lonely sky sailors! May the yellow night frog leave you many droppings of peace and prosperity."

I stared out at the lone figure and smiled.

"Son of a gun," Will muttered incredulously. "It's Rufus!"

As the craft came abeam, Rufus recognized us as well. His large, friendly eyes lit with appreciation and his face cleaved into that big, gap-toothed grin, salt-misted dreadlocks curling down around his ears onto his shoulders. He had on a new Bob Marley T-shirt, but very possibly the same weary shorts we had last seen him wearing.

"Aaahhh! My olden friends, Mississippi and Wills! Blessings to you that we should visualize ourselves again!" Then he immediately shot us his unique peace sign, two fingers to the forehead salute.

"Hi, Rufus!" I said. "It's Kansas and Will."

"Ya mon!" Rufus said, not missing a beat.

"Never been to Mississippi," I muttered.

He nodded thoughtfully. "Aaahhh, then it is good you changed your name."

I opened my mouth. My partner put his hand on my arm. I shut my mouth.

"We're out of gas," Will called. "Do you think you could tow us in?"

Twenty minutes later our skiff was secured to the stern of *The Virtuous Mango* and we were in the small wheelhouse, chatting with Rufus as he cheerfully steered toward Spanish Harbor Bridge. A pale yellow moon climbed from the darkening horizon and Rufus' old radio scratched out Grace Slick's powerful, introspective melody "Somebody to Love."

I passed back a tightly rolled sliver of Jamaica's contribution to world peace and exhaled. "So, where'd you get the boat, Rufus?"

Our friend smiled pensively. "The Grand Messenger of the Wisdom of Ganja say, 'Patience and faith are the hungry monkey's companions while he seeks the virtue of timing.'" He paused. "One night, Rufus is sleeping, mon, dreaming maybe, when there is big storm—see bright lights, hear splashing sounds. I think, ya mon, maybe this be ganja vision, or maybe… but it too much excitement for one who lives in Maytag box, so I just close my eyes."

I chuckled at the erudite self-analysis. Rufus continued.

"Next morning I go to relieve the tension of my rectum and I am given to the vision of this lovingly splendorous craft in mangroves. I yell, nobody answer. I sit and wait all day. I sleep in vision that night—roof leak. Next morning I fix roof with coconut tree branches and sea grape sap, then get high with tide and push out." He glanced around proudly. "Ya, mon. Very much improvement over Maytag box."

"A gift from the gods, I guess," I said.

Rufus's eyes changed slightly—a sense of insight replacing frivolity for a moment. "Gods and man—I think may be more combined than we realize. We think, aaahhh, we are so clever. But we are just monkeys dancing in the moonlight." Suddenly the seriousness faded and the old Rufus was back. "But now, I am joyous possessor of new habitation and gainfully filled employment—catch little finny brothers in ocean and sell them to fish houses."

"Outta sight, man! Good for you!" Will exclaimed, experiencing a little Jamaican euphoria.

"Ya mon! Ya mon!" Rufus replied enthusiastically. "The Grand Messenger says, 'The perfect mango is freed by the wind and kisses the earth at dawn—it awaits the warmth of the sun, and the fortunate worm.' The worm is me! I am the worm! Blessed is the virtuous mango!"

An hour later we were home—our boat safely docked to the canal seawall. We gave Rufus twenty dollars for towing us in, which he took reluctantly. Our Jamaican friend wished us the best, then carefully turned his craft around. But before he departed, he shifted into neutral and leaned out from the cabin overhead. Once again issuing his famous salute, he smiled and shouted. "Do not take any wooden blowfish!"

We returned the salute and the smile.

I called the Coast Guard and found they had located Calico and his boys. They were being brought in aboard a cutter. We cleaned up, then went out for cheeseburgers, milkshakes, and Eskimo Pies.

CHAPTER FIVE

Drugs, Sex, and Rock and Roll

(And Magic Dust)

We had a friend named Kip—a huge, three-hundred-pound walrus of a man who dove lobster for a living. He was such an ungainly creature on land, but in the water he was beautiful, as graceful as a seal, and that was where he spent a good portion of his time. He knew the swirling eddies of the channels and the pockets in the flats like the scars on the bar top at the Big Pine Inn. Kip wore a gold doubloon on a chain around his neck and claimed it was from a cache he'd stumbled upon near the outside of Hawk Channel, and that he sold the rest to a friend in Miami who had a penchant for yellow.

It cost us a bottle of rum and a Key West hooker, but Kip gave us the phone number.

We sold eight of our coins to a guy who met with us in the rear seat of a '69 Fairlane at a Frisch's Big Boy in Homestead, and said names weren't important. He counted out sixty crisp Franklins, took our leather bag and wished us well. We washed down our success with cheeseburgers and milkshakes, then headed back to the Keys. Will and I kept one coin each, as a memento of our adventure. I've been through some flush times and some lean times in my life, but that coin has never been for sale.

We weren't forever wealthy from our little transaction, but it did afford us the opportunity to improve our lives in a number of fashions. There wasn't enough money for Will's little red Mustang, but he did manage a used blue one. We also paid off our boat and bought a hookah rig, which was a vast improvement in our professional arena. In addition, I decided I would learn to fly airplanes. We were burning up at least one day a week traveling back and forth to Miami delivering fish. If we delivered to Tampa, we lost closer to three days. By renting a plane, all that was reduced to hours. Our wholesalers had already agreed to split the cost of a rental with us—because less time in transit ensured lower mortality rates.

A week after selling our coins, I drove down to the Key West Airport FBO and flight school—a little closet with a few windows opening onto the runway. There was an older guy, maybe early forties, reclining in the waiting area wearing a baseball cap, flowered shirt, and tired-looking slacks. He had a toothpick dangling from his mouth and his feet were propped up on a low table littered with yellow copies of *Trade-A-Plane* and weathered *Pilot* magazines. He looked up, not moving.

"Can I help you?"

"How much does it cost to get your private pilot's license?" I asked.

He took the toothpick out of his mouth, slowly. "Depends."

"On what?"

"If you're a quick learner and you fly regularly—so you remember what you learned the lesson before—seven, maybe eight hundred dollars."

I've always been a little impatient. "What's the quickest anyone's ever done it—got their license?"

He paused. "One guy did it in six weeks."

"When can I start?"

He thought for a moment, glanced out at the tarmac to a little blue and white Cessna 150 perched on the ramp, then turned back to me, slowly. "We can start in the 150 tomorrow morning. How about nine a.m.?"

That single decision opened up more vistas in my life than anything I had ever done before. It led to remarkable adventures, wonderful stories, and ultimately some considerable financial improvement here and there. But what I discovered initially was that flying scared the shit out of me. Maybe not flying exactly, but flying badly, with very little assurance from my calm to almost comatose instructor that I wasn't going to kill him and myself sometime during each lesson. The greatest example I can offer is my introduction to stalls—where an aircraft is forced upward at such an angle, and/or reduced speed, that the relative wind can no longer support the wings and the plane basically decides to become a rock. You learn how to do stalls so you can recognize the characteristics in advance and correct them before you become a statistic.

It was my sixth or seventh lesson. I was just beginning to fly without a death grip on the controls, and had begun stopping for only one beer at the end of the flight, instead of two or three.

"We're gonna do stalls today," said George, my instructor. "You know what that is?"

I'd read something about the 'wing-relative wind' thing in the training manual. How hard could it be? "Well, yeah. I guess."

He smiled. I never saw him do that before. "Okay, take it up to five thousand feet."

At five thousand, George told me to pull back on the controls. As the plane began an unusually steep assent he casually said, "Pull back some more."

I did as requested, but I was starting to feel seriously uncomfortable. The aircraft was damned near reaching a nosebleed angle and the wings were shuddering.

"A little more," George said.

I thought, *A little more, my ass! We're almost flying straight up!* About that time, the stall warning buzzer started screaming in my ear. (I had no idea what that was. I was convinced we'd broken something). Suddenly the plane simply quit flying, rolled over on one wing, and began a terrifying spinning descent toward the ocean below. In the process of screaming unintelligible things, I began jerking back on the controls, trying to physically force the airplane up while pulling the yoke into my abdomen hard enough to crack ribs.

George was sitting there, calmly, perpetual toothpick dangling, shaking his head slowly. "Nope, that ain't how you do it. You didn't read your lesson plan for today."

The ocean was spiraling up at us with remarkable speed. The world around me was blurring like a bad tequila high. I offered a poignant reply to his statement. "Aaahhhgh! Shiiittt! Aaahhhgh!" *Which lesson, you son of a bitch! We're about to die and you're getting friggin' intellectual on me*?

"Let me have the controls," George said.

I surrendered gladly. I had nothing to lose. Tiny fingers were pulling back the skin on my face, and the morning's oatmeal was moving toward critical mass.

"You want me to show you now?" he said.

I thought, *I'm gonna kick your ass when we get to hell.* I nodded vigorously. "Aahhhgh!"

George backed off the power, applied a little right rudder and drew the plane gently into the direction of the spin, then added a little power and rolled down and out, into straight and level flight. He looked at me. "See, not so difficult when you know what you're doing."

I smiled wanly and threw up on him.

Regardless of my strained relationship with George, I still managed my private pilot's license six weeks from the day I started. In November of 1972, Will and I began renting a four-passenger

Cessna 172 and ferrying our fish out of Marathon. We became such regulars that when I reserved the plane, they would have the backseat pulled out (for the Igloo fish coolers), and the aircraft fueled and waiting. The wholesalers would have a panel truck waiting for us at Tamiami Airport, where they would count out our fish and write us a check. Lord, we thought we were hotshot tropical fish collectors.

We weathered our second winter—a colder experience than the first—and we spent fewer days in the water. To occupy our time, Will and I took up the hobby of antique bottle hunting—scouring the out-islands around Big Pine Key for old home sites dating back as far as the 1700s. It was a couple of our neighbors, Pete and Pam Pinholster, who introduced us to the endeavor. From them and other locals we learned what to look for, and trained ourselves to recognize the dull glint of sun off antique black glass or rich amber, what identified the old homesteads, and where to dig. Ultimately, what we found were pieces of people's lives in another time—a tangible history of the generations before us—and it was fascinating. It was archeology without the restraints of a one-inch brush and an ice pick.

To this day all I have to do is have a little rum in me, then pick up one of those precious old bottles that adorn the shelves of my den, hold it tightly, and close my eyes. Quietly, in the backcountry of my mind, I begin to hear the distant chorus of the catboats' riggings singing to the early morning wind. I see that clean, kind, sparkling sea, and smell the tart, gray mud that births the mangroves and the buttonwoods—sometimes sour, sometimes sweet, oftentimes filled with hope, because the nets are dry, the wind is right, the sky's clear—and there's a good catch coming.

Spring came quickly in 1973, pushing out the cold northers that cleaved the Gulf in long furrows of windy froth. Subtle changes in the color of the sky and the hue of frond and leaf heralded a new season. Mottled lizards scuttled forth from their lairs, seeking the new array of mosquito hatchlings that had been held at bay by the cooler weather. Seabirds returned in abundance to feast on the shoals' baitfish in the shallows, and as the bougainvillea bloomed in riotous colors, clinging to bough and trellis with new vigor, what few tourists there were began their exodus to the north, leaving the locals to the perennial heat.

That year, the U.S., North Vietnam, South Vietnam, and the Viet Cong signed a peace treaty in Paris, Vice President Spiro T. Agnew resigned in disgrace over charges of racketeering and tax evasion, and *The Exorcist* was the number-one movie at the box office. It was also the year we met the lovely, incomparable Banyan McDaniel, and the weasel bastard Justin Mames—both of whom changed our lives.

The truth is, no matter how diligent you are you can only direct your future so much. Just about the time you're strolling down the street of life, hands in your pockets, not a care in the world, somebody pushes a piano out of a sixth-story window....

We had a buddy named Turtle (Winfield, actually, but everyone preferred Turtle) who was a tropical fish diver, like ourselves. He was a man with an innocent heart—a straightforward human being in a world full of pretenders. Turtle was of average height, wore his dark hair long, like most of us, and carried himself with a surety borne not of ego but of honesty. He was certain of who he was and he was at peace with the world. I guess you would have called him a handsome fellow. He had large brown eyes capable of displaying a vast spectrum of emotion, and a smile that looked like a toothpaste ad. In nothing more than Hang Ten shorts and a T-shirt, he was very tough competition on outings to Key West, but he was wonderful flypaper. Nearly every girl who wanted to chat with him had a friend.

At least once a month we'd all get together and make a night of it, but in April of that year there was an exceptional band playing at Captain Tony's, so we began going in each weekend. As a result, two things happened—we met Banyan and Turtle fell in love.

We arrived at Captain Tony's one Friday evening after treating ourselves to dinner at the Black Angus on Roosevelt Boulevard. We had barely taken a seat and begun to enjoy the sultry music of the new band—a group out of Georgia called *The Naked Penguins,* who wore tuxedo shirts, black bow ties, and black Speedo bathing suits—when a lovely cocktail waitress on the far side of the bar saw Turtle. As the band finished their number and announced a break, she put down her tray and excused herself from her customers, and slowly, deliberately glided toward our table. Turtle saw her coming, and with a wide smile he stood and opened his arms. She virtually floated into his embrace. Lord, she was lovely—a petite blond with a Saint Croix tan and the tightly-proportioned body of a figure skater, dressed in a snug, two-part, white-flowered green sarong. They held each other for a moment, then she gave him a delicious kiss on the neck and pulled back, still staring at him. "How ya doin' handsome?" she said with a voice that was both sultry and genuine, without a hint of pretense—much in keeping with the character of the man in front of her. "Looking for some action tonight?"

He grinned, still holding her hands. "Nah. I took vows of celibacy last week. I'm going to become a nun."

"You mean a priest."

"No. I mean a nun. It's the only way I'll be able to keep them."

She giggled throatily, gazing up at him. "You're gonna drive them crazy at the abbey."

I was enthralled with her—the way she carried herself and the honesty she projected. I would have said she was in her early twenties, but the girl possessed that rare, almost revered child-woman quality, and could have just as well been eighteen. I realized that, when you took in the whole package, I had seen more attractive women, but she had some very nice parts. Her eyes were reef line blue, and she had a cute, slightly upturned nose, but her mouth was by far her most outstanding quality. A woman's mouth is the most provocative and seductive feature she has. It prompts more imagination and promises a wider variety of delights than any other part of her body. Not all women understand this and use it to their full advantage, but this woman did. She had a wide, Carly Simon smile and full, petulant lips. She enunciated each word carefully, rolling vowels with her mouth, making casual conversation sensual.

Turtle finally let go of her hands and put his arm around her waist, presenting the lady to us. "Will, Kansas, this is my sister, Banyan McDaniel."

His sister! His sister! I was suddenly, unequivocally convinced there really was a God. I nodded and mumbled something about "nice" and "meeting"—the words kind of dribbled out of my mouth and dropped onto the table. I glanced over at Will, who, I'm quite sure, judging from the indelible junction in his eyes, didn't even know his own name then, let alone command the capacity for speech. He nodded and smiled. His mouth worked a little, but he wisely stopped it before he blurted anything. I'm certain at that point Banyan thought her brother had taken to consorting with imbeciles.

She was as kind as she was attractive, and jump-started the conversation. "You're the two tropical fish divers on Big Pine my brother's told me about. It's so cool, what you guys do—catching fish and flying them across the country.

"Yeah, we're pretty lucky, I guess," I said, finally finding my equilibrium.

Turtle broke in enthusiastically. "Yeah, man. These two are fast becoming the guys to watch—the cutting edge of the business. But they need to get drunk and laid more often, and that's part of my task tonight."

As she laughed and punched him playfully, I wanted to say, "No! It's not true! I'm not that kind of guy! I'm a nice guy! The kind you might like to date." But I didn't. Because I was that kind of guy.

"So what are you doing here?" Turtle said to her. "Does Dad know you're peddling liquor to drunken sailors?"

She sighed. "Yeah, he knows. He doesn't like it, but he knows." She turned to us. "Our family owns a nursery on Big Coppitt and I've worked there for years, but I wanted a new car, so I picked up an extra job for the down payment. So," she said, displaying her hands theatrically like Vanna White, "can I get you sailors something to drink?"

We ordered. Will and I managed to choose drinks without stuttering, which both of us considered a sizable victory. As she walked away, we leered ever so briefly, trying to stay within the boundaries of propriety. She suddenly glanced back and caught us. There was no chastisement, but rather a hint of a smile and a wonderfully mischievous glint in her eyes, but I couldn't tell who it was for, or if it was for anyone. But I wanted to believe it was for me. As Banyan continued on her way, I turned to her brother, who grinned knowingly at us.

"Lord, Turtle! You never told us you had a goddess for a sister!" I whined exasperatedly.

He grinned. "You guys need sexual distraction, not cardiac contraction. What are you gonna do, draw straws for her, break up a perfectly good partnership while one of you marries her and lives happily ever after?"

"I'm not ready to ask for her hand in marriage," Will said seriously. "I need a couple more hours."

Turtle was about to answer when three characters walked into the saloon. The one in the middle stopped, surveying the scene, making sure of an entrance. The others immediately halted at his side. He was about thirty years old—tanned "Miami" complexion, aquiline nose that gave his face character, average height but a touch overweight. Still, he carried himself with a bandy sense of importance. His salon-styled, sable hair shone slightly with pomade, and his dark eyes were bright with intelligence, but slightly dispassionate. He was dressed more uptown—beige slacks, white shirt open, a couple of buttons displaying a sizable gold chain, Florsheims. The guy on his right was tall, maybe six feet. He was dressed casually, in blue jeans, a Hawaiian shirt, and tennis shoes, but there was a wary, hard look about him. The third fellow was a Latin with some African mixed in, with hair that curled in dark ringlets, a pudgy, pockmarked face, an Errol Flynn mustache, and dark eyes. He was wearing blue jeans, a slightly wrinkled polo shirt and leather sandals. Man, that guy looked familiar to me, but I just couldn't place him. One of the managers drifted over and shook hands with the guy in the center, delivering them to a table in the rear of the bar. As they were getting settled, Banyan returned with drinks, accompanied by another goddess in a yellow sarong. "This is Brandi," she said. "You're in her section and she promises to take very good care of you. I'll see you guys when I get a break, in about a half hour." With a smile and a wink (which I was certain was for me) she was gone.

Brandi was taller, with lustrous, shoulder-length, auburn hair, dark, almond-shaped eyes, and a figure that would defy description by Homer. She was undeniably beautiful, but my heart was already taken. My musings were interrupted by a nudge from Will. "Man, did you see Banyan wink at me when she left? She felt the magic too, man."

I whipped around. "What magic? She was lookin' at me! The only magic you're feeling is the Dramamine patch I stuffed in your beer."

"You wouldn't do that."

"I might. Anything's fair in love and war and this could be either before the night is done, dude."

During our bantering we weren't paying attention to some serious emotional alchemy occurring on the other side of the table. Turtle was holding his glass as Brandi slowly poured his beer. Neither was paying too much attention to where the beer was going. They stared at each other as she poured until there was no more room in the glass and the remainder fizzed over. Finally, she caught herself and pulled back, setting the bottle down. "I'm sorry. Messy of me," she said as she wiped the excess from the table and his hand. She stopped and looked at Turtle again, who hadn't taken his eyes from her. "I'm sorry, but do I know you from somewhere? It's just you look so familiar… and…."

With complete seriousness Turtle replied, "Two lifetimes ago in Paris—during the fall of Louis the Sixteenth. The peasants were taking the city—killing the wealthy people, like us—but we escaped on a little fishing sloop onto the Seine. You were pregnant with our first child."

She had leaned forward as if drawn into him. Their faces were almost touching. "Don't say things like that," she whispered. "I believe in reincarnation. Things like that can be true."

"I hope it is true because it means I've found you again."

Brandi exhaled. "You might be the most romantic person I've ever met."

"Or I might be just trying to get into your pants."

"Give me one solid thing you remember about us that we'll both recall and you can have my pants and all that goes with them."

He smiled. "Too easy, my lady, for what has passed before. Too easy." He paused, reminiscently, eyes somewhere else. "You loved the bridges—the different colored bridges in Paris, and the way the sun used to reflect off of them. It's one of the reasons you chose to return to the Keys this time. For the bridges, and for me."

She was silent for a moment. "I'm seeing someone."

"Yeah, I know—me."

She pulled back. "No. It's complicated and if you're not the right one, I stand to lose a lot."

"Let your heart do the choosing," Turtle whispered.

"I will if I have one left." She moved her head toward the three men in the corner. "I'm seeing Justin Mames and he requires a degree of fidelity on my part."

Turtle scoffed. "Justin Mames, Key West's most infamous attorney, wants fidelity? That's a bit bogus. He's better connected to the smugglers he defends than he is to the judges he works with. I hear the big news is, he wants to be mayor. Only in Key West, man."

"See, there is something to lose," she said.

Turtle just stared at her. "What time do you get off work?"

Brandi glanced over toward Justin's table. He was involved in a conversation with his two friends. "Ten o'clock."

"I'll be waiting for you at the Bull and Whistle."

As she turned and drifted into the crowd, Will exhaled. "What in the hell was that, man? You made the hair on my arms stand up. That was the most amazing thing I've ever seen. I think maybe I love you. Or at least I'd like you to teach me how to do that. Maybe, just maybe, that was the greatest pick-up line I've ever heard."

Turtle just stared at her as she walked away. "Not sure it was a line."

Banyan visited with us when she took her break. When she and Brandi finished their shift, we all ended up at the Bull and Whistle. Will and I took turns telling outlandish stories, dancing with Banyan, and drinking way too much. Turtle and Brandi couldn't have cared if they were at Mardi Gras on Mars. They weren't much interested in what was taking place around them. By the end of the evening, Will and I had decided we needed to buy some nursery trees and bushes for our home, and we needed to visit Captain Tony's at least twice a week.

As the next few weeks played themselves out, there was some good news and some bad news. The good news was, we had both found the girl of our dreams. The bad news was, it was the same girl. Turtle had also found the light of his life, but she belonged to someone else, and that someone had a reputation for making people's problems disappear.

It was a strange situation, this thing with Banyan, Will, and me. It didn't take long to realize that we all got along wonderfully. She had the same acerbic, bright wit and sense of honesty that had become the cornerstone of my friendship with Will, and there was simply no struggle in conversation. We started visiting with her occasionally while she worked at the nursery, then going out for drinks. That led to dinner a couple of times a week, before she went to work at Captain Tony's.

She was the most genuine of women, and we had nothing of any consequence to offer, other than our affection, so the time spent with us was pure. Nor had she offered more than friendship—to either of us—which was acceptable on one hand (as opposed to having a winner, and a loser) yet perplexing and somewhat unfulfilling on the other. But as the weeks passed, it was obvious something both singularly magical and infinitely complicated was taking place. Second stage affection was beginning to play itself out. We'd be having dinner at the Pierhouse down by the small beach lagoon, and she would suddenly reach out and take my hand, drawing it into her while I told a particularly amusing or exciting story. I could see the irrefutable affection for me in her eyes. Then, the girl whom I was fairly certain must be falling for me, would suddenly grab my best friend around the waist and drag him out into the lagoon, falling and laughing and getting her T-shirt sexy wet. She'd come out of the water and those perky little breasts would stand up like small horns, and all of a sudden just being friends really sucked.

Will and I tried not to talk about it—our emotional *ménage a trois*—but one day while we were working on the boat engine, it just came tumbling out of his mouth. He put down his wrench, sighed and turned to me. "Kansas, you're my good friend. My best friend, and I don't want to hurt you, but you know how I feel about her." He paused. "I'm going to ask her out, on a date—just her and me. Because the suspense is killing me."

I sat back against the gunnel for a moment, staggered by the broadside, but not entirely surprised. "I don't want to see anything change with our friendship either. But the best I can offer is to name one of our children after you."

He gave me that same old cockeyed smile as he pushed the sun-bleached hair from his eyes with one hand, but there was just a touch of melancholy there. "I just gotta do it, man. I just gotta."

That afternoon Will called Banyan and asked her out for the evening. She said yes. I got drunk—seriously drunk. He came home late, and happy—the whistling kind of happy. Almost the "I got laid" kind of happy. We weren't able to dive the next day because the weather closed and a front rolled in. I retaliated and asked Banyan out. She said yes. Will got very drunk. He had to be carried home from the Big Pine Inn that night.

It was a wonderful evening. The front passed through, leaving brush strokes of white-gray cirrus clouds suspended beneath the stars, illuminated by a waning full moon. Banyan and I had a quiet dinner at a little Italian restaurant called Aunt Rose's. We ordered seafood lasagna and a bottle of red wine, and talked about the small, important things you tell someone you care about—because you understand they really want to know.

I gazed at her, watching the yellow flickering of the candles cast soft shadows across her tanned face and bare shoulders. The soft reminiscence of "In My Life" by The Beatles floated almost ethereally around us. We had moved our chairs closer, elbows on the table, leaning toward each other in the soft conspiracy of romance. She took a sip of wine and tilted her head in question. "So Kansas, how did you end up with the name of a square, Midwestern state?"

I shrugged. "They wanted to call me Mississippi but there weren't enough letter spaces on the birth certificate."

She giggled. "No, really."

"The truth is, our family had a distant relative, a bank robber in the late eighteen hundreds whose name was Kansas, and I guess my dad thought it was kind of a romantically bold name. That's what I hear." I turned slightly to her. "And you? How did you end up with a name that fits you so well? Banyan—beauty, substance, perennial grace."

"When I was young, I was told it was just a pretty name. Later I found out my parents sought the refuge of a Banyan tree during a storm, while visiting Cuba before I was born." She smiled mischievously. "It was a long storm and they decided to occupy some of their time. That's what I hear."

We ended up taking a walk on White Street Pier, watching the stars reflect off the dark water and listening to the waves gently brush the shore. We were about halfway along the pier when Banyan just turned to me in that inimitable fashion of hers, looked into my eyes and said, "I need you to kiss me." Although it was all I had been thinking about for the last half hour, I was still a little taken by surprise. There was absolutely nothing left to say. I pulled her to me slowly, and she lifted up and brought her mouth to mine. Her lips were softer than I would have dreamed possible, and I had dreamed about it more than a little. As our mouths melded I pulled her in tightly to me, feeling the firmness of her breasts against my chest. As intense as it was, neither of us was lost to a passion of teeth-banging, tongue-swallowing lustfulness. It was a wonderful, romantic, damned near perfect kiss. We pulled back just a touch and gazed at each other, then did it again, just to make sure. Without a word, her hand slid into mine again and we began to walk toward the end of the pier. I think we both knew what was coming.

"What did Will tell you about our date?" she asked softly.

"Nothing," I replied, a little fear replacing some of my immediate euphoria. "He didn't offer any details and I didn't ask. But he was happier than I was comfortable with. You know, of course, you're driving us both mad?"

She sighed. "I know. And it was never my intention. I wasn't even looking to get involved with one man, let alone two. I couldn't have imagined something like this would happen to me. It doesn't seem possible—it's straight out of some bad B movie. There is so much that I love about both of you, I just don't know what to do."

(Lord, she used the word, love.)

"I feel like Dorothy Lamour in a Bing Crosby/Bob Hope movie," she chuckled. "*The Road To Key West*." There was a pause. "So Kansas, what are we going to do?"

"You're asking the wrong guy if you want an unbiased answer. I say we name a kid after him. And if we all really tighten up, maybe he can have you on weekends."

"You better be joking," she said.

"Yeah. I am."

She stared out at the water for a moment. "I'm deliriously happy, terribly confused, and rotting with guilt. There's no way to keep you both and make everyone happy all the time. But I'm not ready to make a decision. I'm just not sure I can."

"Well, I can say for sure that the concept of making us both happy is going to cost you more sleep than you'll like." Then I paused, more serious. "The danger here as well is that ultimately, Will and I could lose our partnership, our friendship, over this, and I'm not ready for that either."

"So take me home, Kansas," she sighed, "and maybe by the time we get there, you'll be able to tell me what we're going to do."

I took her home and a small decision was made. We made love—gentle, passionate, eventually tongue-swallowing, teeth-banging love. But we did nothing about the bigger decision that sat quietly in the room with us like a mastodon.

As it turned out, something happened that changed perspectives on everything and put our morass of emotions on the back burner. Turtle got arrested with twenty pounds of Colombian gold in the trunk of his car.

While my friend and I had been blissfully courting Banyan, Turtle and Brandi had been seeing each other regularly. It took Brandi about two weeks of trading affections between Turtle and Justin Mames before coming to a decision and announcing to Key West's nefarious attorney and recently declared mayoral candidate that it was over. Mr. Mames said she would be sorry.

Turtle smoked pot occasionally, as did nearly everyone in the Keys. It was the '70s. It was a civil amenity. With the exception of the Annual Policemen's Ball, it was standard decorum at almost any festive occasion. Local law enforcement hardly ever arrested people for smoking pot. They might take it away from you. They might even keep it. But they were cool. They were looking at the bigger picture and trying to nail the guys who brought it in and distributed it—that's where you could find yourself in trouble. That's where Turtle found himself—in the Key West Jail.

Banyan called us the day after she and I had gone out. She was frantic. Her parents were freaking out, but they had the presence of mind to begin the process of bail—twenty thousand dollars, which was extremely high, given the situation. The next day Turtle was out and we went over to see him that evening. Banyan and Brandi were already there. After hugs all around, we sat down and Turtle began to explain.

He looked at us, no deception in his eyes, no agenda. "Man, I've got no idea where that pot came from." He exhaled angrily.

"Dammit, man, where would I get that much pot? Better yet, where would I get seven or eight thousand dollars to pay for it? All I know is that I had been into Key West to see Brandi. I spent most of the night with her. We were talking about her moving up to Big Pine to live with me. I left about three in the morning. I had just gotten to Roosevelt Boulevard and was heading onto Stock Island, when suddenly there were red lights all around me. They pulled me over and asked for identification, then immediately wanted to know what was in my trunk—not even a perfunctory search of the car, straight to the trunk. The next thing I know, I'm in handcuffs and being checked into a single room with a bad view. Talk about a bummer…"

I was beginning to gather some thoughts of my own on the situation. "Turtle, look me in the eyes and tell me one more time that you weren't involved in moving that pot."

He stood up and stared at me. "Kan, I swear to you that I had nothing, absolutely nothing, to do with this."

I gazed around at everybody. "Okay, I'm going to tell you what I think. I think he's been set up by Justin Mames." I looked at Turtle. "Didn't you tell me you got some subtle warnings from friends of his?"

"Yeah. I was sitting at the bar one night and this squirrely-looking Latin guy sits down next to me. He sets his shot glass down, puts his cigarette out in my ashtray and looks at me. He's got this lisp. He leans over and says, 'Chu better not pluck around con another man's woman, man. Bad tings can happen.' Turtle smiled despite the situation, recalling. "He picks up his shot glass and gives me this macho toast/salute, like something out of a bad Western, and says, 'To good health, amigo.' As he starts to throw back the shot, somebody in the crowd bumps him and he drops the drink in his crotch. He looks down, mumbles, '*Coño, coño, coño*,' then just gets up and leaves."

I smiled, suddenly remembering who the guy was with Mames that first night in Captain Tony's—the crab races robber—obviously coming up in the world, but not getting much better at it. "You've already got an attorney, right?"

"Yeah. My folks hired one."

"Okay, here's what we need to do. We need a transcript of the police report. It's available to the attorney. We need to know how this came about—to be certain. Have you got a court date yet?"

"Yeah, oddly enough they've already scheduled me for May fifteenth, two weeks from now. For some reason, this whole thing seems well greased."

Well greased, indeed. Talk on the street in the next few days was that the movers and shakers of Key West justice had decided to make an example of a few bag boys in town who'd been picked up moving stuff. Justin Mames and one of the local judges, Milton Thompson (ironically, the one set to try Turtle), were speaking out about stronger sentences for those "who deserved them," and a "safer, more tourist-friendly Key West." The police records revealed there had been a tip-off to the department. Someone had dropped a dime on Turtle—location, time, even estimated quantity. It was pretty obvious that our friend had been booked a seat on the railroad to hell. Even his attorney told him he was concerned. It was possible Turtle might get a couple of years in prison. That would give Mames considerable time to console Brandi, if that was his plan. But we all knew with Mames, it could simply be revenge. We needed a plan. Ironically enough, it was Brandi who set the wheels in motion. When you spend time around someone with a large ego, you inevitably learn a lot about them. When a woman spends much time with a man, she generally learns his weaknesses as well as strengths.

We were all gathered together at Banyan's house a few days later, drinking wine and reviewing what the attorney had told Turtle to that point. None of it looked promising.

"We need a bargaining chip. We need to find Mames' Achilles heel," I said, frustrated. I looked to Brandi. "What can you tell me about Justin? Did he talk about any of his deals with judges or smugglers? Does he have any kind of secret about him that we can exploit?"

She eased back in her seat for a moment and thought. "He never came right out and told me what he was doing, but I'm certain from all the little innuendos that he gets paid in pot sometimes and has a team that moves it. And I think he's got something on at least one of the judges." She paused and smiled. "He got high one night with me and mentioned something about being an excellent record-keeper, and Judge Thompson knew it. And he bragged about the quality of the safe in his office. Impenetrable is what he called it."

"Now, that's interesting," I said. "But I'm sure there's no one here that couldn't throw a dime over the moon easier than crack a safe. So I don't know how it helps."

"There is one other thing, but I don't know how it would play into this," Brandi said. "There's something that almost nobody knows about him. He goes to a hypnotherapist once a week—to try to quit smoking. He hasn't had success any other way, and she seems to be helping. He told me offhandedly that he's considered a 'sleeper' in hypnotherapy circles. He goes under really deeply and is extremely sensitive to suggestion."

Will looked at me and smiled. I knew that smile. We were on our way to a plan. He turned to Brandi. "What's her name—the therapist?"

"Sunni Beach," she said with a smile. We all looked at her. Brandi put her hands up. "Really. That's her name, her real name. She's fairly young, but she's reportedly very good at what she does. She has an office out of her home on Simonton Street."

"How often does he see her?" I asked.

"He has a regular one-hour appointment on Friday afternoons at four o'clock."

I thought for a moment, then looked at Will. He nodded and leaned forward conspiratorially. "This is a long shot, but it may be our only shot. Here's what I suggest."

Two days later, on Friday afternoon at three-thirty, Banyan, Will, and I were having a drink at an innocuous watering hole on Duval Street, reviewing our plan one last time. I was admittedly a little nervous and decided to go to the bathroom once more before things were set into motion.

I was standing at the urinal when the door opened behind me. I paid little attention. I was occupied. Another person joined me two urinals over. I still wasn't paying much attention. It's one of those places where guys try to avoid being too interested in each other. Eyes down or indifferently staring at the wall tile is *de rigor*. Then I heard a familiar voice.

"Aahhh, my good friend. May your circulatory apparatus find peaceful thumping!"

I looked over and smiled at our dread-locked Jamaican buddy, who had once again shown up out of nowhere. "What's happenin', Rufus?"

"I thought that I might encounter your presence today," he said, slightly serious, glancing my way.

"Why?"

"I'm lucky that way, mon."

I opened my mouth—then shut it.

He looked at me and his eyes did that strange thing, passing from light and breezy to intuitive and sort of formidable in a fraction of a second—like the veil had been lifted. "Kansas, even the hasty seagull knows preparation and timing are the keys to having a fish, or not having a fish..."

It was a little eerie. I would have sworn that he understood what was happening. I put everything away and stepped back from the urinal. I didn't know exactly what to say. "So, how you doin', Rufus?"

He finished and turned. "I am at peace, mon, but peace changes like the tides. Sometimes you can dip your hands in the current and still come up without any of it on your fingers."

"Ain't that right on," I said, once again a little amazed at his insight. "Well man, I gotta split—got things to take care of today. Good sailing, my friend."

As I turned to leave, Rufus called out behind me. "Kansas, I possess a thing of import to the triangulations of your endeavors."

I turned back. Rufus reached into his shirt and pulled out the pyramid-shaped amulet I had seen him wearing the first time we met—the one I was certain I had seen glowing. He opened the hinged top, and from his pocket took a cocktail straw that had been cut in half. One end had been twisted closed. He dipped the straw in the amulet then pulled it out, holding it upright and shaking it slightly, then he folded the top of the straw to seal it. Closing the amulet and returning it to his shirt he handed me the straw.

I blanched a little, shaking my head. "No thanks, man. Not into coke."

"No mon, magic dust," he said. "Pour in palm of your hand and blow—only at one person." He looked sternly at me. "Do not breathe in. No secrets, no will but yours with magic dust, mon."

"Whatta you mean? I—I don't think so, Rufus."

He put his hand out. "Put uneasiness aside. It is a potion of my homeland. It is what you need."

Dumbfounded, and certainly a little circumspect, I put the straw in my shirt pocket. "Rufus … how is it…that you—" I shrugged, not knowing exactly where to take the conversation from there. "Well, I gotta go. Take care."

He gave me his famous toothy grin. "Cool driftings, mon. May the goddess of great decisions hold a lantern for you in the grotto of uncertainty."

"What kept you?" asked Will when I returned to the table. "It's time."

"Ran into Rufus in the restroom."

"Yeah? What's he up to?"

I shrugged. "Stopped by to give me some magic dust."
"Really?"
"Yeah."

Sunni Beach was a small, thin, but not unattractive brunette with large blue eyes that carried a soft sadness about them—as if perhaps she'd heard too much of the secret distress of the world. She lived alone in a nice little hibiscus-shrouded home tucked away beneath two huge rubber trees. She had converted the back bedroom into a study, where she held her sessions. There was a circular coral rock driveway lined with traditional conch shells, and a multitude of vines, flowers, and ferns throughout the yard. We drove by slowly and Banyan confirmed that Mames' car was out front—a sporty little two-door Mercedes. We already knew the layout. I had stopped by a few days before (working for the water company that day), looking for a leak that had been reported. Brandi told us that Mames was her last client of the day—no one would interrupt us. We parked the car at a small Cuban convenience store two blocks away. I left first with Banyan. Will followed a few minutes later.

Banyan and I casually made our way off the street and slipped behind the house. As we eased our way back toward the study, I noticed there was an "In Session: Please Do Not Disturb" sign on the front door.

It was a mild spring day and Sunni had her windows open, taking advantage of the lovely breeze. We could hear a soft, soothing voice as we neared the study window. I peeked over the windowsill. Mames was reclining on a beige leather couch, eyes closed, while Sunni, dressed in a soft chiffon blouse and a white skirt, sat across from him in a high-backed Victorian-type chair, speaking quietly. I nodded to Banyan and she slipped back to the corner of the house, signaling Will as he approached. I watched from outside the window as Sunni heard the first knock.

Her brow furrowed. She paused for a moment and listened. She resumed, "You will look at cigarettes as if each one carried—" There was the knocking again. She sighed with resignation. "Justin, I want you to take a deep breath and relax for a moment. You will go into a deep, comfortable rest and imagine yourself completely free of the desire for nicotine." She rose quietly and left the room, closing the door behind her.

I immediately pried off the screen with a screwdriver, helped Banyan through the window, then followed.

Sunni opened the front door. It was like the curtain rising on a stage.

There stood Will, attired in the flowing brown robes of a monk, complemented by a Jewish skullcap, a handful of rosary beads, and a scraggly fake beard. He opened his arms wide, robe flowing out. "Shalom! By the blessed light of the Virgin, greetings from the temple of the Baptist Ministry's Jehovah's Witness Program! We're a wonderful new religion whose philosophy is 'You know you're gonna die, so why take any chances. Cover all the bases!'"

"Please," Sunni said in hushed tones. "I'm a therapist and I'm with a client—"

"A therapist! That's wonderful!" cried Will. "We have a branch in Southern California—The Therapeutic Snake Charmers and Faith Healers Guild! We'd love to have you as a member. You can treat the ones that get snakebit!"

Meanwhile, in the back room, Banyan quietly sat down next to Mames. "Justin, this is Sunni. You will continue in your deep relaxation. You will listen to every word I say now, and you will do exactly as I say." Mames' eyes were still closed but the rhythm of his breathing had changed and he was shifting just a little in the seat. Perhaps it was the different voice, but he was becoming slightly agitated.

Up front, Sunni started to close the door. "I'm sorry," she whispered tersely. "I'm not interested. I—"

Will's eyes suddenly bulged. He slapped his hand to his heart, while putting his foot inside the door. "Ohhh God! Aaahhh, the old pacemaker … stopped…" he wheezed, dropping to his knees dramatically. "Forgot to change the battery… Ohhh, God… help … in the pocket of my robe."

Sunni quite naturally freaked out. She quickly knelt beside him and began riffling through his pockets.

Will kept moaning, "The other one, must be the other one … little battery… Ooohhh, Jesus, take away the pain! The paaain!" as he thumped on the porch deck with his fist. "Ohhhhh Jesus, John, and Ringo!" (More thumping—Sunni was getting frantic, ripping through his pockets.) "Lord! Take away the frigging pain!"

Mames' head began to move back and forth. He was coming around. Banyan looked at me in a panic. I did the only thing I could think of. I took out the straw that Rufus had given me, knelt by Justin, took a breath, poured the sparkly, almost luminescent dust into my palm, and as Mames began to rise, blew it in his face. His eyes shot open like he'd just been goosed with a broomstick. There was a deep, distant, shocked expression in them, as if he was seeing a freight train strike a baby carriage, then suddenly it all passed. He sighed softly and blinked—blank, without comprehension, then slowly closed his eyes and put his head back down on the couch.

Banyan looked at me in awe, mouth agape. "What in the hell did you just do?" she whispered.

I shrugged, eyebrows up. "Magic dust?"

Meanwhile, Will lay on the porch clutching at Sunni's arms and groaning, "This is the big one! I'm a' goin'—I can see the light! Oohhh Loorrd! There's the tunnel! Thump me on the chest. Bite me with a snake! Oohhh God! I don't wanna die!"

Sunni tried to stand. "I'll call an ambulance. We'll get help!"

Will grabbed her around the ankles and cried, "Noooo, don't leave me. Get Jesus on the line! Tell Elvis I'm a' comin'!"

Meanwhile, Banyan composed herself and started again. "Justin, let yourself drift into that safe, warm place. You will continue in your deep relaxation. You will listen to every word I say now, and you will do exactly as I say. Do you understand?"

Mames sighed, contented. "Yes."

I slipped out of the window.

Out front, Will glanced over and saw me stick my head around the corner of the house and nod. "Ohhh God," he cried, releasing Sunni's legs. "The pain! The pain is gone! It's gone! Sweet Jesus! I'm healed! It's a miracle! A flippin' miracle!" He quickly rose and brushed down his robes. "Well, sorry you're not interested in any of this. Most of it's crap anyway, but the snakes are really cool. Best of luck to you!" Before Sunni could close her mouth, he was gone—just the wisp of a robe around the corner hedge.

The following night, Will and I visited Justin Mames' office via the back window. On the way home I turned to my friend. "Do you really think this is going to work?"

"Which part?"

"Any of it."

Will was driving. He got that crooked smile of his, tilted his head slightly and shook it slowly. "It's a great story even if it doesn't—especially the part about the magic dust."

I nodded thoughtfully. "I'm gonna tell you something. I always knew that Rufus danced to the beat of a different drummer, but I'm beginning to think he might know the guy who makes the drums."

Will looked out at the dark road, illuminated only by an occasional arched streetlamp. "Only the blowfish knows, man. Only the blowfish knows."

Monday morning at nine o'clock the trial of Winfield T. McDaniels began. In what was a slightly unusual but not unheard of situation, Justin Mames was serving as an assistant to the prosecutor. It didn't take long for it to begin to look bad. There were eight-by-ten black and white photos, police testimony, and the prosecuting attorney's speculation that Turtle was a part of a much larger operation. The defense did what they could, showing a solid citizen, no record, and claimed that the contraband had been planted—but that was an old song inside those walls.

The prosecution was about halfway through their closing statements when a young boy in a Sloppy Joe's T-shirt and tan shorts brought a yellow manila folder into the courtroom and deposited it on Justin Mames' desk. With absolutely no emotion he bent over and whispered, "You need to read this, now." Then he quietly left. Justin shrugged at the other attorneys and opened the folder. He pulled out a couple of typed sheets, indifferent and unconcerned, and gazed at them. Indifference fell off his face and shattered on the table. Unconcerned just slid down like warm potter's clay and melted into his lap. He took out two more pages. Anxious was right up there, followed by very confused, and the last page he drew out was an easy read—scared and screwed. He put the pages away and stood, requesting to approach the bench.

Judge Thompson took one look at his face and called him forward. There was a hushed, one-minute conversation at the bench, then the judge looked out to the courtroom. "There will be a ten-minute recess in my chambers."

"Bam!" went the gavel. Nine minutes later, the two attorneys and the judge were back, all slightly ashen-faced. Judge Thompson swung his gavel, and as it resounded nicely he announced, "Case against Winfield McDaniels is dismissed on an evidence submission technicality. McDaniels, sir, you're free to go."

Sitting in the back row of the courtroom, we could hardly keep from applauding. It was amazing. It really worked! I smiled and thought back to how cooperative Mames had been at Sunni's, when we had asked him a couple of simple questions about wall safe combinations and alarm devices in his building. The next night, we snuck in, popped open the safe, and made a couple copies of his "special books" before putting them back. Mames had made more deals than General Electric, and he had some names in his pocket that, when it came down to it, would sell him out or take him out in a heartbeat. But the best was yet to come.

Mames was scheduled to publicly announce his mayoral candidacy for Key West directly after the trial. There had been a platform set up in front of the courthouse with American flags draped on the rails and two podiums. Key West television was covering the event. It was eleven o'clock when he and Judge Thompson stepped out onto the platform and moved forward to the podiums set with microphones.

Mames took a breath and began, "Regardless of the outcome of today's trial, which was lost to a technicality—*Arrooff!*"

I stood there in disbelief. Justin Mames had just barked into the microphone. A murmur of surprise rolled through the crowd along with some poorly suppressed giggling.

Getting his balance, Mames moved on. "But we intend to take this town into a new era where drug smugglers are hard to find, because we've arrested them—*Arrf! Arrf!*" He hadn't gotten the last word out of his mouth and he was down on his hands and knees, in his fifty-dollar Dockers slacks, barking like a dog—woofing with the enthusiasm of a hungry puppy.

The crowd was freaked out a little at first, but they sensed something extraordinary was happening. Mames was more well-known than he was well-liked. What had brought most of them there—curiosity, interest—was now morphing into a truly unprecedented opportunity to feel superior to someone who had spent the better part of his life deliberately making them feel inferior. It was like hounds closing in on a fox.

Catcalls erupted from the audience.

"Speak up, Alpo breath!"

"You're barking up the wrong tree here, man!"

Will grinned from ear to ear. "I didn't really think it was possible to use hypnosis to make a person do what they normally wouldn't."

"Maybe he always wanted to bark like a dog," I replied. " Personally, I'm not ruling out the magic dust."

"I don't care what it is," cried Will over the babble. "I want to ask him a question." Working his way into the crowd, Will shouted, "Are you gonna quit selling drugs if elected mayor?"

Mames struggled to his feet again, the effects of the first few questions having begun to wear off. (We had programmed him for ten seconds of barking on all fours for every lie).

"Why yes, of course—aahh, I mean I do not sell drugs. I will enforce laws harshly against those who—"

Wham, down again, bouncing around like Lassie on bennies. About that time people began catching on and the congregation started getting cruel. Justin barely managed to get off his hands and knees for the next fifteen minutes. Judge Thompson had long since abandoned him. The police had to break it up.

The next morning we were sitting at a table in a little waterfront café off Malory Square—all of us, Turtle, Brandi, Banyan, Will and me. We were drinking mimosas, eating Cuban toast, and reading the paper. Much of it was about Mames, and the obvious demise of his career in our area. The headlines were: "Key West Politics Goes To The Dogs." Aside from the scathing text, there were some marvelous eight-by-ten color photos of him during his performance. One clever journalist did give him "Best of Show."

I put the paper down. "Whoever said, 'there's no such thing as bad publicity,' didn't catch that act."

Will gave me that classic Lee Marvin grin and raised his glass in a toast. "Bark like a dog, baby! Bark like a dog!"

Mames wisely abandoned his aspirations for mayor, packed up his office, and quietly moved his practice to Fort Lauderdale. But his influence in the Keys and his business regarding late-night deliveries of bulky, duct-taped burlap bundles was far from over.

CHAPTER SIX

Dear Ma, I Never Really Wanted To Be A Criminal

That fall, Richard Nixon was elected president in a landslide victory over George McGovern (despite the brewing Watergate controversy), Turtle and Brandi got married, and Banyan finally made a decision. You're walking along, hands in your pockets, doing your best to mind your own business, and here comes that piano out of nowhere.

We had solved Turtle's problems, but our complicated *ménage* had simply become more complicated. It was a trying affair—a vortex extraordinaire. One of us was always trying to get a commitment from Banyan while the other was trying to get as drunk as possible. When I look back on it all, I realize Will and I had a remarkable friendship in that it was capable of enduring such a cleavage. Perhaps rift would be a better term, but cleavage is pretty accurate.

We decided a viable solution might be for us to get away for a while—to give our lady's heart a chance to grow fonder for one of us—to go somewhere so sufficiently removed that neither of us could drug the other and catch a bus back to Banyan. Our wholesaler in Miami helped make the decision when he offered to pay half our fare to Costa Rica if we would determine the viability of setting up a collection station on that country's west coast. The company was hoping to import a highly prized tropical fish from that area called a Cortez Angel. They explained that our mission, should we choose to accept it, would be to rendezvous in the west coast city of Puntarenas with a local aquarium store owner named Sergio Mendoza, and dive the bay islands for a week to ten days. Both Will and I spoke passable Spanish. It seemed simple enough—a few days south of the border, a little diving. How much trouble could we get into, really?

We called Banyan and told her of our plan, asking for a decision from her on our return. We left our dog, a scruffy black and white terrier named Lizard, with our neighbor, Nick Crow. Nick was a card-carrying member of the "good life" club—a Tom Selleck kind of guy—tall, tanned, fruit-juicy shirts, bell-bottomed blue jeans, Keno sandals, sandy-colored hair. He had explained to us that a rich, recently departed uncle had left him a tidy sum of money and thanks to a savvy investment company, money was no longer an issue. Nick had a nice little 41-foot Morgan sailboat tied up at his dock and he ran a continuous classified advertisement in the *Key West Citizen* for female companion/sailing mates to accompany him on an upcoming Bahamas/Caribbean cruise. Consequently, he had a conga line of tanned backsides and pointy bikinis who were more than willing participants of day sails and overnighters—to determine their "sailing skills and compatibility." Nick also owned a small, twin-engine Piper Aztec in which he and his companions occasionally skipped around the islands. They would disappear for a few days, then suddenly show up tanned and refreshed, just in time for tennis at the Marathon Country Club. Nick told us that after college, and before his inheritance, he had joined the Air Force and earned his wings. He had flown spotter aircraft—Cessna 172s and 337s in Vietnam for a year, before checking out of the service and moving to the Keys.

I once asked him when he figured to make the big cruise that he was always advertising.

Nick looked at me and grinned—cool, way ahead of the curve. "I got a pig in the backyard I'm teaching to fly. When his wings are long enough, I'll be on my way."

We were scheduled to land in San Jose on Saturday, then take a bus to Puntarenas and meet Sergio on Sunday evening. After giving it some thought, I called our Costa Rican contact before the plane departed and told him it would be Monday or Tuesday evening before we'd be checking in with him. Will and I had made a pact. "What happens in Central America stays in Central America."

"Sure we're in love with her," Will said as the pretty, dark-haired stewardess offered us another cocktail at 32,000 feet. "But your sense of loyalty suffers somewhat when you know your girl is also boffing your best friend."

I nodded as I held out my glass as well. "I dig it, man. I mean, think about it. I'd like to have two sisters thumping the stuffing out of me on a regular basis, and all I had to do to keep them was say I loved them both and just couldn't make up my mind."

Will cocked his head. "You don't think we're being used?"

I looked at him.

"Naaahhh," we said in unison.

"Banyan wouldn't do that," Will added.

"Not her style," I said confidently.

Nonetheless, we both agreed that this trip would be a complimentary cocktail on the journey of life, a free gift for the spirit and the body, beginning with a tour of San Jose's nightlife. It seemed a pretty fair hedge on the situation. There was a good chance only one of us would have a girlfriend when we got back. If that were the case, only one of us would actually be cheating, and if neither of us knew who the lucky winner would be, how could anyone actually be held accountable?

As the captain announced preparation for landing, the lush tropical hills of Central America rolled up at us. Thick, verdant foliage arched and cantered with the terrain, parting reluctantly for the swirling waters of narrow rivers that wound their way east like dark serpents, gradually widening into glistening Caribbean bays surrounded with mangroves and yellow beaches. The capital city lay nestled into the Cordillera Mountain Range, inviting high, cool breezes, offering a vista of a countryside blanketed with ponderous rain clouds that day. Still, the sun broke through as we were landing and graced the hills with brilliant, mist-filled trellises. It was a magical beginning for the most extraordinary journey that was to come.

By day, San Jose is an aging but magnificent countess, with grand cathedrals, ancient cobblestone roads, and majestic Spanish architecture. But at night she becomes a beguiling dark-haired vixen beneath the glow of a street lamp—a lovely, spirited, alley princess. The old countess was nice to spend the afternoon with, but at nightfall, I'll take a vixen every time—and I did. Then I opted for a spirited princess for most of the next day. For the two days we were there, I don't think Will slept at all. He was like a deviant Boy Scout earning sex merit badges, and he wanted every damned one of them. When it was over, our intrepid explorer was named American "*pene* of the week" in three out of five of the downtown bordellos.

We dragged ourselves aboard a very used, smaller version of a Greyhound bus Tuesday morning, and slept most of the way to the coast. Occasionally, I would drift into consciousness and find us winding our way down through the mists of low clouds, the moist splendor of the tropical forest all but engulfing us. Flights of exotic-colored parrots burst from the jungle and soared into the air, spiraling beyond sheer cliffs that suddenly appeared out of nowhere off the road ahead. Huge outcroppings of granite thrust their way out of vine and broad leaf, adorned with pods of large, mottled iguanas that eyed us suspiciously as we passed. An occasional clan of monkeys would drop from the heavy boughs on the edges of the green labyrinth like nervous brown wraiths, and skitter across the roadway.

Every once in a while the jungle surrendered and we meandered into a small town. Bamboo houses and cinderblock businesses sprawled along the roadway—grocers, bars, and open-air restaurants with old wooden tables and faded signs advertising the local beer. Small, gaily colored homes of green, blue, and pink bled into tin-roofed shanties that scaled the hillsides, jutting out precariously on tenuous wooden stilts. The brown-skinned villagers clad in bright shirts and dresses stared without significant interest as we passed. The children waved and chased after us. They had all carved an existence out of the relentless jungle—trading, fishing, and catering to the tourists who arrived in the Greyhound bus imitations.

I called Sergio when we arrived in Puntarenas. Half an hour later an aging Toyota station wagon pulled up at the bus depot. The fellow driving rolled down the window and stuck out his head. He was a pale Hispanic in his mid-twenties—thin and slightly balding, a wide, enthusiastic smile and dark eyes accented by classic Coke-bottle glasses—dressed in a white pullover and beige shorts.

"Hey! You guys America from?"

"That's us!" Will said.

Sergio nodded emphatically like a Gecko with something stuck in his throat, then smiled broadly. "Loaded is the boat. We go tropical fish catch!" And with no more ado than a shake of hands and a toss of the gear into the back, we went to tropical fish catch.

Sergio was a distant cousin of one of our wholesalers in Miami. He did a little snorkeling around the shoreline of the bay, but he wasn't really a diver. His fledgling aquarium shop carried a bit of exotic freshwater stuff seined or netted from the local rivers or lakes, but Sergio hoped to become our wholesaler's shipping connection for saltwater tropicals. The high side was, he had a map of the islands and had borrowed an 18-foot outboard skiff from another cousin, loaded it with a tent, a cooler of supplies, added a case of beer, and considered himself/us ready for the great adventure of the Puntarenas Bay islands.

When we reached the dock, Sergio insisted on piloting—after all, it was his cousin's boat. This proved to be a major problem.

What Sergio lacked in rudimentary planning and intelligence, he made up with unmitigated, empty-headed audacity. Our Costa Rican buddy knew only two speeds—throttle against the front wall and throttle against the rear wall. Steering could only be described as a defense mechanism—try to avoid the things that are bigger than you and stationary, then yell and wave at the smaller things like other boats, sea lions, or turtles, hoping they will see you and flee. As we rocketed out into the bay, Sergio stood there clutching the wheel, head doing the Gecko bounce, eyes bugging, Coke-bottle glasses fogged over by spray. With the roar of the engine, there was no reasoning with him. When he ran over the second turtle, I did the only thing I could think of; I pulled a beer out of the cooler and looked at Will. He nodded. I smacked our mad friend in the head with the bottle.

When Sergio awoke a few minutes later, he rubbed his head gingerly and winced a little. "Something hit me."

"Don't understand it," said Will. "One minute you were perfectly okay and the next you were lying on the deck, out cold."

I knelt down next to him. "It was probably a rare case of flotsam and jetsam," I said. "We were worried about you."

"Fletsem and jetsem?"

"Yeah, sometimes boats get to moving so fast that they pass by something—like a floating board."

"Or a bottle," said Will.

"Yeah, or a bottle. And the speed of the boat's vortex sucks that object into the craft. Very dangerous."

Sergio touched his head again, and looked at his fingers to see if there was any blood. "Feltsem and jetsem, huh?"

For the next five days we set out on a leisurely exploration of Puntarenas Bay, punctuated by the somewhat harrowing transit between islands. We kept a dive log of the areas where we encountered quality tropicals, especially Cortez Angels. All in all, it was a wonderful experience for us, and a much-needed hiatus from the emotional entanglement Will and I had left in the Keys. The bay islands were remarkable. Strands of coconut palms stretched out along beaches, leaning wistfully toward the sea. Verdant expanses of sparse jungle met the sand, furling into picturesque coves, ascending rapidly into hillsides that rose to meet monoliths of dark granite. It was very near Hollywood perfect.

There was, of course, Sergio, who ran a little hot in temperament and a quart low in common sense most of the time. But having experienced a couple of additional bouts with "fletsem and jetsem," he recognized the possibility that he was dealing with a serious condition and was making some effort to prevent recurrences. It was, however, Sergio's last unadulterated screw-up that devastated us with one hand, and set in motion our most unique Costa Rican adventure with the other.

It was the last day of the trip and we were headed back to the city of Puntarenas. We were tired, looking forward to something other than fish or canned beef stew, and desperately in need of a shower. Sergio was piloting, and as usual, traveling just under the speed of light. Will was saying to Sergio that he might experience another case of his nagging condition at that speed.

Sergio wiped the spray from his glasses and shook his head. "No, no *problemo*—just ahead beach."

Will picked a hefty beer bottle and was about to flotsam Sergio's head when the boat suddenly struck a submerged log, ripping off the engine and most of the transom. The craft went flying, rolling over in midair. Everything fell out—Will, Sergio, me, coolers, dive gear, clothes, wallets, money, passports. It was a miracle we weren't killed. Five minutes after we hit that log we were penniless, unidentifiable, and unverifiable in a foreign country.

A sightseeing boat picked us up and took us to shore. Sergio had sprained a shoulder and had to be taken to the hospital, where they decided to keep him overnight for observation. At least he had a place to stay.

It was about mid-afternoon when Will and I left the hospital. We just sort of wandered away with no real plan other than maybe trying to find the American Embassy. We passed a bar and Will paused, reaching down, pulling off his tennis shoe.

"You got a rock?" I asked.

He smiled. "No. I just remembered I've got 500 *colones*," he said reaching into the shoe and pulling out a crinkled Costa Rican bill. "I stuck it away for an emergency. How about a drink?"

"Maybe we should save it for an emergency."

He got that goofy grin. "Naahh. Let's be frivolous."

We sat in the little downtown cantina with a mixture of somber locals nursing *cervezas* and a handful of older, tour bus *touristas* adorned in flowered muumuus and "I love Costa Rica" T-shirts. They were disgustingly jovial and typically loud. The locals would have gladly poisoned their margaritas for a little peace and quiet. Will and I were discussing exactly how many rum and Cokes 500 *colones* would buy, because if we nursed them, we could fill up on the free nachos, when a gentleman who had been sitting quietly in the corner across from us rose and came over to our table. The first thing I thought of when I saw him was *Casablanca*. The guy looked like an overweight Bogart. He was only about five-nine, but was a rotund 200 pounds, easily—not so much fat as heavy, in a formidable fashion. He had on a white dinner jacket, which had seen some wear, a red flowered shirt that strained to contain him, a pair of cut-off shorts that might have, at one time, been a relative to the jacket, and leather sandals. An old Panama hat that was a little weary around the edges was perched atop his head, tilted back slightly, covering most of his longish, straw-colored hair. He carried himself with a practiced assuredness. He was cool, easy—like Bogie, or maybe Brando. He took the *cigarillo* out of his mouth and exhaled a blue cloud at the ceiling fan, which immediately sucked up the smoke and dissected it. Glancing briefly at both of us with confident, pale blue eyes, he pulled back a chair and sat down without invitation. "Do you mind if I sit down?" His accent was a little clipped, almost British, but carrying the occasional inflection and cadence of a person who has spent a good deal of time south of the border. "I couldn't help but hear you talking about your present predicament." He sighed, a little on the dramatic side. "The lack of finances does have a way of spoiling these beautiful Costa Rican days—and they are beautiful, no?"

Not certain what was happening Will and I just nodded, as if we were safer with fewer words.

"Next to no money, ill health is life's greatest plague, I think." He took another draw from his *cigarillo*. "I've been without finances once or twice in my life—I know what it feels like, but that's not one of my problems now. Health, however, cannot be bought and paid for like a burrito at a roadside stand. Good health can be more elusive than money." As the waiter passed by, he raised his hand "*Aqui, por favor.* Two more for my friends." He brought his attention back to us, making a slight twist of his neck, turning his head to the right, then the left a fraction, as if it was a subconscious adjustment. "The name's Sundance—just a nickname, but I like it. From Canada—Vancouver. What about you?"

"Kansas, and Will," I said, motioning toward my partner. "The Florida Keys. On a diving trip and having a pretty damned good time, until we lost all our belongings in a boat wreck."

The man nodded sagely as the waiter delivered two more drinks for us, and a shot of tequila for him. "That's a shame, but all is not lost," he said. "You strike me as kindred spirits, adventurers, not without verve and pluck, and I like that, so maybe I'll help you." He slugged his tequila, hissed and slapped the table as it burned its way down, and did the little neck adjustment twist again, like a boxer before a fight.

"You're a long way from home," I said.

He looked out the window of the cantina at the street. "What's home to the wanderer but a place that feels good for the moment? Down here, we're all expatriates from somewhere or someone, no? Sometimes we have luck, sometimes we make it." He slapped his hand on the table and turned back to us. "But today providence has smiled on you, because it just so happens I'm on the way to make a withdrawal from my bank, which is right across the street. Now, if I lent you some money, would you promise on the soul of your favorite whore to pay it back?"

Will shrugged almost imperceptibly. "I don't have a favorite whore," he said. "I love 'em all."

Sundance smiled, displaying a remarkable collection of pearly teeth. "Ha! A man after my own heart!"

"Yeah, we'll pay you back," I said. "Every last penny, as soon as we get back to the States."

Sundance nodded somberly. "Then I would be pleased to withdraw a little extra for you boys, and release you from your present encumbrances." He reached into his jacket and pulled out a small flask. "*Mescal* helps keep poison out of your system," he whispered as he leaned over conspiratorially. "I was bitten by a rat last week. Do you have any idea how many diseases rats carry? Bubonic Plague, salmonella, hepatitis (eyes rolling). God knows what else." He poured himself a shot, belted it, hissed and slapped the table again. He paused for a moment, staring at his hand, then muttered angrily, "A rat! God! Of all the bloody creatures." He shook his head, then sighed. "Been feeling a little flush, a little feverish lately." He suddenly leaned over and grabbed Will's hand, placing it against his forehead. "Do I feel hot to you?"

Will paused just long enough to be polite, then pulled back. "No. No, you feel just fine—maybe a little warm."

Sundance rolled his eyes again. "Aahhh, I knew it. It's probably salmonella—can be fatal, you know. Salmonella—God! I'd rather kiss an adder!" Filling his glass with *mescal*, and tipping a little into ours, he held out his glass. "A toast before I die—to *mescal*—and adventure! God bless adventure!"

I looked at Will. He shrugged. We all bolted the shots, hissed and slapped the table.

Sundance stood up, weaving just a little. "Time to go get some money from my bank and start enjoying life again. Any takers?"

Five minutes later we were walking through the doors of the First National Bank of Puntarenas. The five tellers looked out from their stations, friendly, smiling. A withered old guard stood slouched against the wall in the corner. Two executives chatted from their desks on the other side.

Sundance turned to Will and I. "You guys just go get the money."

I was about to say, "What money?" when our new friend pulled a large revolver from the opposite side of the *mescal* in his coat and fired twice into the ceiling. *"Este' es un robo!"* he shouted in what I thought was excellent Spanish. "Hands up!"

Everyone just stood gaping for a moment. Sundance fired into the ceiling again. That brought the hands up. "Drop your gun!" he yelled at the guard, who gingerly took out his *pistola* and let it fall to the floor. Pulling a flour sack from his coat pocket, Sundance threw it to Will and me. "Get the money from the tellers!"

I turned around, facing him. "What do you mean get the money? I'm not robbing a freaking ba—"

Bam! Bam! Bam! There were three neat holes in the floor by my shoes.

"Just get the money!" he yelled. "You wanna be rich or walk with a limp?"

While Will and I were politely asking for cash from the tellers—trying to explain that this was all a misunderstanding, that we really didn't know our accomplice was a madman, and we weren't really bank robbers—Sundance pulled out his flask and took a long shot of *mescal*, then tucked it under his armpit as he flicked out the cylinder on the revolver and ejected the six empty casings. He was rummaging through his pockets, trying to find more bullets, when the old guard started slowly bringing his hands down, reaching for his gun on the floor.

Sundance swung around and drew down on him, cylinder of the pistol still open, empty. "Don't do it, old man, or I'll shoot!" he said, still rummaging for cartridges.

The old guy reached down a little more. Sundance's voice was rising.

"I'm telling you, don't do it or I'll drop you!" (He found two rounds but in the process of trying to get them into the cylinder, he dropped them on the floor.)

The guard finally had the gun and was rising, albeit a little shaky and uncertain.

"I warned you, didn't I!" screamed Sundance as he stomped over three paces, aimed the gun point-blank at the guard, and yelled, "Bang! Bang!" as loud as he could.

The old man recoiled and cried "Arrrhhh!" stumbling backwards, losing his balance and falling against the banister of the teller windows, knocking himself out.

Sundance turned to us—us with the bag of money—and smiled. "Man, am I good or what? I shot him with an empty gun! No?" He fumbled for a moment longer and found his bullets, then quickly reloaded. Snapping the cylinder closed, he yelled, "Viva la *revolucion!"* and tossed the mescal flask high into the air. Raising his pistol he fired twice in quick succession. The bottle tumbled to the floor unscathed—two more bullet holes in the ceiling. He looked at us, and smiled, eyebrows up like Groucho Marx. "You've got to admit it would have been impressive, no?"

Two minutes later we were in the back of a taxi and Sundance was waving his pistol at the freaked-out driver, giving him directions. Then he turned to us in the back. "That was glorious! Just glorious! We were a great team today. I can see the headlines in tomorrow's paper, *'Tres Banditos* Strike!' We can rob these beaner banks for years! *El Tres Banditos!* We may go down in a hail of bullets eventually, but we will have had our time—left our mark!"

"I don't want to be a bank robber," I said.

Will leaned forward and grabbed the top of the front seat. "I don't want to go down in a hail of bullets."

Sundance just laughed. "C'mon, where's your adventurous spirit?"

"I think it got sucked up my little puckered asshole when you started shooting holes in the ceiling of a bank and demanding their money," I said.

Sundance shook his head and smiled. "No *cojones*, no *colones*, man. That's how it is in the bank-robbing business."

Will was quietly banging his head on the window of the cab and whispering, "I just robbed a friggin' bank—I robbed a friggin' bank!"

Suddenly, Sundance got a little, concerned furrow between his eyes. "God! My heart is still pounding!" He put his hand to his chest. "I'm fairly certain I have high blood pressure—hypertension—it's the number-one killer of people with stressful jobs, you know."

“You qualify there,” Will mumbled from the back.

“Besides, I’m still feeling the effects of the Salmonella.” He took off his hat and wiped the sweat from his forehead with the back of his sleeve. “God! Salmonella and hypertension! I might as well cut my own bloody wrists!” He swung around suddenly, bumping the taxi driver and nearly taking us off the narrow street, while stretching his arm out to me and pulling back his sleeve. “Here! Take my pulse. I gotta know how high my pressure is. If I die, you guys won’t know how to get to the hideout.”

“The hideout?” Will cried. “The hideout? Sweet Lord! I’m with Jesse James incarnate!”

I pushed his arm away. “I’m not taking your pulse. I got no idea how to take a pulse. Trust me, yours isn’t any higher than mine right now. We want outta here. Right now!”

Sundance shook his head disgustedly. “Boy, you two are really whiny, ungrateful sons of bitches. I rescue you from your dilemma, get you enough money to enjoy life again and all you do is complain. What are you gonna do? Go to the police and say, ‘Gee, we’re sorry. We really didn’t mean to rob your bank.’ Ha! You’ll do twenty hard ones just because.”

I opened my mouth. Will put his hand on my arm and shook his head. I shut my mouth.

Ten minutes later we were out of town and winding down a narrow gravel road that led toward the ocean. In the middle of nowhere, with dense foliage on both sides of us, Sundance yelled for the taxi driver to stop. “This is it, boys. Let’s go.”

“Go where?” I cried. “We’re in the middle of the flippin’ jungle!”

Sundance just smiled condescendingly. “Gotta trust your partner if you wanna stay in this business.”

Will sighed, picked up the bag of money and opened the door, mumbling. “Dear Mom. I’m writing from the prison in San Jose. I wasn’t always a bank robber…”

Sundance threw a handful of money into the cab then pointed his pistol at the taxi driver and told him to buy his wife something nice and forget this fare if he knew what was good for him. When the taxi was out of sight, our bank-robbing accomplice led us down a small path that wound through the jungle to the water’s edge, where a small outboard skiff sat in the mangroves. We all boarded and Sundance fired it up, beginning to steer toward one of the small bay islands just offshore. The sun was setting, the water was still as glass, and in one of those rare moments the sky bled into the ocean without discernible verge, forming one huge assembly of rich, riotous colors that stretched from the bow of the boat into the heavens. It was like sailing into the empyrean—one of the most remarkable sunsets I have ever witnessed. Had I not been so concerned with my present plight and our new profession, I might have been moved to tears.

Sundance slapped himself on the neck and cursed, drawing me out of my reverie.

"Damned mosquitoes. I hate the little sons of bitches. They carry malaria—terrible disease." He slapped again, on his arm. "I'm pretty sure I already have it. I've been reading about the symptoms—fever, chills, nausea, dizziness. I've got 'em all." He pulled off his hat and wiped the sweat from his brow again. "That and the bloody salmonella! Why shouldn't I rob banks? I'll be dead long before they can catch me—huddled in some corner shaking with chills and fever, skin as yellow as parchment paper. I don't know why I just don't shoot us all and put us out of our misery."

Will looked at me with some discernible concern, then to Sundance. "How about because we don't have malaria?"

Sundance did the little neck-twist thing again. "Oh, you will. You just stick around here long enough, you'll get 'em all—malaria, hepatitis, salmonella. God knows what else." He suddenly took his hand off the outboard control arm and stepped over to Will, plopping down on the small bench seat next to him and nearly swamping the boat. "Look at my neck! Look at my eyes! Yellow as a phonebook! I'm telling you, a bloody phonebook! I'm in the final stages. All because of these frigging little bugs—bloody little malaria-infested, winged demons."

The boat, with no one at the helm, began to course in a large circle. From the bow, I pointed to the control arm. "Sundance…"

"Yeah, yeah, yeah. I know. You want to get to the hideout so we can split the dough. No compassion for your fellow man. Just like all my other partners."

"Other partners?" Will said, head cocked slightly. "You've had other partners?"

"Yeah, a few."

"What happened to them?"

"No staying power. Didn't have the heart for it. One I had to shoot because he kept whining. You take somebody that's just getting by, give them a new, exciting profession—you'd think they'd be grateful."

It was a small, innocuous island about three miles offshore. We pulled the boat up the sloping beach and tied it to a palm tree. There was a two-room, ramshackle hut with a corrugated tin roof set back in the trees. Sundance got to the slightly askew door. "Now, where did I leave my key?" he mumbled, scratching his temple, then laughed heartily and kicked it open. Tossing the money sack on an old wooden table in the middle of the room, he pulled a fresh *cigarillo* from his shirt pocket, moved to a weathered bureau on the far side and dug a bottle of *mescal* from one of the drawers. "Have a seat," he yelled over his shoulder. "Count that money and take a slice for yourselves. There's lots more where that came from."

"I don't want to count it," I said. "I don't want to touch it."

Will took the bag and poured the cash on the table. "They won't arrest us for counting it or spending it, only for stealing it."

An hour later, we all had a pleasant *mescal* glow and a verified six thousand *colones*. We had even laughed about the old guard knocking himself out and Sundance missing the bottle with the pistol. Sundance gave us three thousand *colones*, which I didn't want to take, but Will reminded me that our pictures were going to be in all the post offices whether we spent the money or not. Our partner in crime relaxed and proceeded to get seriously drunk, polishing off most of a bottle by himself. By ten o'clock he was slurring out the symptoms of alcohol poisoning—certain it was his latest ailment. By eleven he was snoring soundly from the bed in the other room. I leaned over to Will and whispered, "Now would be a good time to get out of here."

When we reached the boat, a breeze had come up, ruffling the tops of the palms that were silhouetted by a nearly full moon. Ghost-gray clouds whisked across the stars in soft banners. Somewhere a night bird called forlornly, and another replied.

I tossed the money onto the floorboards by the transom. "Get the bow untied," I whispered tersely over the wind. "I'll pull, you push."

It was a bit of an effort without the inertia of our large friend, but we managed. We had just reached the tide line, turned the skiff around and put the bow into the water. I was starting to feel there was a chance when we heard the voice.

"Now this is exactly why I had to shoot my other partners."

Will looked up. "I thought you said you only shot one of them."

"I lied," said Sundance as he emerged from the darkness, barefoot, in shorts and unbuttoned flowered shirt, half a *cigarillo* clenched in his teeth, blond hair in disarray, pistol in hand. "You took all the money."

"We were going to give it back to the authorities."

Sundance did that unconscious neck-twist thing—one side, then the other. "Sure you were."

I put my hands out, imploringly. "Listen, Sundance, we don't want the money. We just want to leave."

He smiled, not nicely. "Consider yourselves gone."

"Sundance…"

He motioned with the gun. "Well, seeing as how you have the boat aimed out at the channel, that's as good a place as any."

"Sundance, we're not going to say anything to anybody. Couldn't we just talk about this—"

"We'll talk when we get to the channel. Now get in."

Will and I were sitting in the bow facing Sundance. He pushed the skiff into the water, crawled in and pulled the starting cord on the outboard, keeping the gun on us. Unfortunately, the engine fired first pull. "Aahhh, what a shame," he said with a sigh as we moved away from the shore. "I thought you two fellows might have been different—more pluck and verve, but alas, (dramatic pause) it's not the case. Not the case at all."

In just a few moments we had reached deep water. The wind was kicking the seas a little, throwing a light spray over the gunnels as the small craft worked to steady itself. The moon's reflection danced across the tops of the waves. Sundance put the engine in neutral and stood up carefully, bracing his legs for balance. "Stand up my friends and say, 'good night, Johnny.'"

I was about to stand when Will kicked my foot gently. I followed his quick glance and saw the bow rope next to us had been strewn out along the gunnel to the stern, where the end lay in a curl on the floorboards. Sundance was standing on it.

Will stood up. "I want you to shoot me first. It doesn't matter, because I'm going out knowing that you're right behind me."

"Oh yeah?" Sundance said, tilting his head slightly. "How's that?"

"You've got smallpox. Haven't you noticed the shortness of breath, the veins in your eyes enlarging, that rash on the side of your neck? I've seen it all before."

Sundance started visibly. "Whatta you mean, smallpox? Don't bullshit me. I'm gonna kill you twice for that." Still, he paused and involuntarily raised a hand to his neck.

"Your neck is sore a lot," Will continued. "That's where the disease sets in first. It's still common in Central and South America.

Look at the back of your hands and see how dark and large the veins are. You got it, man."

Sundance couldn't resist. As he turned his hands to look at the back of them, inadvertently aiming the gun away from us, I reached down and jerked the rope. The big man lost his balance and grasped for the gunnel. He missed by about three inches and his inertia carried him over the side and into the water. Without hesitation, Will picked up the boat paddle and when Sundance came to the surface gasping and sputtering, my partner smacked him like he was packing dirt in a driveway. I was at the engine before Will finished his second swing. I hit the throttle and we were gone into the night. The last we heard of Sundance was an angry wail floating across the water. "I'll get you sons of bitches! … I will! … God! … Smallpox!…"

When we reached the mainland and were tying the boat to the mangroves, I turned to Will. "How'd you know so much about smallpox?"

"I don't know squat about it. I just made it up."

I laughed. "That's really funny. He'll have rashes and veins in his eyes for weeks."

Will smiled. "Yeah, I hope what he doesn't know hurts him a lot."

The good news was we weren't dead. The bad news was, the morning's paper had some remarkably accurate sketches of Sundance and us on the front page. The first thing we did was purchase a pair of scissors and some hair dye at a local *pharmacia.* We rented a room in a dilapidated guesthouse and two hours later emerged with short, Latino-black hair that looked like it had been cut with a wood chipper. I found a box, Will wrote a nice letter of apology, unsigned of course, and we mailed the money (less 500 *colones* for running expenses) to the First National Bank of Puntarenas. Then, desperate to the edge, we called our neighbor, Nick Crow.

After I explained what had happened to us, Nick had me repeat it again, slowly. There was a pause.

"Nick? Are you still there?"

"Yeah. I'm here. Okay, there's no getting out of the country conventionally. This is what you do. Write this down. You have to make it to Limon, on the east coast. There's a small airport about ten clicks north of the city just outside a hole called Quentos. You find a guy there, an American, named Burt Hendren. Look for the local bar. If he's not there, they'll tell you where the other bar is. Find him and tell him to fly you to a place on the coast of Northern Honduras called Trujillo. There's a grass strip exactly one mile west of the town. He has to be there at sundown, Thursday." (Pause) "You tell him I'm calling in my card for Chin Lai—you understand? Chin Lai."

"What's Chin Lai?"

There was another pause. "It was a small suburb of hell in North Vietnam. I did him and a couple of other guys a favor. He'll understand."

Early the following morning we boarded a bus for Limon via San Jose. The old Greyhound imitation curled up into the mountains in low gear, once again winding through the villages and the jungle we had passed on the way down into Puntarenas. Lines of brown-skinned women ambled along the roadway, carrying their colorful laundry back from the river on their heads—as their mothers had, and their mothers before them. The children chased the bus and waved. The iguanas stared stoically, the monkeys shrugged indifferently and dragged their brood back into the foliage. They'd seen it all before. At the terminal in the capital city, we grabbed a late lunch in a small cantina then caught another bus headed out of the mountains, toward the east coast. The mountains once again gave way to rolling hills and farmland. We followed the ever-widening rivers that carved their way into the farm country, then through sparse jungles, and finally, across the humid, flat coastline. Late that evening, we rumbled into a dilapidated station in Limon.
Exiting as inconspicuously as possible, we found a room for the evening at a little hotel on the edge of town.

Will and I sat on our beds, facing each other in the tiny room, eating greasy meat pies and drinking warm soda purchased from the only store still open at our end of the village. On the street below, someone began to strum on a lonely guitar and the exotic melody wafted upward like a breeze lifting a sail. The stranger started to sing—something about smuggling grass, and loving younger women, and being a pirate centuries too late. It was an engaging melody and interesting lyrics. When the song ended, I went to the window and looked down, catching a glimpse of a blond-haired fellow in an old, white sports coat, drifting down the street with his guitar.

Will took a sip and sat his bottle on the floor. "Next time, we need to plan a vacation with a little excitement in it."

"Yeah, maybe we could find a small country and invade it, not just steal from its national banking system and elude its law enforcement by relying on the advice of a sociopathic bank robber, no?"

My partner smiled. "Well, look on the bright side. We still have to find a drunken ex-Vietnam pilot who will fly us five hundred miles across Nicaraguan and Honduran jungle—assuming old Bart can still fly."

"Burt," I said. "Assuming Burt can fly. Then he's got to put us in just the right spot at the right time to get us winged back innocuously to the States by Crow and his little Aztec.

Will took a swig of his soda. "Finish your meat pie, you're going to need the energy. We gotta go looking for old Bart tonight."

"Burt."

Will sighed and looked out the window at the full moon that hung over the street like a Spanish *Pilar* dollar. "Wonder what Banyan's doing tonight?"

"I'm pretty sure she's busy finalizing our wedding plans—buying dozens of those tubes of exotic body oils she wants to rub all over me on our honeymoon. But don't worry, we'll take lots of pictures."

Will shook his head condescendingly. "You're the one that's gonna need pictures because that's all you're gonna have." He winked at me "We got da magic, man. Did I tell you she's a bona fide card-carrying member of the California Kama Sutra Club? I think that girl's mother was a ferret, or a pretzel. Did you know she can—"

I put my hands over my ears. "Ya-ya-ya-ya-ya-ya-ya-ya!" I yelled.

Will laughed. "I win."

"Okay. You win. No more about Banyan."

Will nodded. "Okay. No more about Banyan… except did you know, she can actually put her—"

"Ya-ya-ya-ya-ya-ya-ya-ya-ya!"

Quentos was a hole, just as Nick had described it. There was a small, daytime grocery, a fish market, and three bars. You could buy a woman and a rum and Coke from any of them and still get change from an American ten spot. Will and I picked the bar with music coming from it. There was a rummy-looking three-piece band in the corner—an old white guy strumming on a guitar, a young Latin conga man, and a huge black man playing the accordion. The whole thing sounded like Polish calypso on acid. The crowd was a rich blend of West-African/Latino heritage salted with a few Caucasian locals and a smattering of fairly uncomfortable tourists who had been looking for the wild side and had accidentally found it. The bar covered one wall and a handful of tables and chairs half-circled a weathered dance floor. A huge Banyan tree grew into, or out of, the far end of the building. Its trunk extended up through the roof, and benches had been nailed to the legs of the tree.

Leaning up against a rail of the bar, Will looked around and smiled. "My kind of place. I can see why *Senor* Bart would be so taken with it."

I waved to the bartender, who worked his way down to us. "Do you know *Senor* Burt Hendren?"

He nodded, a little reserved. "*Si*, we all know *Senor* Burt well. He has been good friend to many of us."

Realizing I was making some progress, I added, "Will we see him here tonight?"

"But of course. The special ceremony for him is at nine. Drinks are on the house until then."

I smiled, my first rum and Coke was coming home, and I was starting to enjoy the easy, Bob Marley polka in the background. I looked at Will. "Damn. This is good timing—a special award ceremony for our boy and free drinks to boot. What a deal!" There was a fairly good crowd, albeit a little more somber than I would have expected. With all the free drinks, I figured some would be dancing on the bar in no time. At nine on the dot the bartender rang a ship's bell, everyone got quiet and raised their glasses, turning to the door in the back of the room. I smiled and nudged the fellow next to me. "Man, this guy must be one cool dude. Where I'm from you'd have to be dead to get this much attention."

The guy was still staring at me like I was an absolute cretin when the pallbearers brought out the coffin and placed it on the stage. The good news was, we'd found Burt. The bad news was, he wasn't flying us anywhere. He'd been robbed and shot the night before, on his way home. Rumors were it may have been the *Tres Banditos*.

"Well, that frigging tears it," I muttered angrily.

Will slapped down his drink. "Yeah, sure does. Now we've got to find his plane and you gotta fly us out of here."

"So, now we add aircraft theft to the list of our felonies?"

"At this point, what's one more. We've got less than twenty hours to make Trujillo."

The gray stillness of early dawn found us at the dirt strip outside Quentos. The sun had yet to crest the horizon. Wet mists curled in and out of the jungle, drifting across the runway in lazy, translucent sheets. Shadows slowly began to diminish, almost magically, and the last of the night creatures cried plaintively in reluctant surrender to the new day, tucking themselves away in burrow and bough. We stood before an aging twin-engine Cessna 337 under an open hangar with a slanting corrugated tin roof. It was, fortunately, the easiest type of twin to fly because the engines were mounted in tandem instead of on the leading edge of each wing, giving it the take-off and landing characteristics of a single-engine aircraft. We jimmied the lock and checked out the cockpit. The fuel gauges read full.

Will looked at me as I studied a Central American navigational chart. "Can you fly it?"

I shrugged. "It's really not point A to point B that's tricky. It's getting it off the ground and putting it back down, seeing as how I've never flown one before."

"But the twin-engine thing won't be a problem, huh?"

"Well, it does mean I have one more engine to worry about than I've generally had to worry about before. But how hard can that be?"

Will exhaled nervously. "You're not going to kill us, are you?"

"Not intentionally."

A few minutes later we were sitting in the cockpit, doors of the plane open while I went over the prop pitch and fuel mixture levers, when we heard something behind us—a chuckle, then a familiar voice. "My, my, my, if it isn't the *tres banditos,* together again."

"Aaahh crap," Will moaned, turning to me. "It can't be."

"Ah, but it is, my whiny expatriate partners," said Sundance, brandishing his trusty revolver and moving up next to Will. "Your old friend, back once again. Missed me, haven't you?" Leaning toward us and arching his eyebrows in that Groucho Marx fashion, he added, "Tell me the truth, hmmmm?"

I turned around. "How in the hell did you find us?"

Sundance tilted back his Panama hat with the barrel of the pistol and smiled, displaying a blemished face that looked remarkably similar to smallpox. "You're not exactly Batman and Robin. You took the only local taxi to the bus station and bought tickets to Limon. I followed. How hard is that?"

"So, now what?" I said. "Don't you have a bank you should be robbing or a doctor you should be seeing? Or did you just follow us all this way to kill us?"

He stepped back and stared pensively. “To answer your questions in order; yes, yes, and yes. I like revenge. Revenge is considered a worthy endeavor within almost all cultures and religions, except for maybe Buddhists, and look where it got them—thumping on bloody tambourines and begging for money at airports.”

“Those are Hare Krishnas,” I muttered.

“That’s partly why I’m going to shoot you, just because you’re a smart ass. That, and the fact you guys hit me with a paddle and tried to drown me.”

“Let me refresh your memory. You were going to shoot us!”

Sundance continued, unaffected by my logic. “Well, it was all for one and one for all when we robbed the bank, then I wake up in my shack and find it’s two for two and squat for one. Besides, you can identify me.” He threw his hands up in a sweeping gesture toward the plane. “But! Seeing as you’ve acquired a means of transportation out of the country, I might hitch a ride first.” He snorted angrily. “I’ve had it with Costa Rica—the unmitigated gall of its flipping newspapers! Look at this! Just look at this!” he spat, dragging a newspaper out of his breast pocket and shaking it open. “Who in the hell draws this shit? My ears are nowhere near that big! And look at the bloody nose they gave me! Karl Malden has a better snout than that, no? Karl bloody Malden! If I’d had more time, and was feeling better, I would have tracked down the artist and shot him.” He paused for a dramatic sigh and let the newspaper fall to the ground. “I think I might try the banks and the beaches of Mexico. Might suit my temperament and my health better. ”

“We’re not going that far.”

Sundance raised his gun menacingly. “You are if I say you are.”

“How’s the smallpox?”

He twisted his neck and shoulders in that unconscious boxer reflex motion. “Not much better, thank you. But I’m betting you’ll be dirt-napping before me, smallpox or not.” He straightened up and his eyes went hard again. “Now, you wanna fly or you wanna die?”

I looked at Will. He nodded. “Okay, let’s get this thing wound up and in the air before the locals show up and find us borrowing their *aeroplano*.”

Sundance shoved Will with the barrel of the pistol. “You! In the back. I ride shotgun on this.”

Will shrugged and moved into the bench seat in the interior of the aircraft. Sundance climbed in ponderously and melted into the seat up front.

I moved my hand toward the fuel primer and stopped. "Shit. I forgot to remove the chocks."

Sundance brought up his gun. "Don't be doing anything stupid. Disappear, and I'll shoot your friend twice—once for you and once for him."

As I climbed out and bent down to pull the chocks from under the wheels, I picked up the newspaper Sundance had dropped, crumpled it tightly and quickly stuffed it in the left wheel well. Aboard once more, I hit the primer then the starter on each engine in succession. They coughed and fired cooperatively. All the gauges perked up responsively. I taxied out, checking instruments and magnetos, swinging the plane around at the threshold of the strip. After wiping the sweat from my forehead, and silently offering a few words to the aeronautical threshold deity familiar to all pilots, I mumbled, "Hold on, boys. Here we go."

Moments later I had the levers forward and we were bouncing down the airstrip, into the wind. Other than a little more aileron pressure, it wasn't too much different than the 172 I was accustomed to flying. She slid out from under me a little, pulling toward the starboard side of the narrow runway, but I got her in the air before it became a big issue. Everyone was smiling somewhat cautiously, pleased with the initial results, until I hit the gear switch. There was the standard rumbling announcing the retracting of the gear, but the red gear light warning on the dash began to blink angrily. I had her up to about 500 feet.

"We've got a problem!" I yelled over the roar of the engines. "I don't think the gear has gone up properly. If I take this up to speed, we risk stalling, or worse, ripping out the bottom of the plane!" As I reduced speed and altitude, bringing the aircraft out over the clear, blue waters of the coast, I turned to Sundance. "Someone's got to get a look at the gear to see if it's up. It's right under you. All you've got to do is open your door slightly and lean out—"

"Screw you!" yelled Sundance. "I'm not leaning anywhere. Just fly it like it is."

"We can't! If there's a problem we'll never get over the mountains!"

Sundance jabbed his thumb toward the rear of the plane. "Have him do it."

"Can't!" I yelled back, frustrated. "The sliding door's locked. We don't have the key. We had to jimmy the locks of the cabin doors as it was. Just open the damned door and look down. You don't, you won't have to worry about the smallpox. We'll all be indelibly imprinted in the mountains."

"You whiny sons of bitches!" muttered Sundance. "You got any idea what this is doing to my blood pressure. If there's nothing wrong, I'm gonna shoot you somewhere just for the hell of it." He sighed angrily. "All right. Let's get it over with."

I took the plane down to a hundred feet off the water, a few hundred yards off the beach, flying just above stall speed, and nodded to Sundance. He unlatched his door and leaned against it, opening it about a foot. Looking down, he yelled, "I don't see anything!"

"Push out more—a little farther underneath."

"*Mierda,* man! I don't see a bloody thing underneath the bloody—"

Just then I threw the controls to the right, slamming the opposite rudder and turning the plane up on its side. As we rolled vertically, I unsnapped the latch on Sundance's seat belt with my other hand. With a surprised grunt, his own inertia sucked him out the door as if he'd been greased. The last thing I saw was the soles of his shoes as gravity and the airplane's slipstream whisked him into freefall and the force of the wind snapped the door shut behind him.

Will was still yelling incoherently from the back as I corrected into straight and level flight about fifty feet above the water. He clutched the back of my seat. "Holy shit, man! Holy friggin' shit. Don't ever do that again!"

I turned back to him. "Quit flipping out and get up here. Make sure that cabin door's shut."

Will climbed gingerly into the front seat and quickly locked his seat belt. Then he smiled and looked at me. "You dumped that boy like an ugly date! Kicked him out like he never paid rent!

Will was still making comparisons as I circled back. There below us was Sundance, splashing his way toward shore, pausing long enough to shoot us a one-digit salute and yell something unintelligible.

Will shook his head and grinned. "The son of a bitch is still alive after being dropped from a hundred feet. He's like some damned Costa Rican cat." There was a pause, and Will muttered, "The son of a bitch came all that way to shoot us, again! Man, that pisses me off. Listen, make one quick pass right over the top of him—at fifty feet. Okay?"

"I've got to land pretty quick. I put a wad of newspaper in the wheel well to make the gear light blink. Gotta get it out, then we have to get out of here."

"C'mon. Just do it."

I shrugged and banked around. As we soared over the top of Sundance, Will opened the door. "Shark! Shark!" he yelled, jabbing his finger at a spot behind our Costa Rican nemesis. "Shark! Shark!"

It's always amazing the effect that word has on an open water swimmer. Sundance, eyes the size of mayonnaise lids, came pirouetting out of the sea like Yosemite Sam in a Bugs Bunny cartoon, then took off toward the shore in a fashion reminiscent of those National Geographic lizards.

Will turned to me and smiled, settling into his seat. "I feel much better now. Let's book, *amigo*."

For the next five hours, we cruised over absolutely spectacular terrain, skimming across the azure Caribbean Sea dotted with dozens of Hollywood perfect islands, then sweeping over Nicaragua's famed Mosquito Coast—an isolated green tapestry punctuated with a thousand mysterious bays that threaded their way inland in thinning, emerald tendrils. Finally, we turned and climbed toward the mountains of Honduras, brilliant in color and contrast, but daunting in their brutal isolation. A plane lost there was a plane soon forgotten. The mountain jungle would pull it down in an embrace of vine and bough, and kiss it goodnight forever.

But before we had an opportunity to become too maudlin (not bloody Karl—just maudlin) regarding lost flights, the aircraft broke over the mountains and we soared into the valleys on the other side. The widening coastline and blue water in the distance lifted our spirits. The DME on the dash said Trujillo was dead ahead, sixty miles. We were an hour ahead of sundown. I adjusted the pitch on the props a little, settling them into a pleasant sync, pulled back on the throttles slightly and set up at about 120 mph. The old girl verily vibrated with the desire to serve—obedient and responsive. There was no hurry. We were right on time, and we were being taken care of by a classy lady, who had been well treated by her man. I could tell.

Half an hour later, as we dropped toward the clandestine landing site framed with flares, I found myself wishing I could have known old Burt a little better. I gazed around the cockpit of that craft and wondered what stories it could have told—about the character of men when it all falls in a pinch—the ones who hold their courses and the ones who don't. And the ones who drink a beer or two and talk about it all a little loud afterward, as if to convince themselves of their daring, and the ones who don't talk about it at all.

The sun was just topping the ridges of the mountains when a final smoke flare gave us our bearings and wind. As I set the plane in a slight slip to accommodate the wind, adjusted throttle and pitch, and dropped some flaps, I could see Nick Crow's Aztec on the ground by a small hangar, next to a military-type supply truck. There were several men around him—men with guns. There were probably another dozen surrounding the strip at the edge of the jungle. Suddenly, I was a little anxious.

I dropped the plane in a bit hard, bounced once, then settled onto the strip, and taxied over to the hanger. As we shut down, opened the doors, and got out, Nick and three of his friends came walking over. Crow was dressed in his standard blue jeans and tropical shirt, his sandy hair ruffled by the light breeze. His buddies, whom I assumed were Honduran, didn't say anything. They just stared, slightly indifferent. Nick stepped forward, shaking our hands.

"Will, Kansas! How ya doin'?" He looked around. "Where's Burt?"

"Dead," I said. "He was robbed and killed the night before we got to Quentos, while coming home from the bar. We stayed for his funeral, then decided to borrow his airplane. I think he would have understood."

Nick shook his head sadly, "Son of a bitch! After surviving all the shit he went through—to be killed coming home from a bar! Damn! That's just too frigging incredible!" He looked up. "But you're right. He would have thought stealing his airplane was a damned cool thing to do."

"Borrowing," I said.

"Yeah, whatever," Nick replied with a cocky grin. "I'll see if I can get someone to fly it back, later. But I can't make any promises." He took a cigarette from his breast pocket and lit it, drawing deeply. Shaking his head again, he exhaled and muttered, "Damn, Burt, gone. I can't believe it." Nick took another slow drag then glanced at our plane, assessing it. "Okay, yours hasn't got the fuel capacity to make it back to the Keys, so we take mine as planned. We've got to get loaded and get out of here." He turned and rattled off a quick burst of Spanish to the guy next to him. The fellow nodded and took off with the other two.

I was about to ask about the "get loaded" part when the convoy truck pulled up next to the Nick's Aztec and his friends started transferring bulky, burlap and duct-taped bundles from the truck to the plane, which had two large cargo nets spread out in the back where the seats used to be. I looked at Nick. "I thought you said you got all your money from an uncle."

Nick smiled and pushed his hair out of his eyes with one hand. "I do. That's my uncle," he said, pointing to the guy overseeing the loaders.

"You said he was dead."

"No, I said he was recently departed. He used to live in the Keys, now he lives in Honduras."

"Lord!" Will moaned. "So now we go from robbing banks and stealing airplanes to smuggling marijuana!"

"You're the ones who needed an inconspicuous ride home," Nick said. "I have to pay for my trip somehow. Unless you still have some of that bank money you stole."

"No, we sent it back to the bank."

"Now that's really great," Nick muttered with a grin. "You guys are something else. You rob banks, and then you give the money back. You're making great stories for your grandchildren."

Twenty minutes later Will and I were sitting on eight bales of rich-smelling Central American pot packaged tightly in two small Army issue parachute cargo drop nets—four bales to a net. The sun was gone and the shadows were crawling from the jungle. Small, diaphanous-winged bats jagged and crisscrossed in the air above the field, working the night insects. The creatures of the evening had begun their cries.

I could hear the faint, scratchy lyrics of Don McLean's "American Pie" waxing softly from the hangar in the distance, and they suddenly made me lonesome for home. I wanted it all to be over. I wanted to be sitting on my lounge chair by our canal, feeding breadcrumbs to the schooling mullet with my dog, and Banyan…

Nick's voice drew me out of my reverie. "If you boys don't have any more pressing engagements with Central American banks, we're good to go."

"Yeah, let's get out of here," Will said. "Will there be refreshments served on this flight?"

"No refreshments, no stops, and if you need to take a piss you better do it now."

We'd been flying for two hours at ten thousand feet. I was sitting in the co-pilot seat, dozing a little. Will was stretched out on the bales in the back. I came around to see Nick tapping the fuel gauges on the dash with a much too serious look. "What's up?"

He tapped the gauge again then exhaled angrily. "We got about five hours to go, but with this damned headwind, we're using way too much fuel. Looks like it's going to be close."

That brought Will up from the back. "Whatta' you mean, 'gonna be close'? You mean like, not make our original destination—like we have to land somewhere else?"

Nick eased back the throttles a little. "No. More like real close. We can stay high for now and conserve fuel, but in an hour or so, when we make the turn around the western end of Cuba, we've got to hit the deck for the rest of the way in, or Key West radar will pick us up. It's going to take more fuel. Can't lean the mixture out like you can up here. Here's the thing: my pick-up people are going to be in boats off Big Torch Key. The plan is to come in quick and low, kick out the pot, cut across the Keys and pick up a little altitude out to sea, like we're coming in from one of the small Bahamas out-islands, or Miami, then head on into Marathon, where I keep the plane." Nick eased back into his seat and I watched a transformation take place. He got comfortable, and he was smiling to himself. "Relax, gentlemen," he said over his shoulder. "This is nothing. If Burt was here, he would tell you this ain't shit—just an evening's entertainment."

I looked at him. "What happened at Chin Lai?"

Nick didn't answer, like he hadn't heard me. He just stared straight ahead out the windshield at the dark moonlit ocean, but I could see the smoke from a distant fire in his eyes. Then, very quietly, he started talking. "We flew spotters, sometimes 337s, like that little one of yours, with rocket pods and 30-cals. We got a little too far along one evening and got shot down. Survived the crash, but got captured by an NVA patrol and ended up in a hellhole just into North Vietnam. It was a small camp, probably a dozen regular guards and only four American prisoners left out of the original twenty. The others had been starved or beaten to death. We heard after we got there that they were terminating the camp in about ten days, killing the remaining prisoners and pulling out. Burt hurt his leg in the crash, couldn't make a break with me, but he insisted I go. One night I just slipped out under the wire and headed south, as hard and as fast as my body would take me. I got lucky. Three days out I was near dead from exhaustion when I stumbled into a team of Special Forces. They got me fixed up and took me to a firebase. They sent me by truck to Long Binh, but I'd used up six of my ten days getting there. I spent two more trying to convince the base commander we had men alive out there who needed rescuing. He wouldn't buy it. Said it would take a week just to get permission from DaNang for a mission like that. So I gave up."

He paused, running his fingers over the mixture throttles softly, adjusting them just a touch. "I went and got an M-16 and a handful of magazines. Then I stole a rocket pod 337 and headed back. I got there the next day, just as dawn was breaking. I just came in hot and blew the crap out of the barracks and the guard towers with every rocket I had before setting down on the little strip next to the camp. I had killed most all of the guards with the rockets—all but two. I killed them with my rifle. I found Burt. He helped me free the other prisoners and drag them over to the plane. We turned into the wind just about the time a couple of trucks of NVAs came roaring down the road. They were two minutes too late. We were gone." He paused again. There was a soft exhale, almost melancholy.

"That particular event made me several lifetime friends, but it cost me my military career. The big wigs weren't sure what to do with me—make me a hero or court-martial me. They decided on neither, buried the whole affair and gave me an honorable discharge." He looked at me and chuckled. "Almost everyone I know in this business is Vietnam vintage. You see, they gave us guns, boats, or planes, then sent us on missions—forced us to live by our wits, taught us to respect but not fear danger. They taught us to live on the edge and like it, so we could perform to the optimum. What they couldn't know then is that the jazz would become our mistress—the jazz was the greatest high of all." He paused again. "Then they said, 'It's over soldier—no more living to the nines, no more jazz. Just go home and get a job. Be a shoe salesman or work in a bank.'"

He took a moment, fingering the trim tab for a minor adjustment, then continued. "We tried it. But it just didn't work for some of us. Hell, there's little more danger in delivering the fifty thousand dollar cash crop in the back of this plane than there was in one mission in Nam. Where's the incentive to become a shoe salesman, man?" He turned to me. "And you know what the worst of it is? I'm addicted. Not to the product, but to the jazz." He smiled. "If they paid me in Popsicle sticks I'd probably still have to do one every other month, just for the hell of it."

For the next hour it was quiet in the cockpit. Bathed in the luminous light of the instruments and lulled by the steady hum of the engines, I eased back and watched us race through long wisps of high cirrus clouds. I did, however, notice that Nick had brought his hand to his stomach and was burping a lot.

I eased around in my seat. "Hey, you okay?"

Crow grimaced just a little. "Yeah, Yeah. I think so. I ate some rice and beans with the boys before leaving. Didn't seem to set well with me. Normally I avoid that—just in case...." He brought his hand to his mouth and burped uneasily again, but managed a confident grin. "I've eaten worse. I'll be okay."

But he wasn't. Inside an hour Nick began to throw up. I don't mean a little dribble in a cup. I mean like rice and beans and unidentifiable meat on the instrument panel. He began to double over with cramps. We managed to get him into the co-pilot's seat at first, but he was in such bad shape we had to stretch him out on the bales in the back.

Will looked at me from the co-pilot's seat as he cleaned the dash with a rag. "I'm not taking any more vacations with you. I don't give a shit if you're just going to Miami for the weekend."

I raised my eyebrows and turned. "Oh, now it's my fault? You're the one who said this would be a great way to take our minds off Banyan. Visit Costa Rica for fun and profit."

He shrugged. "Well, you have to admit it has taken our minds off Banyan, and if we hadn't given the money back to the bank, it certainly would have been profitable." He paused. "Can you fly this thing okay?"

"Well, it's not so much the point A to point B. It's just that I've got about an hour or two of left seat time in an asymmetrical twin. It acts a whole lot different on landings and take-offs. It's going to be a little spooky, I think, when we get to that part. Then, of course, there's still the matter of dropping off some pot somewhere."

"You're not going to kill us, are you?"

"Not intentionally."

Crow coughed and moaned from the back. He looked at his watch and struggled to a sitting position. "Time to drop down to the deck—no higher than five hundred feet." he gasped. "Course of zero-four-five and stay with it for the next three hours. No radio communications. I'll be all right by then."

But he wasn't. Three hours later he couldn't keep water down and was still drifting in and out of consciousness. We had less than a quarter tank of fuel left on each side, and on top of that, our weather radar showed a huge storm moving down over the Keys—cumulus clouds, heavy wind, and rain.

"What's going to be frigging next?" moaned Will as he studied the weather images.

"Next is a pot drop," Nick whispered hoarsely from the back, as he tried to sit up without success.

Will reached around and held him by the shoulder.

"We should be about forty miles southeast of Big Torch," Crow muttered. He pointed weakly to the starboard. "Lights of Key West…there…"

I looked out and could vaguely see a dim glow on the horizon.

He was wracked with a spasm again and dry-heaved for a moment, then wiped his mouth and turned back to me. "Full moon tonight, easy target. You know the long, straight roads on Big Torch Key?"

I nodded. "Yeah."

"All you got to find is the first one at the top of the island—aims out at eighty degrees, right at Big Pine Key across the channel. You fly down that road, and as soon as you're over water in the channel, you kick the pot out." He paused and took a couple of ragged breaths. "Get the cargo door open well in advance. Be ready. Look for a blinking spotlight."

I nodded again, nervous to hives. "Yeah. Okay. Soon as we're clear of land, Will pushes out the cargo."

Nick coughed again and moaned, clutching his stomach, breathing heavily. "I'll never eat friggin' rice and beans again for as long as I live." He motioned to the cockpit. "Put me in the right seat. Give me the mike. Will, you get back here. Be ready."

After Will eased him into the seat, I handed Crow the microphone. He set up a frequency and keyed his mike three times, waited ten seconds then keyed it again. "Night Owl, here. Night Owl to Waterbug."

He waited a few moments. Nothing. I could see lightning flashing out of the huge cumulus wall building in the distance, headed at us. The first fat pellets of rain slapped the windshield intermittently, a preamble to the fury ahead.

"Waterbug, come in, good buddy."

Still nothing.

Nick was bringing up the mike again, when faintly, we all heard, "Night Owl, this is Waterbug. Come back."

Nick smiled, despite it all. "We're twenty out, Waterbug."

"Roger that," came the faint reply. "Looking forward to visiting with you."

Nick turned to me. "Damn, man! I hate to leave you with this," he gasped. "But I gotta puke again."

Ten minutes later, the moon broke through the cloud cover and I recognized the distinct shape of Raccoon Key, just above Big Torch. Banking down and carving out another twenty degrees to the east, I spotted the long, runway-straight road at the end of the island. Rain was starting to slap the windshield solidly. The plane rocked as Will moved to the back, forced open the cargo door, then moved between the bales and the fuselage to provide some leverage. Wind screamed through the aircraft like a hurricane. My heart was hammering out a steady Grand Funk Railroad beat. I backed off the power, trimmed her out, and did my best to keep it straight and level. I felt Nick's hand on my arm. "Steady, now. Steady," he croaked over the commotion. Lightning flashed in front of the plane so close I thought we'd been struck.

"Holy mother of God!" Will screamed from the back. "I'm never going on another vacation with you—ever again!"

We swept down on the road no more than two hundred feet above the Australian pines bent to the storm below. I slowed some more and dropped ten degrees of flaps. The controls shook in my hands as the plane shuddered and pitched, close to a stall. As I pushed the nose down a bit, I could feel rivulets of nervous sweat running down my temples and the back of my neck. Suddenly, in the moonlit channel ahead, I could see a spotlight flashing. We cleared the land and I yelled over the wind and the storm, "Now! Get it out now!"

I heard Will cry out with exertion, "I'm never leaving home again!"

The plane suddenly lurched upward as the first package went out and our load instantly lightened. Nick instinctively hit the controls forward, to keep us from stalling, then leveled us out. The second package went out and the plane lurched again, but this time I was ready for it. Will fought his way against the wind to the cargo door and managed to get it closed as I retracted the flaps and banked over Big Pine Key toward open water. Suddenly it seemed so quiet.

Will pulled himself up between us, breathing heavily. "I think I may have peed my pants. When I get home, man, I'm locking all the frigging doors, phoning for pizza, and never going outside again."

Nick eased back against the seat and wiped some vomit from the side of his mouth with the back of his hand. He glanced over at me. "Just a night's entertainment," he whispered with a faint smile.

We swung out wide, past the reef line, to the periphery of the storm, then worked our way up the coast toward Marathon, climbing as we went. Weather still hammered the plane and the lightning was terrifying, but the worst was behind us. We had less than an eighth of a tank showing on each gauge when I set up our descent and we made our long final approach toward the small ribbon of tarmac that was Marathon Airport. With Nick coaching me, I trimmed her out, backed her off, dropped some flaps, and bounced and skidded my way onto the strip. It wasn't pretty, but we ended up on the ground in one piece. I was taxiing down and turning into the spot on the tarmac where Nick kept his plane when the starboard fuel gauge flopped over and that engine coughed and quit. We all stared at each other for a moment.

Crow shook his head. "That's slicing it about as thin as you can slice it."

"I can tell you right now," Will said as he leaned in between us. "Of the two, I prefer bank robbing."

We slept through the entire day and got up about six that afternoon. Will called for pizza—two pizzas. We drank beer, ate, and recounted our incredible adventures until we were laughing so hard we had tears in our eyes. We had become adventurers extraordinaire. We had survived the near impossible and created tales our grandchildren would most certainly consider lies.

It was nine o'clock before Will sighed and looked at me, finally voicing what was on both our minds. "I can't stand the suspense. I think it's time we call Banyan."

I exhaled and nodded. "Yeah. Me too." I motioned to the phone. "You go ahead. Make the call."

There was no answer at Banyan's, so Will called Turtle. After the standard greetings, Will asked about Banyan. I watched his expression suddenly change and his shoulders sag as he tucked the phone in close, mumbling one-syllable responses, eyes distant. Somewhere, I heard a piano falling.

I picked up the second phone in the kitchen. Turtle was in mid-sentence. "...and I'm so sorry, for both of you. I would have gladly taken either one of you as a brother-in-law. She came to me a week after you left, anxious, but I could tell she was excited. And I thought, *Oh Lord, not again. Not this time.*" He paused. "It was a conga player named Reginald Damascus—plays for a Latin group touring the Caribbean. They were headed back down to Barbados, where his twin brother/conga player, Archie, owns a nightclub. She told me to tell you she just wasn't good at waiting, and that she loved you both, and that was the problem."

"What the hell! We weren't gone eight months," moaned Will. "Two lousy weeks and she falls in love with a Cuban conga player."

"And probably his twin brother," Turtle said softly.

I turned the phone toward me as if it was an entity. "Turtle, what do you know that we don't?"

There was a sigh of resignation on the other end, then a pause that sounded eerily like a preface to honesty. "You're not the first 'two guys' she's fallen in love with. There were two brothers a year and a half ago. And there were two jocks in her senior year of high school. She's not a bad person, it's just there's a small piece of her psyche that's, well, twisted a little. It's not that she can't love passionately, it's that she loves too often. She never even allows a relationship to wear out, to wind down naturally, before she's found a replacement and she's all gaga at her new life." He paused again. "I really hoped you two might be the ones who would break this psyche thing. You are real, level-headed, compassionate dudes, and you could have helped her—that one of you might have been 'the one.' But it didn't work. It just didn't work out. She left for Barbados with Reginald last Friday."

We thanked Turtle for his honesty and hung up. Having just had our insides sucked out by the queen spider of them all—beautiful, sweet, slightly overrated and somewhat loosely wound Banyan McDaniel—we moved a bottle of tequila and the lounge chairs to the edge of the canal. Will and I sat silently watching the last of the sun ooze out into the channel in orange and violet pastels, drawing back into Mother Ocean and sliding peacefully over the distant rim of the earth, as the sky above struggled futilely to hold the same colors alive. From a house down the canal, the poignant sounds of "Lady," by Styx, drifted across the water.

It was pretty melancholy stuff until Nick Crow came walking up. "Hey, what's up? You don't look like two guys who have lived in the nines for the last twenty-four hours."

Will looked up. "Yeah, well, we got some unexpected bad news when we got back, about our girlfriend. She dumped us both." He chuckled sadly. "Like two cross-eyed mud ducks."

"Sorry to hear that," Crow said as he pulled out a cigarette and lit it, drawing in slowly. "But maybe there's a way I can help a little." He pointed at the sleek sailboat gently nudging his dock. "I'm getting a little overbooked on my day sails and overnighters for 'the big Caribbean cruise,' and I was wondering if you guys could maybe take up some of the slack for me—probably no more than a trip a week—two, three girls. Help keep you at your, uh, peak."

From his back pocket, he pulled two bundles of one-hundred-dollar bills, each bound with rubber bands. "Here's a little something for your trouble the other night." He threw one to Will and one to me.

I started to get up. "What's this? We don't need… we didn't—"

He waved me down casually. "Trust me. You earned it. As far as I'm concerned, you're bona fide members of the Popsicle Stick Club." Then he straightened up, gazing squarely at us. "I will, however, issue this one word of warning. You participated with me in something illegal, for which you could turn me in to the authorities. But I'm not worrying about that, because first off, you both have great character, and secondly, I'm the only one who knows you robbed a Costa Rican bank and stole an airplane to escape from the country." He paused and let that sink in. "So we're cool, right?"

"We are so cool," I said.

"Until the last sunrise, Nick," said Will. "Until the last sunrise."

Lady… when you're with me I'm smiling…
Touch me… and my troubles all fade…
You gave… all the love that I needed…
So shy… like a child who has grown…
Lady…

CHAPTER SEVEN

New Homes and Crazy Monkeys

With the fresh stacks of Franklins from Nick burning holes in our pockets, we decided we might like to have our own trailer—something a little nicer than the eight-foot-wide green tunnel we'd been living in for the past two years. A couple of months before our Costa Rican adventure I had phoned my parents, who lived in Oklahoma, and they told me my uncle, who lived in Miami, wanted to move home but was having a hard time selling his place. I had inquired about it—a 55-foot by 10-foot mobile home only five years old. We went up and had a look, but simply couldn't afford it at the time.

I called my uncle and made him an offer, which he accepted. We had already found a nice lot for rent on an exceptionally clear canal located on the northern side of Big Pine.

The only problem was getting the trailer down to the Keys. But Uncle Ted said he had a friend who owned a ton-and-a-half pickup and he was sure the guy would tow it down to Big Pine Key for a hundred dollars. He would have him call me. Sure enough, the next day I got a jingle from Ralph, who was ready and willing to drag our mobile home to the Keys for a "C-note and a case of beer—and a case for the return trip."

I called Ted back and we agreed to pick up the mobile home the following weekend. In the process of the conversation, my uncle paused. "Listen, Kan," he said in a slightly confidential tone. "Ralph's a good guy, but here's the thing. He just got discharged from the Army after spending a few months in Nam. It's a bit of a story. The poor guy's taking a crap in the jungle when his platoon is hit by mortars. He gets separated from his team and listed as missing in action—ends up living with a Montagnard tribe for a month or so before they can get him out. The whole thing didn't sit well with him." Ted paused for a moment. "You gotta understand man, he was a baker. He worked for Krispy Kreme Donuts before getting drafted. Every once in a while, now, he has these little nervous spells."

"What exactly is a nervous spell, Ted?"

"Nothing. Listen, forget I said anything. He's a great guy—maybe a little fidgety sometimes. But he takes medicine for it. You'll like him. Salt of the earth. Look, it's only a few hours, then you'll have your trailer and he'll be on his way."

Ultimately, I agreed. I wanted that trailer down there. Uncle Ted said it would probably be a good idea for one of us to ride with Ralph, just to keep him company—so he didn't drink all the beer in the first fifty miles. We flipped a coin. I got Ralph.

The following morning my uncle met us at the trailer. The first thing I noticed was the large pickup already locked down and chained on the front of the mobile home. *Efficient,* I thought. *This is going to be okay*. Then Ralph peeked around from the back of the truck. He looked beyond us, then back behind himself, then took a quick look under the mobile home before stepping out to meet us. He moved like a small, wild animal watching for a predator. Skittish—very cautious. Nervous was a good word.

At first glance, I immediately thought of the six o'clock news. Ralph was a carbon copy of the American soldiers they showed dug in at the forward bases in Vietnam—khaki-colored T-shirt, camouflage pants, jungle boots, cigarette dangling from his mouth. He was a smallish, wiry-looking guy, maybe five-foot-five-inches tall. He had a tangle of long brown hair protruding from his floppy, green jungle hat, a pale complexion, and large hazel eyes that were—what was the word I wanted? Nervous, that was it.

He edged over. "I'm Ralph. You got the beer and the money?"

"Kansas," I said, shaking his hand. "This is Will. Yeah, we got the beer and the money. You get some of the beer as we go along, and the money at the end of the trip. I'll ride with you. Will's gonna follow in the bus."

He frowned a little at that. There was a brusqueness about him that was countered by a voice a little too shrill, darting eyes, and a continuous swallowing that made his Adam's apple bounce up and down in his slightly longish neck. I felt like I was in the middle of Mayberry.

"Okay. Let's move out," he said. Then he suddenly emitted a small, spontaneous sound under his breath—"Eckk!"—like he'd just found a lizard in his mashed potatoes. He continued on as if nothing had happened. "But you'll have to share the seat with No Shit."

I looked at Will and raised my eyebrows. I started to turn to Ted. "Who's No Shi—" when Ralph stepped over to the truck cab and opened the door. Out jumped a monkey—a brown spider monkey about two feet tall with a long, curled tail.

Ralph looked at us. "He goes where I go…Eckk."

Lord! It's bad enough I'm going to have to spend ten hours in a truck with a paranoid Barney Fife—but a flippin' monkey too? I spun around to Ted. He put his hands up palms out, defensively.

"It was given to him by the Montagnards. It lives with him. Sorry."

I glanced at the monkey then turned to Ralph. "No Shit?"

"Yeah," he said with something close to a grin. "When I got back, people would come over. First thing they'd say, 'You got a monkey in the house!' 'No shit,' I'd say. I'm stopped at a traffic light and the bozos in the car next to me look over—'Man! You got a monkey in the car!' 'No shit!' Everywhere I go, man, it's the same. Pretty soon the monkey starts responding to that more than his name. So I figure, what the hell. It'll make him easier to house train."

Will smiled. "One of my luckier coin tosses." He shot me a peace sign, then put the two fingers to his forehead. "May the one-eyed toad bless the bowels of your movement."

"You and the horse you rode in on," I said.

Actually, most of the trip went better than I had hoped for, considering the possibilities. Little No Shit was calmer than I expected, and equally as good a conversationalist as Ralph—he answered my questions enthusiastically, I just couldn't understand him. Ralph drove cautiously, checking mirrors constantly, smoking cigarettes, and slowly eliminating the beers in the cooler on the floor (which he shared with No Shit), sometimes complementing them with little white and green pills, showing no particular signs from either. I sat quietly next to the door, watching the alcoholic monkey upend beers with both hands then pass them back to his master, who would finish them and toss the can out the window. Over the constant melodies of the Guess Who and Three Dog Night, I did get an occasional, spontaneous lecture on the advantages of a BAR machine gun as opposed to a standard M16, the average deadly range of a grenade, and the difference between trip wires, Bouncing Betties, and Claymore mines—all of this punctuated with an occasional "eckk!" The number of "eckks" seemed to be directly proportional to how animated he got while delivering the information.

After three long hours, our little caravan was approaching Bahia Honda Bridge, the huge, mile-long monument to Henry Flagler's ingenuity—a graceful, tiered hump of concrete and metal rising 150 feet above the swift channel below. The bridge was silhouetted by a distant summer storm tumbling across the horizon, encasing a golden sun, setting the towering cumulus clouds on fire and illuminating brilliant shafts of silver rain as they cascaded into the sea. I realized again that there is no artist to compare with Mother Nature, but she paints only for the moment.

Unfortunately, I wasn't able to enjoy the scene as much as I would have liked. The monkey was getting fidgety and making way too much conversation. Ralph had finished almost all the beers and apparently most of the pills, reaching a state of agitated catatonia—bloodshot, distant eyes staring straight ahead, a much too solid grip on the wheel, an occasional dry "eckk" from a clenched mouth. I was really glad we only had another five miles to go.

We had just reached the peak of the bridge, when we suddenly encountered a semi-truck barreling up from the other direction. The narrow structure, built in a time when smaller vehicles were the order of the day, could barely accommodate the two trucks, let alone their extended mirrors. There was no time to react and nowhere to go. We missed the semi but the mirrors of the two vehicles collided in a loud explosion of showering glass.

"Ecccckkk!" Ralph shrieked, eyes widening. "Ecccckkk!"

"Eccckkk!" The monkey screeched and hammered the seat with its little hands, jumping up and down, throwing himself at the windshield.

"Eccckkk!" cried Ralph again.

I managed to grab No Shit, and for a moment I thought Ralph was going to make it. We were over the high point of the bridge and headed downward. But suddenly, I noticed Ralph's right cheek had begun to twitch—that same eye was beginning to tic independently, as if it was watching a tennis game by itself. This was soon accompanied by a continuous burbling whisper of. "Eckk, eckk, eckk, eckk..." and a death grip on the wheel. I knew I was in trouble. Then, quietly, from deep inside him came a low whine, building rapidly into a howling crescendo of "INCOMING! INCOMING!" As if that was his cue, the monkey screeched like he'd just been branded and went totally berserk, bouncing off the seat and the dash then launching himself at Ralph. No Shit wrapped himself around Ralph's face—humping his master's head while screeching and yanking out sizable tufts of hair. Ralph was shrieking, "Aahhhh! V.C.! V.C.! Eccckkk! Fubar! Fubar! Aahhhh! Pop smoke!" As we were careening down the sharp incline of the bridge, Ralph had one hand on the wheel while trying to rip the monkey off his head with the other, not the least bit concerned with the unique device on the floor called a brake pedal. The trailer was reaching an acceptable speed for moon rocket launches, and swaying so badly it was grating on the old metal rails—the only thing between us and a hundred-foot fall into the deep, churning water below. *Good God, it can't get any worse than this*! I thought. *He died while trying to save fifty bucks on a trailer delivery...*

Ralph somehow managed to get a grip on No Shit and ripped him off his face. I realized then that they were both completely mad. He threw the monkey on the floor, but No Shit seized his leg with renewed frenzy and laid his sharp little canines into Mr. Flashback's calf. Ralph screamed, completely forgot the steering wheel, opened the cab door and lurched out onto the running board. Grabbing the top of the cab with both hands, yelling about "friggin' V.C. monkeys" and "ungrateful hairy little bastards" he began trying to shake the monkey off his leg. No Shit, who had a remarkably firm grip, was still screeching between bites (and my guess would be, arguing in return about what it's like to live with a crazy person). I slid over and grabbed the wheel, thinking, *Maybe I have a small chance,* but when I looked up, ahead of us, walking in the center of the bridge, was a procession of about a dozen people in white robes. The long-haired guy preceding the congregation by about fifty feet was carrying a large brown urn. *Oh God! A cremation—ashes off the bridge ceremony!*

It was too late to do anything. I couldn't just slam on the brakes or the trailer would jackknife and we'd all go over the side. We were coming down the incline but still about thirty feet above the water. The guy with the urn looked up. I couldn't hear it because the trailer was grating on the bridge, but I could see his mouth frame a healthy scream and his eyes do the Daffy Duck bulge. He threw the urn into the air, jacked up his robes and bolted for the side of the bridge, shooting us a defiant middle finger as he went over the side like some giant, ungainly heron. The others behind him recognized they had a serious problem about the same time the urn hit the front of the truck. There was a white explosion. A huge mushroom cloud enveloped the entire pickup in fine gray ash. *Holy crap! They must have been burying Fat Albert.* I thought. Ralph and No Shit were totally covered in dust—shocked to silence for a moment like a couple of avant-garde statues glued to the cab door. Meanwhile, as we careened downward, the people in front of us were following their leader's example, robes up, scrambling for the sides of the bridge and leaping off like a flock of suicidal Hare Krishnas. I could barely see at that point, so I hit the windshield wipers, which helped just enough for me to begin braking and eventually guide the truck to a stop at the mouth of the bridge.

Ralph and No Shit were still semi-frozen to the door. The monkey finally let go of Ralph's leg and hopped down to the ground, shaking himself. Ralph slowly turned to me. He was still completely covered in gray ash with the exception of his wide, shell-shocked eyes. His hat was gone, his ash-white hair spiked, windblown, and disheveled. He swallowed, then blinked. "Eckk?" he whispered.

An hour and a half later, after making sure all the cremation people made it to shore and driving the final few miles, I backed the trailer onto our lot. A subdued Ralph sat next to me. No Shit was on the floor talking to himself and trying to open a final beer he found in the cooler. We got the mobile home in place and unhooked the truck just as the warm darkness of evening overtook us. We drove over to our old trailer and made some sandwiches for supper. Needless to say, everyone was fairly exhausted. There was little conversation after dinner, and by nine o'clock we had all found a corner in which to curl up.

The following morning, I was awakened by the gentle warmth of an early summer sun cascading through the window of my closet-bedroom. I rolled over and glanced down the hallway, through the trellises of cigarette smoke, to the living room. Ralph, perpetual fag dangling from his lips, was gathering his gear.

An hour later, No Shit and Ralph were "locked and loaded," with a second case of beer secured on the floorboard, and with little ado, they wished us the best and headed back to Miami. I had given Will a brief recounting of the ride from hell while Ralph packed his truck. As the dust of the pickup receded in the distance, I sighed. "I'm going to miss those two—the depth of conversation and the serenity."

"Yeah," Will said. "I'm especially disappointed I didn't get to see little No Shit wrapped around Ralph, ripping out his hair and dry-humping his head. That would have been far out."

"Yeah, well, there are some poignant memories that, unfortunately, you'll never get to share with me. Luck of the draw."

Will grinned. "Only the hasty frog knows the taste of the morning fly."

"You've been visiting Rufus again, haven't you?"

CHAPTER EIGHT

Me, You, and Voodoo...

The winter of '73 rolled in early—cold and audacious. By mid-December daytime temperatures had plunged to the sixties, northern winds raked frothy furrows across the Gulf and everyone was talking about moving south. Continuous gray crowns of high cirrus stretched across the sky and sucked the warmth from the islands for weeks at a time. The winds were relentless, the water took on that silt gray color, and visibility dropped to a few feet at best. When the skies broke behind those fronts, the air was crystal clear for miles but glacial, and the sun struggled in vain to warm the sands and sea. Throughout January and February, we occupied ourselves with equipment repairs, board games, and bottle hunting. We paid our bills by wading the flats for anemones and collecting flame scallops in the old, abandoned submarine pits at Key West Naval Air Station.

One rainy February afternoon, in the midst of a challenging game of Monopoly with Robert and Dede Bunter, we got to talking about Cay Sal Island. It was the tiny center point for the Bahamian bank where we dove with that scoundrel, Calico Curt. The island was about a seventy-five-mile run from Big Pine, but Robert had made it several times in his big Aquasport 22.

"Man, the tropical diving off that little speck is absolutely bitchin'," Bunter said as he moved his 'top hat' to Park Place and started counting out money to buy it. "There are thousands of Royal Grammas a hundred feet offshore, and Black Caps in fifty feet of water."

Neither of those species was readily found in the Keys, and they were big money fish for us. A hundred Grammas were the equivalent of a full week's work.

"I've always picked my weather carefully, shot over, dove for a day or two then headed back," Bunter added. "But it's an exhausting five or six-hour ride if there's any seas at all. Beats the crap out of you and the fish." He paused. "Bet you guys didn't know there's an airstrip there, did you?"

We both looked up.

"An airstrip, huh?" I said.

Bunter nodded, still occupied with counting money. "Yeah. Was the last time I was there, but it's been about six months—not a trip you want to make in winter seas."

I put down the dice for a moment. "We could get a 172 in there?"

"Yeah, I don't see why not. But there are two things you need to know about Cay Sal Island. There's a caretaker there who doesn't like strangers—name's Thomas Harcord. He'll run you off sure as shit, the moment you land, if you don't show up with half a dozen Playboy magazines and a couple bottles of J&B Scotch."

"You're kidding."

Dede and Robert chuckled.

"No, man. That's the ticket," Bunter said. "If I want to go on the island, that's what I have to have. It'll be the same with you." Then for a moment he became a little more serious. "There's one other thing. I've never stayed overnight there—always slept in my boat, offshore. It's a real small key—maybe two miles square. There are about fifty Bahamians living in a little village at the east end." He paused. "I found out most of them practice *Santeria*, a religion which originated in Cuba, created by Africans who were brought to the Caribbean as slaves, with a little Haitian voodoo mixed in—to really keep the congregation on their feet and clapping." Robert shook his head a little. "It's cult-like stuff. Way too far out for me, man. I've seen them dancing around a bonfire by an old house near the beach at night. They're into sacrifices—small animals, chickens. One night I heard somebody screaming and it didn't sound like a chicken. If I was going to stay overnight, I'd keep to the west end, near Harcord's house and the airstrip."

"Royal Grammas and Black Caps, huh?" Will said, as if he hadn't heard anything else. "If we could haul back a couple hundred of those, that would be far out."

Finally, by the middle of March, the winds subsided, rolled around to the south and warmed. Spring in the islands was, as always, a subtle affair. The wan sun found its vigor again, mangoes and papayas budded, key limes began their bloom, and everywhere miniature coconut and banana trees sprouted from the moist soil around their parents. Hermit crabs found their way from beneath weathered log and leaf, and once again could be seen scurrying across tide lines, one step ahead of the raccoons. Lizards perched on coral outcroppings and reveled in the sun as seabirds danced through the sky above them, celebrating the new season with a cacophony of whistles and shrills. I remember how that spring sun worked its way around to my bedroom window in the mornings and softly touched me. I've never been awakened more kindly.

For breakfast, we would most often whip up a plateful of pancakes, but occasionally, when the money was rolling, we might stop at Island Jim's—a one room, hibiscus-encased, screened eatery of about a dozen tables owned by Shelly Jane, a woman possessed of remarkable culinary talent and mild schizophrenia. She kept a small plastic baseball bat (the kind designed for Whiffle Ball) behind the counter. There were times you could tell her there was a fly in your scrambled eggs, and she would laugh apologetically and bring you a new order. But I also saw her beat the pudding out of our huge diving buddy, Kip—whopping on that boy with that plastic bat like he was a loose-bladdered house dog, because she heard him pass gas in her restaurant.

I guess in truth, it was all pretty good-natured stuff. We all loved Shelly because she added dimension to our lives. It's the characters of your life that make the stories you remember, and the very best you can hope for, is to be one of those characters.

Will and I were having a quiet breakfast at Island Jim's one flawless April morning when Bunter came in. He sat down with us, looking tired, but all smiles.

Will swallowed a mouthful of eggs. "So what's happening, Rob?"

Robert ordered coffee and settled back into his chair with a sigh. "Just got back from a marathon trip to Cay Sal Island. Six hours over, dove for six hours, then turned around and did six more back. I'm stoved, man, worn to the nub. But man, was it worth it."

The weather had been flat calm. Obviously, his timing was good. Shelly dropped off his coffee and took an order. I pushed the cream over to him as our friend poured copious amounts of sugar into his cup. "So what did you get?"

Robert smiled again, obviously pleased with himself. "Two hundred Royal Grammas and a hundred Black Caps. Nearly eight hundred dollars—maybe seven after gas and expenses—but it still makes for a really great day of diving."

It was a more than a great day of diving. A day like that could keep us in supplies for weeks. We could upgrade our Miller beer and throw a steak on the barbie occasionally with some of Nick's sailing compatibility girls, which had proved to be one of our more entertaining endeavors.

Will turned to me and got that Lee Marvin smile. He stared for a moment.

I nodded. "Okay. We go Tuesday, next week, weather permitting."

My partner tilted his head a little, still staring.

"Okay. Two days, one night on shore. We take our chances. How bad can it be?"

Tuesday morning I aimed the nose of our rented Cessna down the runway in Marathon just as the sun crested the sea, turning to bright pink the thin ribbons of clouds that floated on a brilliant turquoise horizon. As we lifted off, I threw the 172 into a thirty-degree bank and aimed for Cay Sal. We were looking for another story in the chapters of our lives.

The flight over was uneventful. The near cloudless sky drifted into pale blue with the distant horizon going soft and hazy on the edges. The winds were light, and the sparkling panorama of indigo drop-offs and staggered Bahamas reefs at five thousand feet was Hollywood. I set a course vectoring with Marathon and Key West to be certain, because we were aiming for a little dot in the middle of nowhere. Less than an hour later, the little dot appeared out of nowhere, just like in the movies.

The good news was, it was a beautiful little island surrounded by waters so clear we could make out coral heads and patch reefs on approach, and the strip was easily long enough, normally. The bad news was, someone had recently bulldozed a ten-foot-high mound of sand across the center of the runway. It wasn't difficult to figure out why. With smuggling being as popular as it was, the island made a perfect drop-off point for long hauls from Jamaica and Colombia. It may have been a coup for the authorities, but it didn't do much for our plans.

As we passed over the airstrip, Will craned his neck. "Craaap!" he muttered. "That really pisses me off!"

I banked around and flew by once more, taking a good look at the situation. "I can get in there and stop before we hit the sand," I said. "Might even be able to get out. It was designed to discourage twins with heavy payloads. Besides, I know a trick."

"Might be able to get out?" said Will shrilly, ignoring the possibility of a trick. "Might be able? You're aware, of course, what happens when you're traveling seventy miles an hour and 'might be able' turns into 'ooopps, figured wrong, here,' aren't you? Are you going to try to kill us again?"

"Not intentionally," I said as I banked around and backed off my speed.

Will looked at me. "You're going to land, aren't you?"

"Yeah," I said, concentrating on my airspeed and approach. "I think so."

Will unconsciously checked his seatbelt. "Okay, now would be a good time to tell me about the trick."

I dropped some flaps and set up for a long final. "The guy who taught me to fly used to tell stories about his barnstorming days. He said he used to 'hop' haystacks on wheat fields in old Piper Cubs by running at the haystack full out, then at the last minute, slapping down twenty degrees of flaps and snapping back on the stick. He said it just makes you bounce like magic, right over the top. I think we can get out by doing that."

Will cocked his head at me. "And how many times have you done this?"

"Including the attempt we're going to make later, here?"

Will nodded. "Yeah."

"Once."

My partner slapped the dash. "I knew it! I knew it! You don't even know if it works! And we're going to be loaded down with water and fish!"

"It'll work. I know it will. The principle is perfect," I said as the plane dropped toward the strip.

Will nervously pushed himself against his seat as I lowered the last of the flaps and the runway reared up at us. "Oh, that makes me feel a lot better. That's what they'll say when they're spreading our ashes off some frigging bridge. 'Can't figure out how this happened, 'cause they had perfect frigging principles!'"

I put the wheels down on the edge of the strip, then eased onto the brakes and continued pressure until I was standing on them. We were bouncing and skidding down the runway and the sand mound was rushing at us a little faster than I had hoped. I glanced over at Will, who was staring straight ahead, rigid as rigor mortis, grasping the hand rests hard enough to make permanent indentations.

"Quit admiring my profile and stop this damned thing," he muttered through gritted teeth.

I had to smile, and for just a moment I was washed with a sense of honest affection for him, and pride that he was my friend. For all his feigned complaining, he was so damned courageous. It's a lot easier when you're flying the thing rather than sitting there and trusting somebody with your life. It all came down to that one thing—he trusted me.

The plane slipped sideways just a little. Instinctively I worked the ailerons but there wasn't enough speed for them to help. I stood on the opposite brake a little harder and she came back around a bit, finally losing momentum. The plane surged and skidded another hundred feet before the earth drew her down and she rolled to a stop, about fifty feet from the mound of sand.

Will let out the breath he'd held for the last minute or so, still staring straight ahead. "Did I tell you I've ordered a correspondence course in television repair."

I had no sooner taxied the plane over to a cleared area by a stand of coconut palms and killed the engine, when a beat-up old Jeep with no top and no doors came rumbling across the field from the south side of the island. There was a big, formidable-looking black guy driving—maybe mid-forties, a halo of short curly hair, Eric Clapton T-shirt, cut-off shorts supported by a strip of nylon anchor rope, and flip-flops. We opened the doors as the Jeep pulled up. The Bahamian guy got out, obviously not happy.

"What you think you doin', mon? Dis ain't no damned Miami International, and you ain't doin' no damn business here, mon! So you get your—"

I pulled the Playboy magazines and two bottles of scotch from the cabin. "Hello, Thomas!" I shouted as gleefully as I could muster. "Robert Bunter sends his greetings and says these are for you!"

From the moment our friend saw the gifts, there was an immediate and remarkable transformation. His big, dark eyes widened with appreciation, and a genuine smile broadened his face, displaying a mouthful of large white teeth. "Aaahhhh. You friends of Mr. Robert?"

"That we are," I replied, stepping out and handing him the bottles and magazines. "And these are small tokens of our appreciation for being allowed to dive off your island for a day or two."

Thomas put one bottle down and tucked the magazines under his arm. He examined the other bottle for a moment, then twisted it open and took a healthy swig. "Ahhsshh!" he uttered through clenched teeth, then smiled again. "No problem, mon. No problem. Get your gear an' put it in da Jeep. I take you around to da best damn camping site for da best damn diving." Holding the bottle, he flipped open a Playboy and let the centerfold fall out, admiring it with a shake of his head. "Dat wooman spent one night with da black snake of Thomas Harcord, she never want a white boy again. Ooooohhh, she come live on da beach, eat turtle soup an' diddle with Thomas day and night."

"Until I catch you with her white ass and cut off that skinny needlefish of yours with my bait knife," yelled an older, but not unattractive black woman coming over the sand dunes by the beach, carrying a plastic gallon pail.

Thomas flinched. "Lordy!" he muttered. "Dat damn woman got radar! I just think about another girl an' she appear out a' nowhere like some damn Juju spirit an' wanna prune me to da stump."

Modeen Harcord, long hair held up by a colorful scarf, dressed in a soft, white cotton shift and sandals, smiled at the description despite herself. Her face was austere at the moment, but it didn't deny the ageless beauty underneath—regal slim nose, intuitive eyes, and an engaging, albeit perturbed smile. She walked over and shook a finger somewhat sternly. "It still be mornin', Thomas Harcord! You put dat damn bottle away, or dat damn snake not gonna be no good for nobody by sunset." Without missing a beat she turned to us. "You boys got dope in dat plane? 'Cause if you do—"

"No, Mama, no," said Thomas, putting his hands up in entreaty. "Dey be friends of Mr. Robert. Dey wanna dive."

"Humph," she replied, rolling her eyes with just a touch of drama. "Oh yeah. Dat make sense. I can see dey got liquor and pictures of naked white women for you, just like dat smooth-talking Robert Bunter." She stepped over to us and shook her finger again, but I could see the humor in her eyes. "Why don't you boys get together and just bring him a white woman, so he can get dis out of his system."

"Oh, Mama, dat-dat not necessary," Thomas stammered. "I don' need … You da one—"

"Oh, you damn right dat not necessary, you nappy-headed fool!" said Modeen, really hitting a roll. "I catch you with another woman—I don' care if she be paisley-colored—you gonna be able to drink all you want, 'cause dere ain't gonna be no dog in your pants ta' bark at strangers." She turned to us and suddenly winked. "Get your gear in dat Jeep. Give dat damn fool somethin' to do."

"Yes, ma'am," Will and I said in harmony.

Thomas took us to a little sand cove about a quarter-mile west of his house, which was an older but well-maintained gray conch home with a widow walk, white shutters, and a weathered, friendly front porch that looked out over the sea. Another half mile east of his place lay the little Bahamian village. As we reached the cove he looked over at me. "I ain't no damn pilot, mon, but watchin' dat landing, it look to me like you gonna have a tough time gettin' outta dat strip."

I nodded. "Yeah, it looks a little tight. Maybe too tight, if we're loaded with water and fish too."

"Yeah, man," said Will as he leaned forward from the back of the Jeep. "We'd hate to mess up your sand dune with our airplane."

Thomas smiled while steering along the rutted dirt road. "I'll see 'bout gettin' da dozer out tomorrow—push it down before you take off. I don' need no damn broken airplanes litterin' my island."

As we were unloading our dive tanks and equipment bags from the Jeep, I saw a cat peek a head over the dune behind us—there for a moment, then gone. A few minutes later, as Thomas helped us organize our campsite, the cat, a young calico with orange stripes on her sides, appeared on the dune again, just sitting there watching us.

Thomas glanced over and saw me looking at the little feline. "Don' know how dat animal survives. She won't come to us, an' it's a damn miracle someone here ain't thrown her in a pot before now and ate her skinny ass."

The creature, indifferent to the conversation, sat and watched us with curious, chartreuse eyes.

The campsite had been used many times before. There was a nice coral-ringed fire pit, a latrine had been dug a discrete distance from the camp, and a flat area had been cleared just below the dunes but above the tide line for a tent. We had just finished gathering a little driftwood for the fire and Thomas was preparing to head home, when around the bend came a bevy of four young Bahamian girls carrying plastic buckets. They were working the craggy shallows for conch and lobster, wading in and reaching down under ledges and coral pockets. They wore short, cotton sarong wraps around their waists and a typical Caribbean cotton wrap across their breasts. Their dark skin, moist from seawater, glistened in the sun as they bantered with each other, lithely stretching like sleek felines, bending down, reaching into the water …

Will and I had stopped what we were doing and were observing the wiles of nature. The girls looked up at us and waved, and I was suddenly reminded of the Haitian paintings I had seen in Key West gift shops—svelte mahogany figures, long-limbed and supple, complemented by vibrant colors, posed knee deep in the clear, lucent waters of the Caribbean.

It was one of those rare moments that the subconscious captures and puts away, to present you with when you least expect it, maybe twenty years forward, when you really need it.

There was a short burst of chatter about us, and a round of intimate laughter, then the girls moved on their way, glancing back occasionally. But there was one who paused and turned around, gazing at Will—clearly at Will. She was probably no more than 18, yet by anyone's standards she was lovely—satiny, milk chocolate skin, high cheekbones and full lips that were her African/Caribbean heritage, and a slim, young figure just beginning to ripen into maturity. But it was her eyes that were so striking. They were a hazel green, like languid river pools at the edge of the sea, and they were remarkable conversationalists. The message to Will was crystal clear. Only the time and place were yet to be established. With a final glance, full of promise, she reluctantly turned away and caught up with her friends.

Old Thomas didn't miss any of that conversation either. He went over and put his arm around Will's shoulders. "How much trouble you really want in your life, boy?"

"As little as possible while getting as much as I can," said Will with a grin.

Thomas shook his head. "Tell your little dog to pass on this one. Do not sit up, do not bark, mon." Thomas suddenly got serious. "Trust me on this, as one who knows when to bark and when not to. You want plenty bad Juju, this is an easy place to find it. Catch your fish and go home. Plenty other time for moonlight diddlin'."

Will shrugged. "Yeah, okay. Maybe you're right." But he was still staring at the tall girl with the hazel green eyes—moist with heat, like the jungle after a rain.

The girls drifted on, Thomas returned home to Modeen, and we went diving—and what an experience it was. Just when you're becoming a little jaded, when you begin to feel you've seen the better part of it, The Good Lord offers you a spectacular reminder.

We donned our gear, waded into the water, and slipped beneath the surface as soon as it was deep enough. In moments the sandy ocean floor moved gently down into a gin clear abyss, and in thirty feet of water we were surrounded by hundreds of huge orange coral heads—like monstrous mushrooms in tales of Alice. Gorgonia and sea fans swayed in constant ballet with the current while hundreds of iridescent tropicals descended on us in seething waves, only to be shattered into perfectly synchronized, gaily colored shards by the noise of our regulators. It was nature's own accompaniment to Pink Floyd music. As we moved deeper I noticed that the coral heads around us were alive with primarily one variety of fish—the prestigious Royal Gramma. Three and four-inch purple and yellow flashes zipped across the weathered coral seeking protection in a constant game of musical holes. We had found what we came for.

We stretched the air in our tanks for the better part of an hour and a half, working from one coral head to the next, sliding deeper into the darkening chasm. Finally, when our nets were churning with purple and gold and our air had thinned, we came to the drop-off Thomas had told us about—the true abyss—a wall that descended vertically into blue-black nothingness. We knew that's where the Black Caps would be, along that wall. We knew there were other things down there as well—things that danced to da-da, da-da, da-da.

I pointed toward the shore. Will nodded in emphatic agreement. We had just turned toward the island when I suddenly caught a glimpse of something…deep down … big and gray… just a glimpse. I was very pleased to be headed back to shore.

We slipped off our flippers and unstrapped our tanks in the light surf, then walked out onto the beach next to the campsite. The first thing I noticed was the cat. The same calico was perched above my bedroll, curled in the sand, staring at us with those almost phosphorescent eyes. We quickly transferred our catch to some sturdy plastic screen nets we had brought with us, tying them to coral outcroppings in about four feet of water. The cages would float, allowing circulation and protection. Surprisingly enough, when we slipped out of our wetsuits and moved up to the camp, the calico refused to give up her perch near my sleeping bag. Only when I came over to her did she reluctantly surrender and move off cautiously. She stopped about twenty feet away and stared again.

"It's okay, baby," I said soothingly. "You can hang around if you want." She looked up at me and trilled, deep in her throat, still sitting there.

As we started to prepare a meager supper of sandwiches and potato chips, Thomas and Modeen showed up with a barbecued chicken and two huge baked yams. The sun was just a notch above the horizon, streaking the long, white ribbons of stratus clouds that stretched out across the dome of the sky, with rose and violet pastels.

Thomas, attired in his formal evening shorts and a baggy T-shirt, smiled. "So, I be glad to see you boys still here. Didn't go chasin' no mermaids instead of diving, huh?" There was just a hint of J&B bliss to his voice.

Modeen put the chicken, wrapped in tinfoil, by the fire and smoothed down her soft, white cotton shift. "You boys put dem damn white bread bologna sandwiches away and eat dis chicken. It much betta' for you. Give you enough strength to snatch dem tiny fish an' chase mermaids."

Thomas shook his head. "Oh, Mama. Don' be encouragin' dees boys. Don' be encouraging 'em. Dat Islamora Bensen already been by making hot eyes at Will here. He don' need dat kind of luck."

Modeen listened, nodding in agreement. She looked at Thomas and tilted her head at Will. "Does he know who she belong to? Has he been told da number of minutes it gonna take him to lose his hairy little lizard after he touches her?" She swung around at Will. "Let me talk to you for a moment, you hungry little horn-dog. Dat girl you saw is da daughter of Umbouki Bensen—da local witch docta, if you will. He da head of dem *Santeria* people in da village. Dat crazy sucka one step away from a leopard skin and a spear. He got enough bad Juju in him to scare da pus out a leg boil. One a dem boys in da village tried playin' hide da lizard wit' Islamora. Now he just sits on da rocks on da west end, looks at his pants and cries. Don' be stupid boy. Don' be stupid. Plenty other mangoes in da basket."

Will lowered his sandwich thoughtfully and shrugged. "Gee, how was I to know? She just walked by and sort of offered an invitation."

"So, you decline, like da 'telligent boy you are," Modeen said. Then she smiled and winked again. "Sometimes you gotta have help siftin' da good ones from da bad ones." She jabbed a thumb at Thomas. "Dat's what I hadda do for dis good lookin', curly-headed fool."

Thomas smiled sheepishly.

Modeen glanced over toward my bedroll and changed the subject adroitly. "I see you makin' a friend dere." The calico was back, curled next to my sleeping bag. "Cats be damn smart creatures," she said. "Dey know good Juju from bad in folks. You two boys must be okay souls. Maybe old souls." She took a look at the sun, which was just slipping over the rim of the world, smearing the sky in brilliant crimson, and sighed. "Com'n Thomas, let's go finish our walk and let dese young folks eat dere meal in peace and put all dis beauty in da back of dere heads, so dey can see it years from now, when it'll be a damn site more important to 'em."

As they walked away, hand in hand, I realized Modeen Harcord was a beautiful, damn smart woman. I should be so lucky someday.

We ate our chicken quietly—the three of us. The cat had come down to share a bite, and I was able to touch her for the first time.

She was young, maybe a year old, and highly vocal. She purred contentedly when I touched her, arching her back to my hand, trilling softly while she ate a handful of chicken. Afterwards, she settled in the sand beside me and we watched the Caribbean evening steal in, slowly turning the clear, aquamarine water to somber gray and charcoal. The wind surrendered in that brief hiatus between night and day, graceful black and white egrets gave up on the baitfish in the shallows and winged above us in silent silhouettes as they sought high refuge amongst the mangrove and buttonwood, and we were enveloped in the still, winsome fragrance of sea and sand—another indelible moment.

We built up the fire and watched a huge full moon, incandescent as a lantern, rise out of the sea and creep up into the heavens. As that ancient orb slid in and out from behind coveys of wistful gray clouds, we talked of the day's adventures, laying plans for the following morning. Will produced a pint of Southern Comfort, which we shared, adding to the euphoria. Our plans were to dive for a few more hours, using our second tanks, then snorkel a little. By early afternoon we'd pack the fish into ice chests with minimal water, load the plane and head home.

The silver moon continued its ascent as night breezes lifted the heat from the air, and our Southern Comfort provided the last of the intoxication. I don't even remember falling asleep.

I do, however, remember waking up. It was two in the morning. The moon had peaked and was descending, but when it drew away from the clouds, its luminescence still brightened the sand and sea like daylight. But it wasn't the moon that woke me—it was the drums. There was a distant tempo—a soft hypnotic rhythm carried by the breeze from the heart of the island, and there were voices above it—strange discordant harmonies chanted in phrases first carved along the primal trails of Africa, forged in the bellies of slave ships, and refined by a thousand night fires hidden in the jungles of Haiti, Jamaica, Rotan, and Cuba.

"Hey Will, you hear that?" I mumbled.

There was no answer. I sat up and looked around. My friend was gone. By his bed, in the sand, was a single yellow hibiscus—the same type of flower Islamora Benson had in her hair when she passed by our camp. As I sat there, more than a little angry that Will had set out on a night of nooky without at least letting me know, I noticed the cat was gone as well. I waited for a half hour, listening to the drums, calling cautiously into the darkness around the periphery of the camp, but there was no response. Finally, still upset that I was the one losing sleep and not the one getting laid, but becoming a little concerned as well, I put on my tennis shoes and set off toward the drums. The moon crested the clouds for just a moment and its brilliance rolled across the landscape of deserted beach and Australian pines like a searchlight. Suddenly the drums stopped and there was an eerie stillness broken only by the soft lapping of gentle waves against the sand, and the distant, high chanting…

About five minutes later I was passing by Thomas' house on the beach path when a figure rose from an old chair on the porch. Already a little on edge, it was enough to startle me to a yelp. I heard the smile in Thomas's voice.

"What you doin' out dere, boy?"

I really didn't know how much to tell him. In the distance, the drums started again.

Thomas shook his head. "Dis ain't a good time for white boys to be wanderin' around in da dark. Dem natives is plenty restless tonight."

I took a deep breath and exhaled. "I woke up half an hour ago and Will was gone. I think he's met up with Islamora."

"Dat one damn stupid horn-dog, I tell you," muttered Thomas, looking off into the distance toward the drums, the smile lines in his countenance fading to a frown. "If dey caught him with Islamora, somebody gonna be missin' valuable appendages."

I could hear the concern in his voice.

"You need to find dat horn-dog, slap him in da head and get him back to his own sleepin' bag." There was a pause. "I jus' take care of dis island, mon. I don' got no control over dem crazy people."

The wind had come up a bit, whipping my hair and shirt. Lightning in the cumulus on the water to the east showed signs of an approaching storm. I nodded. "I understand. Well, I gotta go."

"Good luck, boy," he said, almost in a whisper.

As I began to trek down the beach again, the drums stopped abruptly, followed by a collective cry from the voices. There was something about that cry, almost a statement of finality that made the hair on my arms stand up. Robert Bunter's words suddenly danced into my head. "They're into sacrifices—chickens and small animals."

"C'mon Kansas," I muttered, chiding myself. "This isn't a Tarzan movie."

When I rounded the point on the beach, ten minutes from Thomas, I could see the bonfire in the distance. Just off the beach, fifty yards from a stand of huge banyan trees that prefaced a long stretch of mangroves curving around the east side of the island, there were twenty or thirty figures moving around the fire.

As I turned inland with the intention of coming out from the mangroves, I began to try to get a grip on all that was taking place. I suddenly realized that I could easily be making more of this than was necessary. If a bunch of villagers wanted to get together and dance in the moonlight it really wasn't my business. Even if they lopped off the head of a chicken or two, it still wasn't my business. I shook my head and grumbled. "That son of a bitch is probably on the beach somewhere, getting royally laid, while I tromp through the mangroves looking for him."

Nonetheless, I stayed in the mangroves as I moved closer to the fire. The stand of Banyan trees was off to the left of the dancers. Apparently, a crude alter had been constructed from a dozen lobster traps stacked on top of each other in steps. At the top stood a man, between two traps, wearing a red toga, held together by a shell clasp on the shoulder. He was tall and thin, almost skeletal, and the heat of the fire made his ebony skin sheen. His hand rested atop a heavy, knotted, buttonwood staff. His head was shaved and his eyes, though drawn and hollow, had the same wild, hazel green fire as his daughter's. He looked like a character out of a Bela Lugosi movie produced by Spike Lee.

The dancers, clothed in white smocks, swayed around the fire as if lost to trance, undulating inward and outward from the flames, chanting in cadence to their movement.

I stared hard through the darkness and the glow of the fire but I couldn't find Will. Certain now that he had slipped away with his prize and was boarding her at his leisure, I smiled and started to turn back toward camp. But at that moment I caught a glimpse of a familiar figure amid the shadows of the banyan trees—tall and thin, very close to naked, with a very awkward posture. Something was definitely amiss. I worked my way around the mangroves, closer to the stand of trees while Umbouki Benson shouted ritualistic shibboleths at the moon and prepared to decapitate a chicken. The dancers were still lost to rapture. I moved quietly forward.

There was Will, no clothes, his hands tied behind his back, but that wasn't the worst of it. They (I assumed Umbouki) had taken a light string, like packaging twine, looped it around Will's vulnerable undercarriage and pulled it tight, then tied it tautly to a stake that had been hammered into the ground between his legs. Another piece of twine was bound firmly around the same location—tight enough to question the probability of future generations, and tied to a tree, high and taut enough to very nearly keep him on his toes. There was a long, sharp knife stuck in the tree—definitely a bad omen. I started to move out of the mangroves toward my friend, when I saw the massive sentry leaning against the tree only a few feet from Will, watching the ceremony.

Suddenly the drums stopped, the chicken screeched and lost its head.

"Okay, okay," I whispered nervously to myself. "I need a plan—a quick plan." I could see there were two more chickens in the cage by the altar. It appeared I had a little time before the main act. The drums commenced that "Zanzibar" rhythm again and the dancers slowly started undulating to the tempo. I made a quick decision, slipped back into the buttonwoods and set out at a run to the west, through the sparse mangroves toward the airplane.

The furtive moonlight cast distorted shadows on the harsh coral ground. More than once I lost my balance, paying with the flesh on my knees and hands. Craggy arms of mangrove and buttonwood reached at me, clawing at my clothes and skin, and the summer mosquitoes set on me with a vengeance, but in a few moments I reached the high, clear ground of the island and set a quick pace for the plane. Once again, clouds swallowed the moon and I ran in darkness for the next few minutes, crossing the runway and almost stumbling into the aircraft in my haste. She sat there on the coral strip like a huge night bird, tethered to the palms, waiting patiently. I quickly found a water jug and drained a gallon of fuel into it from the right wing tank. I grabbed the portable radio in the back seat of the aircraft and two minutes later I was on the run again, this time headed to the west of the *Santeria* reunion. I remembered seeing a huge pile of driftwood just off the beach about 150 yards from Umbouki's weenie roast.

I arrived at the driftwood pile panting heavily, spent—overexertion getting the better of adrenalin. I caught my breath for a moment, then pulled the lid from the bottle of fuel. As I prepared to pour the contents on the driftwood, someone stepped out from behind the pyre.

"Aahhhgh," I cried, dumping gas on myself.

"What da hell you doin' now, boy?" muttered Thomas. "I think maybe you spend too much time under da water, breathin' bad air."

"Man, glad to see you," I gasped, "Ombouki has him—about to make him a Cabaret singer. Gotta help."

Thomas's brow furrowed as he gave me a questioning look. "Cabaret?" Then he put the package together. "Hmmm, Cabaret... Not good." He looked at the jug in my hand, then glanced at the driftwood—a very quick study. "Okay, mon. I pour da gas an' start da fire, then turn da radio up loud as it goes. Dat oughta get deir attention. But I'm not stayin'. When da show starts, you gonna have to grab your boy, get to dat damn airplane and get outta here. You hear? Don't worry 'bout your gear; I'll gather it up for you an' save it."

I paused for just a moment and stared at him. "Thomas," I whispered. "I know you're taking a chance doing this. I just want you to know that... I think you're way too cool for this island."

Thomas gave me that wide-mouthed, Colgate grin of his and said, "Maybe dis island way too cool for me—you know, it always teachin' me things, mon." He straightened up. "Okay. Ain' no way aroun' but through it. Get goin'." He put out his hand, which I shook, and held for a moment.

"Thanks, Thomas."

In the next minute, I was running hard across the island, through the mangroves toward the stand of buttonwoods and banyans near the fire. Behind me I could see the flames licking up the driftwood, sparks crackling and exploding upward, sending showers of glowing embers into the darkness, and I could hear the sounds of Jethro Tull's "Aqualung" ripping asunder the still summer night.

In the shuffling madness of the locomotive breath,
Runs the all-time loser, headlong to his death.

By the bonfire, the rhythm of the drums faltered, falling out of meter, and halted. Umbouki came to his feet slowly, staring out into the darkness, listening. His dancers wavered and slowed. A swift gust of wind blew through the gathering, and in the distance, lightning arched out of somber clouds and seared the sea. The chickens clucked nervously. Everyone, including Umbouki, turned toward the flames and noise in the distance. Once again the wind rose and brushed the gathering, carrying the lyrics:

He hears the silence howling—catches angels as they fall.
And the all-time winner has got him by the balls...

Umbouki snorted in anger. He raised his staff and with a shout, he and his minions, including Will's guard, turned *en masse* and charged into the darkness after that brazen interloper, Jethro Tull.

A moment later, I stole up silently from behind Will. He, too, was absorbed by the distraction.

"Hey!" I whispered to him.

My partner jumped, muffling a scream as the twine bit. He turned, and his eyes widened. "Oh, man! Am I glad to see you."

"Yeah," I scoffed. "I'm real glad to see you too. I've been crawling all over this bloody island trying to find you while you've been using your dick for a compass."

I nodded at his groin. "Little uncomfortable there, Marco Polo?"

"What do you think?"

"Why didn't you just tell her no?" I smiled. "Sounds like a song …"

"Lord!" he moaned, exasperated. "Give it a rest, Elvis, and get me out of here!"

"Don't get testy with me. I'm not the one with my lizard tied to a tree. I'm not the main act at the class of '63 *Santeria* reunion and midnight weenie roast."

"Are you done?" Will whined under his breath, just a little past impatient.

"Almost. Can you say, eunuch?"

I pulled the knife from the tree and cut the twine binding his wrists. As Will untied himself, I looked down and saw a burlap bag off to the side of the tree. Something inside it moved. "What's in there?"

Will was still in the process of freeing himself somewhat delicately. He glanced at the bag. "It's the cat. The calico. She followed me and Islamora—they took us both."

I reached over and touched the bag. She trilled anxiously from inside.

Will nodded. "She was gonna be the warm-up act."

"Not gonna happen," I said as I snatched up the bag and turned to my friend, who had found his shorts and was pulling them on. "Okay, lover boy, it's time to streak like never before. We're headed for the plane and we're not stopping for a beer, a Snickers bar, or to get laid. We're getting out of here. Because if those folks catch us before I get that damned thing in the air, there'll be no more barkin' dogs in our pants—ever." I paused and let that sink in, more than just a little frightened, and angry. "You ready?"

Will nodded. "Man, am I ready. Let's book." Still, he paused for a moment and shook his head. "But I gotta tell you, man—that Islamora—Lord, that's something else. Do you know she can actually—"

"Would you just save it!" I hissed. "I don't want a—" Will had stopped in mid-sentence, looking behind me, his mouth slightly agape, eyes displaying a little more concern than I was comfortable with. I turned, and there was Umbouki, with the huge Bahamian who had been guarding Will. Lightning flashed again, closer, and the first fat droplets of warm summer rain pelted us.

Umbouki smiled menacingly and brought his staff around with both hands. The big guy, who looked like "The Midnight Mauler" on Saturday Night Wrestling, flexed, and the firelight reflected off his muscles as he took a step forward, slightly to Umbouki's left.

Neither Will nor I were wusses, but we weren't really fighters either. We'd always been big on talking our way out of things. Somehow I didn't see that as an option here. But there were times I forgot how clever Will was. He used to say, "You have to be able to think in 3-D."

Will took a quick glance at the position of the sentry and deliberately stepped into range of Umbouki's staff. "I figure you're about to kick my ass anyway, so I just want you to know that your daughter is possibly the best piece of ass I've ever had. Do you know she can actually—"

The gaunt man with the heavy buttonwood staff roared incoherently and swung at Will with no other thought than crushing that white boy's skull. Will, on the other hand, had planned on that. When the staff came whizzing at him, he ducked with perfect timing, dropping down and grabbing a handful of fine beach sand.

But there was no stopping the malevolence and momentum in that swing, which didn't slow an iota until it impacted the big guard's forehead. The staff snapped cleanly in half, one piece sailed off into the darkness toward the beach. The fellow was lifted completely off his feet, almost horizontally, before he dropped to the sand like a sack of cement. Umbouki was left there, astounded. He no longer had a weapon and no longer had backup, but he wasn't out for the count. He drew himself up, holding what was left of his club preparing to do battle, but Will was way ahead of the curve. He rose and hurled the handful of sand into Umbouki's face. The Bahama Bela Lugosi dropped his stick and brought his hands to his eyes with a cry, momentarily blinded. Will stepped in and kicked him in the groin hard enough to ensure him a part in *The Barber of Seville* (we're talking falsetto for months.) Umbouki grunted, his eyes got that Daffy Duck bulge, pain edging out surprise, and he crumpled to the ground with a low moan, like someone had let the air out of him.

I shook my head and smiled. "Dude, sometimes you absolutely amaze me."

"Yeah, well, I think I may have over-amazed myself this time,"

Will muttered, looking a little pale. "I think I need to puke."

"Save it until we get to the plane, wild man," I said as I clutched the burlap bag with both hands. "Let's blow this place, dude. Run!"

The driftwood/radio diversion was to the southwest of us, near the beach. The airplane was northwest of us toward the center of the island. If the folks at the sacrificial beach party figured out what we were up to, they wouldn't have to run far to catch us. It all came down to reaching the plane and getting out as quickly as possible. There was one other somewhat significant situation—the ten-foot sand dune smack dab in the middle of the runway.

Adrenalin does wonderful things to the body. We ran like two greyhounds on crack. Small trees, bushes, mangroves, and the steady slap of rain didn't even slow us. By the time we neared the plane, I had a much better understanding of Jethro Tull's locomotive breath. My lungs seared with every gasp, my heart painfully slapped my ribs with each beat, and my legs were becoming "double tequilas" rubbery. The roaring in my ears was so loud I was certain Will could hear it. Will's heaving was just as audible, but he wasn't breaking his pace by much. This was not a race we could afford to lose.

Finally, we pushed through the last of the buttonwood and there it was—our *Pegasus,* waiting to be unleashed from the palms and deliver us from our misadventures. Staggering the last stretch, we untied the tethers, wrenched open the doors and piled in. I tossed the cat onto the back seat, where she complained bitterly, but there was no time for amenities. Will set the NAV while I primed the engine and cranked it over. The storm began to rise over the end of the island. Jagged bolts of lightning lanced hotly through the distant cumulus, lighting them up iridescently from the inside out. I glanced over at Will nervously. "You okay, buddy?"

Despite it all, he smiled. "Yeah. Yeah, I am," he said determinedly. And then his smile softened and warmed. "Thanks, Kan—for back there."

I paused, realizing for a moment how deep and powerful our friendship was.

He got that Lee Marvin grin, reading me without effort. "Don't get all warm and fuzzy on me now. Just fly the damned plane and get us out of here!"

I chuckled. "Yes, sir!" I pushed in the throttle and the roar of the engine drowned the steady, rhythmic pop of rain against the hull and windshield, lending a sense of security to the inside of the fragile aluminum and Plexiglas pod we were about to force out into a raging storm and the dark, pearled sky. Swinging the plane around to the very back of the strip, to give us as much running room at the sand pile as possible, I straightened out, checked the magnetos, then slammed the throttle to the wall and stood solidly on the brakes, creating every ounce of energy. The engine screamed and the aircraft was vibrating so badly the cowling rivets were dancing in their sockets. I was just about to release the brakes and shoot down the strip when lightning struck not fifty feet from us. As I shrieked and glanced over to make sure the wing was still there, a second bolt hammered even closer, and suddenly in the midst of the eerie blue blast, the last person I ever wanted to see rose up like a specter against my window.

The rain laid Umbouki's coarse hair flat to his head, and beaded off his face. His green eyes bulged with a touch of additional madness (as if being regularly crazy just wouldn't do). He also wielded a new club—a heavy, gnarled-looking thing that appeared as if he'd personally wrenched it out of the heart of a living tree. When he began bludgeoning the plane, smashing the cowling and cracking the windshield, I'll admit I screamed, and I'm not ignoring the possibility that I might have wet my pants. He'd have probably beaten us apart like an old blue crab, had he not become quite so Quixotic. After another slash at the cockpit, he turned those crazy eyes to the rapidly whirling prop. I guess we all have our windmills...

With a howl, he stumbled forward in the rain to do battle with three blades being pushed at maximum revolutions by a 150 horsepower engine. He raised his club, screamed, and swung. The result was a lot like putting a toothpick in a blender. The moment the club struck the prop there was a resounding explosion. In the blink of an eye, there was no club left to speak of, just small fragments stuck here and there—embedded in the ground, the trees, the plane, and last but not least, good old Umbouki. Our crazed antagonist was hurled away by the impact like an ugly little Umbouki doll. He wasn't dead, but he had suffered a sufficient number of embedded splinters to keep him occupied with needle-nosed pliers and a bottle of iodine for weeks. He lay there in the rain, the muck, and the blood, yelling at us in falsetto, those crazy green eyes following us as I let go of the brakes and we shot down that strip like we'd been catapulted.

Still, the dirt mound seemed to be coming up a lot faster than I had figured, and the damned rain was making it difficult to judge distance. I glanced over at Will. Never taking his eyes off the strip, he gritted through clenched teeth, "Now would be a good time to show me that trick, buddy."

It was all a roll of the dice at that point—the luck was there, or it wasn't.

The moon cleaved the clouds for a moment and we could see the sand dune as it charged up at our windshield with uncanny speed. I threw twenty degrees of flaps, jerked back the controls, and blinked. Lightning struck again and in the midst of the electric blue corona that seemed to inundate the moment, I noticed, in a very calm, second person fashion, that the plane had bounced into the air and popped right over the sand dune with room to spare. Unfortunately, the trick hop had cost us the momentum we needed for flight and we were settling back down on the other side. The last of the runway was rapidly evaporating into a marshy swath of mangroves that ended abruptly at a small, 50-foot cliff descending into the sea. Swarthy, sullen clouds swallowed the moon again, enveloping us in darkness. Blinding rain continued to slash at the windshield. I could feel the plane sinking and my gut tightening. If I pulled up there was a fifty-fifty chance we would stall.

The ancient moon broke through a patch of hazy gray clouds and showered the somber landscape in chartreuse just as the stall buzzer screamed in our ears. The wheels of the plane scraped the tops of the taller mangroves, then we sailed off the cliff, plunging toward the dark sea with the stall buzzer still shrieking. As the bitter bile of fear rose in my throat, Will turned toward me, desperately holding onto the last vestiges of cool.

"Go for it, Kansas!" he whispered. Then louder, "Go for it!"

I pushed the controls forward for a second, the buzzer stopped, and I pulled back. There was a terrifying moment of silence as the ocean rushed up at us, punctuated only by a brief expletive from Will. Just when I was certain we were destined to be a part of tomorrow's gruesome news, a gust of wind caught our wings not ten feet from the water and the old girl began to fly, slowly rising up toward the distant moon. We howled with delight and defiance as I drew the aircraft upward, climbing toward the center of that timeless bauble in God's own mobile, and we were gone—lost to the glow of green cheese.

An hour later we broke through the storm into the still clarity of a dark summer sky laced with sparkling celestial gems. Again, our friend the moon lit the course toward the narrow band of tarmac that was Marathon Airport. It had never looked so inviting.

It was almost dawn when we finally got back to Big Pine, so we cleaned up a little and let the cat out of the bag. After all she'd been through, we were afraid she might freak out and disappear, so we released her in the living room. The little calico shook herself, looked around for a moment, then hopped up in the lounge chair by the television. She glanced at me and trilled, deep in her throat, then settled into the chair and began to preen herself, as if she'd been there all along. It was the beginning of my understanding of just how cool cats actually are.

Will grabbed a couple of beers and we found our way to the lawn chairs by the sea wall. The last of a waxen moon was surrendering to the dawn, fading into the deepening hues of a pale morning sky. A vibrant summer sun shimmered out of the eastern horizon, melting the distant haze with yellows and reds, silhouetting the stands of palms at the end of the canal. It was simply spectacular and I couldn't help it. I sighed like a teenager. I was home, and safe again, after another preposterous adventure. While we enjoyed the pleasure of a perfect Caribbean sunrise, Will took a sip of his beer and quietly asked, "Do you think we should be writing this stuff down?"

I smiled without humor and shook my head. "Nah, I don't think so. Nobody would believe it."

"Yeah, you're probably right. Just a night's entertainment."

I took a sip of my beer, still staring at the sunrise. "So, tell me about Islamora."

CHAPTER NINE

Revenge, Rescue, and Pyramid Power

With the exception of our little adventure on Cay Sal Island, the remainder of 1974 was relatively uneventful. Even the rest of the world seemed to ebb for a while. There were, of course, a few events that caught our attention. Nineteen-year-old Patty Hearst, heir to the William Hearst fortune, was kidnapped by the Symbionese Liberation Army. I could only surmise that after forming their organization they couldn't find any Symbionese to liberate, so they took up kidnapping and bank robbing. I always thought it was a shame they never ran into our Costa Rican buddy, Sundance. I'm certain he would have added an interesting dimension.

That same year, President Nixon resigned after White House tapes proved he had obstructed justice in the Watergate investigation. Shortly after assuming the presidency, Gerald Ford, confusing his position with that of the Pope, granted a pardon for Nixon, then declared an amnesty for Vietnam deserters and draft evaders. During that summer, the marijuana business in South Florida took a quantum leap. More folks than ever decided to take their fishing boats south for a quick visit with the mango man. Some were getting rich—some were getting time. Our attorney friend Justin Mames made the Miami Herald on a couple of occasions—once for a big pot case he was defending, and once for being arrested as a co-conspirator and an accessory to the importation of illicit substances. He won the noted trial and beat the charges against him without working up a sweat. He was becoming a big name in a lot of circles.

Beyond those items, there was only one other event that caught our attention. It wasn't as momentous as some of the news that year, but Will and I found it intriguing.

While excavating what was thought to be an ancient Incan mining shaft in Peru, South America, archeologists broke into a narrow underground chamber and discovered a small, solid gold pyramid. It had six-inch sides, and most remarkably, the top third was comprised of a perfectly cut, flawless emerald—the third largest ever found. The pyramid was mounted atop a two-foot-square base of solid marble (of a geological strata not found in South America) and was estimated to be over ten thousand years old, but it was discovered within a culture thought to be no older than two thousand years. Needless to say, the find initiated reverberations in archeological communities throughout the world, and most everyone found the story alluring. But for anyone who had ever found a crafted piece of precious metal shaped by the ancient hands of another time, the tale was purely fascinating. Will and I, of course, fell into that category.

During much of that year we continued to assist our buddy, Nick, with the overflow of shapely cruise mates, who somehow never quite made it to the big cruise. Nonetheless, a good time was had by all. The little calico cat, whom we named Triller, settled in and began to provide one and all with lessons on the feline species. To understand cats you have to speak the language of subtlety, you have to learn boundaries, and patience. You have to accept what you receive in affection, understanding that what you want and what the other is capable of giving may be two different things. You learn to give simply for the pleasure of giving, to satisfy another creature because you like the way it responds to you when you touch it in a certain way. At some point, you come to understand the delicate nuances of appreciation, body language, and a carefully managed sense of emotion.

I discovered that owning a cat should be mandatory for every male at age sixteen. It's the supreme field study on the opposite sex. If you pay attention at all, you come away with volumes of knowledge on care, nurturing, artful communication, and proper approaches to sex (with the girl, not the cat).

They don't like being chased too much. They want to be left alone sometimes, and they want love at their pace and time. Their feelings are easily hurt, but if you don't speak the language of subtlety you'll rarely know when that is. Never hold them so tightly that they feel the need to free themselves—always gently, sometimes firmly, and always part with a caress. And if they move away, let them. It's the only way to assure they'll be back. Cats like things they can't always have. That's why they chase butterflies—because they only get about half of them.

For cats, and women, you want to represent a more difficult than average butterfly.

The winter of '74 –'75 was kinder than most. Temperatures hardly fell below seventy degrees, which made for pleasant diving. During that time, the world news rose a notch in entertainment—Teamster Jimmy Hoffa disappeared (with a little help from his friends). Former Charles Manson follower, Squeaky Fromme, tried unsuccessfully to assassinate President Ford, and that magnificent golden pyramid found less than a year before, was stolen while en route to the Peruvian National Museum. Scientists discovered that it possessed strange electromagnetic properties, most of which no one understood. Watches ran backwards when near it and electronics like radios and telephones received remarkable bursts of energy. But before anyone could determine its real values, it was secreted away. I was certain it had ended up in some hoary, old, fabulously rich collector's mahogany-walled personal showing room.

Summer rolled through without incident and both Will and I were beginning to feel that perhaps our propensity for extraordinary adventures had ebbed a bit. Life appeared to be balancing out. We had just stuffed our hands in our pockets, whistling a little as we strolled along the sidewalk, when, all of a sudden, there was the mother of all pianos.

It was a Friday night in late October. We'd had a good week and decided to burn a little money on dinner, drinks, and women in Key West. We were just on our way out of the door when the phone rang. Motioning Will to wait, I went back inside. It was Brandi, Turtle's wife. She wasn't crying, but she was close.

"Kansas, Turtle didn't come home last night."

"What do you mean, 'didn't come home'? Where did he go?"

She sighed, her voice softly laced with conscience. "We've been having some problems. Nothing major, just a rough spot. He lost his job with the boat builder and hadn't been working real hard on finding another. I said I was going back to cocktail waitressing, and we argued." She took another deep breath. "You know, it's happened before—once or twice. He goes and has a drink or two, then comes back. We make it up to each other in imaginative ways and it's forgotten. But he didn't come home, and I haven't heard from him all day."

Will came through the door and looked at me questioningly. I held up a finger, turning my attention to the phone again. "Where's he go, Brandi?"

She paused. "I guess the usual, you know—the Bull and Whistle, Tony's, The Green Parrot."

"Okay, we're headed into Key West as we speak. We'll check things out, see if we can find him and get him pointed home. I'll give you a call later on."

There was that sigh again. "If you find him, tell him I'm sorry, okay? And tell him to get his ass home."

I explained the situation to Will as we drove south on U.S. 1.

"Doesn't sound like Turtle, to be gone into the next day," said Will, absently drumming his fingers on the steering wheel. "You don't think the magic has worn off, do you?"

I looked at him. "I want you to just picture Brandi in your head for a moment."

"Yeah, right. If he were Liberace, the magic wouldn't have worn off. So, I guess we hit a few bars on Duval and ask a couple questions."

Dressed in our usual evening excursion attire of khaki shorts, flowered tropical shirts, and leather sandals, we grabbed a quick bite to eat at a little open-air Cuban restaurant near the foot of the docks off Mallory Square—savory, spicy chicken buried in steaming mounds of black beans and yellow rice, like a choir of piquant angels in your mouth. We splashed on hot sauce with abandon, savoring each bite as we watched towering cumulus rise out of a distant storm bank, slowly catching the failing sun in pink cotton candy. There was just enough breeze to rustle the palms, and from the jukebox we could hear the soft, melodic strains of Eric Clapton's "I Shot The Sheriff." We washed it all down with a couple of beers, then headed for Duval.

There were two new waitresses at Captain Tony's—very nice, but not informative. No one had seen Turtle last night or that day. One of our connections at the Bull and Whistle said he had seen Turtle the night before—that our boy had been working his way toward seriously drunk—telling a story of some sort about Justin Mames. That made the hair on my neck stand up. We all got away with that little affair because we swore not to tell a soul about it. If it ever got back to Mames… Then the news got worse. Mames and his crew were in town last night. He was beginning to frequent Key West more often again. The word was, Turtle was last seen at the Green Parrot.

We entered the dimly lit saloon and glanced around. There was a handful of regulars seated at the big, oval bar. The rest were spread out around the pool tables in the back. The Parrot's clientele generally consisted of tough old shrimpers, a handful of tourists trying to find "the real Key West," a wave of boisterous, inimitable pot smugglers, and a smattering of undercover narcs attempting to be boisterous and inimitable. It was a fun game and they all played it. Too bad, every once in a while somebody had to lose.

We sat at the bar and ordered drinks. When the bartender came back with our tequilas, Will leaned over, put a ten in his hand and whispered in his ear. The guy—muddy-colored frizzy hair, Dead-Head muscle shirt—looked around carefully, then whispered back. Will nodded, shot his tequila and turned to me as the bartender moved away.

"We got problems. Maybe big problems," he said, looking a little uneasy. "I think we're going to have to quit looking in the bars and start checking hospitals."

I put down my drink. "Whatta you mean hospitals, man?"

Will leaned into me, whispering. "The Bull and Whistle wasn't the only place Turtle told the story, and by the time he got to telling it here, half his audience worked for Mames. Apparently, three or four of them took him for a walk and that was the last anyone saw of him."

"How long ago?"

"About two a.m. What's gonna get done is done in that time. Sure as fire they left him somewhere, beaten up or dead." He paused. "And maybe, by this time, they're looking for us."

We left quietly, by the back door that led out onto a residential section of town. There was a pay phone a block away. The second hospital Will called said they had a badly beaten John Doe. Keeping to the back streets and paralleling Duval, we worked our way back toward the car.

We were about a block from Will's Mustang, passing by an alley, when a voice called out from the darkness, "Hegh, help me, man. Help me."

Will stopped and glanced at me. "Did you hear that, man?

Fairly certain I'd heard that voice before, I took Will's elbow. "You have to trust me. There's nothing in there you want to know about."

I was pulling him away when the voice called out again. "Hegh man, help me, please." Will stopped and turned back, toward the alley.

I sighed, and quickly stepped over to him, grabbing his shirt. "Lets' get the hell out—" Just then Hector Zarapata, lisping Salvadorian-Cuban refugee robber-gone smuggler, evidently gone robber again, stepped from the gloom with a gun. One that possibly had bullets in it this time.

"Don' you make no stinkin' move or I'ne dwenna choot chu six tines, man. Dimme all chur plucking monie!"

Will and I looked at each other in befuddlement. Hector puffed up, eyes wide, waving his gun erratically in front of us. "Don' pluck with me! I'ne a berry dangerous man!"

I squinted into the gloom of the alley. "Didn't you used to work for Justin Mames? What are you doing out on the street robbing people—again?"

Hector exhaled angrily, looking up and away, raising his hands dramatically. "Chu make one stinkin' little mistake—lose a little pot—and he wants to choot chur plucking head off."

Will nodded. "How much pot did you lose?"

Hector puffed up again, waving the gun in Will's direction. "It's none a' chur buisiness, man." He got quiet. Then he opened up. "Eight bales of Colombian Gold, man. (Hands/gun in the air again.) It wasn' my fault. We were in bad seas, gettin' chased by da plucking Coasta Guarda, so we dumped de bales to get away. Next day, Mames get all purple, with eyes bulgin', look like he dwenna give birth of a goat from his rectum. Then he's yellin' how he duenna have me chot—says I cost him sixty beeg ones. While they havin' a beeg conperence on a special deal, I slip away fron' de guard and get out batroom window."

Suddenly, he was gun-waving angry again. "Enough of dis confession chit. Dimme el dinero or chu dwenna be dead plenty ahead of me." His eyes went wide again. "I'ne a berry dangerous man!"

"Yeah, yeah, we can see that," said Will without much enthusiasm, which really yanked Hector's chain.

"Chu don' tink I choot chur skinny ass? Chu in for bad stinkin' surprise, man." He raised the gun over his head and pulled the trigger for effect, but nothing happened. Hector pulled again. Still nothing. He brought the gun down, anger and exasperation running neck and neck. But anger took it by a nose. Our Cuban *bandito* brought the gun up aimed between Will and me, and pulled the trigger again. Still nothing. At that point, Hector started doing this weird little frustrated dance around in a circle, stomping his feet and muttering, "Chit! Chit! Chit! Chit!" As he "chitted" loudly he pointed the gun at the sidewalk, and pulled the trigger a few more times. The third time he got the "bad stinkin' surprise" he was referencing earlier. The gun went off and he shot himself in the foot. The .38 made a sizable hole in the top of Hector's shoe. Everything froze. The little Latin's eyes got that look Wile E. Coyote gets just after he's stepped off the cliff. His skin instantly went clammy as he gazed down at the blood oozing out the top of his shoe. "Dod gamnit! I just chot my stinkin' toes off," he whispered in the amazement. "*Mierda*," he mumbled quietly before his knees buckled and he passed out, face first onto the pavement.

The shot was sure to bring people—and the police. I looked around nervously. "Let's get out of here, man."

Will started toward me, then stopped. "Aahhh crap, man. We can't just leave him here. He's bleeding pretty bad, and he'll get arrested."

"Who are you—Florence frigging Nightingale?" I cried, a little louder than I'd planned. "He just tried to rob us, dude! He was going to shoot us!"

"C'mon, Kan. The guy's about as dangerous as Peter Pan. We're headed to the hospital anyway, right? The car's only a block away."

"Okay, okay. But we better wake him up and get the hell out of here or we'll be accomplices to our own robbery."

Will squatted down next to Hector, rolled him over and patted his face, bringing him around. I picked up the gun and threw it as far as I could down the alley. It bounced off the wall and hit the pavement fifty feet away, and went off again. "Whoa!" I yelled involuntarily as we both ducked. Will looked at me with exasperation. I shrugged my shoulders.

Hector came to, eyelids fluttering. "Wha' happen, man?"

"You shot yourself," Will said. "We have to get you to the hospital."

"Ohhh chit." Hector's eyelids fluttered and he was out again.

"Grab his feet, I'll take his arms," ordered Will tersely.

"Ohhh, yeah, I get the end that's bleeding."

Will grabbed Hector under the armpits. "Shut up and lift. Let's get out of here."

We managed to get him down the street and to the car without incident. In Key West, it's not terribly unusual to see a couple of people carrying a comrade who has fallen to the tequila god. The police sirens could be heard in the background as we were shoving Hector into the back seat.

Our little acquaintance was awake when we reached Florida Keys Hospital. We stopped at the emergency entrance and I turned back to him. "We can't go in with you—don't want to be involved. Tell them you accidentally shot yourself."

Hector opened the door, painfully slid his feet out and stood up. He looked back at us and paused. "Chu guys okay. Hector Zarapata neber dwenna rob you again."

Will grinned despite Hector's display of sincerity. "That's a relief. I'm sure we'll both sleep better."

Hector let a small smile escape—more like a grimace—then he was gone, hobbling his way through the emergency room doors.

We drove around front and parked. The nurse at the front desk referred us to room 202. An on-call doctor met us there and we went in. It was Turtle all right, but he had been beaten so badly he was nearly unrecognizable. A crab fisherman had discovered him that morning on the back side of Sand Key. He'd been left in the water by the shoreline—apparently in hopes that the incoming tide would have finished the job.

Seeing him battered and unconscious was frightening, but it made me furious, as well. I knew we could be next, but more than anything, I wanted Justin Mames to pay for what he'd done. I looked at the doctor. "He's our friend. Is he going to be okay?"

The doctor scratched his chin, ruminating. "Yes, I imagine. But it's going to take some time. He's got a concussion, a fractured jaw, and a broken right arm, aside from all the obvious damage. Do you know who did this?"

Will glanced at me.

I looked back to the doctor. "No. I don't."

I called Brandi and a half hour later she was at Turtle's bedside, crying and gently caressing his swollen face. We stayed with them throughout the night. Just after sunrise the following morning, he came around.

Turtle opened his eyes, squinting through puffed and bruised flesh, and saw Brandi. "Where have you been," he whispered. "I hate drinking alone." Brandi burst into tears and threw her arms around him. As she held him, we went over to the bed and he looked up. "I'm sorry," he whispered. "Got drunk and the story just came tumbling out. I liked the way it felt. Everybody really enjoyed the part about Mames…" He chuckled and it ended in a small, painful cough. "Everyone but Mames." He gazed at us and answered the question without our asking. "I guess I mentioned your names a couple of times."

We knew what that meant. Will exhaled hard, ran his hand through his hair nervously, and his blue eyes darkened with concern. There was a sound behind us. Hector Zarapata was leaning against the frame of the doorway, on crutches, foot in a cast. He worked his way in a few feet and stopped, glancing back at the hall, then turning to us, speaking quietly. "I heard chu talking 'bout Mames in de car. I know chu got itssues. I'ne dwenna tell chu sonethin'—sonethin' I heard when I was waitin' to be chot. (Finger to his temple in demonstration, complete with recoil, eyes rolling back.) Mames got a especial chipment coning in on next Tuesday, man. Not drugs—sonethin' *mas importante.* Dey said sonethin' 'bout gold—a lil' gold pyramid—fron Peru, man. Only hin an' his two buddies know about it. I thin' dis berry *importante* to him."

I glanced at Will. "Man, you don't think ..."

My partner nodded emphatically. "I bet it is. The son of a bitch stole it, emerald and all."

Hector came close to a grin again. "Emerald, yeah, it got a emerald. Chu wanna esplode Justin Mames' *cojones?* Chu wanna see him give birth of a goat fron his rectum? Chu get his lil' pyramid. He say tomorrow, fron Bahamas Air Freight to Cayo Hueso."

Will looked at me questioningly.

I shook my head. "No way, man! I'm not stealing anything from Justin Mames, least of all something every bloody law enforcement agency in the world is after."

"For sure, man. I gotta agree." Will said. "I'd like to get that SOB, but right now, I think we should consider a small vacation. All of us." He turned to Brandi. "We need to get Turtle out of here and we all need to book a flight to someplace like Disneyworld—lots of innocuous little motels, loads of indifferent people. Let things cool a bit.

"I like Disneyworld," mumbled Turtle, lost to the nepenthe realms of pain medicine. "Can we go see Mickey?"

There was a pause. Will and I exchanged a glance. He shrugged. "Disney's good. We just need to get this guy a wheelchair and get him discharged."

The next day found us rounding up money, packing clothes, and booking tickets. Key West to Orlando, leaving 5:45 p.m. I called Nick Crow and asked him to take care of Triller and our dog. We packed everyone into our VW bus and made the airport by 5:15—just enough time to check the bags and get to the departure gate. We were pulling into the parking lot when I saw Mames' Mercedes parked by the airfreight concourse. I remembered it from the hypnotherapy sessions at Sunni's. He was here for his prize—a stolen golden pyramid whose creators lived long before the first coral polyp stuck its head above water in what would be the Florida Keys. We got Turtle out of the car and into a wheelchair. Brandi pushed him to the ticket counter. While she was working with the agent on their tickets, I suddenly realized I needed to go to the john. Sometimes I just get peeing nervous. I headed for the restroom at the far end of the small concourse near the bar. I was about to open the bathroom door when I glanced through the glass walls that separated the bar from the lobby, and there was Mames, having a drink with one his bodyguard friends—a big blond guy in blue jeans and a muscle shirt, who looked like he spent most of his time in a gym. Mames was sitting on a stool with his dark hair slicked back, Izod pullover, neatly pressed slacks, and his standard shiny Florsheims, talking casually with his buddy, so damned calm and assured. I knew unequivocally he was going to walk out of that airport with that damned ancient pyramid, and somehow it just really pissed me off. I glanced back down the concourse at my friends, anxiously waiting to flee, and something just snapped. I closed the bathroom door and headed back to Will, Turtle, and Brandi. I walked up to Turtle and asked, "You've got your sleeping pills with you, right?"

Turtle smiled. "Oohh yeaah, man—wonderful little babies. You take one of those, you got about five minutes before you're stupid as a mud duck. Ten minutes later, it's good night sweet prince."

"I need six or eight of them." I turned to Will. "Mames is in the airport bar."

Will straightened up. "I know that look, man. You're gonna go for it, aren't you?"

"Yeah. Unfinished business."

"Then I'm in too, man," Will said. "I'm not lettin' you get ahead of me on the great barroom stories of our lives."

I couldn't help but smile. I knew, sure as the sun rises, that he would be there. I knew the words before he said them. And I suddenly realized that was exactly why I had the courage to take the chance from the onset—because Will would be at my back. "You're gonna miss Mickey and Goofy."

My partner got that crooked grin and shrugged. "Disney World's just a state of mind. You can buy me a couple shots of tequila at Sloppy Joe's when we're done." He turned to Brandi and Turtle. "You guys get on over to your departure gate, enjoy your vacation. Let us know where you are when you get settled."

Turtle shook out half of his sleeping pills into my hand. I put them in my pocket, gave Brandi a hug, and patted Turtle on his good shoulder. "Well, see you soon. Peace."

As we walked away toward the bar, Will leaned over, "I guess you got a plan, right?"

"Yeah, sort of."

"You're not gonna get us killed, are you?"

"Not intentionally."

Will settled into his long-legged gait next to me. "I knew a fellow who once said, 'Revenge is considered a worthy endeavor by almost all religions.'"

I smiled again.

As we walked, I explained what I had in mind. "We'll be relying on Mames not knowing what we actually look like. Now, I noticed the bartender had on a tropical shirt, like mine, so this is what I want you to do…."

When I finished, Will chuckled. "I can do that. This may actually be fun."

I popped a rubber band off an old newspaper on a concourse chair and pulled my long hair back into a ponytail, then tucked in my shirt. Will went into the bar ahead of me and took a seat at a table adjacent to an older, well-dressed couple, obviously wealthy, having a cocktail before take-off. After a moment or two, I followed. It was too early for serious drinking. The small, dimly lit lounge only had a smattering of patrons at the tables. Mames and his partner sat alone at the bar. I came bouncing in and went right over to the bar, sliding under the partition that put me on the bartender's side. He was an older fellow—tallish, hair graying a little on the sides—slightly detached, like he wished he were somewhere else, or maybe someone else. He looked at me, startled.

"Hi! Billy's the name—Billy Ray," I said as I glanced over at the chalkboard roster for the daily bartender shifts, grabbing a name. "Rich won't be in. Actually, he won't be in at all. The boss caught him pouring drinks and pocketing the cash this week."

The guy blanched a little at that. "I'll be taking his shift," I added with a disarming smile.

"Okay," the bartender replied hesitantly. "Chuck," he said, introducing himself.

"Oh, yeah, Chuck," I said picking up a bar towel. "The boss said I was supposed to tell you someone was asking for you at the TWA counter—a friend of yours. Evidently, there's a problem with an I.D. He said get it straightened out and get right back. I can hold the fort for a few minutes."

The fellow didn't seem quite sure what to do. "Asking for me? I don't know anything about—"

I put my hands up, palms out. "Hey, I'm new here. I'm not telling you what to do. I'll go back up and tell him you don't have the time."

"No, no. I'll go," he sighed angrily. "There's always friggin' something. Always something." He put down the towel with which he was drying glasses. "Don't change anything. Don't touch anything but the glasses and the bottles while I'm gone, and don't open the register. I'll be right back."

With the last of the bartender headed out the door, I casually began working my way down the bar to where Mames and his buddy sat. I looked up while polishing a glass, allowing a dawn of recognition on my countenance. "Wow. You're Justin Mames, the famous attorney, aren't you?"

Mames liked that—brought him right around. He nodded, a small smile of ego escaping. "Yeah."

"Man, I've always liked your style," I continued earnestly. "You're your own man. Nobody sets rules for you. I think you'd have been a great mayor for Key West."

He nodded again. "Thanks."

As he turned back to his conversation, I interrupted once more. "Mr. Mames, would you allow me to buy you a drink? It would be my privilege—something I could tell my friends about." He hesitated. "Just one, sir," I picked up quickly. "A shot for all of us." I nodded to his friend, to include him. "Your choice."

Mames was somewhere close to annoyed, but agreed anyway. "Okay. Bacardi Dark."

"Yes sir! Coming right up," I said as I turned to the shelf behind me and pulled out three shot glasses, glancing casually at Will in the far corner.

Will really missed his calling. He should have been an actor. Suddenly, my partner bolted straight up out of his chair, eyes bulging. He dropped his drink on the floor, grabbed his throat with one hand and threw the other straight out as if he was trying to stop a bus, then stumbled stiff-legged into the table with the wealthy older couple. As their drinks went flying, Will fell to his knees, trying to slap himself on the back and making excellent little gasping/wheezing sounds.

The couple lurched from their seats and stood back, staring, aghast. "Wilber, the man's choking!" the woman cried. "He's choking on something!"

Will immediately pantomimed an emphatic nod, shuffling toward them on his knees, one hand out, pleading, the other balled into a fist, hammering himself in the chest.

Will's remarkable demonstration on how not to swallow a foreign or domestic object had the entire room's attention, including Mames and his friend, both of whom had turned away from me, engrossed in the performance. I quickly took out Turtle's pills and dropped three in each of their glasses, crushing them quickly with a spoon. Then I poured the three shots, stirring the appropriate ones.

Finally, a large fellow at an adjacent table stood up, walked over, grabbed Will by the collar and slammed him with a stiff-arm between the shoulder blades hard enough to jiggle his eyeballs. With perfect timing, Will spat an olive at least twenty feet across the room. There was a smattering of applause. Will recovered nicely, thanked the man, apologized to the older couple and offered to buy them drinks. They declined. Still looking at Will as if he might possess some sort of contagious disease, they grabbed their belongings and left.

I turned to Mames and his large friend, placing their shots on the counter. I raised mine. "Here's to the good times between heaven and hell."

Mames smiled. They picked up their tumblers and shot them.

"I can't tell you how important this was to me," I said sincerely.

Five minutes later, I noticed the conversation had slowed with my two new friends. Through the large windows in the back, I watched a Bahamas Air flight land and taxi in. Mames and his buddy missed it. They were beginning to slur a little and Mames was having a tough time getting his rum and Coke to his mouth.

I leaned in, elbow on the bar. "So, what are you up to tonight, Justin?"

Mames swayed a bit and smiled as if amused by the question. "Got to pick up somethin'."

"Would that be on the Bahamas Air flight?"

He perked up just a little. "Maybe."

I nodded to Will, then slipped under the bar partition and came around to my attorney friend's side. "C'mon, you're late—plane's already landed. I'll help you."

He shook his head drunkenly, as if fending off an imaginary fly. "Don' want help... Secret." He knocked over his glass and didn't even notice.

His bodyguard friend wasn't doing much better. He slid out of his seat and was standing on wobbly legs leaning against the bar. "Gotta pee," he whispered.

Will was suddenly at his side supporting him. "C'mon buddy, we'll get you to the head. No peeing on the lounge rug. Bad for business." As Will moved him out the door, I heard him ask the big guy if he had beaten up a fellow named Turtle. The fellow smiled, and slurred, "Yeah, me and Marty did him—little weasel."

A moment later I had Mames convinced that I had his best interests in mind, and we were headed out the door and down the corridor.

As Will opened the bathroom door for his new friend, I heard him say, "A little weasel, huh?" He took a quick glance both ways, then picked up a large metal ashtray with a thin trunk and a heavy base, before following the man inside.

A few moments later Will showed up alone and helped me support Mames as we neared the Bahamas Air Freight counter. Justin swung around, pupils like Little Orphan Annie, barely able to hold his head up. "Where's Frank?" he muttered.

Will looked at me and there was a strangely savage gaze in his eyes. "Frank had to pee for a while, then he got a headache. He may have to rest for a while. But we'll take care of you, Justin. I promise. I wanna take care of you."

Mames shrugged, nearing the indifference of narcosis, but he hadn't lost focus. "Gotta get the nose cone—damn, just so sleepy."

I looked at Will and mouthed, "Nose cone?"

As we eased Justin into a chair across from the Bahamas Air Counter, we heard a ruckus taking place at one of the boarding gates just inside the wing we faced. Someone was getting loud and indignant, and there were a couple of airport security guards moving in to control the situation. I got a brief glance at the troublemakers and heard a voice—a very distinct voice—one I remembered from another time. Calico—Calico Curk. The next thing I knew the little pirate and his two sons, Kenny and Lenny, came hustling out of the security gate. There was a screechy, very unhappy female voice in the cacophony behind them. Calico was cursing a blue streak—something about it not being his fault her toy Yorkie looked like a rat. The upshot was Calico and his boys were being asked to deplane ahead of the other passengers.

"Lord! That's all we need," I moaned. "What the hell are they doing here?"

Will shook his head. "Don't know. I heard they took their insurance money from the boat and headed up to Tampa. But now is not the time for a confrontation. Make like incognito, man—heads down."

He was right. We just lowered our profiles and Calico's gang rolled right by us and out the doors of the airport into the muggy October night. A moment later the last of their chattering was swallowed by a taxicab. I lifted Mames' chin and looked at him. "I'm gonna go get your nose cone, Justin. What's the company name it's under?"

"Tortuga Enterprises," stumbled out of his mouth.

"You got paperwork?"

He nodded drunkenly, pointing to his breast pocket. I reached in and pulled out a sheaf of papers, then whispered quickly to Will, who took a seat with Mames. I strolled over to the counter.

There was a big Bahamian slouched against the wall reading a newspaper. I waited for a moment. He straightened up. "What can I do for you, sir?"

"Here to pick up a package for Tortuga Enterprises."

He tilted his head, studying me. "You don' look like the guy—"

"The guy is sitting over there. Got a bowl of bad chili in the lounge." I waved. Will very subtly brought up Justin's hand and wiggled it enough for a halfhearted gesture. Taking out a twenty-dollar bill I said, "We're taking care of business for him, because he's very close to us, and rich, and he appreciates people who get done what he needs to get done—you understand?"

The Bahamian sighed. (It sounded like someone puncturing a tire.) "Okay, okay. You got papers?"

I handed him the papers. He paged through them, stamped a couple, then disappeared into the back. Five minutes later a guy with a small dolly appeared from the hanger. On the dolly was a foot-square wooden box with Tortuga Enterprises stamped on the side. The porter pushed the dolly out to the sidewalk while Will and I discreetly carried Mames, who had been reduced to unintelligible mumbling and the rigidity of rice pudding. While Will held our new friend, I went to the parking lot and brought the van around. We thanked and tipped the porter, loaded the box and Mames into the back, got in and drove away. Mames, spread out on the back seat like a melted Hershey Bar, was no longer an issue. That old Halloween moon had just started to crawl out of the sea and silhouette the lines of palm trees along the airport drive. It was so beautiful for a moment, it took my breath away, and I almost forgot that I was in the process of kidnapping a Miami attorney after stealing an object of some importance from him, which he had already stolen, and the whole world wanted back.

"Well, that certainly went better than expected," Will muttered with relief.

I took my first normal breath in about a half hour. "Yeah. Surprisingly well. Actually absolutely frigging amazingly well."

My partner looked at the box, then back at me. "I can't stand the suspense." He crawled over the seat as I stopped the car in the parking lot at Smather's Beach, then pulled a large screwdriver out of the toolbox and cracked open the sides of the crate. Sure enough, there it was—a nose cone for a twin-engine Cessna. Will looked at me as he felt the texture of the cone. "Plaster of Paris—painted nicely." Without a word or the slightest invitation, he picked up a small hammer and slapped it against the cone, which cracked nicely into two halves. The pieces fell off, leaving something underneath—something dusty from the plaster of Paris, but gold and gleaming nonetheless.

"I'll be a …" I muttered to no one in particular as Will brushed off the object and lifted it carefully over to me. It was smaller than I imagined, but heavy. Just then the moonlight caught the emerald. The van was suddenly flooded with a radiant green light. Brilliant sharp tiers of crystal lagoon green lanced out from the emerald engulfing everything. Then there was a humming—deep, robust, infused with life—like the sweet cacophony of an all-knowing, all-aware hive of bees. It scared the shit out of me and I quickly set it down on the floorboard. Instantly everything dimmed.

"Holy frigging monkey shit!" Will cried. "What in the hell is that?

"It's more than we bargained for," I said quietly, subdued, knowing suddenly with great certainty that it was a piece of machinery from a race of people with a far greater understanding of the big picture; a much bigger slice of the cosmic pie than us two little earthlings.

About that time Mames rolled over on the floor and burped up a little pill spittle around the edges of his mouth, reminding us that we had equally pressing problems on that account as well.

Will pointed to the back. "What do we do with him? He's gonna kill us if he wakes up and remembers any of this."

"That's why it's got to be really good."

My partner got that crooked, mischievous grin. "You gotta plan, don't you?

"Why don't you call Nick Crow," I said. "Tell him we need five pounds of pot, a parachute and fifty feet of heavy, one-inch anchor rope. Use the pay phone over there, by the concession stand. Tell him I'm calling in my cards for Trujillo. Tell him … it's nothing more than an evening's entertainment."

Crow had the stuff we wanted waiting on the floor of his garage when we arrived.

"You got a little jump planned, boys? And by the way, that's a thousand dollars for the pot." Then Nick caught a glance of Mames in the back. "Holy shit! How is it that you have come to possess a wasted Justin Mames in the back seat of your car?" He put his hands up, palms out. "I don't even want to know what you're going to do. I just want you to know that my admiration for you both has peaked another notch simply because you're doing it! This is just cool to the bone." He smiled mischievously. "Let's drop him in the ocean, huh?"

I shook my head. "Naahh. We need to have him noticed, and consequently out of the way for a while. So, this is what we have in mind...."

You couldn't have chiseled the grin off of Crow's face. Then he got serious. "The son of a bitch stole a whole shipment from me one time because it landed near a couple of his boats one night. We're gonna make that ten pounds you need."

When the sun came up the next morning and graced that remarkable span of concrete and steel known as Bahia Honda Bridge, there was a single adornment hanging slightly off-kilter from the center point of the highest part of the span, easily 100 feet from the water. A passing shrimper noticed the silk from an unfurled parachute that lay tangled on the steel railings at the top of the bridge. Swinging freely below in pendulum fashion, the guy lines led down to a single soul impossibly tangled in the harness and strings, and in truth, so hopelessly high on sleeping pills it really didn't matter to him that the police would soon haul him up, check what was in his backpack and find ten pounds of Colombian Gold. A reporter for the Marathon newspaper happened to be on his way to work when they were hauling Mames up and over the railing. Needless to say, the picture for the front page was in the bag. Even for Justin Mames, it was going to take a day or two to get resolved.

Hopefully it would buy us the time we needed to get rid of the pyramid.

There was no going home. Mames' people could easily be watching the house. So we rented a sleazy motel room on Big Coppit Key and slept for a few hours.

I awoke about 11 a.m. to find Will sitting on the floor with the pyramid in front of him. He had it covered with a blanket from his bed.

Without looking up, he mumbled, "*Buenos dias.*" Still focused in front of him, he lifted the blanket slightly and let the sunlight touch the pyramid. Instantly it began to hum and the emerald diffused the sunlight a hundred times over, glowing like a mythological Greek lighthouse, showering the room with an intense, brilliant green fire. He quickly put the blanket over it again and everything ceased.

"Will," I said. "That's not a five and dime store toy. I would be careful lest you turn yourself into a frog. Or worse, turn me into a frog with you."

He sighed strangely. "Yeah, I know you're right, but there's something about this—just looking at it takes me beyond where I am, who I am. You can feel the agelessness of the universe coming from it. It's like suddenly becoming an integral part of the cosmos. You suddenly know, beyond a shadow of a doubt—that there's more…"

"That's beautiful, Copernicus, but it's not a bloody lava lamp," I said dryly. "It is a stolen archeological artifact. Now we have to talk about getting this thing back to the authorities before we become an integral part of the cosmos in the Miami Federal Detention Center. I'm thinking we just take it into the Key West Police Department and—"

"Yeah. Right. How exactly are you going to explain stealing it from Mames? And who's really going to believe you?" Will humphed sarcastically. "You'll do fifteen years just because."

"You got a better suggestion?"

"We call the police and talk to a detective, arrange a meeting—something we can control a little. We just tell him we found it. We cut a deal. They get the pyramid and we get immunity against any possible charges."

I thought about it for a moment then reached over and picked the phone off the nightstand. "Hello, operator. Give me the Key West police station, please. No, it's not an emergency." I looked at Will. "Not at this very moment."

Key West Detective Ralph Landon picked up the phone. Landon was tall and thin with sparse, sandy hair, which was making a futile attempt to cover his balding scalp. His longish nose, cautious dark eyes, and pockmarked, conical face made one think of a fox at first glance, but a wolf would have probably been closer. He leaned back in his chair and took the toothpick out of his mouth. "Landon here."

He listened for a moment. "Yeah, I know the pyramid you're talking about." He continued to listen, then glanced around the room. Most everyone else was gone to lunch. The boys at the front desk were busy booking a kid who had stolen a car the night before. His eyes narrowed instinctively. "If this is a bullshit prank, I will trace this call, find you, and kick your ass, you understand?" He paused, listening again. "Okay. Okay. White Street Pier off Smather's Beach. Just after sunset." He paused again. "You better not be screwing with me, you understand? Yeah. Okay. White Street Pier."

He put the phone in its cradle with a perplexed but intrigued smile. Then he shrugged and picked it up once more.

Will and I spent the afternoon working on the precise wording of a profuse apology to the police. As the sun began to bury itself in a distant squall line on the horizon, I found myself standing about three-quarters of the way out on White Street Pier, dressed like a fruit-juicy tourist with a small wicker picnic basket, as I told Landon I would be. A storm was building and heavy rain clouds were emerging from the squall line, swallowing the early stars in mottled grayness. As the last of the sunlight surrendered, Landon pulled up in his Chevrolet Impala and got out. He was dressed in a cream-colored, short-sleeved shirt and gray polyester slacks. He moved with a casual, indifferent fashion, but his eyes belied that appearance. They were quick, darting, canvassing the area. He worked his way up the nearly deserted pier, stopping a few feet from me as I leaned on the railing, looking out over the darkening water. I glanced at him and nodded. He nodded back.

"So, you find something interesting recently?"

"I think so," I said.

"Why don't we cut to the chase and let me have a look in the basket?"

I turned toward him. "Soon, but first I want some assurance. Look, we like, found this thing. We don't want it. We want to return it to its rightful owners. But we don't want to find ourselves being arrested for something we had nothing to do with."

"Yeah, no problem," Landon said with something similar to a smile. "You give us the pyramid and there'll be no charges filed. Might even be a reward."

Strange, I thought. *He said 'you give us the pyramid'—not, 'when you turn it in to the authorities, the police, etc.'* Something just didn't fit with that sentence—the way he said it. I was about to ask for some I.D. when I noticed two big guys—T-shirts and jeans—moving casually toward me from my left. I suddenly realized I had seen one of them before, a little over a year ago. He was with Justin Mames at Captain Tony's—the night we met Banyan.

I threw up my hand, and held the basket out with the other, shouting. "Okay! Everybody hold it!" To my surprise, everybody stopped. I decided to adlib. I threw out a peace sign then drew it to my forehead, Rufus style. "We come in peace." I cried in a higher voice than I had planned. "We wish the earth no harm. Do not make us use the Loton Rays!"

"What the hell!" muttered Landon as he put his hand out, restraining his crew. I realized there was a third guy dressed like a fisherman to my right—floppy hat covering his face. He looked up. Mames!

I backed up against the railing. "How about a deal? You get the pyramid, I just beam up to the mothership."

Mames smiled—not a nice smile. "It's not that simple," he whispered threateningly as he reached into his pocket and discreetly pulled out a small handgun. "I owe you."

I held my hand up, palm out, in supplication. "But it is that simple. Let me show you." I cautiously set the basket down in front of them. "Here it is—what you want."

Sometimes timing in life is everything. At that moment an Air Jamaica jet decided to make a low approach into Key West Airport, directly behind us. Buried in the overcast, the approaching roar of the engines was disquieting at best. But when the landing lights suddenly broke through the clouds and bathed the pier in eerie luminescence, I decided to bet on the adlib again.

"The mothership!" I shouted in my best whiny outer space voice, jabbing my finger at the sky.

It was just too much for them. They had to turn and look, and before anyone could say "Houdini," I did a quick flip over the rail and dropped into the sea. Night had nearly claimed the pier but the floodlights hadn't come on yet, which added considerable suspense to my disappearing act. I swam underwater for the first three or four pilings, coming up next to Will in the little day skiff he had rented—just in case.

He leaned over and grabbed me, dragging me aboard. "I heard the conversation. We come in peace? Loton Rays? The mothership? You been reading too much Asimov or drinking too much Smirnoff, or both."

"Just get us the hell out of here," I hissed. "That was Mames in the flesh up there. He's been keeping score. Got the damned police force working for him."

"No problem," said Will with a grin. "I'll just beam us up to the mothership." He hit the starter and we zoomed out into the moonless night like a Halloween wraith, lost to the mists of the approaching storm front.

We were still just within earshot when Justin Mames opened the basket. Even over the sound of the motor I distinctly heard our names being used in vain. For his trouble, he had received a pretty piece of coral rock and a Polaroid shot of the real thing.

We headed around the island, dropping off the boat at a small marina near Mallory Square. Ten minutes later we were in our VW bus and headed out of town. Will shook his head apprehensively. "Well, so much for that well-laid plan. Now we have Mames and the authorities after us and now they know exactly who we are, if they didn't before. You know you can only trick a guy like Justin Mames so many times."

"How many times is that? Because at this point we're doing pretty good."

Will frowned and started to answer.

I held my hand up. "I know, I know. Just joking. Truth is, maybe we should be thinking about living in Panama, or maybe Costa Rica for a while."

Suddenly, from the shadows of the back seat, a voice said, "Aahhh, Costa Rica, we do have a few fond memories there, don't we, my expatriated friends?"

Time froze. We froze.

"No, man, it can't really be," Will whined.

"Aahhhh but it is my whiny brethren. The *tres banditos* back together again."

The van filled with light as Sundance drew back the blanket that covered the small pyramid. He shook his head in admiration. "I would say this is certainly one of the most advanced designed Lava Lamps I've ever seen." Then his voice became surly. "If it hadn't come from a one-thousand-foot hole in the Andes and wasn't made 10,000 years ago, give or take a month or two. And wasn't worth millions to private collectors and miscellaneous governments around the world."

I turned around and opened my mouth. Sundance cut me off, finger pointing. "If you even whisper about wanting to give this back to anyone I will shoot you here and now." He waved his favorite revolver around casually with the other hand. "I may still shoot you later. Lord knows I should shoot you. But if I can get this to the right market, it's permanent vacation time, and maybe I'll forgive you of your sins—write you occasionally from Fiji, France, or maybe Switzerland." He smiled and tipped back what appeared to be a new Panama hat. "I was leaving on a flight from Key West the other night—had become bored with watching people play miniature golf from my bedroom window and eating conch fritters at some Cuban cantina—and lo and behold, who did I see but my old expatriated buddies dragging someone and his important-looking box out of the airport. So I got back in my car and followed for a while, and my respect increased five-fold when I realized what you had stolen from him. Sundance emitted a sigh that bled into a cough. "Aaahh, I think I may have congestive heart failure, that and the leprosy you gave me."

Will exhaled, exasperated. "We didn't give you leprosy. It was smallpox."

Our old nemesis tilted his head. "And that's supposed to make me feel better? Well, in any case, I must make the best of the time I have left, before the various parts of my body become all soft and blotchy like milk toast and decide to rot off. God bloody awful disease!" He grabbed the pyramid. "I'm going to steal this mystical triangle and find a buyer quickly, so that I can begin the joyous, lavishly wealthy funeral procession which will consume my final time here in flames of iniquity and promiscuity, and march the barge that is me into the River of Styx with a thousand saxophones performing "Dark Side of the Moon."

"That'll be an expensive funeral," I said dryly.

He smiled subtly, eyebrows raised. "Money will be no object. And I want to thank you for your assistance in procuring the object that will provide the money. That's probably why I'm not going to shoot you right now." He sighed. "Just stop the van and get out."

We were coming around the backside of Key West on Roosevelt Boulevard. It was late; there was almost no traffic. I looked at Will, who was driving, and he hesitated. If we lost the pyramid we were as good as dead. It was our only bargaining chip in any of this. The sudden report from Sundance's pistol and the bullet ripping through the top of the van drew us from our indecision. Will pulled over and we got out.

Sundance took the driver's seat and grinned, leaning out the window. "Not too much despair, old friends, we'll meet again. You are ingenious fellows. You'll find a way out of this and one day we'll meet each other at another little cantina and share some *mescal*." He leaned out a little farther, eyes wide, eyebrows arching like Groucho Marx. "Maybe rob a bank, ehh?" With that, he pulled a flask from his jacket and lithely tossed it high into the air. Bam! Bam! Two shots rang out from his revolver. The flask landed unscathed and intact on the lawn next to the sidewalk. He looked at us and shrugged with that same wacky smile, eyebrows up. "You've got to admit it would have been impressive, no?"

Without another word, he turned up the stereo, swung around, and drove off amid the bright lights of Roosevelt Boulevard. The last we heard from Sundance was the Steve Miller Band rolling out the windows of our van…

Singin' go on take the money and run
Go on take the money and run
Go on take the money and run…

CHAPTER TEN

Cuban Vacations...

The following morning found us at another sleazy motel. We knew we needed to get to our place on Big Pine and get Will's Mustang. What we didn't know, which was considerably more important, was that Mames and Landon had decided it would be easier to steal the pyramid from the police contraband room after we'd been arrested, rather than chase us all over the country.

We were having a quick breakfast of eggs and Cuban toast at Merioso's Café when Will brought over the paper and opened it. There we were in all our glory—sketches quite well rendered.

"Cayo Hueso Bandits Steal Famous Colombian Pyramid"

"Reward promised by authorities for information leading to…"

By 10 o'clock everyone who ever knew us was going to be looking for us. We'd be going to jail with or without a pyramid.

Will threw the paper on the table and turned to me. "We've got only one shot here. We have to find Sundance and get that pyramid back, then bargain our way out of this mess."

I shook my head. "He could be anywhere by now—up the Keys into Miami, hiding out in Key West. He'll want to ditch our van as soon as possible and get another, probably a rental."

"Wait!" said Will, finger in the air, pausing to collect his thoughts. "Last night he said he was tired of watching miniature golf and eating conch fritters! Think about it! That's Summerland Key—the little goony golf place and Coco's Cantina. There's a motel just on the other side of the street—Sindy's Seabreeze Apartments. I'll bet you dollars to donuts that's where he's been staying. You know what else? It's Halloween tomorrow night and there will be a street party to beat all street parties on Duval—free-flowing booze, half-naked girls, and live music from about dusk until dawn. I just know Sundance wouldn't miss that, man. It wouldn't be cool for him to miss that, and you know how cool he thinks he is."

"You may have a point. I think it's time to check with Sindy—after we pick up your car.

We tucked our hair up into a couple of ball caps and hitched up to Big Pine, hiking in the final mile to the house. Sure enough, there was a guy watching our trailer, slouched in an old beat-up Corvair a block away. He'd been there a while—there was a pile of cigarette butts littering the pavement outside his window. Will's Mustang was sitting in the driveway and he had his keys with him. We needed a distraction.

We worked our way into the mangroves to the left of the car, far enough back to where the sentry could still hear, but not see us. I looked at Will. "Okay, you want to be the girl or the guy?"

He shrugged indifferently. "I'll be the guy."

"Damn," I muttered. "Why do you have to be the guy? I could do the guy just as well."

He put his hands on his hips exasperatedly. "Well, you asked and I chose! You wanna be the guy? Be the guy!"

"Naahh, never mind. I'll be the girl." I took a breath. "Okay. You ready?"

Conan Jones, formally a full-time lobster fisherman, presently a part-time drug smuggler, was drawing a cigarette out of his fourth pack when he heard something in the mangrove and buttonwood jungle next to him—voices…

There was a saucy, high-pitched woman's voice—like Flip Wilson's Geraldine…

"Take your frigging filthy hands off of me, you fool! I ain't gonna screw you in these filthy, bug-infested woods."

And a deep, heavy, man's voice—think Barry White…

"C'mon baby. I know you want me. Look at this, baby. Look what I gonna give you. I'm gonna give you aaahlll of it, baby."

"Ooohhh my gawd! You ain't gonna touch me with that filthy, long…thang. My gawd! How you keep that from draggin' on the groun'! You sure yo mama wasn't a yak?"

"C'mon baby, don' fight me—I know what you want."

"Stop! Stop! Ooohhh Gawd! Don't you do that! Don't you put that filthy, long, tuberous, veined thang in me! Don't you dare! Don't you…oooohhhh! Ooooohhhhh Gaaaawd!"

Well, the entertainment in the woods was just too much for a curious person like Conan. He cocked his head and listened to my introduction, and by the time I got to the second "oooohhh gawd," he was out of his car and creeping through the mangroves toward the voices. At that point I lured him in a little deeper.

"Ooohhh please, sweet Jessssus! I cain't take it! I cain't take it! It alive! It got a mind of its own! Oooohhh Gawwdd! Noooo! Nooooo!" (Pause) "Aaahh… Aaahh, yes… Yeeesss! Yeeesss!"

As I coaxed Conan into the mangroves, Will worked his way out of the mangroves on the side nearest the house and got his Mustang started. I gave our curious friend a couple more choruses then left him fairly lost. I circled back and got into his car. Conan Jones was still standing in the woods wondering where the girl was when we drove away with both cars. We left his about three miles down the road at a gas station. That would at least buy us a little time before he could call Mames.

Even though Key West's Halloween Bash was set for that evening, Sindy's Seabreeze Apartments were only about half full. One of the first things we noticed was our VW bus parked outside room 32. We got a room on the other side of the pool and waited, taking turns watching Sundance's door. Every half hour the bar boy would deliver a margarita with a fruit-juicy umbrella. Sundance would take the drink and deposit money on the boy's tray. We were still in the process of formulating a plan when a van pulled up at room 32. The lettering on the van read:

Little Tony's Antiquities—Miami, Florida
Sell it at Tony's, where possession is nine-tenths of the value.

"Lord! He's already got a buyer here!" Will hissed from the curtain in our room. I rushed over and peered out cautiously. Sure enough, Little Tony, who weighed about 400 pounds and looked like a dark-haired manatee in a Polo shirt, poured himself out of the van and wiped the sweat off his forehead. A smaller guy with longish blond hair, sport shirt, blue jeans, and a briefcase, got out the other side. They knocked on the door and Sundance let them in.

Will stood up. "Okay, we got to think fast. We need a plan, dude. This guy gets away with the pyramid and we'll never see it, or the outside of a jail cell, ever again."

I put my hand out, palm forward. "Okay, Okay. Here's the thing. Little Tony is never going to make it back to Miami without stopping to eat. We follow them, then snatch the pyramid when they stop to eat, or pee, or whatever."

"I don't know. What if they don't stop?"

"They will! They will! You got a better plan? You wanna just bust open the door and demand the pyramid back because we stole it first, or second. Think about it—'Little Tony.' They're probably mob connected. They've probably got bigger guns than Sundance."

My partner nodded thoughtfully. "Good point." He paused, then exhaled hard and ran one hand through his long hair like he always did when he was in a quandary. "Okay, we follow them."

We didn't have long to wait. Ten minutes later Little Tony and his partner emerged from the room with a small, nondescript carryall bag. They got into the van and unceremoniously drove off. We followed. An hour later, as we entered Marathon, they pulled into the famous Seven Mile Grill on the southern end of the sprawling little town. It was headed toward evening and the sun was drifting into the dark green Gulf waters. The pale sky turned emerald, and high feathers of cirrus clouds clinging to the heavens began a transformation from soft white to rose, and finally to the deepest, most profound shades of purple, turning the calm sea to velvet gray and silhouetting the distant islands. It was an extraordinary sunset and any other time I would have just pulled up a seat and watched Mother Nature do what she does best. But we had issues. We had a pyramid to steal—again.

Tony and his partner parked in front of the restaurant. Will cruised down another block and pulled into the adjacent lobster boat docks. We parked, got out, and casually worked our way back to The Grill. Before we entered the restaurant I realized I had to pee—that nervous bladder thing again. Will went to get us a table and I hit the head.

I was standing at one of the urinals when I heard the door open and close behind me. There was a pause. Somehow I just knew who it was, even before I heard the voice.

"By the blessings of the great one-eyed night toad, is that not you, Kansas?"

I zipped up and turned. "Well, hello, Rufus."

Rufus—Bob Marley T-shirt, baggy shorts, same halo of dreadlocks, same big chocolate eyes and broad, toothy smile—held out his arms. "What a coincidence we should again encounter each other's presence in the process of blissfully eliminating urinary waste."

"So what brings you here?"

Rufus shrugged noncommittally. "I be delivering catch of finny brothers to restaurant. Fishing good lately." There was a pause, then he spoke again quietly, more seriously. "And I think I maybe encounter your personality today, here."

"Somehow, why am I not surprised?"

He let the question roll by. "I have a delivery unto you, important to the triangulations of your quest."

I threw my hands out and stared at him. "Okay, Rufus. What is this all about? Why? Why me? How do I fit into this whole thing? Better yet, how do you fit into this whole thing?" I exhaled hard. "This is all about the pyramid, isn't it?"

Rufus didn't answer right away. He just gazed at me strangely and said, "We are all part of great cosmic pinball machine. Sometimes it is tiny levers that deflect ball bearing of fate just a little." He shrugged again. "You, me… tiny levers."

"What the hell is the deal with this pyramid? What the hell is so important about it? Who the hell are you anyway?"

He closed his eyes for a moment and took a deep breath, exhaling slowly. When he looked up, there was a different person in front of me. His eyes had made that change again and there was a glint of purpose in them. He rose up and his posture shifted from indifferent to capable. The amiable, slightly nonsensical character melted away and in its place was a much more confident and deliberate individual.

"Let me tell you a story," he said quietly, much of the old sing-song rhythm of his voice replaced by a smooth, cadenced delivery. "Ten thousand years before the first Pharaoh built a tomb to glorify his name, this planet was populated by a unique race of people. No one remembers their origin, but over the centuries they gleaned great powers through the knowledge and the application of the elements—not in competition with nature, but in alliance with it. They lived on a single continent surrounded by water, but they had means to travel swiftly and were able to observe the rest of mankind as it made its progress from caves and mud huts to cities of stone. They had no need of acclaim, no desire for prestige; they wished only to serve as caretakers to their new brethren, and they remained in the shadows as the rest of the planet developed. As fledgling societies grew, they sometimes posed as gods and encouraged them with simple ideas in building and tools, and concepts on morality—to improve and advance their cultures. They were the ones who provided the knowledge to build the colossal, almost indestructible monuments in Asia, Egypt, and Central and South America—to remain as testimony to powers beyond simple human labor. They were the myths of Greece, the voices the prophets heard. They were Easter Island and Stonehenge."

He paused dramatically. "But as mankind developed, a great tragedy struck the caretakers. Their continent was destroyed in a sudden shifting of the earth and it sank beneath the sea. There were some who escaped before the final collapse—what you might call spiritual leaders. They took with them several small, golden pyramids that contained blueprints for powers beyond imagination. The secrets to life—construction, sound, momentum, energy, and planetary information—that would assist future generations when they had risen to an acceptable intellectual and sympathetic plane to understand and apply this knowledge conscientiously. They buried one of these deep within the earth on three different continents. The last of these people blended into the new and rising cultures innocuously, passing down the knowledge and responsibility from their ancestors to their children."

Rufus drew a breath slowly and continued. "They were the caretakers, the guardians of the great secrets. My family is one of the last existing caretakers. Like the others before us, we have waited and watched for the moment when the secrets would be unearthed and with our assistance, practiced for the betterment of the species." He paused again. "But progress on this planet has been slow. You are not ready yet—too mucked-up with greed and hatred, and jealousy—too many gods and not enough spirit."

I started to say something, but Rufus put up his finger, stopping me. "So when one of the vital tools to enlightenment was recently discovered in Peru, there were few caretaker families left who had survived the ravages of time, and this species. Location dictated that my family be responsible for returning it to the safety of the earth until the people of this planet had grown sufficiently to accept the responsibility of its power and energy." He smiled mischievously and ran his fingers through his long dreadlocks. "You ask why you? Why not you? You're intelligent, clever, and expendable—lots of good qualities." Then he became more solemn. "Truth is, even we could succumb to the powers of 'the gift.' We have taken an oath not to personally intervene, but if necessary, have those from the existing society serve us, in a test of their progress and evolution."

He gazed at me for a moment with what seemed like a touch of sadness. "Nonetheless, we must find the pyramid and return it to the bowels of the earth if possible. You are not yet ready for its powers."

I stepped back involuntarily, confused, a little dumbfounded, and maybe a little angry.

"Rufus, if this is a bunch of Rastaman ganja bullshit, I'm gonna personally—"

He held up a hand, stopping me again. "This is no ganja bullshit, mon. I wish it was. My life would be so much simpler. I did not choose this place either. Fate has chosen it for both of us. Where our ancestors came from is not as important as what we do with our accumulated wealth of character. After all, we are both just people of earth."

"That's all really interesting," I said. " But let's get back to me for a moment. I hate to sound too self-serving, but what do Will and

I get for our troubles? Let me remind you that life has not exactly been a picnic for us lately. The police think we stole this bloody pyramid. This whole thing has been a classic bummer."

My Jamaican friend became pensive for a moment. "I think there is a plan. You—you get very cool memories for sure, and maybe a gift. I think there is something very special for you—ya mon—an appropriate gift."

Reaching into his pocket, Rufus pulled out two small, round balls, about an inch in diameter. One of them was black and the second was golden colored. Holding them in the palm of his hand, he said, "For now, I have magic dust for you." He picked up the dark one and held it out.

"You remember magic dust?" he said, casually lapsing back into his unique island vernacular. "Okay, this is magic dust gumball." He looked at me very seriously and shook his finger sternly. "Do not eat! Do not eat! This is econo-size magic dust—one size fits everybody. Good for maybe a dozen people in small building. Take deep breath. Hold it. Throw magic ball on ground. No thoughts but yours matter then. Do not breathe, or you be standing around dazed, waiting for instructions too. That would be very bad. Can be used to make impressionable zombie friends for about fifteen minutes and leave residual 'suggestions' for a later date.

Then, carefully, he picked up the golden colored gumball and his countenance became somber. "This is, 'all has failed to get pyramid back' destruction gumball. It is just not good for this mucked-up species to have pyramid knowledge yet. If there is no other way, this gumball has flat side. Put it on side of pyramid and get out. You have maybe one hour to get far away before a small explosion of possibly one square mile—similar to nuclear, but with no radiation."

Rufus smiled sadly. "Your life egg has broken, mon, and your journey begins. You must make it across moonless beach and throw yourself into the tide. Use the gifts wisely, timely, and your tiny levering will bring the shiny ball bearing home to the great cosmic throat of life." He sighed. "Stay close to the Western Key. I will find you, and help as much as I can. Cool driftings, mon." Then he was gone—out the door with nary a look back—leaving me in the shabby bathroom of a fish house with a handful of magic balls.

Will sat anxiously waiting at a table by the door, close to the van and hopefully the pyramid. Little Tony and his friend chose stools at the bar, where they could glance back every once in a while and check things out. I eased into a chair.

"What took you so long, man?" Will asked.

"I ran into Rufus."

"Rufus, huh? How's he doing?"

"I'd say his stock has gone up some. He's working with a group from out of town—way out of town."

"Okay, I'll bite. I got a little time."

Still staring at the bar, I said, "Well, to begin with, Rufus gave us some special gifts to help us on our quest for the pyramid. The rest of the story is a little more difficult to digest, but I'll give it a shot."

When I finished giving Will the *Reader's Digest* version, he looked at me incredulously. "Oh, c'mon, man. Why us?"

I shrugged. "That's what I said. He claims we're intelligent and clever, and expendable. Besides, at this point we're in this up to our little eyeballs anyway and we got to go through it to get out of it."

Just then Little Tony and his friend were served fish sandwiches by the waiter—one for the little guy, three for Tony. I looked at Will.

"We'll have to pick this up later. Right now, we gotta solve our immediate problem."

Will raised his eyebrows. "Are we gonna use magic dust?"

"Nah, I think we better save it. I got a small plan, but I think I'm gonna need a distraction."

After I explained the plan, Will said, "You do your part, I'll do mine." He got that Lee Marvin grin. "Distractions are one of my specialties." Gazing around slowly, his eyes stopped on a tourist family about three tables from us. He smiled again. "Give me five minutes."

Will got up and casually walked over to the family—a man, a woman, and their two children. I couldn't hear what he was saying, but he bent down next to their little girl. She was about six or seven years old. She had a life-sized doll—a Chatty Cathy wrapped in a pink blanket—that she held affectionately. After a few moments of conversation, he put a twenty-dollar bill on the table and the little girl somewhat reluctantly, at the urging of the parents, gave him the doll. Will glanced over at Tony and his friend. They were still absorbed in their sandwiches. My friend quietly excused himself and went out and around the side of the building, quickly entering the side door that led to the kitchen. He hadn't managed a dozen steps into the galley before the burly head cook met him head-on.

"What are you doing in here?" she said, hands on her hips.

Will never even hesitated. He smiled disarmingly, produced two more twenty-dollar bills and said, "I need some lipstick, a waitress uniform, and some lighter fluid."

Little Tony had just ripped a White Shark-sized hunk out of his second fish sandwich when the swinging double doors to the kitchen suddenly burst open and possibly the ugliest waitress I had ever seen came stumbling out—holding at arm's length a burning baby wrapped in a pink blanket, screaming, "My babeee! My babeee's on fire!" (Think Flip Wilson's Geraldine again.) My lipsticked partner staggered over to the bar, spitting distance from Tony, slapped the blanket-wrapped, flaming, smoking doll on the bar top, and started whacking it with a bar towel, screaming, "Aahhhh! My babeee's burning up! Gotta save my babeee!"

Chatty Cathy was responding, albeit a little inconsistently, with, "Whaaaa (whack!)—love you momm—(whack!) momm (whack!)—meee..."

Tony and his partner were, at that point, mesmerized—eyes like saucers, sandwiches forgotten, mouths hanging open, tartar sauce dribbling down their chins. There wasn't anyone in the restaurant who wasn't into that floorshow. I figured that was a good time for me to get started on my end of the project. As I headed for the back of Tony's van with a screwdriver, Will released another bloodcurdling scream.

"I gotta get you to the water, babee girl! Hold on babeee!" He snatched up Chatty Cathy, and while little wisps of smoke drifted out of her nostrils like something out of *The Exorcist*, he ran out the other end of the room and headed for the docks and the water, which were no more than a dozen steps from the open-air bar. The restaurant patrons, including Tony and his buddy, got up *en masse* and ran after Will, who was shrieking incoherently about scars and flames and stumbling toward the water. I noticed my buddy took a quick glance back—to make sure he still had his audience and I was on my part—then he threw his head up and screamed, "Into the water, babeee girl!"

Swinging the flame-belching doll by the feet like a discus, Will let go and stepped back as Chatty Cathy sailed out over the water, tiny arms flailing dramatically. She smacked down solidly on her back, plumes of smoke rising from her seared curly locks, a final wisp of smoke lifting from those small flared nostrils. It was just too much for the congregation. There was a collective gasp of horror, and two spectators dove to the rescue—an old shrimper and a guy in an Army uniform.

"Swim, babee, swim!" screeched Will as the crowd surged forward, past him, to the edge of the docks. "I'll go get some aloe," he said quietly as he began backing away.

I had already popped the lock on the back window of Tony's van and crawled inside. The carry bag was lying on the floor between the seats. I quickly opened it and there was the pyramid, wrapped in a blanket. I grabbed the bag and crawled out as quickly as possible. By the time I had my feet on the ground, Will had melted through the crowd and inconspicuously worked his way back to me. Smoothing down his skirt, he looked up at me. "Can you believe it? No tips again tonight."

"I can't understand it, because that lipstick really does bring out the pink in your eyes. Maybe you need to consider shaving your chest."

He nodded. "Yeah, you might be right. You got the rock, dude?"

"Yeah. I'll put it in the trunk. We need to split, now."

We still weren't seriously missed by the time our tires hit the highway but it would only be a few minutes before most of the restaurant patrons realized they had been sucked into some sort of weird Jerry Springer entertainment, and two people in particular would discover they'd been had—big time.

I turned south toward Key West as Will wiped off his makeup and changed into jeans and a T-shirt. He got his furrowed brow look and said, "Where the hell you going, man? They're looking for us there. They know what we look like."

"Rufus said to stay close to the 'Western Key'—Key West—and he would find us. Besides man, it's Halloween. We can grab a couple costumes and become incognito."

Will paused for a moment, then nodded with that crooked grin. "Sounds okay to me. I could use a margarita."

Little did we know that while we laid plans to disappear for a while, there were several others laying plans to discover us at the earliest possibility.

In a small conch house off Simonton Street in Key West, Justin Mames was meeting with Detective Landon and a number of specially selected individuals.

Mames, overdressed in gray Brooks Brothers slacks and a blue silk shirt, paced the living room angrily. He ran a hand through his dark, slicked-back hair, grabbing the nape of his neck with a frustrated motion. "I want these sons of bitches and I want them now!" he hissed, riveting Landon with his black eyes. "I don't want any more excuses."

"It's not an excuse," said Landon defensively, recoiling more than he intended as he slouched back in an overstuffed lounger. "It's frigging Halloween and every booze weasel from Miami south is here in Key West for the festival. We've got people watching the roads out of Marathon and north into Key Largo, but nobody's seen their car. We just found their VW bus at a motel on Summerland Key. Some damned Canadian claimed they sold it to him for two hundred bucks. We impounded the bus and questioned him, but there was nothing to hold him on. The traffic is backed up everywhere. It's a mess, Justin."

"Just find them, and get me back my damned pyramid!" Mames hissed again. His gaze sliced across the room. "The rest of you, spread out through the Lower Keys. Keep moving, pay attention. Twenty thousand, cash, to the person who brings them to me. Now go!"

We had every intention of dumping the car. We knew it was the right thing to do, but it started raining so we drove a little farther. We had just entered Stock Island and I had just finished explaining in full Rufus' latest gifts.

Will was a little incredulous. "Okay, dude, you're telling me we got a gumball bomb, and more magic dust, huh? And in the end, after we risk our lives and our freedom, we maybe get a present of some sort for all this. I think you may be slipping tracks on me, man. Are you doing acid and not telling me?"

Before I could rally a sensible defense, we saw a woman—five-foot-six, maybe mid-twenties, standing in the rain next to a broken down Volkswagen Beetle by the side of the road. Her shoulder-length, auburn hair was matted, mascara surrendering to the rain, but she had a decidedly nice figure represented in detail by her clinging, wet clothes. Will was driving. He looked at me, eyebrows up.

I shrugged. "What the hell. Let's give her a ride. Years from now she can tell her children she was picked up by the infamous *dos banditos* who had stolen the famous South American pyramid."

He glanced at me with the furrowed brows thing again. "Don't say things like that, dude! It's not funny."

We stopped and she quickly ran over to the side of the Mustang. I rolled down the window, and she smiled desperately, beautifully. Despite the flagging makeup, I hadn't seen a smile like that since … Banyan.

"Oh, thanks so much," she gasped. "Ran out of gas. The bastard Jerry gauge said I had an eighth of a tank left. I do think the bloody

Germans make things like that deliberately, just to get us back for winning the war." She had a slight English accent that made the talk of Jerry bastards so earnest and authentic, and hazel-bronze eyes flashing with indignation like shiny agates. Very intriguing. She got in front and I took the back seat. As she combed her hair I asked her name and where she was headed.

"Polly—Polly Pilgrams. I'm supposed to meet a mate at the Sands Motel—Halloween, you know—don our costumes then it's off to Duval for a devilish time." She winked seductively, those incredible eyes flashing again.

I smiled wanly, trying to keep some semblance of hormonal balance as Will introduced us. "Would that be your boyfriend you're meeting?" I asked casually.

She grinned, fully aware of the thrust. "No. Girlfriend. But she doesn't mind being the boy when it suits her, and other times she just likes us to be two girls, doing what girls do." She turned and put her arm up on the seat so she could see us both. "So, what about you two? Coming into Key West for the party?" She made it sound like an invitation.

Will looked back at me in the mirror for just a second, then turned to her. "Yeah, that's exactly what we're doing."

We dropped her off at the Sands office and waited with sugarplums dancing in our heads as she checked what room her friend had reserved. We had promised to go back and get her car after she settled in. Will looked at me with a lecherous smile. "Lord! If her friend is as hot as she is, we're going to have… a devilish time!"

"Ya mon," I said. "But we got a couple of immediate problems."

Will nodded, deflating a little. "Yeah. I'm still not sure we shouldn't just call the authorities in Miami, like the F.B.I., and just turn the damned pyramid over to them."

I sighed, exasperated. "They think we stole it too, man! How do we talk our way out of that?"

"Well, what the hell are we supposed to do then?"

"I think we're going to have to try to hold on for just a little while and see if our boy Rufus comes through. As long a shot as it is."

Will grabbed his forehead and ran his hand through his hair again, frustrated. "Man! Are you hearing yourself? We're waiting for people to save us whose spokesman is a ganja-blasted Rastaman."

Just then Polly came out of the manager's office smiling and waving a key. We looked at each other and shrugged.

My partner smiled. "I'll take immediate gratification to confusing, long-range thinking anytime."

"Ya, mon."

One twenty-eight looked like the lucky number for the evening. Polly opened the door and let us in. She excused herself to the restroom with her carryall to freshen up and change clothes, while we sat in relatively uncomfortable chairs and waited.

Polly emerged refreshed and considerably more appealing in her red miniskirt and white tube top. "I think I know where my mate is," she said with a promising smile. "I'll make a quick call." She dialed a number and waited for a moment, turning away from us a little. "Hi, luv. Well, I'm over at the Sands and I have some friends here with me. Why don't you come over and visit with us?" She listened for a moment. "That's smashing, see you soon."

Immediately after she hung up I saw an uncomfortable look in Will's eyes. He glanced at me and I knew something was wrong. One of Will's unique qualities was that he had the hearing of a Basenji. It had to be something about the phone call. He looked at me again and stood up, pasting a pleasant smile on his face. "Well, why don't Kansas and I get some ice and a bottle of rum—to get the party started."

It was a well-done façade, but I wasn't sure Polly bought it.

"Sure," she said with a smile. "Sounds like a groovy idea. Let me give you some money." She reached into her carryall. Before either of us could utter the first syllable of "Oooohh craaap," she pulled out a formidable-looking little snub-nosed revolver. Her smile evaporated. "Okay, mates, the party's over. I'm a Key West police detective. I want you both to very slowly sit back down. And I want to know where the pyramid is."

Will shook his head. "I knew that was a guy's voice on the phone."

"Yes," she said. "Detective Landon. He'll be here in a few minutes.

"Oh Lord!" I muttered. "Landon!"

Polly brought her gun up menacingly. "Sit down, both of you. Now!"

We immediately responded as obediently as terriers.

"Polly ..." I said, imploringly.

"The name's Detective Angie Hanes."

"Angie. Detective Hanes. Landon's working for the person who actually stole the pyramid from the Peruvian museum. Did you know that?"

She waved the gun. "Save the bullshit for the booking statement."

"What do you know about Justin Mames? Because he's the one who actually stole the pyramid."

That got her attention for some reason. "Mames? What do you know about Justin Mames?"

"I know he and Landon are partners. Or at the very least Landon has been bought by him. Mames tried to kill one of our friends. We stole the pyramid from him when he brought it into the country, to get him back for what he did. We were going to turn it in, just to fry his potatoes. We called the Key West police and got Landon. When we rendezvoused to give it back and negotiate our immunity, he and Mames tried to kill me. "

She paused, uncertain. "You're lying."

"For God's sake, woman! We don't give a shit about the pyramid." Will cried, exasperated. "We just want out of this whole thing without being buried in a fifty-five-gallon drum on the back side of the reef!"

"Son of a … Landon and bloody Mames!" she whispered pensively, lowering the gun a little. "I've been trying to bust the South American connections in this town for years. And there's been a couple of times I've wondered about Mames and Landon." She brought the gun back up suddenly, those bronze eyes flaring. "If you're lying to me I'm going to shoot you both and *I'll* bury you on the bloody reef!"

"Woman, you're going to have to get in line," I muttered. "Every time I turn around somebody's pointing a frigging gun at me."

Detective Hanes stared hard at us for a moment, as if making a decision. "Do you have the pyramid?"

I looked at Will, then back to the detective. "In a manner of speaking. But as soon as we give that to Landon, it's gonna disappear, and we're gonna be fish food, or in jail forever—or fish food in jail. It's the only negotiating tool we have."

She thought about it, then nodded. "Okay, I'm not buying any of this until I can verify it. But you two have bought yourselves a little time. We've got to get out of here before Landon arrives—figure out a way to make a trade for your immunity. If you're for real."

We piled into the Mustang. Will drove. I sat in the front seat while our detective took the back so she could keep an eye—and a gun—on us. Still, I thought things were going pretty well—we weren't arrested and we weren't dead yet, and we still had the pyramid—all good signs. As we drove, we told detective Hanes about pyramids, and people from long, long ago, and a little about magic dust. Fifteen minutes later we pulled into the parking area at Smather's Beach. The moon was just dropping into the ocean, silhouetting the palms along the beach, and bathing the inky, still waters with its luminescence. Will turned off the car and we swung around, looking at our new acquaintance.

She sighed incredulously and collapsed back into the seat. "Oh, sweet Lord, what have I gotten myself into? You're both bloody lunatics!" After a pause she said, "If all that you tell me is true, about this Rufus, and these pyramid people—and I guess it bloody well might be—how do you propose to give this pyramid back to them and not be prosecuted for its theft from the Peruvian National Museum—both here and there? And where the hell is the pyramid now?"

Watching her, I was once again taken with how much she reminded me of Banyan—the same high cheekbones, and incredible eyes. Her hair was different, auburn instead of blond, but she had that same smooth Saint Kitts tan.

"Well?" she said, interrupting my musings.

"Those are good questions, but we've been told the 'caretakers' have a plan," I replied with more confidence than I felt. "And the pyramid is safely tucked away right now—yes, again, we have it. I told you we would get it when we're ready."

Hanes stared at me for a moment then let it go. "Okay. Well, we need a plan now if we're going to get through the next few days. And I'm going to need to see the pyramid at some point—to be sure." She looked across the island to downtown, which was all lit up, gilding the low clouds with the reflection of a Halloween party in full swing. "We need to hide you somewhere for a few days. Completely out of reach of everybody," she said, still staring at the glowing sky. Then she swung around abruptly, as if making a decision. "I'm gonna give someone a ring. You two sit tight for a few minutes."

She walked across to the concession area pay phone, dropped in a dime and conversed briefly with someone. She hung up, dropped in another dime and again spoke briefly to someone. When she hung up the second time, she came back, smiling, and got in behind the driver's seat. "Okay, we're getting out of here, but we have to wait until tomorrow morning to leave. I have a friend who owns a seaplane," she said noncommittally. "He's going to fly us to Cuba tomorrow morning."

"Cuba?" both Will and I harmonized.

"Like in Fidel, and shoot Americans Cuba?" I said a little too shrilly.

She smiled again—beguiling but determined. "There's a small island on the western end of the Sabana Archipelago, about seventy miles from Key West. Justin Mames' family owns a house there. His father still has some ties to Cuba."

I cocked my head. "How is it that you know about this?"

"I've been there a couple times." Before either Will or I could utter a pressing question or two, she answered them, her eyes offering no excuses. "We had a thing for a while, when I was still a green detective and before I discovered he was an unmitigated duffer."

Will and I glanced at each other—a little uncertain.

"Get over it," she said. "I'm still your best shot at surviving this, regardless." She edged out a sigh. "Okay, this is what we're going to do. We can't go back to my flat, because Mames or Landon may get suspicious and check it. So tonight we're going to hide in the herd—Duval Street. But first, we have to swing by my chum's shop and grab some costumes." She smiled. "A few feathers and some spray paint for me, and whatever we can find to disguise you lads. Then at dawn tomorrow, we're out of here—and you better have the pyramid with you when we leave."

"Let's get back to Cuba for just a moment," I said. "What about the Cuban MIG fighters, gunboats, and perhaps firing squads? Or the very least, eating beans and rice in an eight-foot cell for the rest of our lives?"

"Listen, we're going to go in about fifty feet off the water. The plane will be in and out so quickly, you won't know whether to throw up from air sickness or sea sickness. Their radar isn't even going to blink. Only two gunboats patrol that section of Cuba, and they don't bother with Bandera Cay. We can spend a week or two there and let things cool. A nice little vacation—no phone, no pool, no pets. Maybe even get things taken care of with your Rastaman friend. You've got the pyramid tucked away someplace safe, right? "

I nodded and glanced at Will. He shrugged. "I always wanted an adventurous life."

Aaahhh, Halloween in Key West—an amalgam of unfettered

decadence and delight—a riotous but remarkably amicable tequila and lime collective consciousness. The last of that old hallowed moon gazed down as the first cool winds of fall caressed the sand and the palms, and it smiled like the cover of a King Crimson album, offering blessings to its prodigal children—glorious island pagans lost to their annual rites.

We found costumes of sorts at the shop owned by Hanes' friend. I was an acceptable pirate. With my long hair shrouded by a scarf, roped britches, eye patch, and the darkening of my mustache, I was fairly well disguised. Will was exceptionally disguised in a somewhat gangly gorilla suit. Hanes, true to her promise, consigned her adornment to feathers and spray paint. She looked like some exotic tropical flower, concealing her pistils with only blossoms—a breath-taking, titillating, pagan extraordinaire.

I couldn't help but stare when she came out from the dressing room. "Lord, I have never appreciated Halloween as much as I do at this moment," I said with barely contained hanker.

Gorilla Will, who was holding his head in his hand, looked at her and a glow that had been dim for some time in his eyes glimmered faintly—like the lamp of a lighthouse breaking through the evening fog. He gazed, unabashed, then spoke quietly. "Have I mentioned that I think I knew you in a past life—two lifetimes ago in Paris. During the fall of Louis the Sixteenth. The peasants were taking the city, killing the wealthy people, like us. But we escaped on a little fishing sloop into the Seine. You were pregnant with our first child."

Angie leaned forward slightly, as if drawn into what he was saying.

Will paused, reminiscently, eyes somewhere else. "You loved the bridges—the different colored bridges in Paris, and the way the sun used to reflect off of them. It's one of the reasons you chose to return to the Keys this time—for the bridges, and for me."

Angie stared at him for a second, then turned to me. "Is he daft? Does he need special medicine that he's not keeping up with?"

I could barely stifle a grin.

She looked back at Will. "Put on your head, gorilla boy. Save the song and dance for the barroom smut queens." Then she turned toward the door. "C'mon, it's time to get lost in the crowd."

I nudged Will. "I told you it doesn't work all the time."

He shrugged. "Guess not."

We joined the press of revelry as it wound its way in and out of the bars along Duval Street, becoming part of the mindless, collective inertia—less frantic than lemmings but certainly no more intelligent. We drank sparingly at several watering holes, gorged ourselves on oysters on the half shell and conch fritters, then drank less sparingly until we closed the last bar. As the sun climbed hesitantly from ruby-colored early morning mists, it found us bleary-eyed and weary on a small beach near Garrison Bight. We had unloaded a few things from the car that we might need on a lonely island—suntan lotion, some munchies, a change of clothes or two—Will had the carryall/pyramid bag in his hand.

Angie and our seaplane pilot spoke in hushed tones as Will and I examined the Cessna 182 that would provide us exodus from our present plight. After her conversation with the pilot, Angie came over and, without further courtesy, said curtly, "Okay, we're nearly ready to go. So where's the triangular object of interest? At this point I need some proof."

"We have it, and it's safe," Will said. "You're going to have to trust us on this. Do you think for a moment we'd be daring or stupid enough to go through all this if we didn't have it?"

"I'm taking a lot of chances here," she said tensely. "And you haven't produced a bloody thing." She looked at the bag in Will's hand. "What's in there?"

"Suntan lotion, underwear, and about forty Almond Joys." He thrust it out at her. "Here. You wanna look at the skid stains on my underwear? Go ahead."

She hesitated.

I took a step forward. "Listen, Angie, we'll make a deal with you. When we get to the island and we find everything is copasetic, you get your look at the pyramid. I promise."

"How are you going to manage that?"

I smiled. "You forget. We're connected to the people who built the damned thing. Trust me, we can arrange a look for you."

She did that signature angry sigh of hers and glanced back at the pilot standing somewhat impatiently by the plane. "Okay, okay. Let's get this show underway. Load up."

As we climbed aboard the aircraft, I nodded to the pilot—a tall, tanned, serious-looking fellow dressed in tropical khakis and a Captain Tony's ball cap. "Kansas," I said.

The pilot looked at us. "I don't know you. I never met you, and I never did what we're about to do."

"The pleasure's all yours, dude," Will said sarcastically.

Will and I settled into the back seat, Angie and the pilot up front.

He scooted the plane around with the sun at our backs, pushed in the throttle, and after a prone surge and a series of quick water slaps on the pontoons, we planed, everything smoothed, and we lifted off. As the aircraft began to rise I glanced back at the beach and for a moment I thought I saw a figure step out from the foliage along the shore—short and bald—a strange smile as he looked up at us.

"Lord, that looked like Calico," I muttered to myself. But it was such a brief glimpse I wasn't at all sure.

"What'd you say?" Will asked, leaning over to compensate for the roar of the engine.

"Nothing. Nah, nothing," I said shaking my head. "Just getting a little jumpy—with all this excitement."

I don't think we flew any higher than two hundred feet the entire trip. A half hour out, the pilot adjusted pitch again and nosed her down to about fifty feet above the rolling green swells of slick glass below us. There wasn't much conversation. My impression was he owed Angie for something and this was the payback. Another fifteen minutes into the trip he nodded toward a gray-green smear on the horizon. "That's the place—Sabana Archipelago. Bandera Cay is the big one on the far right. You might as well grab your stuff and unbuckle. I'm gonna make one pass at the beach. You better be out and wading before the prop slows."

"Okay, okay," Angie said, a little tense. "Let's do it." She looked hard at the pilot "Ten days from now, exactly. No more. Okay?"

He just adjusted his Ray Ban sunglasses with one hand and nodded.

"It was nice never knowing you," Will mumbled from the back.

From the quick look I got coming in, it was a pretty island, probably a mile or two in length with a small green ridge in the center, a couple of tiny bays, and an abundance of tropical flora. As the plane hit the water and slowed sufficiently to turn around, we were out onto the pontoons and into the waist-deep water, dragging our gear—a couple of overnight bags and an ice chest with food—headed toward an old stilt house with an expansive wooden deck set into a pod of coconut trees just off the beach. I suddenly felt like Bogie in *Key Largo*. I liked the way it felt—that electric mixture of illegitimacy and adventure. I turned so I could manage a cool nonchalant wave to the pilot, but he had already swung around and was headed out.

Mames' caretaker, a thin, grizzled, gray-haired fellow with a leathery tan and expressionless dark eyes, found his way down to the beach as we waded ashore. He took off his straw hat when he saw Angie. “Ahhh, Miss Angie. I not expect to see you again.” He didn’t seem pleased or displeased—it was just a statement. He looked at us then back to her. “I will prepare a couple of rooms. There are towels on the deck—to dry off.” With that, he stuffed on his tattered hat and turned toward the house. We followed.

“It was nice to never meet you too,” Will mumbled again.

Sanchez never proved to be much of a talker but he cooked a mean fillet of snapper and had a very acceptable wine room from which we confiscated a bottle of Chardonnay. By the end of the day, we were secured in comfortable rooms and enjoying a wonderful dinner on the deck, watching the last of the sun pierce the first gray translucent arches of an incoming storm. The wind fell and the water stilled to a dark blue glass that mirrored flights of gulls and egrets on their way to the safety of solid ground before nightfall. As the darkness engulfed us, we lit oil lanterns, drank more wine and listened to the movement of the sea, watching the squall line become incandescent with slashes of angry lightning. But there was something else in the clouds—a distant heavy humming that heaved upward in tone and volume, leaving searing radiant lines of purple flashes emanating outward from the core of the storm. Unearthly beautiful, and it was the unearthly part that had me concerned.

Will echoed my thoughts. “That’s some strange stuff, dudes. Do you think that’s Rufus’ calling card?”

I nodded pensively. “Could be, man. Could be.”

But neither Rufus nor any of his connections showed up, and for the next few days we all languished in the Cuban Tropics like characters from a Hemingway book, and got to know each other. The days were warm, the heat broken only by the slow, methodical turning of the ceiling fans that were powered by a generator Sanchez fired up once or twice a day. The island was the consummate tropical paradise. It had long, sandy beaches covered with tall, arching palms shading the sand and stretching out toward the crystalline waters that surrounded us. There were two small bays—complete microcosms of Caribbean sea life. We walked along the shore, exploring, gathering coconuts and mangos. We splashed in the warm sea, borrowed masks and a couple Hawaiian slings from Sanchez and found grouper and lobster in the reef grottos. Detective Hanes was still interested in seeing the pyramid but Will and I explained that we were waiting for word from our Rastaman connection, and she seemed to accept that, reluctantly, for the time being. Sanchez was consistently taciturn but not unfriendly, occasionally offering a suggestion on where to find the best fish or fruit. He created island feasts from the products of our efforts, we drank Cuban beer, witnessed glorious sunsets, and somewhere along the line, detective Hanes became just Angie.

Our new acquaintance was a delight—petite, but not shy, well read, confident, and possessed of an unforgiving, acerbic wit that complemented our own. In just a few days we were thoroughly enjoying ourselves. Angie's tan darkened after days in the sun, highlighting the soft, auburn hair that caressed her shoulders as she moved. Her bronze eyes would change to amber when she became animated with laughter or ire, and although her teeth were less than perfect—she had somewhat of an overbite—it somehow managed to add to, rather than detract from, the package. She possessed that same economically perfect figure as Banyan did. All in all, she proved to be a remarkable woman, and, as usual, Will and I began our typical, almost instinctive competition.

Much to my chagrin, it was obvious after a couple of days, that Will and Angie were hitting it off better than planned. I like to think of myself as a clever boy—not without intuition. It wasn't that Angie and I didn't get along well—we did. We genuinely began to enjoy each other's company, but I realized that there was a warmth in Angie's smile when she looked at Will, her touches lingered a little longer with him, and she seemed to find his anecdotes more amusing—which really pissed me off. It brought back a lot of memories of Banyan and our times in Key West. I tried to ignore it, to be happy for him. So he got the girl this time. But it all struck a melancholy chord within me. I started to explore the interior of the island on my own, which seemed to suit Will and Angie.

One evening after supper, about a week into our visit, I went back to the room Will and I shared. The others were still out on the deck. But a few moments later Will knocked discreetly then came in. I was sitting on one of the small beds. He came over and sat on the other. He looked at me with a touch more concern in that crooked grin than normal. "Angie and I are going to take a walk." He paused, then smiled a little self-consciously. "I think there's a good chance I won't be back here tonight. Just didn't want you to worry if I don't show up."

I nodded. "That's cool. Enjoy yourself, buddy. Thanks for letting me know."

He sighed softly. "Are you okay with this? You and I, we always seem to…there's always some competition. I don't want it to change anything."

"If your father hadn't been a yak, I would still have a chance," I muttered with a smile.

Will chuckled, relaxing. "Yeah, well, luck of the draw. Now if I could just lick my eyebrows." There was a pause. "You know, man, I really like her. I don't know if it's like 'the one,' but she's really cool, and Lord, she's a minx! Did I tell you she can actually—"

I waved up my hands. "No, no, no—too much information. Just go away and do what yaks do. I'll catch up on my reading."

My partner grinned and stood up. "Okay, dude. Wish me luck. See you in the morning."

I don't know how one person finds another and senses that completeness in a short period of time. Maybe it's karma, chemistry, or just blind sensuality. Maybe it's ultimately a combination of timing and need. But after that night there was little pretense and little attempt to veil the affection that was growing between my friend and his new girl. They held hands, shared food sensually, and publically caressed each other to an almost disgusting degree. Will never returned to his bed in our room. Still, if she had just laughed a little more at my jokes, I would have been okay with it.

On the evening of our eighth day, we had gathered on the deck to watch the sunset, which had become a ritual of sorts. We all shared a pitcher of margaritas, including Sanchez, but there was little improvement to his somber nature. In fact, he seemed more subdued—content to sit in a deck chair and sip his drink quietly as the rest of us talked. As the sky darkened, engulfing the final tendrils of a surrendering sun, and the heavy gray banks of an evening storm coalesced on the horizon, we all sensed that distant, ponderous humming we had heard on the first evening of our arrival. It pitched upward in tone and volume as it had before, leaving the same searing radiant lines of purple flashes in the center of the storm.

"That sure ain't natural stuff," Will said.

"I wish we had the pyramid here now," Angie said quietly.

Will glanced at me, and at that moment his eyes reflected a decision. Before I could get my hand up or open my mouth to say, "No, no, no," he quietly replied, "We do."

She looked up sharply. "I thought you hid it somewhere in Key West before we left?"

"Crap!" I whispered under my breath.

"It's okay, man," Will said, hands out in front of him in a

placating fashion. "It's okay—she's on our side." He looked over to her and shrugged. "I just stuck it in my overnight bag. Tomorrow morning we'll show you."

I gazed at the horizon and the unearthly storm clouds as they were again pierced by that eerie, scarlet iridescence. Exhaling heavily, I muttered. "I'm thinking we may have visitors."

CHAPTER ELEVEN

Viva La Resistencia

Just before dawn the next morning, I awoke to the sound of voices on the deck outside. *Sanchez,* I thought, *hopefully preparing breakfast.* I was pretty sure I heard Angie's voice as well. I smiled and stretched luxuriously in the old four-poster bed, feeling almost safe for the first time in weeks, then leaned up on my elbow and pulled back the gossamer mosquito netting. I crawled out, slipped on my pants and a T-shirt, and ambled through the living room onto the deck.

Sanchez was there. So were Angie and Will—and about a half dozen Cuban Coast Guardsmen, all with weapons aimed in our general direction. Tucked close up in the little bay in front of the house was an austere gray gunboat. I was immediately grabbed and hustled over to my friends, who bore the same frightened and confused look I certainly possessed.

The officer in charge, a smallish, dark-haired fellow with a pinched face and a wiry build, glared at us with squinty little eyes then threw his hands up dramatically and shouted, "Imperialists! Puke-sucking American spies! Yeah! Yeah!"

As innocuous as the term "Yeah" is, this fellow managed to give it a poignant, accusatory tone, his eyes flaring with each utterance. We involuntarily winced. He took a step forward and adjusted his tight "Fidel" cap with another dramatic flair, then threw his shoulders back and puffed out his chest. It was supposed to be an imposing gesture, but there just wasn't enough height to pull it off, and his eyes were just too damned close together—they looked like they were continually competing for the bridge of his nose. In addition, there was a sense of impatient nervousness about him. His head pivoted too much, like a squirrel guarding a nut, and his left foot periodically tapped out a staccato Morse code. Even with the gravity of the situation, I felt like I was in a Woody Allen movie.

"I yan Captain Enrique Villadosa ob de Guardia National de Cuba," he shouted in a voice just a pitch too high. "And you," he cried, jabbing a bony finger at us, "are goink be some dead son-a-bitches! Yeah! Yeah!" He swung around to the rising sun, throwing his hands up again. "I'ne finally goink to get to execute sonbody. It about time!" Pivoting around at us again, he jabbed at his boat in the harbor, and shouted (a little exuberant spittle flying from his thin lips), "Seben years! Seben years on that piece a chit, leaking tin can and I neber catch nobody importante. I neber get to execute nobody! But now..." He grew quieter, more intense—his beady eyes flaring then narrowing as he whispered with malicious glee, eyebrows dancing up and down. "But now ... Oohh, I'ne goink to execute you so good!"

I thought, *Good God! Just our luck! We've been captured by some crazy Fidelian psychopath,* when Will suddenly drew himself up and echoed my thoughts,

"Are you crazy? We're American citizens. We have rights. You can't just shoot us!"

Captain Villadosa smiled, his lips curling back from surprisingly pearly teeth. Still, he looked more like a Chihuahua snarling over a bone. He glanced around at his men. "How many ob you see American citizens on this deck?"

They hesitated, sensing where this was going, and no one raised a hand.

Villadosa nodded, satisfied. "Now, how many ob you see puke-sucking American spies?"

Of course, all hands quickly rose.

The captain turned back toward us. "I know who you are—Sanchez called us."

Remembering I'd seen a CB base station radio in the kitchen, I glared at our caretaker. "Thanks, Sanchez."

He looked down and mumbled, "I have a family."

The implication was clear.

"Tie them up!" Villadosa shouted in Spanish. "Take them down to the beach." He swung around to us again. "I'ne goink to hab a nice breakfast that Sanchez is goink make for me. Then we goink to have a lil' execution." Without another word, he strode into the living room. As the guards closed in on us we could still hear the captain mumbling loudly, "Oh, my lucky, lucky day. I finally get to execute sonbody! Maybe one at a time. Yeah. Yeah!"

As they tied our hands, Will looked at Angie and rolled his head to one side sarcastically. "Oh, there's no gunboats near Bandera Cay. A nice week's vacation—no phone, no pool no pets."

A half hour later, Villadosa had finished his breakfast and we were tied securely to three adjacent palm trees on the beach. Borne by the prospect of an entertaining execution, the captain was in an excellent, somewhat accommodating mood. His men were spread out in a semi-circle around us, guns at the ready. Their leader ambled over and smiled disarmingly, adjusting his hat for more of a jaunty look, running a finger down his pencil-thin mustache. "Well, it time. I decide I'ne goink to make it quick for you. It not goink to hurt."

I scoffed. "How do you know it's 'not goink to hurt'? When was the last time you were executed?"

Ignoring me completely, Villadosa went on. "You want a cigarette? Chewing gum?"

Will blinked. "Sure. Why not? I'll have a cigarette."

Angie just exhaled exasperatedly and looked up at the sky.

"I'll have a cigarette, then some chewing gum," I said.

Needless to say, we nursed the Cuban cigarettes until the final glowing embers burned our lips and we were forced to spit them out.

Villadosa threw the last of his cigarette in the sand and twisted it to death with the heel of his boot. "Okay, that was good. Now time for execution."

"Nuh-uh," I said, shaking my head. "I haven't had my gum."

Villadosa frowned. "You don't need no stinkin' gums."

"You promised, man! You said I could have gum!"

The captain threw up his hands in acquiescent anger. "Okay! Okay!" He fumbled around in his fatigues jacket for a moment and came up with a pack, ripped out a piece and stuck it in my mouth. "Eat your gum, then shut up and die like a man."

As I nursed the Cuban imitation of Wrigley's Spearmint, Angie twisted around to us and spoke somberly. "I'm sorry, guys. There were a lot of things that were supposed to happen, but this just wasn't one of them. I'm really sorry."

"Nobody's fault—just a bad roll of the dice," I muttered.

"I'm a little scared," she said quietly.

No one answered.

The sun was just cresting the vast blue horizon, turning the sand to gold as our executioners chambered rounds.

"I hate to say it my friend, but this looks like the last sunrise," Will said while staring straight ahead. "Of all the things I imagined … I never thought…." He paused for a moment as the first warm rays of the sun reached us, abating the morning chill—and a little of the fear—then a sad, wistful little smile touched his lips. "Of all the people I've known this time around, I just want you to know…"

I was trying to keep my eyes from glassing. "Yeah, I know, partner. I know."

Villadosa effectively crushed any additional sentiment as he stepped forward brusquely. "Okay! Okay! Enough of this useless emotional chit. It time to get chot! Yeah! Yeah!"

The little Cuban stepped back and gazed at us for a moment, rocking his head from side to side in uncertainty, his left foot doing its staccato Morse code thing. "One at a time?" He paused. "Or all together?"

Suddenly he clapped his hands decisively and said, "All together! Yeah! Yeah! All together!" He turned to his men and raised his arm. They brought up their guns. All I remember distinctly about that moment was how terrible and large the muzzles of all those weapons seemed. I closed my eyes.

Just then, Villadosa yelled, "Wait! Wait! We forgot blinfolds!"

I slowly opened my eyes and looked over at Will. "Blinfolds?"

While his men stood there, uncertain, guns still aimed at us, Villadosa strode over to us muttering, "Chit! What was I thinkin'? You gotta hab blinfolds." He screeched to a halt in front of us, waving his hands. "You want blinfolds, right?"

Will cocked his head and shrugged at me. "What the hell is a blinfold?"

Villadosa stomped his feet in frustration. "Blinfolds! You know, blinfolds to cober your eyes. A good execution has to hab blinfolds!"

Angie sighed angrily, then riveted the captain with her eyes. "Just shoot us and get it over with, you mad little twit!"

The captain started at her vehemence. "Hmmmph! You really a puke-suckin' American spy bitch and you don' get no blinfold now." He glanced over to Will and I. "You want blinfolds? C'mon, don' none of you wan' a blinfold?"

"Would it make you happy if I wore one?" Will asked.

"Yeah. You wan' a blinfold?"

My partner smiled, shook his head, and answered in his best Cuban accent, "We don' need no stinkin' blinfolds."

Villadosa puffed up indignantly and his eyes narrowed. "Okay. Okay. We just goink to choot you like puke-suckin' dogs." With no further ado, he backed away from the line of fire and raised his arm again. "Ready! Aim!"

But before he could get out the "Fire," his Cuban Coast Guard cutter, sitting at anchor less than 200 yards from us, exploded in a fiery ball and a deafening roar that drowned everything out. Suddenly, a gaudy red and white cigarette boat roared out from behind the smoke and fire of the burning cutter and swept by the beach. Villadosa was shouting, but the crackle of automatic rifle fire was again drowning him out. Two of the firing squad were struck and knocked off their feet as bullets ripped up the sand around our captors and us. I could see five or six men in the cigarette boat shooting—one with what appeared to be a heavy caliber machine gun mounted on the bow. Unfortunately, being tied to a tree left little mobility. We watched in terror, flinching helplessly as bullets zinged around us like angry hornets. Another of the Cubans cried out and fell, and the rest, the diminutive captain in the lead, dropped their weapons and scrambled helter-skelter for the jungle.

As the last of the Cubans disappeared into the dense green foliage, the cigarette boat swung around and nosed into the beach. A tall, gaunt-looking fellow with a short, military-style haircut, intense black eyes, and a tightly cropped dark beard turned off the engines as one of his men vaulted out with the anchor, securing it in the sand.

Venezuela Tango (Veney to his friends) smiled. This was his moment in the sun. He was going to go down in the annals of the anti-Castro Cuban resistance movement. He had just saved the famous freedom fighter Juan Ricardo Herrera's life. Or so he thought.

Up until last week, Veney was the leader of a relatively nondescript anti-Castro Cuban resistance movement. They called themselves Ortega 9—after the relatively famous Omega 7, whom they admired greatly. Veney was born in Cuba, but when he turned 15, his father, who was a part of the *Escambry Campesino* anti-Communist Insurgency, was arrested. By the purest of flukes he escaped, gathered up his family, stole a fishing boat, and made his way to Miami, where he requested political immunity. Tango naturally carried an inherent hatred for all that was Fidelian.

Veney's group had been contacted by the Omega 7 organization—there was a situation. One of their secondary leaders, a Juan Ricardo Herrera, had been captured on a reconnaissance mission in waters near Cuba. They discovered he was being "interrogated" on an island in the Sabana Archipelago on the northern side of Cuba. The Omega 7s recognized it as pretty much a suicide mission. Best-case scenario, the Cubans would probably kill Herrera if they knew a rescue was underway, which would keep him from talking. In a worst-case scenario, most of the people trying to rescue him would probably get whacked as well. So, the Omega 7s offered the Ortega 9s the mission as sort of a rite of passage into the big boy's league. Veney and his men were given a cigarette boat, some serious arms and ammunition, and a map of the archipelago. The weather had been exceptional, and they made great time crossing the straits undetected. However, Veney, who was not great with nautical charts to begin with, ended up at the wrong island. Hell, there was a Cuban gunboat in the bay. He figured he had to be in the right place. He eased up behind it and with a zealous exclamation of "*Viva la resistencia!*" let fly a rocket-propelled grenade, then charged the beach, where there appeared to be an execution in progress.

As the boat was secured on the beach, Veney leapt out and very dramatically marched up to those of us who were still tied to trees. He paused, hands on hips and studied us with those dark emotionless eyes. (Okay, he studied Angie a little longer.) "Which one of you is Juan Ricardo?"

We had just seen a number of people shot and that didn't lend us a lot of confidence. I tilted my head at Will and Will tilted his head at me. "He is," we both said in harmony.

Veney blinked a couple of times. "I am the leader of the Ortega 9 Cuban Resistance Movement from Miami," he said in remarkably good English. "My name is Venezuela Tango. I am here to rescue Juan Herrera."

"Okay, I'm Juan," I said.

Veney's tanned and angular face broke into what was probably his closest excuse for a smile and he raised a clenched fist to the sky. "*Viva la resistencia!*" he shouted—loud enough to make us all flinch.

The other members of his team, who had gathered around at this point, shouted in return. "Hiiiaaahh! *Viva la resistencia!*"

I figured this was a good time to join the club. *"Viva la resistencia!"* I shouted.

Will, always a quick study, chimed in. "Hiiiaahh! Down with Castro!"

"Hiiiaaahh!" shouted everyone—and so typically, Will really got into it.

"*Viva la free Cuba*!"

"Hiiiaaahh!" sang the chorus.

Will threw his head back. "*Viva Miami!!*"

"Hiiiaaahh!"

"*Viva Ann Margaret!*"

The enthusiasm of the chorus drifted away somewhat at that point, and Will quit while he was ahead. Veney pulled an ugly, very sharp-looking knife from his belt and moved toward us.

"I love Cubans," I said quietly, apprehensively, to no one in particular, which was followed by a sigh of relief as Veney cut my bonds and nothing else of importance.

As his men cut Angie and Will loose, he spoke to me in Spanish. "You don't look Cuban to me, and neither do your friends."

I shrugged and answered in my best Spanish. "*Mi madre es Cubana. Me padres es Americano.* I gestured at Will and Angie. "*Mis amigos son Americanos solamente, pero ellos conscientes el situacion—simpatico.*"

Veney nodded, mollified. Will and Angie came over and stood next to me, uncertain.

The tall Cuban took another slow minute to look us over. "I thought they would have tortured you by now."

"Oh, man. They did!" Will replied. "It was terrible!"

Veney looked at him skeptically. "I don't see no marks."

Will arched his neck. "Just look at these bruises, man!"

"Looks more like hickies to me, man," Veney muttered suspiciously.

"Hickies! Hickies!" Will scoffed. "They were beating me with a rubber hose! A big rubber hose!"

Our new acquaintance stared at him for a moment then turned to me. "So what else?"

"Water torture," I replied. "One of the most diabolical mental tortures there is. Tied us down—one drop of water every fifteen seconds—splat, in the center of your forehead. An hour into it, you think you're gonna go mad."

"No TV, no Beatles music for a whole week, man," Will moaned dramatically.

I glanced at my friend and narrowed my eyes. He went quiet.

"We told them nothing," I spat. "Nothing! So they were going to shoot us when you showed up."

Veney nodded, pensively, still staring at us. "It is good. Before the week is out we will all be heroes of the resistance. *Viva la resistencia!*" he shouted again, and his men cheered.

Will took a deep breath, and I caught him with a look. He did that tilt of his head and shrugged.

At that point, Venezuela Tango drew his shoulders back and straightened up, staring to the south and the distant Cuban mountains that rose out of the haze on the horizon. "We will exact our revenge before we leave these waters—tonight we invade Cuba to strike a blow for the resistance. It is *El Malecon Havana Carnival* all this week and Castro will speak in the plaza tomorrow. We will assassinate Castro as he speaks!"

"Oh, Lord," I heard Will moan behind me. "All I ever wanted to be was a simple tropical fish collector."

Veney motioned to a couple of his men and pointed to the bodies lying in the sand. "Get those off the beach and set out guards to watch for those other *federales* pigs. We will rest here until midnight, then make the run for the Cuban coast."

We all returned to the house. Sanchez had disappeared. I figured there was no point in mentioning him. After Veney's men had made a thorough search of our end of the island, one of his boys cooked some lunch. I tried to keep the conversation away from revolution as much as possible.

Veney looked up from the plate of *frijoles* he was hunched over. "You should know that Philippe of Omega 7 sent us. You are well appreciated in your organization."

I nodded humbly, noncommittally. "Yeah, Philippe is a good man."

"How long have you been with the Omega?"

"Too long. But not long enough yet to accomplish our goal of a free Cuba."

Our new Cuban compatriot nodded enthusiastically while chewing a wad of bread. "But tomorrow we will strike the blow that brings the Cuban people much closer to freedom!"

Amid the enthusiastic thumping on the table by Veney's companions, I glanced at Will and Angie. When the applause had died, I stood and rubbed my stomach. "I think I need to take a walk—to work off some of these *frijoles*."

Will and Angie stood on cue. "I could use a stretch myself," Will said. "We'll come with you."

When we reached the beach and began strolling along the tide line, well away from the others, Will turned to me and whispered urgently. "Okay, 'Juan,' we need to get our asses out of here before the rest of those crazies up there attack Cuba and get us all killed."

"I'm open for suggestions," I said. "You got a plan?"

Will paused for a moment. "We've still got the economy-size magic dust, right?"

"Yeah," I said hesitantly, "but I got a strange feeling the opera ain't over yet. I hate to use up all our backup."

He glanced out at the cigarette boat lying at anchor about fifty yards offshore, then gave me that Lee Marvin grin. "Okay, I got a plan, but we're gonna need a diversion."

Veney's boys had shot one of the partially domesticated pigs that roamed on the island and had built a pit fire on a sandy rise about fifty yards from the house—planning a little pre-Castro-shooting luau. It provided me with some diversion inspiration. I had remembered seeing an aged South American shotgun in the corner of Sanchez's room in the cottage, and what appeared to be a box of shells. During the day, while we all lounged around waiting for the sun to set so we could begin our midnight ride into Cuban resistance fame, I worked my way behind the cottage and slipped through a window, deftly pocketing the shells. Even though our plan for escape was gelling, I knew we had to be careful. As overly enthusiastic as he was, Veney was no fool. He had guards posted around the compound and he had two watching the boat. Timing had to be perfect or we could end up gathering flies like Villadosa's luckless men.

When the sun, infinitely too slow for my patience, finally began to edge toward the horizon, I struck up a conversation with the fellow assigned to watch and baste the pig, which had been gutted, smothered in palm leaves, then laid on the bed of coals. We were discussing the distinguishing merits of Cuban rum when, just a few yards into the jungle, Angie screamed.

That caught the attention of the majority of warm bodies in the area, including my companion.

"It's the girl!" I shouted. "Something's happened!"

As my Cuban friend headed at a run for the jungle, I quickly tossed a dozen shotgun shells into the embers of the cooking pit, then followed.

Angie wasn't hard to find. Looking quite frightened, she gazed at the handful of us who had found her. "It was a snake—a bloody huge snake!" she shouted. Pointing at the foliage above her, she added breathlessly, "It dropped on me from those vines."

"Stupid American women," Veney muttered. "Everyone back to their posts!" I put my arm around Angie protectively, as we watched the others drift back to their respective positions.

Angie and I waited until the others had returned to camp. I turned to her. "Okay, girl, we've got maybe a couple of minutes before showtime."

We had just turned and begun to make our way from the clearing toward the beach when suddenly, out of the thick of the jungle pounced a fairly disheveled but certainly angry Captain Enrique Villadosa, jabbing a trusty AK7 at us. His tight "Fidel" cap was gone, his hair tangled, and those squinty little eyes were diffused with even more madness than usual. He stepped forward smartly, almost jabbing the barrel of the gun into my chest, head still doing that nervous pivoting, squirrel-guarding-a-nut thing. "I got no boat, I got no men, I'ne goink to lose my command now," he sputtered, then his eyes narrowed maliciously. "But, I'ne goink to get to execute you after all. Yeah! Yeah! How you like that? Yeah! Yeah!"

"Can I have a blinfold? How about a cigarette?" I said.

I could see that for just a second the idea was, of course, appealing, but he caught himself, jabbing the barrel at my chest again. "No! No blinfolds. No gum! No cigarettes! You gonna die right now!"

As he brought the gun up to his shoulder to fire, Angie, who was standing just a step or two away, did the strangest thing. She reached down and pulled up her T-shirt up, exposing her breasts. "Hey, what do you think of these?" she said, while shimmying seductively.

I have to admit the move took both Villadosa—and me—by surprise. There's just something about a shapely pair of breasts that can be purely distracting. Villadosa glanced over at her and, just for a moment, lost his concentration. He tried to bring it back to me, but his head did that squirrel thing and his eyes just couldn't resist swinging back to Angie once more. At that moment, I slapped the barrel away from my chest and tackled him. I had to admit, for a little guy, he was wiry and surprisingly strong. As we struggled for control of the gun, I realized I could be in trouble. Fortunately, the ever-ready Angie pulled down her shirt, grabbed a coconut and bounced it off Villadosa's head, which took the demented glaze right out of his eyes. I pushed the unconscious captain off my chest and stood up a little shakily. Angie helped me to my feet and for just a moment we stood looking at each other. I smiled. "Quite an amazing … distraction."

She grinned, not at all shyly. "Use what you've got available. That's what they teach you at the police academy."

As we stood in the clearing alone, my shotgun rounds in the pit fire reached critical mass and the explosions began. Angie looked toward the reports, then turned to me. "I guess we should be on our way,"

I smiled. "Yeah! Yeah!"

Will was waiting at the edge of the jungle, watching the Cubans' boat rocking gently in the waves about thirty yards offshore. Two guards sat on the gnarled and tubular base of an aged palm tree at the edge of the beach, smoking cigarettes and staring at the darkening waters. They had held their positions when Angie yelled, and soon after, one of the others checked in with them, explaining what had happened. They shared a ribald comment about snakes and women then returned to their respective tasks. But when the apparent gunfire and shouting suddenly erupted back toward camp, it was too much for them. They bolted upright and charged back down the path toward the house. Will, who claimed the dubious distinction of being able to hotwire a car in sixty seconds, slipped out of the jungle and down onto the beach, wading into the water toward the gently cresting boat.

As Angie and I started out toward the beach I stopped suddenly. "Almost forgot. One last thing, then we're out of here," I said.

She looked at me quizzically as I moved to the base of an old sea grape at the edge of the clearing and began digging with my hands. I pushed the dried and brittle leaves away, pulled the sand back and drew out a small canvas bag.

"The pyramid," she whispered.

I stood and nodded. "Will showed me where he buried it."

We cut through the jungle toward the beach, avoiding the trails. The boat was 100 yards south of us. I could just make out Will's tall, gangly silhouette at the helm. He saw us and waved. We waved back and began running.

As we entered the water, thirty yards from the boat, Will fired it up and pulled the anchor. The tide was high. He had just trimmed up the big inboards and skimmed in closer to pick us up, when Veney and his men came charging out of the jungle and onto the beach. Veney Tango was a pretty quick study—he'd figured it out. He brought up his rifle and started firing. His men quickly followed suit. As bullets smacked the water around us, Angie and I struggled through the waist-deep water. When we reached the side of the craft and Will pulled Angie aboard, I watched a line of bullets stitch the side of the hull not a foot from me. The furious shooting was deafening. Another line of shots slashed the water in front of me. It was all good incentive. The next thing I knew, I was in the boat huddled behind the gunnel as Will swung us around and headed for open water.

With almost orgasmic relief we watched the island that had provided such a cocktail of dangerously demented personalities begin to grow smaller. We could still just see Veney and his group shouting and gesturing in frustration, still shooting at us, but we were out of range.

Will finally backed off the throttles and turned to Angie and me with that wry smile again. "You both okay?"

We nodded.

He grinned. “Damned if our grandchildren aren't going to think we're just bald-faced liars.” Then he spoke a little more seriously. “Let's take a quick look at the boat—we took a few hits back there and we need to make certain we haven't got any serious holes in us before we head out over open water.”

Will and I took off our shirts and jumped over the side, diving down and running our hands over the hull. Ten minutes later we were back in what appeared to be a slightly shot up but fairly sound speedboat.

We were just beginning to feel like we all might live to see another margarita at Captain Tony's. Will had just started the boat and was easing the throttles forward when we saw them. About a mile and a half out on both sides of us were two Cuban gunboats—not the old junkers like wily little Captain Villadosa commanded, but new, very fast, forty-five-footers with 50-caliber machine guns and small, 20 mm cannon on the bows.

“Holy crap!' Will moaned exasperatedly. Then he looked over at Angie. “Not to worry, there's no gunboats near Bandera Cay. A nice week's vacation—no phone, no pool, no pets.”

Angie shook her head. “I'd heard the Cubans were going to bring in some new stuff—to edge out the smugglers using their waters, but I didn't—”

“No you didn't,” I said, more than a little angry myself. “Those guys are as fast as we are—maybe faster. We've still got eight or ten miles to the ADIS, and that's nothing more than an invisible boundary between the U.S. and Cuba.”

Just then we saw a puff of smoke from the bow of one of the gunships, and with a roar, a fountain of water exploded 100 yards off our stern.

“Time to say ‘goodnight Johnny,” Will muttered as he slammed the throttles in and the sleek craft beneath us surged out of the water at a run. For the next five minutes, we played a dangerous game of cat and mouse as Will kept the boat at full throttle while zigzagging every hundred yards to keep the Cuban cannon from zeroing in on us. But in that short time two things were becoming obvious—they were gaining on us, and the guys at the cannon were getting better.

As another angry fountain of water and shrapnel exploded fifty yards ahead of us, Will yelled over the roar of the engine and the explosions. “I don't know what the hell to do—we're at the ADIS and they're not turning back. They're gonna get us sooner or later!”

I was about to reply when Angie looked out at the horizon and grabbed my arm hard enough to make me squeal like a pig.

"Aaahhhh! What the hell are you doing?"

She pointed into the sky ahead of us. "It's Mac! It's Mac!"

At first I didn't know who Mac was, but I quickly put two and two together when I saw the familiar red and white Cessna floatplane that had unceremoniously dropped us at the island almost two weeks before.

"I'll be dammed," I said to no one in particular, quickly grabbing the radio mike at the console and changing the frequency to 122.2, which most pilots monitor. "Mac! Mac! Answer your damned phone!" I yelled with probably a little more gusto that I had planned. "We're in the cigarette boat a mile and a half and 180 degrees out from you. You got us? Come back. You got us?"

We all held our breath. Another cannon round slapped the waters twenty-five yards behind us. The radio offered nothing but static. The two Cuban gunboats had converged, now about a half mile behind, showing no signs of being concerned about international boundaries. I was bringing the mike up again when the radio squelched. "This is Cessna; 360 degrees off your bow. (No call numbers I noticed). Is Angie there?"

Will's lady snatched the mike out of my hand. "This is Angie, you late son of a bitch. Get that plane down here and pick us up!"

The water was dead calm with an occasional low, slow swell—one of those late fall doldrums where the sea looks like glass. The sun was sinking and we were running out of daylight, but it could be done. My hopes started to rise.

"Timing is everything," I muttered with a smile. But then Mac replied.

"No can do," he replied stoically. "By the time I set it down and wait for you guys to get to me those Cubans are going to be all over us with their deck guns. We'll be sitting ducks. I hate to say this, but you're on your own."

Angie's face flushed hotly. "Now you listen to me, you two-bit rummy. I'm gonna—"

I grabbed the mike from her. "Mac. There's another way. It depends on if you're a real pilot or just a hacker. We can get this boat up to 75-80 miles an hour—that should keep you above stall. You come down right on top of us while we're moving. You gotta bring one of those pontoons down and practically balance it on our gunnel. If we can grab that pontoon and climb on, you can pull us out. We never have to stop—we can stay ahead of the gunboats and we can be drinking margaritas in Captain Tony's by nine."

There was a poignant silence at the other end. "Don't know... I don't think so... Too risky. Sorry."

I keyed the mike again. "No guts, huh? You really are just a rummy with an airplane."

Silence. The radio squelched. "Sorry." Silence.

I took a breath to calm myself then brought the mike up again. "You got two choices here, Mac. You can be a hero and accumulate another genuinely outlandish tale for the next barroom, or you can stare at the ceiling fan when you lie in bed at night for the rest of your friggin' life and remember what a coward you were. There are some things that wear on a man worse than death, and you're about to inherit one."

There was still silence on the radio, and to our dismay, the aircraft began to bank away in the distance.

"Bugger!" Angie muttered, frustrated near to tears.

Another round exploded off our starboard.

We looked at each other in grim, shaken silence. There was no way out of this, and we knew it.

"So, we run until they hit us," Will muttered grimly, forcing the throttles against the wall. "I'm not going to prison in Cuba."

Another cannon round slapped the sea fifty yards to port and the race was on.

Will zigzagged for the next minute or so, trying to keep as much of a true course as possible, but the Cubans were gaining on us. I felt Angie's hand on my shoulder. I could see the fear in her eyes, and I knew it was in mine, as well.

Will, on the other hand, seemed to rise to the occasion. He stood there, straight-up, legs flexing to the movement of the boat, grasping the steering wheel and staring straight ahead. I remember the look on his face—there was no fear, just defiance. They were simply not going to have him cheaply or easily. As frightening as it all was, I remember at that moment, how proud I was to have him as my friend. That's how I remember him.

As Mac's Cessna was rising away in the distance I noticed it suddenly dropped a wing and started to bank. The radio squelched.

"Aaahh, what the hell. I got enough bad memories," rasped Mac. "You get that damned boat up as fast as it goes and keep it straight and true. I'm coming in!"

Angie's face flooded with relief and she whispered, "I'd kiss him on the lips if he was closer."

"Hell! I'd kiss him on the lips and probably let him feel me up," yelled Will.

We all laughed despite the situation. Man, it felt good to have a small chance.

Mac banked the airplane around, climbed, and flew over the Cuban gunboats behind us, then he banked around again, and dove straight at our stern.

I turned to Will and Angie, yelling over the engine, "This is going to get tricky. One of us has to stay at the wheel while the first two grab the pontoon. Once they're aboard, Mac will rise up just a little and get them into the cabin. Then he's going to have to drop down for the other person. The one who stays has a lot smaller chance of pulling this off—gonna have to tie the wheel in place and quickly make a jump for the pontoon because even tied, she won't stay on point for very long. I think you need to let me—"

"I'll do it," said Will. "You guys get up near the bow on the leeward side. We can pick up a little speed with you up there."

Angie blanched. "Will, no—"

"Let me do it, Will," I said. "You and your girl get outta here first."

Will shook his head adamantly. "Nope! This time it's me who gets to tell the great barroom story." He gripped the wheel defiantly and motioned with his head. "Now get up front and get ready." He looked back at Angie. "I'll be right behind you."

I paused for a moment. "You're not going to get yourself killed, are you?"

He grinned, typically Will. "Not intentionally."

Another cannon round no more than fifty feet off our stern snapped us all into action. A minute later Mac and his Cessna were tailing us thirty feet above the water, closing carefully. He was a better pilot than I thought. He flawlessly moved his left pontoon to our right side and was keeping pace with the hurtling boat. I was talking him down on the radio. I was to go first, get positioned on the pontoon, then help Angie up. As the float neared the gunnel I swung the bag with the pyramid over my neck, then paused and looked back at Will. "Don't take any extra chances, buddy. Just tie the wheel and get onboard."

He gazed at me with a strange look and his eyes softened. "Till the next sunrise, my friend." Then he straightened up. "Now, get the hell out of here!"

I turned and lunged forward, grabbing the strut and throwing myself onto it, but the instant I settled, a cannon round slammed the water just in front of us. The boat lurched through the spray of the explosion and the plane canted wildly breaking away from the waterborne craft. I was thrown over the side of the pontoon—the only thing that saved me was my tenacious grip on the strut. Dangling in midair, I managed to fight my way back onto the float. I hammered on the side of the fuselage and Mac righted the aircraft, then stubbornly turned back at the cigarette for another try. We eased in over the boat. Angie stood on the bow cushions and reached out. Straddling the float with my legs and holding the strut with my other hand, I grabbed her arm and pulled her aboard. "Two out of three so far," I yelled as the wind ripped at our clothing and Mac leveled out at 100 feet, leaning over and pushing open the cabin door. I grabbed it and we clambered aboard.

"Damned nice job, Mac!" I said as we settled in, Angie in the back and me in the right seat. Without a word, the pilot banked around tightly for another pass. As we leveled and dropped down for the next approach I added, "Now we just got to do it one more ti—" But at that moment we watched a cannon round clip the stern of the cigarette in a fiery explosion. The boat cantered sideways, skidded, then flipped into the air, landing upside down, smoking and fractured. As Angie cried out, I caught a brief glimpse of Will being catapulted out of the craft as it rolled.

I swung around and yelled at the pilot. "Get banked around and get down there—we gotta get him!"

"He's gone," Mac said stoically, pulling the nose up toward the horizon. "We got two out of three, like you said. He's dead, and if he isn't, he'll be in a Cuban jail by nightfall. I'm not joining him."

Angie and I looked at each other. From the back seat, Angie tore off the pilot's hat and grabbed a handful of hair, ripping his head back hard enough to practically snap his neck. As the plane lurched upward, I snatched up an empty Pepsi bottle from between the seats and smashed it against the metal door handle. It fractured leaving nothing but the jagged neck in my hand. I grabbed Mac by the collar of his shirt and buried the broken glass a quarter inch into his neck. "You're going to do exactly what I say or I'm gonna drive this into your frigging throat and kick you out the door," I hissed. "You're gonna set this damned plane down there, now!"

"The Cubans—" he sputtered, as he struggled to keep control of the aircraft. "We'll never get off the water!"

"You let me worry about that. Just set this damned plane down!"

Angie slowly, reluctantly, released his hair and I withdrew the jagged glass in my hand, but I stayed right on top of him, holding his shirt as we made a pass over the capsized boat below. There was an oil slick forming and miscellaneous flotsam and jetsam surrounding the craft, but no sign of Will. We were almost past the crash site when Angie yelled, "There he is! There he is! About fifty yards behind the boat!"

I caught a brief glimpse of Will as we passed. My partner was floating face down in the water, and the gunboats were only a half mile away.

"Set it down now!" I shouted, tossing the bag with the pyramid to Angie in the back and ripping off my shoes and shirt. The sun was almost lost to the horizon, and the water was turning slate gray as the aircraft's floats slapped the surface. We were running out of time in a lot of ways.

Mac practically skidded the plane to a stop about twenty yards from my partner, who still floated motionless, face down in the sea. As I kicked open the door Angie reached over from the back seat, grabbed the pilot by the hair and thrust the bottle neck I gave her against his throat again. "Don't even think about that throttle," she whispered with deadly vehemence.

I hadn't even hit the water when the Cubans realized what was happening and a cannon round struck the remainder of the sinking boat. The terrifying explosion threw a maelstrom of fiberglass and metal into the surrounding waters, showering the plane and me. Seconds later, the first of the 50-caliber machine guns came into range and bullets slapped the surface next to the aircraft.

Angie tightened her grip on Mac. "Relax, sweetheart, we're not going anywhere."

The pilot glanced at the bag on the backseat behind him. "But—"

She just pushed the broken glass tighter against his throat. "Just sit tight."

In seconds I was at Will's side, flipping him over and looking for wounds. A bad gash on his forehead was leaching blood into the water and his eyes were closed. He didn't appear to be breathing but there was nothing I could do at the moment. I put him in a cross-chest carry and dragged him toward the pontoon, where Angie and Mac were waiting.

We unceremoniously dragged a pale, unconscious Will aboard. Angie pulled him into the back and began CPR as Mac hit the throttles. We hadn't even lifted off before a burst of machinegun fire stitched the starboard wing with the snapping sound of popcorn in a microwave. As terrifying as it was, Angie never even missed a beat with Will.

A cannon round exploded to our right and the aircraft shook from the shock wave, bouncing up onto one float for a moment. Mac cursed under his breath as he fought with the rudder and ailerons for control. Finally, as the rhythmic slap of the water on the floats ceased and we became airborne—and I exhaled the breath I had been holding—three or four 50-caliber rounds slammed into the fuselage and shattered the rear window about a foot from my head. That time I yelled. There were another sixty seconds of serious tenseness as we rose into the darkening sky, but at that point, it appeared we'd made it out. I turned and looked back at Angie. She was still furiously working on Will, but I could see the fear in her eyes when she glanced at me. My stomach lurched at that look of desperation. I don't remember feeling more helpless in my entire life—I was watching my closest friend die, and I realized with a sense of hollow, agonizing insight that I was losing the person with whom I had shared the greatest bond in this lifetime so far. That sudden emptiness—the pain and the terrible reality—were overwhelming. Angie paused, tears streaming down her face. She began sobbing, hammering Will's chest and crying out, "Don't do this, Will! Oh God! Don't die, please...don't die..."

I reached back—I don't know why—and took my partner's hand. There were so many things I wanted to say, but my mouth was dry as sawdust. Angie finally stopped, shoulders slumping forward in surrender, still crying.

I was left with nothing but his name on my lips. "Will ..." I whispered hoarsely. "Will..."

And at that moment my friend's head rolled to the side and he coughed, spewing out a lungful of salt water. In my life, there have been times of immense joy and gratefulness, but that moment still stands out.

Angie cried out, reaching over and cradling his head in her hands, tears still streaming from her face. "Oh, thank God," she whispered. "Will... Will!"

Our friend's eyes fluttered open. As the glaze faded and he focused, looking at me, he croaked, "Okay, from now on you get the barroom stories."

I smiled, suddenly realizing that my cheeks were wet. "Don't make any promises you can't keep, *amigo*." I paused. "Good to have you back."

He took a ragged breath. "Did I go somewhere?"

Inside a half hour, Angie, with the aircraft medical kit, had bandaged the gash on Will's head, and my partner was nearly back to his old, precocious self. He looked over at Mac, who had grown even more taciturn as we neared the mainland. "Man that was some amazing timing—you showing up when you did."

"Yeah, Angie called just in time," he muttered. Then he suddenly glanced over at the girl in the back. Will and I turned to her. Surprised would be an understatement.

One of those sighs escaped her. "Yeah, I managed to get a call off from the base station at the shack—before things got real exciting."

Will cocked his head. "Why didn't you say something about it?"

"You may remember we were in the process of trying to get away from several psychopathic groups of Cubans," she spat sarcastically. "Forgive me for not mentioning it while I was tied to a bloody tree, preparing to be shot, or while being chased across a bloody island by frigging revolutionary maniacs—not to mention the Cuban gunboats! Then, of course, there was the little matter of trying to pick you up and revive you while the bloody plane was being shot full of holes like some bloomin' paper duck at a county fair!"

We both backed off and Will apologized. "Okay. The good news is, we're all fine and we're headed back to the mainland."

"Not exactly," Mac said.

That got our attention. So did the large island ahead with the imposing structure on it—Fort Jefferson and the Dry Tortugas.

"What the hell," I whispered. "That's way west of where we're supposed to be!"

Mac took a quick glance at us as he backed the power off and began lowering the nose toward the island and the huge, old civil war bastion/prison that thrusts itself from the sands and mangroves about forty miles from Key West. "You've got a couple more problems yet. The Feds are watching every port of entry like hawks right now and my sources tell me they're monitoring all the air traffic coming in with the radar out at Cudjoe Key. Sorry lady and gentlemen, but I'm not gonna become a part of whatever you're doing. I've arranged for some people to pick you up and scoot you in with an open fisherman. They're waiting for you at the fort. You can make the run in about an hour and a half, weather permitting."

I started to protest when Mac held up his hand, stopping me. "And you've got another small problem no one has discussed with you. Looks like that darkening on the horizon as we took off is working itself into a little storm. It's most likely gonna roll through here in a few hours. You need to either get out quick or you might have to stay here overnight—till it passes through."

I had noticed there were some winds buffeting the plane, but the thought of a storm hadn't crossed my mind. "What the hell is gonna be next?" I muttered exasperatedly.

"Next we land," Mac said.

CHAPTER TWELVE

Old Forts, Old Friends, And Things That Go Bang In The Night

A nearly full moon dragged itself from the horizon and was playing hide and seek with racing gray and white stratus clouds. It broke free for a moment and illuminated the darkened waters near the beach as we came in. The bay was empty, as Mac had promised, with the exception of a weary-looking shrimp boat at anchor on the far side, near the shore, and a fairly sleek-looking open fisherman, approximately twenty-two feet in length by the look of it at a distance, on the other side of the inlet. Mac settled the aircraft in and taxied over to the old fort. The moon bathed the ancient, red brick walls that held so many stories—mostly tragic. Built in the early to mid-1800s, the huge six-sided garrison was originally designed to suppress piracy in the Caribbean, but it was later used in the Civil War to hold Southern prisoners. There's a sense of majesty about it at a distance, but inside those walls there is a definite sense of forlornness and abandonment that plays on the mind. It was rarely a satisfying home to anyone. But as we exited the plane with the wind rising and the first signs of rain moving in, it was beginning to look like our home for the night.

Mac helped us out. That is to say, he held the door open while we scrambled out into the knee-deep water. I caught a fleeting look between him and Angie as we stepped away from the plane.

"Get inside the fort near the east end," he shouted over the idling engine. "They'll be waiting for you there. I'll wait a few minutes before taking off—just to be sure." Without any other fanfare, he simply closed the door and turned away, watching the prop idle into the wind.

We looked at each other, more than a little concerned. "I don't like this," I muttered to no one in particular. "I'm really beginning to feel like Frodo in Mordor."

"Yeah, dude, it's a totally stone-cold bummer," Will grumbled. "I wanna give up that damned pyramid and go home! I'm gonna lock myself in the bedroom and order pizza and beer by phone for the rest of my life."

"I've heard that before," I said sarcastically.

"Yeah, but I mean it this time!"

"Come on, my little Hobbits," Angie said with a grim smile. "This bloody little affair isn't over yet, whether we like it or not."

I shouldered the bag with the ancient pyramid, and we shuffled off toward shore.

As we crossed the single bridge spanning the moat around the fort and worked our way along an old corridor to the east end, we heard Mac's seaplane take off. Wind whistled through the passageway and a shimmering moon peeked through the high portals, lending a dim light and casting distorted shadows on the old, red brick walls. Our footsteps on the stone floor echoed eerily in the corridor. It all added greatly to an already growing apprehension. Then, in the distance, we began to hear the faint sound of music from a scratchy transistor radio. As we got closer, we could make out "The Tin Man," by America.

Oz never did give nothing to the Tin Man that he didn't, didn't already have, and cause never was the reason for the evening, or the topic of Sir Galahad…

We glanced at each other, and proceeded forward, slowly. When we reached the conclave with the music we saw a lantern set on a small, deteriorated wooden table on the far side of the room. It was accompanied by half a bottle of bourbon and three glasses. A figure huddled over the lantern with his back to us—nice leather cardigan, good shoes.

"Come in, we've been waiting for you, actually for some time," he said without looking around.

I had to think about that voice for a second. I was certain I knew it—just a touch of Miami inflection. "Oh my God…" I moaned as the realization struck, and the infamous Justin Mames stood and turned to face us. He took a pull from the cigarette he'd just lit with the lamp and exhaled a bluish cloud at the ceiling as Detective Landon and his big bodyguard guy with the Hawaiian shirt emerged from the shadows. Landon, with the perennial toothpick dangling from his mouth, brandished a nasty-looking chrome-plated revolver.

"Well, Angie, I see you finally delivered. I was beginning to doubt you."

Will and I looked at each other. In an instant, it all sank in. *We'd been played the whole time by the beautiful Brit!*

Will glared at her, pain and anger filling his eyes. "How… how could you? I thought there was something between … Lord, you're an amazing piece of work! You make Mata Hari look like a Sunday school girl."

"You don't understand," Angie cried, moving into the light of the lantern and facing him.

"Oh, I understand perfectly," Will spat bitterly.

"No, you don't!" She held out her hands in supplication. "Yes, yes, at first I was working with Justin. Dammit, man! Nobody can make a living on a bloody policewoman's salary in the Keys, so I decided to moonlight a little. Then this bloody pyramid thing came up—and then you." She took a breath and exhaled hard. "I didn't know it was going to get so complicated! I started off just doing my job—keeping track of you two and trying to find the bloody pyramid, making a quick call every once in a while from a payphone or on old Sanchez's base station. I was going to get a cut. But then something happened … between you and me. For God's sake, man, I found out they were going to kill you two!" She turned, pointing at Mames. "I cut a deal with him. I bargained the pyramid for your lives!"

"About that deal…" Mames said with quiet malevolence as he pulled a pistol from his waistband. "Don't think that's going to work now."

Angie took a step back. "Wait, wait! You can have the bloody pyramid—we've got it, just like I promised. Take it and go. We made a deal! You can't—"

Mames waved the pistol at her, cutting her off. "Now what do you think it would do to my reputation if I let these two *puntas* get away with stealing from me?"

Will shrugged. "Personally, I think your reputation was pretty well shot when they found you hanging from Bahia Honda Bridge in your doper-parachuter outfit."

"Naahh," I said. " I think the barking like a dog thing after the trial was the real turning point."

What the hell—I had little to lose, and besides, I had suddenly recalled what old Rufus said about the gumballs—"Just throw it against the ground. No will but yours, mon, no will but yours."

As my partner added one more anecdote about dragging Mames through the airport after doping him, and something about the attorney doing a great imitation of a boneless chicken, I saw Mames' eyes start to go cold and he thumbed back the hammer on his automatic pistol. At that moment I stepped in front of Will and Angie, facing him.

"Okay, okay, you win. You're gonna take the pyramid no matter what, so here it is."

Justin smiled, hard. "Smart boy."

When I reached into my carry bag, I deftly unzipped the side compartment and grabbed the two magic gumballs we had. I palmed the small, flat-sided gumball with a promised detonation of about a square mile, and grabbed the magic dust ball with two fingers. I was going to save the day. But, as I drew out my hand, my fingers caught on the zipper and the magic dust ball slipped from my grasp, hit the toe of my tennis shoe and rolled over in front of Detective Landon. My eyes went wide as it dropped and I gasped. I exhaled softly when it didn't explode.

Landon reached down and picked it up. "What's this?"

"It's my lucky marble. I've had it since I was ten."

"Well, I'd say at this point it ain't lucky no more." Landon chuckled as he tossed it into the air in front of him.

I stopped breathing. He deftly caught it.

"Well, you never know," I muttered.

But at that point, I realized we had lost our only ace, and the pyramid was going back to the man who was about to kill us.

"The pyramid?" Mames said, hand out, bringing me from my musing.

"Yeah, okay." As I reached into the bag, I pushed the flat side of the golden detonation gumball against the pyramid. It snapped onto the ancient relic like a magnet to steel and there was a minute green flash. The wheels of fate were set in motion.

"Here's your damned pyramid," I muttered. "I hope it takes you to the moon."

As I pulled it from the bag, the moonlight from a portal struck it. Those brilliant lagoon-green tiers of light sprang forth from the crowning emerald, and that deep ethereal humming filled the room.

Mames was taken aback at first, but quickly recovered and took the artifact carefully with one hand, the gun still on me. "Smart move," he said as he slid the pyramid back into my bag, apparently not noticing the little anomaly attached to the side. The light and the humming obediently stopped. He smiled at us. "Well, I'm gonna be going now. What I don't see I can't testify about." He glanced at Landon. "I'll meet you at the boat." Then Mames turned to us again. "Would have liked to have taken the seaplane back—more comfortable, but can't risk the Cudjoe radar with this little prize on board. We'll blend in nicely with the fishing boats headed back for the day."

Apparently, Mac was on the payroll as well. The attorney from hell turned to Detective Landon and his buddy. "Oh, yeah, I almost forgot." He reached into his breast pocket, pulled out a small plastic bag and tossed it to Landon. "Six ounces of coke and twenty hits of acid. Like I said, a drug deal gone bad. Wipe the gun for prints and leave it, and the drugs." He pointed to the whiskey bottle on the table. "Drop a couple tabs of acid in it and make sure they all take a good shot—so it'll look right if there's any blood work done at the morgue." He straightened up and put his hands together pensively, enjoying every second of his final revenge. "Now, I think that's about it. Give me a couple of minutes, then take care of this. See you at the boat."

Landon nodded somberly. "No problem."

Before leaving, Mames paused and said to Angie, "Sorry about this, girl. We had some good times. But I gotta sew up loose ends." Without another look, Justin Mames strode through the arched doorway and disappeared into the gloom of the corridor. We all stood staring at each other until the footsteps faded.

Landon opened the plastic bag and took out a couple of hits of acid. The guy in the Hawaiian shirt took them from him and dropped them in the whiskey bottle, then put the cork back on. He shook it a little, then forced each of us to take a swallow. We all took a hit, looked at each other, and in unison, spit it out.

Landon's brow furrowed and his pale blue eyes went hard. He raised his gun. "Now you're all going to do it again, and this time you're gonna swallow."

Will glared at him. "Or what? You're going to shoot us?"

The detective started to say something, but stopped. Instead, he exhaled, running his hand through his sparse, sandy hair, and said, "Okay, I'm not going to fight you over the small shit. You're gonna be dead in a couple minutes anyway, acid or not." He turned, opening the cylinder on his revolver, and checked its rounds. Snapping it back with the flick of his wrist, he looked up, eyes hard again. "All right, let's get this over with."

"Give me my marble back, please. I want to die with it." I let my voice break a little. "I've had it all these years—my father gave it to me."

For a moment I thought he'd bought it, then he sneered nastily. "Here's what I think of you and your marble, you troublesome little asshole." Suddenly, viciously, he threw it against the wall.

The instant the gumball slammed the wall, there was a bright explosion diffusing the air with millions of minute saffron colored particles. Everyone just stood there, so remarkable and startling was the phenomenon. But the others were still breathing. One glance at Will and I realized he'd had the good sense to hold his breath as well. Angie, unfortunately, didn't.

In less than ten seconds the lightshow disappeared. Landon shook his head oddly, as if trying to clear it, then appeared to be his old self. "Why don't you all just turn around so you don't have to see it coming."

I stared confidently at him. "Why don't you stick your middle finger up your right nostril."

Landon paused and started to scoff, when he suddenly shrugged and did it—just like that.

I wasted no more time. "Give me your gun, Landon."

The detective paused again and there was a momentary flash of confusion in his eyes, but he handed me his pistol anyway.

I quickly pointed at the bodyguard. "Sit down and shut up! Don't get up unless I tell you." He obeyed like a chastised child.

Will exhaled loudly and shook his head in amazement. "Cover me in chocolate and call me a Twinkie. It worked again."

I smiled. "My lucky marble."

Angie just appeared a little dazed, uncertain. I quickly looked around the room. Three of the walls had a small, iron-barred, two-foot portals, to allow airflow. I turned to Landon. "You got handcuffs with you?"

He nodded.

"Give them to me, and the key."

Two minutes later we had the bodyguard in the adjacent room and Landon in the room with us. They were connected through the barred portal by the handcuffs. No one was going anywhere. In the interim, I had pre-programmed them with a "suggestion." When the police came for them, they were to confess the whole story of how Mames stole the pyramid, how we got it and tried to give it back to the authorities, and how Justin tried to kill us to keep the pyramid and cover his tracks.

While we were in the process of securing everybody, our nemesis was nearing the end of the corridor in the fort. Justin could hear the wind rising outside and the moon still cast those same eerie shadows on the walls, leaving even the best of villains uncomfortable. Suddenly, a stocky, diminutive figure appeared out of a doorway and stepped in front of him. "Hi matey," it whispered with a strange combination of pleasantry and malevolence. Mames was reaching for his gun when another ghostly figure appeared from behind him and without ceremony, struck him on the head with a fish club.

After we finished programming Landon and his buddy, Will asked, “There’s gonna be a big explosion in a little while, huh?”

I dropped my eyes to the floor, knowing full well what I’d done. “Yeah. When I realized he was going to kill us, I just couldn’t let him get away with it. Not with the pyramid.”

Will’s anger and resentment toward Angie had cooled somewhat by her fervent attempt to preserve us. But he still wasn’t sure. He turned to me and whispered. “She’s under the spell, isn’t she?”

“Yeah, I guess.”

“I gotta be sure,” he muttered, determined. “Give me the gun.” I complied and Will said, “I gotta check something, you guys wait here. I’ll be right back.” He walked out into the corridor and we heard his footsteps fade. I had no idea what he was up to. A few moments later, he came back in and walked up to Angie. “I want to you to do something for me—do you understand?”

Angie got sort of a perplexed look on her face but nodded anyway.

Will handed her the gun and pointed to Landon. “Kill him.”

She took the gun, blinked a couple of times, then pointed the weapon at Landon and pulled the trigger three times. I gasped then flinched, anticipating the report, but the weapon just clicked impotently.

Will showed us the bullets he’d removed from the gun. Then he gazed at Angie intently and said, “Now I want to ask you a couple questions. First, is everything that you said a few moments ago—about trying to save us by bartering the pyramid. Is that all true?

She looked him in the eyes. “Yes, it is.”

He took a deep breath. “Angie, do you love me?”

Suddenly, she smiled, her eyes filling with warmth and truth. “Oh yes. I do. I love you Will Bell.”

He opened his arms and she rushed willingly into them and they embraced with that rare passion of certain love. And I was glad. But I still had that uncomfortable feeling of a piano falling somewhere.

“Okay you two, break it up,” I said. “Lots of time for that later on. If what Rufus told me is true, we’re counting down on a small nuclear-like explosion and about a square mile of destruction. We’ve got to find Mames and get that damned pyramid back, then get it out to open water.”

“Yeah, you’re right,” Will said. “Let’s get going.” Then he

cocked an ear, holding up a finger for silence. "Listen. There's somebody coming."

Sure enough, in the distance, down the corridor, we could hear voices.

"Douse the lantern," I whispered urgently.

Will turned it off and we moved silently into the shadows of the moonlit room. As the voices came closer, there was without a doubt a familiarity with one of them. As I was thinking to myself, *Lord! It can't be,* we all began to notice the corridor flooding with that surreal, green-lagoon light, and the humming.

"What do we do?" Will whispered.

The problem was solved when Calico Curk peeked his head around the corner, pyramid in one hand and Mames' gun in the other. As the moonlight in the corridor and the light from the emerald reflected off his shiny balding head, he gazed at us with those crazy green eyes, then glanced at Mames' men chained in the portal. He smiled and whispered with a voice as gravelly as sandpaper, "Aaahh, you're still alive." He raised an eyebrow. "I'm surprised. We figured we'd let you folks work this thing out then we'd only have ta take it from one of ya. Why don't ya turn the lantern back on."

Will lit the lantern as Calico's two sons, Lenny and Kenny, appeared behind him. No one had an eye patch and there was no Bennie. Now I knew who owned the shrimp boat in the bay. The boys looked harder than before—longer hair, a couple of new tattoos. Not much conversation.

"Where's Mames?" I asked.

Calico gave me that hollow smile as he put the pyramid back in the carry bag. "He's restin' in the corridor back a ways."

Angie had Landon's gun, and Calico saw it, but Will still had the bullets in his pocket. It was useless, and if we bluffed, it would probably get one or all of us killed.

"Well, I guess what we have here is a Mexican standoff," said the little pirate.

"No, Calico," I said deliberately, passionately. "What we have here is, all of us are going to be dead in less than an hour. A destruction timer has been set on that little pyramid and it's going to explode in a mini-nuclear blast in probably less time than we have to get away from it. We need to toss it in the corner and make a run for it. It's our only chance."

"That's a clever ruse, matey, but I ain't buying it," Calico said as he tucked the pyramid closer, possessively. "Ya ain't gettin' it back."

He looked over at Angie. "Put the gun down, little lady, and maybe you'll live ta tell this tale."

Angie also realized the futility of a bluff. She dropped the weapon.

"Calico!" I shouted. "We're not lying! For God's sake, man, just leave it here and we can make a run for it in your boat!"

He just pursed his lips and shook his head stoically.

"Okay, you keep it. We're going to leave. We don't want it. You can have it. We'll just pack up and head on our way—"

The pirate shook his head again, interrupting me. "I think we'll keep the lass with us, for safekeeping—just to make sure you don't get any crazy ideas."

I could see the look on Will's face at that suggestion, and so did Calico.

"She's a police officer," Will warned. "You take her with you, that's kidnapping a federal agent. I don't think you're that stupid."

Calico waved his gun at us, in control and too pumped to listen to reason. "I can be as stupid as I want, and there's nothin' you can do about it, matey. We'll drop the wench off at a bar in Key West after we're done with a little transaction on a pyramid." He arched an eyebrow again in typical fashion. "We already got ourselves a buyer. Now, get over here, girl."

"Don't do it, Angie," ordered Will angrily.

She walked over to Calico. "You've got me," she said. "So let's get out of here."

"Angie, no!" Will cried.

"Right ya are, ma'am," said Calico. Then he looked up at us, raising the gun again. "You boys are gonna have to be polite now, and let us tie ya up a little. You'll be able ta get undone in a coupla hours, I'm sure."

"What about us?" Landon cried, coming around from the initial effects of the magic dust. "Let us go—we won't do you any harm."

Calico snorted with mirth, eyebrows up. "Right, bucko—hah! You just keep hangin' in the window. Ya won't do me any harm right where ya are." He turned to Lenny, who had just produced some deck cord from his pocket. "Wrap 'em up a bit." He pushed Angie over to Kenny, who grabbed her by the hair and held her securely while Lenny tied her hands, then he picked up the pistol lying on the stone floor and stuffed it in his belt, not aware that there weren't any bullets in it.

While waiting for his sons to secure Angie, Calico spied the bottle of whiskey on the table. "We'll take that too. You ain't gonna be needing it." Then strangely out of character, he gazed at the walls of the old prison with a curious look in his eyes and muttered to himself as much as anyone, "Can't wait to get outta here—too damned many ghosts in a place like this." He strode over and grabbed the bottle of whiskey, turned it up and took a long, deep hit. "Aaarrrhh! Nothing like a little grog ta purify the soul and dull the memory of dastardly deeds that's been done." He tossed it to Kenny who took a solid hit, and from there it went to Lenny who sucked down a third of what was left. "All right! Wrap 'em up!" Calico yelled as he took the bottle back and hit it hard one more time, then tossed it into the corner. He pulled the revolver from his pants and handed it to Kenny. "Let's get gone from this place of unhappy souls, deliver our package, and find ourselves a saloon where the liquor and women are reasonable!"

Five minutes later Will and I were bound hand and foot, and Calico stood in front of us. "We're gonna go now," he said as he looked down at me with an evil grin. "And just so ya know, we've been payin' attention to ya ever since we saw yer pictures in the paper and caught a glimpse of ya on Duval Street Halloween night. Paybacks can be a bitch, matey. It's been nice playin' snooker with ya again."

Both Will and Angie knew there was no percentage in letting Calico know how they felt about each other. They just stared at one another for a long moment before Lenny grabbed the girl and all four disappeared down the corridor.

As soon as they were out of earshot, Will rolled over toward to me. "I'm gonna kill the son of a bitch the first chance I get."

I worked myself into a sitting position against the wall. "Let's worry about getting untied right now. We don't manage that and—"

"Yeah, I know," Will said nervously. "But the odds are moving in our favor. They've each got at least a half-tab of acid in them. Things are going to get interesting for them, no matter what."

Glancing over at Landon, I remembered his right hand was handcuffed to his partner through the barred aperture in the wall, but his left hand was free. I turned to him. "Landon, how about we make a deal?"

Landon stared at me with new interest. "Yeah? What kind of deal?"

"I work my way over to you and you untie me. You do that for me and I'll give you the key to the handcuffs."

"Why should I?"

"Two reasons. One, there's no guarantee that demented pirate wannabe is going to be in any hurry to get out of here, and if he sits around for a few minutes too long, we're all gonna be toast. Secondly, if he does get out of range, it may be days before anybody shows up here. That could be a hot and thirsty couple of days—depending on radiation and wind direction."

Landon stared at me hard. "The bomb's for real, huh?"

"Damned straight."

"Okay. Get your ass over here."

I rolled, squirmed, and wiggled my over to him and managed to get myself upright with the help of the wall. Turning my back to the detective, I was able to lift my tied hands just high enough for him to reach. Two minutes later I was free. Another minute and I had Will untied.

"We gotta get the hell out of here," he cried. "We're running out of time."

My watch indicated we'd already used up almost twenty minutes of the hour we had before blastoff. I reached into Landon's coat pocket and plucked out the bag of cocaine. Will looked at me sideways. "You're gonna have to trust me," I said. "I'm thinking ahead right now."

"Hey! What about me?" shouted Landon. "You made a deal!"

I paused and Will yelled, "You're not going to let those sons of bitches go, are you? You can't be that friggin' crazy!"

"I promised to give him the key. Not set him loose. There were no prerequisites on the condition of the key."

Will grinned. Landon cursed under his breath as I took an old piece of metal bar lying in the corner and quickly hammered the key useless on the rock floor. Then I walked over to the detective and stuck it in his shirt pocket. He reached for me with his other hand and I danced back, out of range. "Save your energy, buddy," I whispered. You're gonna need it."

A moment later we were on the run down the corridor, toward the bridge over the moat. We could hear the wind picking up and whistling through the ports and windows. The moon still shifted past the racing clouds, periodically bathing the corridor with eerie green light. We were at least five minutes behind Calico and the others, maybe more. We had to reach them before they upped anchor and shipped out. Will was holding up well, but I could see he was terrified for Angie—kidnapped by three pirates high on acid, carrying a bomb. After a dead run for a few minutes, I put out my hand and we slowed down. While gasping for air I held a finger up. "Our only chance is surprise. They have two guns, one for sure with bullets—us none. We need a plan, and probably a diversion."

Will paused for a moment, still gulping in air, but I could see the gears rolling. "I remember one of these rooms on the way in had a bunch of junk in it," he muttered to himself. "From people camping here—just ahead I think."

Sure enough, thirty feet down the corridor was a room scattered with debris—tattered, useless clothes and shoes—flip-flops, toeless tennis shoes, a couple ragged, rubber Halloween masks from fantasy nights in Key West. *If those walls could talk,* I thought. There was a torn sail from a sailboat that had been used as a ground tarp, a circle of rocks for a fireplace, and a couple deteriorated sleeping bags I wouldn't even want to stand on, let alone sleep in. Someone had even pulled up the small manhole cover to the old sewer system, using the orifice for a latrine.

My partner got that smile I knew so well. "I remember Lenny telling me that Calico had an unhealthy aversion to spirits—he kept Pecker the parrot because some wacko Haitian priest had told him it would ward off his wife's spirit," he muttered. "I don't think she simply missed her footing on a particularly bad night at sea. Our boys are probably just beginning to feel that acid and we need to play on that. If we can get ahead of them, I'll give you your diversion." Then he squatted, took a stick from the floor and began drawing in the dirt. "Here we are. Here's the bay and Calico's boat. They gotta have a skiff hidden over by the beach near the mangroves, somewhere about here, my guess. They're not in a hurry. They'll walk the corridor to the bridge, then head out to the beach and cut back along the bay to the boat. We need to get out of the corridor here, wade or swim across the moat, work our way through the mangroves to the beach and be waiting for them rather than chasing them on the main path. This is what we need to do…."

Calico and his group had just cleared the fort. The storm Mac promised had apparently passed through, but the winds still pushed feathery, gunmetal clouds across the sky. The old pirate was in the lead, walking along the worn path that wove in and out of mangroves on its way along the beach. Lenny followed, pushing Angie ahead of him. Kenny was in the rear, about twenty feet behind the others, carrying the second pistol and watching for any company on the back of the trail. The acid simmering in their brains had just begun to fog rational thought. Calico had begun to notice how loud the mosquitoes were—they buzzed around his head with the roar of motorcycles. The beach sand had just taken on a strange iridescent glow and he was trying to be careful where he stepped because of the land crabs. Their shells had gone neon and they had psychedelic pictures of rock stars painted on their backs—Joplin, Morrison, Hendricks. They were whispering to him angrily as they scuttled away.

Kenny in the back had suddenly found himself thoroughly taken with the big, round moon above. As he observed, a face on the glowing surface began to appear—heavy intoxicated eyes and a wide lavish mouth with a lolling tongue hanging loosely to one side. It was so close he could almost look in its mouth. He kept stopping and stretching out, to touch it, muttering "That's too cool, dude, wicked cool."

Lenny was having a hard time just keeping one foot in front of the other—with all the colorful electric butterflies fluttering about the sides of the trail.

As they neared their skiff, the mangroves narrowed on both sides, then widened somewhat into a slight curve ahead. It was then that they began to hear a deep thumping sound and a soft wailing coming from the bend ahead. "Ooooohhhhh, ayeeaaahhh…" Thump, thump, thump… (Pause) "Aaaahhhh, ooooohhhh…" Thump, thump, thump… Already plied with enough psychedelics to make even the mundane seem mystifying, the party stopped like it had run into a wall, glancing about nervously.

"What the hell?" Calico muttered, obviously a little spooked, swatting a motorcycle mosquito.

Then suddenly, to the left there was a high-pitched, ethereal wail—"Eeeeeeaaahhhheeeeee!"

That brought their attention around with the precision of a meerkat family on crack. At that moment, as the moon peeked out from the fringes of a motley windblown cloud and an eerie chartreuse glow covered the landscape, an apparition from the very gates of hell suddenly rose up on the path in front of them.

Will, costumed in the old sail (a hole cut for his head like a poncho), draped with strands of damp seaweed and wearing the ugliest of the two masks he had discovered in the fort, raised his hands dramatically and howled, "Aaaiiiieeee! Caallliiccooo! Remember meeee? You killlled meeeee! The parrot can't protect you nowwww. I'm taking you to helllll with meeeee!"

The old pirate stood stock-still, frozen in fear—eyes wide, mouth open, bottom lip quivering. He took a tentative step or two backwards and muttered plaintively, "It was an accident, Mama, I swear."

Lenny and Kenny weren't doing much better. They were already discreetly backing up, hoping that Mama would be appeased with just taking Calico to hell.

Unfortunately, the old seadog responded with more pluck and verve than we'd planned. It seemed for a moment he had forgotten about the gun in his hand, but as Mom/Will brought his hands out like a respectable zombie and took a couple deliberate steps toward the audience, Calico raised his pistol and fired into the center of the apparition—in fact, he fired until the pistol slide snapped back empty.

My heart did a lurch and my breath just stopped in mid-exhale. "Oh no…" I whispered desperately as Angie screamed.

"Mama" had shuddered from the impact of the slugs and staggered backwards. I thought I saw a red spot on the white sail, but there was nothing to do but play out the scene. I stepped from the mangroves behind the boys, and whacked Kenny into next week with a solid piece of driftwood I'd found on the beach. He dropped his gun and collapsed. Lenny was so engrossed with the spectacle in front of him, he responded a little late to the ruckus behind him. He, too, ended up in next week.

The apparition rose up again, arms outstretched like Moses parting the sea, definitely keeping the diminutive sailor's attention, and in a booming, macabre voice bellowed, "I am the god of hellfire! You will burn with me forever!"

I was certain there was a red stain spreading on the shoulder of Mr. Hellfire, but old Calico'd had enough. He let out a healthy scream that rivaled Will's performance, then turned and ran—right into a solid double handed smash from Angie that took the pirate right off his feet and left him out cold. The carry bag with the pyramid plopped at his feet. Our friendly apparition slumped to the ground with a groan.

In the next few seconds, Angie and I were at Will's side. I quickly untied Angie's hands and we ripped off the mask and the sail. Will, who was ever hedging his bets, had tied the old metal manhole cover to his chest. Five of Calico's six shots hit the cover; one missed and just clipped my partner's shoulder. It wasn't life-threatening, but it was bleeding badly and he was going to need some immediate attention. Then we still had the even more pressing problem of a small semi-atomic bomb that was set to detonate in a very short time. There was nowhere to run and no way to get away from it fast enough. As Angie ripped off a piece from the bottom of her blouse, trying to stop the blood flow, Will gazed up at me and whispered, "We're running out of time, partner…." He smiled wanly at Angie then looked back at me "I'm in good hands. You need to take care of that pyramid, before we all go boom."

The sleek Aquasport open fisherman bobbed patiently in the bay, maybe 200 yards in the distance and fifty feet offshore. I looked at my watch; we had maybe a half hour left. I gently patted Will's hand. "Take care, buddy." Then I gazed at Angie—long auburn hair in disarray, worried eyes, no makeup—still one of the prettiest girls I'd ever seen. Like Banyan. "You take care of him, princess. I'm going to see how far away from this island I can get in the next fifteen or twenty minutes."

Will reached out and touched my arm. "You get yourself killed, I'm gonna be bummed."

"Not to worry. All I have to do is shoot out a ways, toss the pyramid into the ocean and get back, fast. How hard can that be?" I stood and pointed at Calico and his boys. "Tie those sons of bitches up right away, before they come to, and get Kenny's gun. If they start to come around, hit 'em until they quit. Then you and Will need to get behind the west wall of the fort." I started to leave, but stopped and pulled Mames' six ounces of cocaine from my pocket. I smiled and handed it to Angie. "Once you've got them tied up, stuff this in Calico's pants."

A minute later I was racing down the beach with the carry bag containing the pyramid clutched in my hand. I had forgotten how heavy solid gold could be. As I wound along the shoreline and the mangroves, already breathing heavily, it appeared the winds were rising again. Angry gray clouds raced before a somber yellow moon, casting a mosaic of shadows and light, but I could clearly see the open fisherman, bobbing on the dark, windblown surface of the little bay. When I got directly offshore from it, I waded into the knee-deep water and forced myself through it the last fifty yards, praying the key was in the ignition and alternately reviewing mentally what Will had shown me about hot-wiring vehicles. It was just starting to rain intermittently—fat, heavy pellets, slapping the water like BBs around me.

When I reached the boat, I drew myself up over the transom and crawled in. It was bigger looking from the inside, and the two 150 horsepower Mercury outboards on the stern meant plenty of power. It would probably cruise at fifty knots plus in a fairly light sea. The console was large, extending from almost side to side with about eighteen inches of space between it and the hull, and the boat had a flat canvas top tied to an aluminum frame. There was some fishing and diving gear strewn around in the bow around a large crumpled piece of canvas. Mames probably had them more for looks than anything. Its high gunnels and big engines gave it a safe, sleek feeling—a classy boat that should get me out and back no problem. If all went well and I hadn't interpolated wrong on the time of detonation.

The key was in the ignition. I breathed a sigh of relief, stuffed the carry bag under the console at my feet and quickly moved forward to the anchor line cleat at the bow. I manhandled the anchor in, tossed it on the deck and took a quick glance at my watch. I'd burned up another ten minutes. I was down to about twenty or so.

As I moved behind the console and fired up the big engines, I muttered, "Best of luck, Kan," then swung it into the wind and headed out on a southeast course, which I hoped would take me into deep water and pretty much away from civilization. The rain was still slapping the water, but without fervor, and the seas were flattening a bit. I was making great time. The old fort behind me was becoming dimmer as distance separated us.

Lord, everything seemed to be staying on course for the moment. I began to feel I might just pull this off, and was just risking the smallest of smiles when suddenly I saw the bundle of canvas in the bow move. At first, I thought it was a trick of the moonlight or the bouncing of the boat—but there it was again. In less time than I could utter an appropriate explicative, the canvas tarp flew back and there was Justin Mames, attorney from hell—no cardigan, shoes and socks gone, his slacks and shirt soaked. Worse yet, in his right hand he held a small revolver, aimed at me. I used the appropriate expletive and backed off the throttles to idle.

Mames stood up, getting his balance in the rolling boat. "Guess I'm gonna get my pyramid after all."

"Don't you ever run out of guns?" I asked, a little pissed to find myself in the same situation again.

Mames shook his head slowly, never taking his eyes from me. "No, I don't. Had one in the boat. There's a great satisfaction in knowing you can shoot someone whenever you want. Just like I'm going to do with you, and then I'm going to get that friggin' little pirate." He exhaled angrily. "Son of a bitch clubbed me. When I came to, I heard voices—you and your partner—making plans to try to get the pyramid back from your pirate friends. So I just tucked back and followed you while you followed them. Figured I'd deal with whoever came out on top. You won and apparently you decided to get out of town without your buddies." He smiled. "Sometimes we just have to make a choice, right, *amigo*? I figured your way out would be my boat. As you headed for the beach, I cut back through the center of the mangroves and beat you back to the shore—swam out so you wouldn't see me as you splashed your way out." He smiled humorlessly again. "And the rest, as they say, is about to become history."

There was no reasoning with him. I glanced at my watch. I needed nearly another five minutes to be out far enough. I suddenly realized that I probably wasn't getting out of this one. It's a terrible sensation to recognize you're pretty much dead while you're still breathing.

"I've grown weary of you, Kansas—shoulda taken care of you a while back," Mames said coldly, standing in the bow facing the console, aiming the gun at my head. "But I'm gonna fix that now."

At that point, there were a very limited number of options. Instinct took over and I simply ducked and slammed the throttles hard full forward, just before the first bullet smacked the Plexiglas windshield. The boat surged like a greyhound out of the gate. Mames was catapulted head over heels into the center console.

Bleeding badly from a gash on his forehead, Mames was down but not out. As he pulled himself up, raising the gun again, I braced myself and threw the throttles to full stop. The inertia sent Justin tumbling backwards as he shot a hole in the canvas top. I shoved the throttles forward again and began to zag hard to the right, then left, still keeping myself headed out to sea and tucked behind the console as much as possible. He got off another three shots that hammered into the windshield. Shards of glass bit me in the face and neck, but miraculously all the rounds missed. Mames was on his hands and knees, crawling toward me, bringing the gun up again. I ducked and slammed the throttles to full stop again. He cooperatively went tumbling over onto his back, firing another round into the sky. I hit the throttles again, trying for a few hundred yards more, but the engines died. You can only jerk a throttle back and forth so many times before the fuel lines rebel.

The boat suddenly settled and it was surprisingly quiet. The moon rolled out from behind a cloud and lit the water in cold luminescence. Justin realized what had happened, and as I frantically ground the starter he gathered himself up and cautiously moved forward. It was time for a new tactic. I reached down and grabbed the carry bag. Lifting it up I moved to the side of the gunnel and held it over the water.

"You shoot me, it's gone forever, Mames."

That gave him pause. As Mames slowly worked his way around toward the stern of the boat, I backed up, frantically trying to calculate how many rounds he'd fired—five or six? The bottom line was, six rounds to a revolver, but I just wasn't certain. Pointing the gun at my chest he held out his other hand. "Give it to me, and I won't kill you."

"Yeah," I said sarcastically. "And it never rains in California." I knew I'd run out of chips. We were probably three miles offshore, so I took a chance. My eyes lit up and I pointed behind him, crying out, "Look! It's the Coast Guard!" I'm certain he knew he shouldn't have, but Mames couldn't help taking a quick glance over his shoulder. At that moment I swung the carry bag and the heavy pyramid with all the momentum I could gather. As it slammed him in the chest, he grunted with surprise, instinctively grabbing the bag, but the inertia forced him backwards and cost him his balance. He stumbled into the gunnel, and with a wide-eyed look that began with surprise and ended up somewhere near anger and terror, he tumbled backwards into the dark water. I immediately grabbed a heavy plastic docking fender hanging on the gunnel, and as he came up sputtering and flailing, I whacked him into Tuesday. It didn't knock him out but he was dizzy enough to be having trouble determining whether to swim, hold the bag and tread water, or hold the bag and try to shoot at me again. I dropped the buoy and hit the starter. "C'mon baby, come on…" I muttered tersely. "Come on!"

Mames was working his way toward the back of the drifting boat—then he had a hand on the transom. I was still grinding the starter frantically as he pulled himself up onto the transom, kneeling, holding the gun in one hand and the bag in the other. He raised his pistol, and the moonlight displayed the triumph and anger etched on his countenance. As the attorney from hell pulled the trigger, I cried out and recoiled. But instead of a loud report, the gun clicked impotently on a spent cartridge. I looked at him and smiled. "It was six shots!"

At that moment, the engines finally fired. Without hesitation, I hammered the throttles to the wall and Mames went flying off the back of the boat like he'd borne wings—a little more terror in his eyes than last time. Over the roar of the engines, I heard him scream, "I'll get you, you bastard! I'll get you!"

He was treading water with thirty pounds of gold that had a bomb attached to it. I allowed myself a feral smile and muttered under my breath, "Don't think so, *amigo*."

I began to fly low over the moonlit water, the hull of the boat barely slapping the waves—little more than the lower units of the engines touching the water. The island and the old fort were growing in the distance, but by my watch, I was out of time.

Angie gathered up our three nemeses as she watched me roar out of the bay in the Aquasport. After staunching Will's bleeding, the detective dragged Calico and the boys over to three palm trees near the high water line, tying their hands and feet with some old lobster trap rope she found in the mangroves next to them. Then, using a trick she learned from an undercover narcotics agent, she propped them up in a sitting position, each one against a tree, tied a piece of rope from their hands to their feet (so they couldn't lift their arms) and secured their necks tightly to the slim but hard trunks with their own belts, notching them to the point of discomfort and wheezy breathing. They weren't going anywhere. Then she helped Will to his feet and they moved back down the trail to the west side of the old fort. Angie got Will seated safely behind the timeworn brick wall, then she moved out beyond the corner and stood there, watching the dark, moonlit sea as it drifted into nothingness and met the stars at the horizon. Arms folded against the chill of the wind, she stood there, staring.

Speeding across the dark waters, the roar of the engines and the slap of the waves against the hull were my only constants, my only encouragement. I was way past time's up, and every minute I bought gave me an edge on survival. My mind kept filling with visions of nuclear blasts in the Arizona desert, the Bikini Islands, and Hiroshima—the mushroom cloud and the sheer outward force of destructive energy emanating from the epicenter. I was still nearly a mile offshore, but I could see the fort clearly in the moonlight. I might have a chance. I got to thinking maybe there never was a bomb. Maybe Rufus just made that part up. I had just permitted myself the smallest of confidence in that theory when a bright light suddenly flashed behind me—like someone had just hit the heavens with a mega spotlight. I backed off the throttles a fraction and turned my head toward the stern, and at that moment I knew the game was over. A malevolent orange halo of devastating energy was rising across the sky—followed by a small but terrifying mushroom cloud—the harbinger of total doom. The force from the blast was already racing out at an incalculable speed, heading toward me.

Angie was still staring at the distant night sky when it lit up in a reddish aura of raw power. She gasped as the explosion illuminated the horizon and was followed by the familiar mushroom cloud. "Oh dear God," she whispered. "Oh no…" She hardly noticed that Will had just moved over to her and was witnessing the disaster as well. The look in his eyes said it all. She reached over and held his hand tightly. A fraction of a second later they could visibly see the shock wave approaching—a diaphanous wall ripping across the sea at them. Angie grabbed Will and pulled him back behind the wall just as the shock wave hit. They watched the palm trees arch to the fury of the wind, branches snapping loose and soaring into the air. The blast created a brief whirlwind of mist and sand, etching new marks in the old stone of the fort, but it could have been much worse. It was obvious that it was a much less powerful bomb than the conventional weapons we knew, and the force of the winds had already diminished significantly as they reached the island.

Calico was brought back to consciousness by the force of the shock wave. Sputtering and spitting, he found himself bound without kindness, neck strapped tightly to a palm tree, staring out at the moonlit waters of the bay. He was just about to mutter a curse when, in the distance, he saw the tidal wave rolling into the bay in its full, terrifying splendor. He screamed, and he screamed once more as the surging waters reached his chin.

As the shock wave hit me, the Aquasport lifted out of the water and canted sideways in midair, virtually flying for a moment, engines screaming with the blades out of the water, but by some miracle, it slapped back down straight ahead, with the stern to the wind. I held the controls with a death grip as the boat splashed into the sea again and buried a gunnel, almost overturning. Manhandling the wheel in the midst of a hurricane blow, I fought to stabilize, and somehow straightened and leveled her. Then, as suddenly as it came, the shock wave was gone, racing ahead, and the seas around me were deathly still and flat. I backed off the engines and collapsed into the captain's chair, hands shaking, my heart hammering like a steel mill rivet gun—but I was alive! I exhaled slowly, beginning to feel I'd survived the worst, when the moon broke clear of a dark cloudbank and brightly illuminated the sea. I heard something behind me—a heavy, rushing sound. I turned, and there was a sailor's vision from hell. Glistening and frothing in the moonlight, rushing at me like a freight train was a small tidal wave, probably ten to twelve feet high, rolling in with undeniable force, extending as far as I could see. I remembered what the old shrimpers always told us about big waves—"Take 'em head-on or they'll founder you." I brought the boat around just in time. As the wave raced in at me I grimaced defiantly and slammed the throttles forward one more time. "I just survived a nuclear blast—how hard can this be?" I muttered.

I will always have a sense of appreciation and a soft spot in my heart for the solid construction and fine lines of an Aquasport. That gallant little lady and I hit the wave bow-on. I do remember screaming a lot at that point, regardless of my faith in her. The open fisherman smashed into the wave, crashing over the crest, becoming airborne and virtually flying again for fifty feet. It was as exhilarating as it was terrifying. Soaked to the bone and numbed by way too much adrenalin for a simple boy and his boat, we both smacked down hard on the other side of the little tsunami—straight and level and basically in one piece on a choppy sea. Again, I backed the throttles to idle and collapsed into the captain's chair, drawing in great gulps of sweet sea air.

After a moment or two, I took stock of my situation. The prop on the number two engine had been bent in the last landing, so I decided to shut it down and take it home on one engine. It appeared the gas tank had been damaged as well—I was nearly out of fuel, but it could have been worse.

Fifteen minutes later I was nosing the craft onto the beach, tossing out the anchor, and gratefully crawling out onto solid land again. As I looked up, there were Will and Angie, moving toward me, their faces filled with the revelation of small miracles. We must have held each other for a minute without saying anything. Finally Angie pulled back—tears in her eyes, looking at me.

"We thought…we thought—"

"I know," I said. "For a moment there, I thought so too."

We hugged once more, spontaneously, then pulled away, suddenly self-conscious.

"Where's Mames?" Angie asked cautiously, pretty much knowing the answer.

"I suspect he's a little bit here and a little bit there. I don't know how religious he was but I'm sure he is much more a part of the cosmos now than the rest of us."

"Couldn't happen to a nicer guy," muttered Will, no disappointment in his voice.

"How about Calico and the boys?" I asked.

Angie grinned. "They're still 'restin'' as Calico would say."

She pointed up the beach a ways and I could just see three figures tied very uncomfortably to palm trees—apparently on just high enough ground to have survived the wave, still on the periphery of their acid cocktails.

Looking at the glow on the horizon that was Key West, I said. "This place is going to be crawling with Feds within the hour. We'll leave them right where they are. I would love to have heard Calico trying to explain away six ounces of coke and a dozen hits of acid in his pocket while he's high as an Alpine kite. I suspect they're gonna be 'eight-by-ten restin'' for a while, compliments of Uncle Sam."

"Ya, mon. I like that!" Will chuckled through his pain.

I noticed Calico's stout little shrimper had weathered the wind and the wave pretty well. She had dragged anchor about sixty to seventy feet, and was only fifty yards offshore, but still in deep enough water to get out. I smiled at the irony. "Well, that looks like our way home, and I recommend the sooner we do it, the better. I don't want to be caught here when the Feds start playing twenty questions."

We hadn't slept in about twenty-four hours and were all near the point of exhaustion, so it took us about ten minutes to find where Calico had beached his skiff. It was dead still and eerily quiet as we pushed out the skiff and boarded. Right before Will set the paddles to the water, I was certain I heard someone strumming on a guitar—chords wafting across the water from the old fort, followed by soft, haunting lyrics about sailing on a midnight boat and not asking any questions, and dreaming about Havana. I stood on the bow and looked out through the mists. Just then, the moon broke through the clouds and I was certain I saw a figure beneath the brick arches of the old fort—long blond hair beneath an old cowboy hat, dressed in a white sports coat and blue jeans—holding a guitar by the neck as he turned and drifted into the shadows. I shook my head and stared again, but the specter was gone. I turned to the others. "Did you see…hear that?"

Will shook his head. "I didn't see anything but I know I heard someone playing a guitar and singing. Who in the hell do you suppose that was?"

I shrugged, still gazing at the fort. "I don't know. But that dude sure looks familiar."

We reached the boat without further conundrums and climbed aboard quietly and cautiously, checking out the deck first—no sign of anyone. I thought we might run into Bennie, but it didn't happen. There was a radio or an eight-track on in the forecastle and we could hear a Linda Ronstadt tune playing softly in the background.

You're no good, You're no good, You're no good. Baby, you're no good.

We stepped into the dimly lit wheelhouse, working our way down toward the galley, when we heard something behind us. We turned and froze. There was a huge Doberman Pinscher lashed to the wheel with just about enough leash to reach the door, or the galley. When he saw us, he rose with a roar and charged, being snapped back by the restraining rope just short of my kneecaps as we all stumbled back. The dog was growling and barking furiously, straining at his leash, but an instant later he yelped and drew back, cowering. I suddenly realized he was wearing one of those new training collars that provided an electric shock from a remote handheld device, when the animal performed below expectations of the master. I shook my head disgustedly.

Feeling better, now that we're through. Feeling better cause I'm over you. I learned my lesson, it left a scar. Now I see how you really are...

"Aahhh, I see you've met our greeter," came a silky, familiar voice from behind us.

"Oh, Lord. No," Will muttered, recognizing the voice.

"So nice to see my old compatriots again, in the midst of no small amount of thievery and deceit, I imagine. Nothing ventured, nothing stolen, I always say."

We all snapped around. Sundance!

I won't say it again. You're no good, You're no good, You're no good. Baby, you're no good.

Our old nemesis sighed, almost contentedly, and stepped out of the shadows with his trusty revolver in one hand and the dog collar remote in the other. He was dressed in white pants and a tropical shirt, and his signature Panama hat. Just behind him stood Bennie, in a T-shirt and shorts, quiet and innocuous as usual, holding a fish club. "Here we are again, at another memorable occasion," Sundance whispered dramatically. "When it all comes down to it, life is really nothing more than a bag of memories. The best you can hope is that the bag is neither too burdensome, nor too redundant in its contents, but that it rests lightly on the back and the mind, and finds you a smile or two when the sun is in your eyes."

"Humph!" I replied angrily. "So now you've gone from bank robber and conman to philosopher, huh?"

Sundance shook his head. "No, dear sir, I have always just been the master of opportunity—a sailor of life with vision and possibility as my shipmates. You two know that all too well."

"Yeah. You tried to rob us! You did rob us!" yelled Will from beside me.

Sundance spread his hands out in front of him. "You would deprive me the gift of chance? Karma? Kismet? Fate? Aaahhh, what does it matter? Here we are back together again—*los tres banditos*."

"No *tres banditos!"* I said firmly. "No more banditos."

Sundance paused, pursing his lips and nodding solemnly, bringing his gun up a little. "Actually you're right. This is definitely where you get off the merry-go-round. But I have a couple questions. First, where's Calico and his nasty offspring, and where's the pyramid?"

"Calico and the boys are tied up on the beach—not much of an issue right now. The pyramid, well, that's another story. How in the hell did you end up here?" I asked, changing the subject. "How'd you find us?"

The big man smiled in a sort of reminiscence. "Well, that is an interesting story. So I'll relate a little of it to you, before you leave. I was having a drink, a small *mescal*, in a local Key West tavern about a week ago, when I overheard the gentlemen at the table next to me having a chat about golden pyramids, the people who stole them, and the chances of getting them back. It was a remarkable, fortuitous coincidence, I admit. Seems it was a pilot they were talking to, who had decided, for a sizable stack of twenty-dollar bills, to tell them where you were going to be on your way back from a visit in Cuba. It's amazing how many people will play both ends against the middle for a little compensation." He paused, drawing a breath and pushing up the brim of his old hat with the barrel of his pistol. Leveling the gun, again he continued. "When the pilot left, I decided to offer them a partnership. We would find you, and I would buy the pyramid from them for $50,000—half of what I got from Little Tony, and they would have an immediate sale with no further entanglement."

"So you've still got the money you made off the pyramid?" Will asked.

"Not your business, really." He paused dramatically. "Yes, I hid it. But during our sale, Little Tony did mention if there was a problem, he was coming back for my tongue and eyeballs, so I realized I had a sizeable quandary when you stole it, if I didn't; A) find the pyramid and give it back to him, or B) get out of town and book a flight for the Ecuadorian Rain Forest, and I don't really want to live in the Ecuadorian Rain Forest—the bloody dampness, the mosquitoes!" He sighed heavily and raised his eyes to the heavens dramatically. "God, I might as well just tie a bloody bed sheet to the ceiling fan and hang my bloody self." Departing from his ramblings, he became serious again, eyes narrowing on us. "Now, what about the pyramid?"

"You're not going to like this answer," said Will, shaking his head. "It's gone, man. That explosion you witnessed about an hour ago was the pyramid disappearing. It had a failsafe bomb attached to it. Long story short, we activated it."

"I don't believe you," Sundance said, motioning with his pistol to Bennie behind him. "These folks and I have a deal." Then, without hesitation, he brought the gun around and fired a round into the floorboards at our feet. "Now, give me the pyramid or I'm going to shoot you—all of you."

"We can't give you what we don't have!" I cried, exasperated.

"Okay," Sundance said, nodding calmly, aiming the gun at Angie, "Then I'll just shoot her first. Then we'll talk again."

I realized at that moment, he was going to do just that, but Will was already ahead of me. My partner threw himself in front of Angie as Sundance aimed and pulled the trigger. But a fraction before the gun went off, Bennie did the most amazing thing. He brought his club up and whacked Sundance in the back of the head. It saved Angie's life. The bullet zinged by her cheek and smashed through the window of the forecastle. With a profound look of surprise, pain, and disappointment, Sundance fell face first onto the floor.

After a moment of intense relief, we just stood there gazing at each other. I picked up Sundance's gun and looked up at Bennie, not certain what to expect next in this situation. "Lord! Bennie, thank you!"

At that point, Bennie did something I'd never seen him do before. He smiled—a real genuine smile. "Consider it a favor repaid," he said haltingly.

I stood there dumbfounded. "Bennie! You can talk! When? I thought you—"

"I couldn't before," he said quietly.

I suddenly noticed there was no constant movement with him—none of the epileptic jitters I remembered. He seemed…serene.

He took a deep breath and began to speak quietly. "I met a guy named Rufus about a week ago. I was sitting on the dock by myself one night while the others were out drinking, and this guy comes up and sits down next to me—kind of a strange Jamaican accent. He said he had something he wanted to give me, 'to aid in the triangulations of my life,' but he wanted a little favor in return." Bennie drew a breath, then exhaled slowly. "He put some dust in the palm of his hand and blew it at me, then he told me that I was free, that there was no reason why I couldn't speak, and I would never have the 'jukebox jitters' again. Most importantly, he told me I could be whatever I wanted to be—it didn't matter what other people thought, it only mattered what I felt. He told me that very soon I was going to have to make a choice, and I needed to make the right one." He paused. "I think I have."

I couldn't help myself. I walked over and gave him a hug, and he returned it. It was a strange, emotional, and satisfying moment. Will and Angie came over, shaking his hand and thanking him again.

After a moment he said, "Rufus gave me the courage to do what I want. I don't belong here." He smiled again—a remarkably amicable, compassionate smile. "He got me an audition for *The Wiz* in New York. That's where I'm headed when this boat touches shore." He paused and looked over at the dog. "There's something else I have to do." He walked over to the big Doberman, who growled under its breath as he approached, then suddenly relaxed as he touched the animal gently and removed the collar.

He was about to toss it over the side, when Will said, "Wait, I think I have just the place for that."

Bennie handed it to my partner and Will smiled. I knew that smile.

"Okay, I think we should crank this baby up and get the hell out of here," I said. "The cavalry, I'm sure, is coming."

We had the anchor up and were bringing the boat around when Sundance, still stretched out on the floor, moaned. Will put the engine in neutral, walked over and knelt by him, affixing the dog collar around his neck. He took a pair of pliers from the table next to him and bent the metal tongue that fit in the adjustment holes, so it couldn't be removed. Then he picked up the remote and backed away just as Sundance opened his eyes, groaned and brought his hand to his head. Will grinned mischievously. "Let's see if he can roll over, or sit up." He pushed the button.

Sundance's eyes flew open and he screamed, writhing like a fat snake as he brought his hands to his neck struggling unsuccessfully to remove the device.

"Sundance!" Will said firmly. "Leave it alone!"

"Screw you!" Sundance yelled, still not quite certain what was happening. "What the bloody hell!"

Will pressed the button again. Angie and I watched from the wheel as our nemesis flopped around on the floor, shrieking obscenities that would make a teamster blush. Will waited a moment or two, enjoying himself. I was having a hard time not laughing. I'm pretty sure I saw the Doberman smiling, too.

Gasping for breath, the big man finally slowed his efforts and looked over at the dog, grasping the situation.

"Get up," Will said.

Sundance glared at him. "I'm gonna rip you a new—"

Will aimed the remote at him. Sundance did his imitation of a beached flounder again. When he had caught his breath sufficiently, Will said, "Stand up!" This time there was no hesitation. Will looked at me. "He's going swimming."

We were about a half mile offshore. "You sure you want to let him go? What if he comes after us again?"

My partner shook his head. "I don't think he will. With the loss of the pyramid he's got bigger worries now—Little Tony. My guess is, he's going to have to opt for the Ecuadorian Rain Forest after all. And he still has a half-mile swim at night to begin with. Then he's got to deal with the Feds."

"Wait! Wait!" said Sundance more earnestly than before. "Don't do this. We could make a deal. I promise I'll disappear. You'll never see me again!"

"Don't think so," Will replied coldly. "Let's go. Out to the deck."

Sundance raised his hands in entreaty. "Wait, please. I'll tell you where the money from Little Tony is."

Again my partner shook his head. "And we have to deal with you until we find out that you were lying? Nope. It's swim time." He looked at me with that roguish grin, then back to Sundance. "The big sharks feed mostly at night—quite a few of them in this area."

Sundance took a breath, bent on another argument. Will brought up the remote again. "Okay! Okay!" the thief cried, hands out. "Okay."

The storm had passed and the moon had risen to its zenith,

dodging puffy pastel clouds and casting a clear, golden glow over the sea. It was picturesque, but I was really glad I wasn't the one going for a swim in those dark waters.

Sundance straddled the rail, pleading one last time for a reprieve. Will refused and the big man became indignant. "I'm not gonna forget this! I'm gonna—" Will pressed the button again. Sundance shrieked, lost his balance and fell headlong into the foreboding sea. He was still screeching, sputtering, and shouting obscenities when he came up.

"Mako!" Will shouted. "A big one coming from the port side!"

Sundance suddenly got quiet as he drifted into the darkness to our stern.

Will pressed the button again—just for fun.

"Aaaagghh! Son of a bitch! Aaaagghh!" the darkness replied.

Standing beside Will, I listened to Sundance's plaintive howling as he drifted into the distance. "Funny thing how we usually part with this guy while he's floating away, screaming curses at us, huh?"

"Will nodded. "I hope this is the last time. Can't say I'll miss him."

Just for the hell of it, he pressed the button one more time.

The sun was just coming up when we dropped anchor at Cow Key, just south of Key West. We were leaving the shrimp boat with Bennie and taking the skiff in. He said he'd take the boat around to a marina after we were quietly away.

As we prepared to debark, Bennie reached into his pocket and brought out a small piece of notebook paper. "Oh yeah, Rufus said for me to tell you to go get your VW bus out of police impoundment as soon as you can, then give it to the 'tiny Cuban with the lisp,' the first chance you get." We looked up at him questioningly. He shrugged. "I don't know. That's just what he said." He held out his hand. "And for me to give you this paper. He said it was your 'appropriate gift,' for your help. He said to tell you, 'cool driftings, mon.'"

Will took the piece of paper. There was no message, no instructions, just a series of six numbers. Somewhat disappointed, he mumbled a thanks, handing it to me. "What the hell is this?" he said. "I thought you told me we were gonna get something really special for all this effort. I nearly got killed. So did you! For what? This is bogus, dude!"

I shrugged, "I don't know, man. Not what I expected either." I stuffed the note in my pocket.

We slipped ashore and half an hour later we paid a taxi and got a room at a nondescript little motel at the edge of Stock Island. I don't even remember my head hitting the pillow.

It was five in the afternoon when we got up and ordered a pizza. While we waited for the delivery, Will went to the office and got a *Key West Citizen*. It was all over the front page.

Mystery Explosion Near Fort Jefferson Believed To Involve Stolen Peruvian Pyramid.
Area Attorney Suspected To Have Been Killed

The Feds had arrived at Fort Jefferson en masse. The article said they had immediately discovered a slightly waterlogged trio of individuals tied to palm trees. The Feds also found six ounces of cocaine on the individuals. They were being booked as the article was being written, but names were not available at press time.

Will straightened the paper and began reading the rest to us. "The authorities also found two men handcuffed to the walls inside Fort Jefferson—Ralph Landon, a Key West police detective, and Gregory Rustle of Key West, bodyguard for the missing Miami attorney, Justin Mames. When questioned, the suspects apparently confessed to being accomplices of Mames in the theft of a solid gold, pre-Incan pyramid that was stolen three months ago en route to the Peruvian National Museum. In addition, Landon and Rustle confessed to the attempted murder of two individuals who had allegedly taken the pyramid from Justin Mames, apparently in hopes of returning it to authorities—a Kansas Stamps and a William Bell of Big Pine Key. Stamps and Bell apparently escaped them aided by Key West Detective Angie Hanes. Neither Stamps, Bell, or Hanes have been located by authorities at this point. It is believed that there was an explosive device in the pyramid that appeared to have detonated when Miami attorney Justin Mames attempted to smuggle it back into the country from an undisclosed island in the Cuban Archipelago.

"A representative of the Coast Guard announced that while they were searching the waters off Fort Jefferson they discovered an additional individual, Rodney Whitcomb, of Vancouver, Canada, who was turned over to federal authorities. Whitcomb is being held for questioning regarding a number of alleged larcenies in Canada and the U.S."

Will put the paper down and smiled broadly. "We're out of the weeds, babies! We're gonna be all right. We might even be heroes!"

Angie sighed with relief as she leaned back on the couch. "I may even still have a job when all this blows over." Then suddenly she leaned forward intently. "Lord, I need to ring my sister! She's likely to hear about all this and will want to know if I'm okay." She looked at us. "I've got a twin sister—not identical, but fraternal. We look a lot alike, but frankly, I'm much prettier now." I couldn't tell if she was joking or serious. "We came from England to the States together. She's living in Fort Lauderdale—works as a wildlife photographer."

My mind did a little flip-flop. H*er sister! She has a sister that is nearly identical.* I was just humming with the possibilities. Some parts of me were humming more than others. Angie went to the pay phone and called. Will and I ate pizza, drank beer, and watched the television news about us—very heady. Angie returned in about twenty minutes, all giddy. Her sister was coming down the following weekend—to visit, and to meet the two amazing guys with whom she'd shared a most adventurous adventure. "You're going to love her, I'm certain. She's a smashing lady," she said. Then she paused. "If her face and legs hadn't been hurt in that terrible automobile accident she would have been the prettier by far. But she's really got such a wonderful personality."

The Lord giveth and the Lord taketh away. My mind did another flip-flop—a self-centered, very shallow flip-flop. For a week I was going to get to be a chaperone for a very nice girl who just happened to be crippled and disfigured. I reached for another beer.

CHAPTER THIRTEEN

Virtuous Mangoes and Fortunate Worms

The next few days were a bit of a whirlwind. We had to meet with the authorities, who questioned us for a few hours, then let us go. The confessions they had already acquired seemed to match our story (imagine that), so we were released with the admonition to "keep our noses clean" and not leave town. That was fine with us. Angie had to be debriefed and do a pile of paperwork pertaining to the event. We went to the police impoundment yard and got our VW van, then we went to Captain Tony's for a drink. I noticed the old van still ran like a top, but the driver's seat seemed more uncomfortable than I remembered. As fate would have it, we ran into little Hector Zarapata. We had a few drinks, and at the end of the night, we gave him our bus, just as Rufus had requested. It seemed like a crazy thing to do, but Rufus hadn't missed on many of his calls to this point, so we went along with it. Hector was clearly beyond grateful. It was his first automobile. He promised he would gladly shoot anybody we needed shot—for free—anytime.

That evening, Hector was driving home, pleased as punch, but there seemed to be something wrong with the seat. "This damn lumpy seat stickin' me in my butt," he muttered, so he pulled over and reached underneath, to see if a spring was broken. What he found were two bags that had been stuffed between the springs and were pushing up against the plastic on the seat. They were heavy bags so he took them out. He was going to throw them into a dumpster, but he decided to look inside first. He opened the first bag and gasped. "Holy cousin of Jesus!" he whispered with incredulousness. "Hector Zarapata gonna get a new stinkin' leash on life!" When he finished counting, he found the bags contained $100,000 in twenty and one-hundred-dollar bills.

There were so many things to catch up on, from making sure the animals at our trailer were all right, and paying our overdue rent and a slew of other bills, to trying to get out to do a little diving to pay the bills coming up, that I forgot about the piece of paper Rufus had given us. I was doing laundry one evening, when I pulled the notebook paper Bennie had given me from a pair of shorts about to be washed. I stared at it for a moment. Six numbers—24* 46. 480'N

- 81* 22. 237'W. All of a sudden it hit me. It was the longitude and latitude for a special spot somewhere. Will was sitting on a lawn chair by the seawall, feeding fish and drinking a beer. The sun was just sinking into the horizon, turning the canal water to a sheet of gold in Mother Nature's remarkable sleight-of-hand fashion when I walked over and sat down next to him. "The present from Rufus—it's a Loran reading. By the numbers, I'm guessing it's not that far from here—in the backcountry I think."

Will turned around slowly. "So we are going to get a little present—maybe our own golden pyramid?"

"No more pyramids, please."

"Yeah, you're right about that. I don't know what it is, but I think we need to check it out. When's Angie's sister, Celeste, due in?"

"Tomorrow afternoon," I said with as much enthusiasm as I could muster.

My partner grinned, picking up on me. "Well, what about after we've had a couple days to show her around, we take the boat out and run down those readings. It'd be a nice trip for us all—get a little sun, be out on the water. Just for the heck of it, I'll borrow a metal detector from Robert Bunter. Can't hurt."

The following day at 4 p.m. we piled into Angie's car and drove over to the Key West Airport. Flight 214 from Fort Lauderdale cruised in on time. We all stood inside the fence by the little airport terminal, watching the passengers debark onto the tarmac. Finally, the last passenger was down the ramp and through the gate, but still no Celeste. Then, at the top of the ramp we saw two flight attendants slowly, carefully helping a person in a wheelchair exit down the ramp. She had a scarf over her face and wore dark sunglasses. She was wrapped in what looked like a London Fog coat and you could barely see her legs. My heart did a final flip-flop out of town. I hate to say it, but I began to think of excuses that would unfortunately draw me away for part of the week. I was sure she was a nice girl, but....

When they finally got the wheelchair down on the tarmac and over to the gate, Angie ran over and put her arms around her sister, hugging her tightly. Then she turned to Will. "And this is the man of my dreams—Will Bell."

I was hanging back just a little. Will stepped forward and gave Celeste a polite hug, saying how nice it was to meet her. Then gesturing at me, Angie smiled strangely, almost mischievously.

"And this is Kansas Stamps, whom I'm proud to call a friend."

I paused for a moment, working on getting my feet to move toward her, when the girl in the wheelchair pulled off her scarf and let it go in the wind, then pulled off the sunglasses. I did a little involuntary gasp. She was beautiful. She was Angie with blond hair. I barely had time to exhale when Celeste rose up out of the wheelchair and peeled off her coat. Underneath was a soft cotton halter top, just taut enough to make things interesting, and a pair of shorts sufficiently succinct to dispel all doubts about the condition of the lady's legs. She walked over to me with a laugh that was sensuous and genuine—bright, sensitive hazel-bronze eyes that promised possibilities at almost every turn. I felt my heart flip-flop right back into town.

Angie and Will were already laughing as Celeste came up and put her arms around me, giving me a soft peck on the cheek. She backed away still smiling. "It's true, I do have a good personality." She glanced at her sister and Will, then turned back to me. "We just couldn't resist a little test of your character."

I had to grin. I'd really been taken. "Well, I'm glad about the personality," I said, pausing for a moment to admire what providence had just placed in front of me. "But considering all the other really nice parts, I would have worked around it."

She chuckled, throaty and inviting, those bronze eyes still holding me.

We stood there staring at each other, not quite ready to let the moment go, experiencing an undeniable connection that was intoxicating, almost mystical—a sensation a person experiences maybe twice in a lifetime, if they're lucky.

Then her countenance changed slightly—still intrigued, but somewhat quizzical. She cocked her head. "What is it about you? Do I know you from somewhere?"

I smiled in recollection. "Two lifetimes ago during the Mexican Revolution, in Guadalajara. The peasants were taking the city—killing the wealthy people, like us. But we escaped on a little fishing sloop up the coast, into California. You were pregnant with our first child."

Celeste had leaned forward as if drawn into the story. "Things like that can be true, you know."

"I hope it is true, because it means I've found you again." I paused. "You loved the warm sea—the coves and bays, and the way the sun used to reflect off of them. It's one of the reasons you chose to return to Florida this time—for the water, and for me."

She smiled and took my hand. “That’s a lovely story, mate. C’mon, I’ll let you charm me with some others.”

And we all walked away. The sun was shining gloriously, the air was as clear as sweet memories, and the wind was soft and gentle—slightly salty and full of promises.

I muttered to Will as we strolled toward the car, “See… sometimes it does work.”

Celeste decided to take some time off and spend the next three weeks in the Keys with us/me. During that remarkable convergence of coincidence and fate, I discovered I had finally found what I was looking for, as Will had—very similar models, same year.

During that time, between the dancing, dining, and the sultry evenings of exploration and surrender, we got out the nautical charts and determined the location of the coordinates Rufus had given us. Ironically enough, the numbers pinpointed to the back of a secluded little bay on a small, uninhabited island called Little Spanish Key, a couple of miles north of Big Pine. It was an easy run of about twenty minutes from our canal. The following day, we packed a lunch and all four of us headed out, chock full of adventure and anticipation. It was a beautiful, clear, calm morning. Gentle rolling waves glistened in the sun, and seabirds called plaintively, sweeping down on baitfish off the bow as we neared the island. A shallow channel led us into the picturesque little bay and we nosed the skiff into the soft sand of the beach. There was no question we were excited; we were undoubtedly on a treasure hunt of some sort. The descendants of people who had walked with the Egyptians and the Phoenicians, and consorted with ancient priests and kings, had left us something. It was very heady.

We moved inland, working our way off the beach and slowly into the sparse mangroves, reaching a buttonwood rise about 100 yards into the island. I nodded at Will. “This is pretty close, I think.”

His eyes flashed with anxiousness as he pulled the metal detector out of its case and balanced out the electronics for that specific terrain. Will began to sweep in wide arcs as he walked, keeping the detector head just an inch or so off the ground.

I don’t know exactly what we expected, but it didn’t happen. After a half hour of sweeping, we had hit no viable targets. We moved a little further inland and worked for another half hour—still nothing. Finally we decided to take a break and have a picnic—ham sandwiches and potato salad that the girls had made, and a bottle of wine. As we sat there gazing around, offering conjecture and suggestions, Will suddenly stopped chewing and pointed into the thicker part of the buttonwood hammock. There stood a large mango tree, its huge, ripe fruit sagging down, reaching for the ground.

"The virtuous mango," Will whispered intently. "Rufus' virtuous mango—freed by the wind, it kisses the earth and awaits the warmth of the sun… and the fortunate worm!" He stood up, bringing the detector around and moving toward the base of the tree. "I am the worm!" he cried. "Blessed is the virtuous mango!"

The girls thought he'd lost it—maybe bad mayonnaise in the sandwich. But I remembered those exact words from Rufus while we stood in his new boat that had been strangely given to him. "A gift from the gods…."

Before the rest of us could even get to our feet, the machine in Will's hand was clanging a beautiful target melody. My partner dropped to his knees and I was right behind him with the shovel. The loam and sand parted easily, and within minutes we had a hole two feet wide and two feet deep. The shovel hit something hard. Working slower, and by hand, we began clearing an object. Eventually, the top took shape, then the sides. It wasn't what we expected, but in the end we weren't disappointed either. It was a large, old Mason jar, with the traditional metal screw lid and rubber gasket. It certainly wasn't ancient, but the contents were.

We brought the jar over to the blanket on which we'd been sitting, clearing a space. With some effort, Will twisted off the lid and poured the contents out onto the blanket. It contained two things—coins (oh, but what coins), and a piece of paper with a final note from Rufus. We all reached down and each of us picked up a handful of the coins. They were all exclusively gold or silver. There were coins from the Egyptian, Persian, and Roman dynasties, Dutch coins from the 15th century, prized Spanish reales, and pieces of eight from the 16th century. There was French and English tender from the 17th and 18th centuries, American Revolution silver dollars, Civil War $20 gold pieces, and much more. It was as if a highly discriminating and dedicated collector had chosen the finest representations of each civilization. There were well over 200 immensely valuable coins—a virtual fortune.

Then, there was the letter from Rufus. I picked it up and began to read out loud.

Kansas and Will,

Here is the "appropriate gift" I promised you. The first part of the gift reminds you how perennial and enduring life is, and that man is continuously crafting and defining what he considers valuable. The second part reminds you that wealth alone is not the greatest gift—knowledge is the most important power of all. The wise fisherman dries his catch and his nets today, but he is always watching the movements of the sea, the tides, and the stars—planning for tomorrow's catch.

My friends, these are portentous, rapidly changing times, and the world promises to become more startling and bizarre tomorrow than it is today. You have become members, albeit somewhat unwillingly, of a very exclusive fraternity. There is a chance we may meet again. Pay attention to the list below and it will free you.

Cool driftings,

R

At first, we were puzzled by the list. Out of about forty names on it, there were a few that we recognized—Coca Cola, Exxon, IBM. But there were others of which we had no conception. Things called Microsoft, Yahoo, Google, Nike, Macintosh/Apple, Dell, and Wal-Mart. We weren't sure exactly what they were, or if they even existed. But of course, as time passed, we realized the full advantage of knowing the names on the list—always watching the news for signs of an emergence of one of the companies on that priceless sheet of paper. Then we cashed in a few coins and bought stock. We became fishermen who watched the tides, the seas, and the stars for our next catch. We became stock-buying worms for every virtuous mango we could find, and life was good.

In June of 1977 we had a two-ceremony wedding at the Pier House in Key West, where Will and I married those fabulous Hanes sisters. They became our wives and our best friends, and I'm pleased to say the friendship between Will and me has never changed. It has never missed a beat through the years—aging like fine wine and providing a peace and a comfort that is the most intrinsic and valuable gift in any relationship.

We did run into Rufus again, but that's another story…

I HOPE YOU HAVE ENJOYED THIS NOVEL. IF YOU WOULD LIKE TO BE ADDED TO MY MAILING LIST (TO STAY APPRISED OF NEW NOVELS, AND TO RECEIVE BI-MONTHLY UPDATES AND MY NEWSPAPER COLUMNS), EMAIL ME AT REISIG@IPA.NET

— Michael Reisig

BE SURE TO READ THE OTHER NOVELS IN THE *ROAD TO KEY WEST* SERIES

FOR WILD CARIBBEAN ADVENTURE AND LAUGH-OUT-LOUD HUMOR:

BACK ON THE ROAD TO KEY WEST (The Golden Scepter) Book II

An ancient map and a lost pirate treasure, a larcenous Bahamian scoundrel with his gang of cutthroats, a wild and crazy journey into South America in search of a magical antediluvian device, and perilous/hilarious encounters with outlandish villains and zany friends will keep you locked to your seat and giggling maniacally. (Not to mention headhunters, smugglers, and beautiful women with poisonous pet spiders.) You'll also welcome back Rufus, the wacky, mystical Jamaican Rastaman, and be captivated by another "complicated romance" as Kansas and Will struggle with finding and keeping "the girls of their dreams."
Kindle Book only $2.99

Click Here To Preview or Purchase From Amazon.com:
http://www.amazon.com/dp/B00FC9D94I

ALONG THE ROAD TO KEY WEST (The Truthmaker) Book III

Fast-paced humor-adventure with wacky pilots, quirky con men, bold women, mad villains, and a gadget to die for...

Florida Keys adventurers Kansas Stamps and Will Bell find their lives turned upside down when they discover a truth device hidden in the temple of an ancient civilization. Enthralled by the virtue (and entertainment value) of personally dispensing truth and justice with this unique tool, they take it all a step too far and discover that everyone wants what they have.

Seasoned with outrageous humor and sultry romances, *Along The Road To Key West* carries you through one wild adventure after another. This time, Kansas and Will are forced to wrest veracity and lies from con artists, divine hustlers, and political power brokers while trying to stay one step ahead of a persistent assembly of very bad guys with guns.

In the process, from Key West, into the Caribbean, and back to America's heartland, our inadvertent heroes gather a bizarre collage of friends and enemies—from a whacked-out, one-eyed pilot, and a mystical Rastaman, to a ruthless problem-solver for a prominent religious sect, a zany flimflamming sociopath, and a Cuban intelligence agent. In the end, it all comes down to a frantic gamble—to save far more than the truth. So pour yourself a margarita and settle back. You're in for a high-intensity Caribbean carnival ride!

Kindle Book only $2.99

Click Here To Preview or Purchase From Amazon.com:
http://www.amazon.com/dp/B00G5B3HEY

SOMEWHERE ON THE ROAD TO KEY WEST
(The Emerald Cave) Book IV

In the fourth book of "The Road To Key West" series, Kansas Stamps and Will Bell once again find themselves hip-deep in madcap adventure—from bizarre to hysterical.

The captivating diary of an amateur archeologist sends our intrepid explorers on a journey into the heart of the Panamanian jungle, in search of *La cueva de Esmeralda* (The Emerald Cave), and a lost Spanish treasure. But local brigand, Tu Phat Shong, and his gang of cutthroats are searching for the same treasure. It's a cat and mouse game—up the perilous Fangaso River, through the jungle and the boisterous mining towns, and into "The Village of the Witches," where nothing is as it seems…

If that weren't enough, one of the Caribbean's nastiest drug lords has a score to settle with our reluctant heroes. (Something to do with an ancient golden medallion they "borrowed.") The word is out. There's a price on Kansas and Will's heads, and a conga line of hit men trailing them. As they careen across the Southern Hemisphere, our adventurers encounter some fascinating ladies as well, and experience an extraordinary romance. Be careful what you wish for…

Kindle Book only $3.99

Other books by Michael Reisig

BE SURE TO READ MICHAEL'S NEW

"CARIBBEAN GOLD" SERIES

CARIBBEAN GOLD — THE TREASURE OF TORTUGA

In 1668 Englishman Trevor Holte and the audacious freebooter Clevin Greymore, sail from London for the West Indies. They set out in search of adventure and wealth, but the challenges they encounter are beyond their wildest dreams—the brutal Spanish, ruthless buccaneers, a pirate king, and the lure of Havana. Then, there was the gold…wealth beyond imagination. But some treasures outlive the men who bury them…

Click Here To Preview or Purchase From Amazon.com:
http://www.amazon.com/dp/B00S6VA6LS

CARIBBEAN GOLD — THE TREASURE OF TIME

In the spring of 1980, three adventurers set out from Key West in search of a lost treasure on the Isle of Tortuga, off the coast of Haiti. Equipped with an ancient parchment and a handful of clues, they embark on a journey that carries them back across time, challenging their courage and their imagination, presenting them with remarkable allies and pitting them against a collage of unrelenting enemies. In the process, they uncover far more than a treasure. They discover the power of friendship and faith, and the unflagging capacity of spirit, and come to realize that, some things are forever…

Click Here To Preview or Purchase From Amazon.com:
http://www.amazon.com/dp/B00S8SR0WW

The New Madrid Run

The New Madrid Run is a tale of desperate survival on an altered planet: In the aftermath of a global cataclysm caused by a shift in the earth's poles, a handful of survivors face the terrible elements of a changed world as they navigate a battered sailboat from the ruins of Florida into the hills of Arkansas via a huge rift in the continent (the New Madrid fault). They survive fierce storms and high seas pirates only to make landfall and discover the greatest challenge of all...

($8.95)

The Hawks of Kamalon

Great Britain, Summer, 1944

A small squadron of British and American aircraft departs at dawn on a long-range strike into Germany, but as they cross the English Channel, the squadron vanishes.

Drawn thousands of light-years across the galaxy by Kamalon's "Sensitive Mothers," ten men and eight aircraft are greeted by a roaring crowd in a field before the provincial capital, on the continent of Azra; a land in desperate need of champions.

Captain Ross Murdock and the '51 Squadron are cast into a whirlwind adventure of intrigue, treachery, and romance as they are "culled" back and forth across the universe, outwitting and outrunning the Germans, while they attempt to foil the invasion of Azra by the neighboring continent of Krete.

The Hawks of Kamalon is a heart-hammering adventure in the classic tradition of Robert Heinlein, but it also examines the parameters of faith and friendship, the qualities that define civilization, and the width and depth of spirit.

($7.99)